Praise f...

The Undead / v...

FLESH FEAST

"Fantastic stories! The zombies are fresh...well, er, they're actually moldy, festering wrecks...but these stories are great takes on the zombie genre. You're gonna like *The Undead: Flesh Feast*...just make sure you have a toothpick handy."

—Joe McKinney, author of *Dead City* and *Murders Squad*

"Bloody and intense, anyone who enjoys a good horror story will get plenty of entertainment from this collection."

—Matt M. McElroy, FlamesRising.com

"If you are a fan of the undead, then you should not miss out on this brilliant collection from today's newest and brightest writers. *The Undead: Flesh Feast* is overflowing with delectable morsels to satisfy the literary palate of the sophisticated zombie fan."

—Eve Black, The Hacker's Source

"With *The Undead: Flesh Feast*, Permuted Press prove that the first anthology was no fluke. Once again they have collected stories by writers, some of which you will know, some will be new to readers, all however contribute good quality stories about our beloved walking corpses. A joy to read!"

—Jude "Pain" Felton, AllThingsZombie.com

"From in-edible humans to a zombie Santa Claus to undead flatfish, [*Flesh Feast*] has everything that a connoisseur of fine zombie literature could want. A must read!"

—Taylor Kent, host of *Snark Infested Waters*

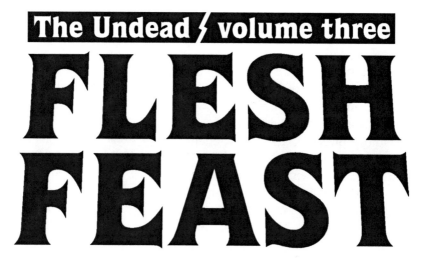

The Undead / volume three
FLESH FEAST

Edited by
D.L. Snell and
Travis Adkins

Permuted Press
The formula has been changed...
Shifted... Altered... *Twisted.*™
www.permutedpress.com

A Permuted Press book
published by arrangement with the authors

ISBN-10: 0-9789707-5-6
ISBN-13: 978-0-9789707-5-8
Library of Congress Control Number: 2007930572

Menu

Bon Appetit

Introduction

by Walter Greatshell

I GOT BITTEN BY ZOMBIES VERY EARLY ON—when I was seven years old, to be exact. So it was inevitable that I'd eventually spawn more.

That's the thing about zombies: they tend to multiply.

I remember it well. My mother and I were living in Hollywood during its late '60s zenith of sleaze, and for some reason she took me to the local grindhouse Rivoli or Tivoli for a showing of *Night of the Living Dead*.

It remains a mystery to me why she did this—could I have heard about it and begged her to go? I doubt it; my tastes at the time ran more towards *101 Dalmatians* than *2000 Maniacs*. I could barely look at a newsstand because of all the lurid horror and true-crime magazines that filled the racks: leering, green-faced witches and slobbering cannibals and pickled human heads—it was all too much for me. Once, I was so creeped-out by a particular movie poster (a picture of a dead woman's half-buried face) that even riding the bus past the theater made me upset. And my mother *knew* this.

Yet she takes me to *Night of the Living Dead* as blithely as if it was a matinee performance of *The Nutcracker?*

Most likely it was totally unintentional, just a chance to park the kid and sit in peace for a couple of hours—as an immigrant and struggling single parent, she probably had more important things on her mind. For all I know, she slept through the whole thing.

Certainly the movie didn't affect her the way it did me, because when that pick-up truck exploded and a horde of pasty-faced ghouls set upon the remains of that wholesome young couple, treating them like roast pigs at a luau, that was it: my brain was forever warped, not just by the grisly images, but by those awful, awful *sounds*.

I was bitten. But like so many other victims of zombie assault, I lived in denial, burying the trauma trying to get on with my life.

Years went by, and the age of cheapie exploitation films came to an end—all those gloomy old movie palaces were torn down and replaced with mall multiplexes showing big-budget blockbusters. Everything was sanitized and packaged and so, so slick.

Then, in 1978, *Dawn of the Dead* came out.

I should have known. Shiny-bright shopping malls or not, zombies will always be there, lurking, waiting to jump out at you. Some bite, others suck, but zombies never go away—the dead can't die.

Day of the Dead, Return of the Living Dead, Evil Dead, Shaun of the Dead, 28 Days Later (to name just a few) ...and back to *Dawn of the Dead*. The films keep coming ...and the books.

Ah, the books.

We can't forget the books. Books are a natural, because it was a book that started it all: *I Am Legend*, by Richard Matheson. That's the one that inspired George Romero, and was also the first zombie tale I ever read. Loving that book as I did, I couldn't understand why there weren't more zombie novels out there—the field was wide open. It was only a matter of time before I started writing my own.

For several years I worked in an old art cinema, the Avon, a throwback to the kind of places my mother took me to as a kid. During those long nights of midnight shows I would sit up in the musty office next to the projection booth and think about the end of the world. Having freelanced for a newspaper and dabbled at fiction, I thought maybe I'd write a story some day, or a script, or even make a low-budget movie, but mainly it was just a game to kill time.

I approached it as a technical challenge, the science of making the dead walk: Zombiology 101. The only problem was, I could never think of a hook, an original angle that would set my zombie story apart.

Then, one day, the local defense contractor was hiring, and I put the zombie dreams aside to focus on making a real living, an actual career. Soon I was working the graveyard shift in a submarine factory. That's when it hit me:

Duh, a *submarine*. What better way to survive a zombie apocalypse?

A year later I had a book, unleashing my *Xombies* upon the world. Because that is what zombies do.

Yes, I'm a zombie. We're all zombies here, resurrecting the dead in order to recapture that first unholy thrill. To relive the experience and spread it like a virus to others. To *you*. Because these stories are infectious:

Just try forgetting about the nightmare vision of Oz in *Killing the Witch*, by A.C. Wise; or the frustrated, impotent Angel of Death in *Brownlee's Blue Flame*, by David Dunwoody; or the grotesque flesh pits in Rick Moore's *Basic Training*; or the wheezing chest of drawers in Michael Stone's *Memory Bones*. Hell, any of them. All of them.

Reading this collection, I was surprised and gratified to find that each and every one of its authors had come to the same conclusion I did: that a zombie story should be more about the *story* than the *zombie*. After all, zombies have very little personality—that's why they're called zombies! They are the element of chaos made flesh... and flesh-eater. It is up to each author to fill in the blanks, invent his or her own zombie lore, furnish the china shop— and then set them loose. Despite Romero's enormous footsteps, there are no laws. Zombies are anarchists.

Insert them into a classic Western revenge tale, such as Tim Curran does in *The Legend of Black Betty*, or into a seafaring yarn like Eric Turowski's *Ile Faim*, or into a hardboiled noir like Matthew Bey's *Deadtown Taxi*, and suddenly all those musty old genre conventions come alive. They get up and walk. And you may find that they follow you around, particularly when you're alone... and it's dark.

Just watch out: they have teeth.

—Walter Greatshell

Street Smarts

by Steven Cavanagh

THE CORPSE LAY SLUMPED on the park bench with its head tilted back and its jaw in a cartoon stretch, as if a throaty snore would rasp from between those yellow-gray teeth. He wore jeans and a dusty brown suit jacket with patches on the elbows. His torn jogging shoes were a grainy film of busy ants. If Jan squinted her eyes, the body looked like a homeless man. Hell, he probably *had* been.

Hamish stepped toward it. "Is it...?"

Jan glared. Hamish was fifteen; old enough to know better. "The answer is *always*—"

The thing lurched upward, pawing toward Hamish with skinless fingers. The boy stood stunned by the hatred in its eyes, which were bloodshot a milky purple by the spores that sparked activity in a dead brain.

Jan stepped in, gave the kid a hard, unapologetic elbow, then swung Six And Out to the corpse's head. The cricket bat connected with a crack, and the dead man arced backward over the bench.

Jan struggled to keep her voice low. "*This* is why I said no kids! What is the *first* thing they teach you about shopping trips?"

Hamish had fallen. He used his axe handle to struggle to his feet, keeping his red face down to avoid her eyes. "I'm sorry. He just looked—"

"Say it!"

"It's kid stuff. I'm not a—"

"Exactly. *Say* it!"

Hamish's face darkened with shame and anger. "Round head, undead. Smashed dome, no one home."

5

Jan crouched to wipe Six And Out on the grass. "Maybe we should find a blackboard," she said. "It's not just a children's rhyme. They can look dead because they *are*, but once a body is spore-animated, it gets hungry thoughts in its head. The only way to get those thoughts out is to knock them out. It'll keep coming at you until you do."

Hamish's enthusiasm for the trip seemed to have evaporated. "They outnumber us and they keep coming?"

"Yes, but they're stupid. Their brain activity is low level, limited to movement and hunger. Keep moving, and *think*. Their brain is no match for yours—if you use it."

Her anger ebbed at the shame in his eyes.

"Look, you're doing okay. You walk real quiet and you haven't screamed once. I just don't want you to take chances, okay? I've seen what happens to people who take chances."

Hamish nodded, imagining.

The way he set his jaw made her nervous. *Teenagers*, she thought. *Scold them about taking chances, and they just want to prove themselves.*

They picked their way through the dandruff of a dead city: leaves, paper, and ash. Silence widened the spaces and lengthened the streets, and here and there they saw the ever-shuffling dead. The two living made no noise to attract them.

After twelve blocks, Jan motioned Hamish within whispering distance. "Okay, time to hunt up supplies. There are two things you need to know. One, we never go out of line-of-sight. If you start heading down into basements alone like a B-movie loser, you *deserve* to get eaten.

"Two, signaling. The dead respond to sounds of the living. That means things they can't do, like speak, or drive a car. If you want me, scrape your weapon three times on the road like this." She did so. "The sound can carry a fair distance, it can't happen by accident, and the dead don't recognize it."

They found some canned food in the remains of an Asian grocery, but it hardly swelled their backpacks. The outskirts had been shopped a few times by scavenging parties. Jan and Hamish had to travel farther in to find loot of any value.

It was almost noon when Hamish scraped his axe handle three times on the road. Jan moved closer so they could talk.

"You hear that?" Hamish asked. A song chimed in the distance.

"What is it?"

"Maybe someone's driving around in a van selling ice cream," Hamish replied. "You feel like a Choc Top?"

"Cute." Jan took her police issue pistol out of her backpack and shoved it into her belt. "Stay close to me, don't run ahead."

They made their way through the giant soldier-rows of buildings toward the sound. The slow, eerie song added a surreal dimension to the echoing streets and provided a bizarre soundtrack to the jerky movements of the dead. Once, Hamish was noticed by a bloated corpse in a wetsuit, but he easily outran the dead man.

"There should be more of them," Jan said. "This doesn't feel right."

They had almost reached the city center when they came across a construction site. A hole some four stories deep had been dug, presumably to lay the foundations for a skyscraper. A section of the safety fence had been knocked down, and a lone zombie teetered on the brink. Suspended in space by a construction crane, just beyond his clawing fingers, something twitched, an object that looked like a small boy dressed in red.

Jan checked the streets and they crossed the road toward it. The small boy, on closer inspection, turned out to be a large Santa Claus doll. It shuddered in a parody of life as it slurred *Winter Wonderland* on dying batteries.

Shaking with adrenaline, Hamish stepped forward and delivered a sharp blow to the back of the oblivious corpse's head. It toppled soundlessly into the pit.

"I got one!" He looked down, and his shoulders sagged. Jan stepped up to him.

The pit contained over a hundred bodies, smashed on the bedrock or impaled on steel reinforcing. Some of them still wriggled, and one dragged its shattered torso along on one arm.

Jan regarded the doll, then the pit. "Nice trap. Now *this* is what I call a bullet saver," she said.

"It didn't work on all of them. The guy I hit was too smart to take that last step."

Jan grunted. "Smart? These are the dead. The word 'smart' doesn't come into it. *Ants* have more intelligence than they do."

Hamish swung the axe handle over his shoulder with new confidence. "That's a bit black and white, isn't it? Surely some are brighter than others. Tell you what, maybe this guy was smarter than average, back when he was ali—"

"Don't," Jan cut him off. Images of her daughter's purple eyes appeared, unbidden. "Don't humanize them. Ever."

* * * * *

They shared a tin of peaches, then resumed the process of listening, signaling, and sneaking as they hunted for essentials.

They covered two blocks in silence and had just entered a paved city square when Hamish scraped his axe handle on the ground three times.

He stood at the smashed glass window of an army disposals store. "Check this out," he said to Jan, motioning to a sword on display. It was five feet long, and the hilt had been shaped into an ornate horned skull. "Cool, huh?"

"Yeah, nice. Let's go."

Hamish dropped the axe handle, and reached into the window.

"What are you doing?"

"It's a *sword*, Jan. I only have a stupid axe handle."

She sighed. "So you see yourself bare-chested and neck deep in bodies, smiting and hewing with that thing? Crom, count the undead?"

"*It* was designed to kill people. *This* was designed to make firewood."

"And it would probably work, for the first two zombies. This is real life, Hamish. In real life swords get stuck in ribs and skulls, and then they'd be all over you. Blunt weapons don't do that."

Embarrassment and hurt flickered over Hamish's face.

"It's your choice, but if I were you I'd stick with the handle and not take chances."

The boy clenched his fists for a moment, then lifted his club and walked away.

Jan smiled. *He's teachable. He'll do okay.*

Hamish stopped. He stepped back to the window and reached in.

"It's not a dichotomy." He slid the blade down the back of his shirt until the skull-hilt rested on his shoulder like a devilish parrot, then he lifted the axe handle again. "We haven't found much stuff, so consider it a souvenir."

"Just don't get tempted and use it, okay?"

"Okay. But you gotta admit, if there'd been a suit of armor, *that* would have been useful, right?"

"A squeaky tin suit that would bring every—"

"You're a glass half empty person, aren't you?"

The blast of a horn echoed across the square. Jan and Hamish whirled, but could not identify the noise.

"Uh... Jan?"

The drifting corpses had responded and noticed the living. They lurched in their direction with the patience of the dead.

Jan motioned Hamish toward the square's northerly exit. She only made it a few feet before figures gathered in the street beyond.

She drew her pistol, decided not to risk attracting more corpses, and returned the weapon to her belt.

She and Hamish turned and turned again. None of the streets were empty. Some of the corpses were only two car lengths away now. Hamish could hear one, a rotting businessman in an expensive suit, grinding its teeth.

"Stay focused," she said. "We're gonna find their weak point and break through it, okay?"

"Stay away!" Hamish blurted. He jumped forward and swung the axe handle—the grinding teeth skittered across the pavement.

Jan downed a groping, eyeless woman. "Don't get separated! Stay with me!"

Hamish swung again, and the axe handle caught in a groping fist. He wrestled with the thing for a moment, then relinquished the weapon and stepped back.

He wrestled the sword free of his shirt as the dead closed in. In spite of the moment, Hamish found himself throwing Jan a guilty look.

"Hey, mate!" someone shouted in an Australian accent.

To their right, a ramp led to rooftop parking. A deep-blue garbage truck rolled down onto the roof's lot from an adjacent building. It stopped abruptly.

"Hey, mate, get in!"

Jan pushed over a fat corpse and drew her pistol. "He's not from our camp," she said to Hamish. "We don't trust him. Take no chances, remember? We check it out, quickly and carefully."

They ran for the ramp, gaining distance from the shuffling dead. "Who are you?!" Jan called to the truck.

"Get in now!"

"Hamish, stay here." Jan moved to the truck and stepped up onto the running board.

The cabin held a shop mannequin in a powder-blue suit and rakish fedora. Beside it sat a large cage. The cockatoo inside raised its yellow comb.

"Get in, mate!"

"Jan, look!" Hamish pointed to bricks in front of the wheels. "These stopped the truck. It wasn't driven, it was *rolled*. Is this another zombie trap?"

"*Bloody hell! Auughno get them away!*" squawked the cockatoo. "*Agggghkill me!*"

A thin corpse in black stood up on top of the vehicle. Black wings unfolded on his back.

Jan's eyes widened.

A crow climbed onto the dead man's shoulder and tugged at the meat on his neck. The corpse opened its mouth and *spoke*.

"*Eeeeeaaaaaatttt.*"

Corpses spilled from the back of the truck, dead bodies that sprang up and ran at her with lolling rotten tongues and filthy teeth and milky purple eyes.

"Run!" Jan said, dropping the first two with headshots from the pistol. Hamish stood with her and swung at the third, but when the sword lodged in its skull, he ran. He sprinted across the square to the drainpipe on an adjacent hotel.

He didn't look back. He was taking no chances.

Jan only had five bullets, but all of them were well used. When she smashed down a sixth corpse with the cricket bat, the dead mob lurched out of range. They spread out, working like a dog pack, and waited until she was completely encircled before moving in together.

Hamish lay curled up on the hotel roof, between the air conditioning outlet and the banner that read:

37th ANNUAL CONVENTION
OF MENSA INTERNATIONAL

Immediate needs: food and water—check. He had the tins in his backpack, and the blocked gutters were full from the rain.

More than once he heard three scrapes on the road below, but he did not take chances. Hamish had learned from the best.

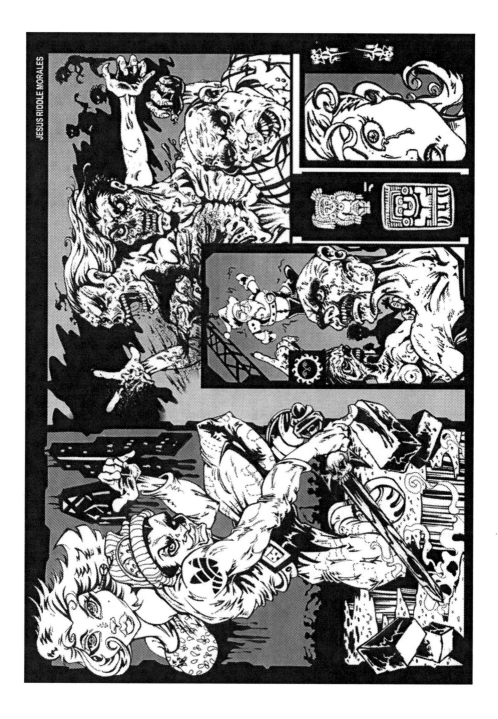

Adam Repentant

by Matthew Masucci

And the Lord God said,
Behold the man is become as one of us,
to know good and evil:
and now, lest he put forth his hand,
and take also of the tree of life,
and live for ever
[...]
So he drove out the man;
and he placed at the east of the
garden of Eden Cherubims,
and a flaming sword which turned every way,
to keep the way of the tree of life.

(Genesis 3:22; 24)

"I found you," Father Gregory Alexander said.

"I let you find me."

Adam pulled an apple from his weathered knapsack, an old leather satchel with black sigils and signs burned into its supple exterior, and he bit into the skin of the Red Delicious. He chewed and smiled, watching the traffic slip by.

"You would think by now I would have an acute aversion to these." Adam took another loud bite. More people arrived at the bus stop and the hum of conversation swelled around the two men.

"You know why I'm looking for you," Father Alexander said, leaning forward, trying to see Adam's eyes. The wind picked up and the priest drew his long coat around his body. Adam appeared to be young, like some of the men at seminary who were always so curious about Father Alexander. He wasn't a virgin. He once had a family, and that made him out of place there. Always an anomaly. Here, he spoke to another anomaly. A man who could provide answers.

"What happened to her?"

Adam swallowed a bite of apple. "Who?"

"I'm not playing games."

"Games are one of the few things that I still have. But, to answer your question, we split up some time ago."

"How long?"

"Well, time is relative, isn't it? Really, what does it matter? I lost interest. We agreed to go our separate ways. She wouldn't have approved of Hitler anyway."

"Hitler?"

"Oh, come on Father, you can't tell me you never heard the rumors about Hitler's obsession with the occult? He was interesting, willing to experiment... but I think it got out of hand."

"How could you?"

"Ennui is inadequate to describe it. I've been alive for far too long. I've been present for every major historical event ever recorded and even many that have been forgotten. I watched the Library of Alexandria burn to the ground. All that knowledge turned to ash in a matter of an hour."

"You did that too?"

"Of course not. That was *your* guy. I want people to *have* knowledge."

"My guy?"

"Don't play dumb, Father. Babel was quite an achievement and would very well be standing today. He gets very jealous, you know. Very possessive."

"I don't believe you."

"Nobody ever does." Adam gazed down the long street, watching the approaching bus. He dropped what was left of his apple and it wobbled under the bus tire as it pulled up to the stop. The fruit split under the tremendous weight.

"Now if you excuse me, I must be going."

The bus door hissed opened and the crowd inside bulged outward, dispersing into the group of commuters waiting to board.

Adam turned to Father Alexander and smiled. He opened his mouth as wide as he could and breathed out. A low hum rode on his breath, filling the priest's inner ear with pressure, like being under water. Father Alexander cupped his hands over his ears to block out the sound. He said a little prayer.

Around him, commuters dropped to the ground. The bus driver's eyes went dark, losing that sparkle of life and recognition; his jaw slackened, and he slumped onto the oversized steering wheel. The bus lurched forward and stalled.

Heavy bodies collapsed, no arms outstretched to break the fall, no tense muscles anticipating the impact. Heads bounced off the ground; bodies landed on top of one another at the bus stop like a mass grave. At first, they were still, but then they began to convulse.

Father Alexander pried his eyes from the bodies snaking around his feet; Adam was gone. Although the haunting sound was still there, still in his ears, somehow he did not faint like the others. He hopped up the bus' stairs, holding onto the chrome handrail that was bolted to the floor and ceiling. Adam was not there.

Outside, he scanned the streets. The sound drained from his ears, and the underwater feeling disappeared. He spotted more collapsed pedestrians heading north, so he broke out into a run, his coat flying loose behind him, something attached at his hip glinting in the light of the setting sun.

As he ran past the twitching unconscious people, foam seeped from their mouths as if they were suffering from seizures. Adam had done something to them. But Father Alexander couldn't help. He couldn't lose track of the man he'd been hunting for more than twenty years.

Up ahead, the front double doors of St. Mary's Church banged shut. Beyond that, people were still crossing the streets, moving toward their destinations, unaware of what occurred a half block from them. He looked back the way he had come, the trail of unconscious bodies twitching.

But something new was happening.

As if the puppeteer called his marionette to life by tugging on its strings, Adam's victims began to rise from the ground. The closest one took a few tentative steps toward Father Alexander, his body jerking, his eyes hazy and lifeless. He was wearing a light-gray business suit and his hair was expertly combed. He swayed, shifting his weight from foot to foot like a baby learning to balance. He stared, his eyes seeing nothing, and small rivulets of blood leaked from the corners of his eyes.

Then, the businessman charged.

Father Alexander reached into the pocket of his coat and pulled out a silver cross. He yelled at the body coming at him, reciting the prayer of exorcism: "Exorcizo te, omnis spiritus immunde, in nominee Dei!" He made the sign of the cross with the crucifix.

The businessman tackled him. Raging, he bit down on the cross and pulled it away, blood now pouring from his mouth, nose, and eye sockets, his gaze lifeless and wandering. Hot blood and spittle rained down on the priest's face, clouding his vision.

He heard the cross clang to the ground somewhere behind them. The businessman bit and gnawed, trying to sink his teeth into still living flesh. The two rolled back and forth on the hard ground, gravel digging into Father Alexander's exposed flesh, lodging under his skin.

The businessman mounted the priest and squeezed his throat until his lungs burned without breath. Father Alexander's arms and legs faded into white noise, a corporeal static in his limbs. The ringing in his ears deafened him until he could only hear his heart thrumming in his head, trying to push the blood through the crushed arteries.

He threw his weight against the bleeding man, using all of his remaining strength to push him off. The priest stood and kicked the businessman in the chest, knocking him back.

His suit now completely soaked in red, the businessman stood again. Father Alexander was surprised that the man's chest wasn't heaving; he couldn't catch his own breath. He wiped the blood from his face and reached beneath his coat. His hand gripped a black leather handle, and from a sheath hidden beneath his cloak, he pulled an ancient steel sword of a cruciform design.

"Forgive me, Father, for I will sin," he said, and with a single, fluid movement, he chopped off the businessman's head. It sounded like a deflated basketball hitting the ground. The body twitched a few times before toppling.

The sound of feet against concrete filtered into his ears after the ringing stopped. What appeared to be a hundred bleeding bodies were running toward him. Some he recognized from the bus stop down the street.

Twenty or so branched off when they spied a woman exit a building. They fell upon her, biting and pulling at her clothes. Her screams drowned in what could only be her blood. The undead, for that was what they were, left her mangled body when she started to twitch. They didn't attack her to feed, as he suspected; they *converted* her. When the shaking stopped, she stood and joined the rest of the walking dead.

Seeing his chance to run dwindle away, his focus a slave to curiosity, he forced his feet into motion and sprinted for the black steel doors of St. Mary's Church.

Once inside, he scanned the room, looking for something to bar the door. The pews were bolted to the floor, and since the doors swung outward, he couldn't stack objects in front of them.

To the left and right of the doors, tall wooden and brass candleholders stood. He jammed one through the levers on the doors and crisscrossed it with the other.

Father Alexander whispered a quick prayer of protection for the door just as the running bodies flung themselves against it. As the undead pulled at the makeshift barricade, the candleholders groaned. But to the priest's amazement, they held.

He took a white handkerchief out of his pocket. A red Chi-Rho symbol was stitched in the corner. No bigger than a dime, the symbol was the only source of color on the immaculate white handkerchief. He wiped the blood from his sword and tossed the handkerchief onto an empty pew. The sword hadn't been used in years, ever since he brought down Arioch, one of the fallen angels, and he could feel the sword's satisfaction, its quiet yearning for blood. All things desire to fulfill their purpose.

"I recognize that," Adam said, staring at the sword in Father Alexander's hand. "Third crusade, Gregory VIII. Back when popes were warlords. I could tell you a story about that, but then again, you probably wouldn't believe me."

Adam stood next to a stained glass window depicting the garden of Eden. Eve was holding an apple between them, a snake wrapped around her naked foot. The glass was so old and distorted that the faces of Adam and Eve were hard to distinguish.

"All the artists of the earth, all the trained and untrained hands, none could ever quite capture the beauty of that woman. That first woman."

Adam's eyes were dry, but the waver was clear in his voice. Father Alexander suspected that he had long ago cried out all of his tears.

"I trusted her when she gave me the fruit from the Tree of Knowledge, but when I later made my way into the garden and took from the Tree of Life, she refused. She would not restore her immortality. I told her that it was what He wanted; otherwise, why would He have put it there. She already knew far too much, and she didn't want any more of God's gifts. I watched her grow old. I buried my wife like I buried so many of our children. If that isn't punishment enough."

His face tightened and deep lines appeared, the only signs of his age. The ravines told stories of his trials.

"I'm sorry I ate that apple. I'm sorry I ate any of the fruit in the Garden. But *I* didn't create us to be so curious. *I* didn't tell us that we couldn't have the fruit of those trees. It wasn't a test, it was a setup. I'm sorry and I've asked forgiveness, but He never granted it. So now I'm going to take it all back. Take it back for all of us."

"Is this a confession, Adam? I can give you penance."

"Do you really believe that? If you do, you haven't understood a thing I've said."

The candleholders began to buckle under the weight of the bodies piling up outside. Limbs squeezed through the bent metal frame of the door, ripped and bloody from pushing through the gap.

"I plan to make an army of his greatest creation, priest. I will march on Eden with an Army of Dead and we will storm the gates of the Kingdom. There I will take control and bring justice and knowledge to the world. It will no longer fall to the whims of a madman. He will no longer cover your eyes and demand that you follow by blind faith. You will be free for the first time in your history. Truly free. And I will bring it to you. We deserve better than this. His kingdom of suffering must end."

"The army won't do you any good here. Eden is in the Fertile Crescent."

"Cripple your opponents before they are your enemies. The basis for a pre-emptive strike. You understand the concept, I'm sure."

"It is my charge to stop you, Adam. I've hunted you, I've searched for you, and now it is time for me to bring another of God's sons home."

"Don't be melodramatic."

The walking dead broke through the doors and entered the church, but they stopped moving when Adam put up his hand. He smiled at his creations, their blank eyes and swinging gait. He loved them, that was clear. In his eyes was the smile of fatherdom.

"You could work with me. You could be the voice of mortals, to write my gospel and proclaim it to the people. I can give you the gift that God never wanted you to have. These fruits never wither, never rot. I can give you knowledge, I can give you life."

"And be the same as these husks?"

"These people are not blessed, they are cursed. Magick is the fingerprint of God. A residue left behind when he created the world. If you choose to harness it, learn how it flows through all living things, you can become like him. Besides, they are a means to an end. Just as God used Cain, Job, Noah, Abraham. I could tell you so many stories, so much suffering unexplained, unjust. All to make a point. Everything you've ever known is about to change. Change with it or become a victim of the change. Your choice."

Adam explored Father Alexander's face with intent curiosity, almost as if he were listening to an indistinct sound.

"Immortality gives you an interesting perspective. And it's not as if God is gone. He's not. He's just become lazy. Idle hands and all that. It's time,

Father. Reclaim the kingdom, for you and for *your* son. I can hear you thinking about him. In time you can tune your own ears and hear the structure, the singing in the I-beams of creation."

Adam took out another apple and started to eat. He sat on the edge of a pew below the stained-glass Eden. Behind Father Alexander, dripping blood on the floor, the bodies stood where Adam had stopped them; they swayed in place, staring at the apple Adam slowly devoured.

Father Alexander thought about his son. The slight brown curls when his hair grew a little too long. The stickiness of his fingers after he ate a small piece of candy. The giggle, soft and innocent, when his father drew his hands away from his face and smiled. The smell of his head while he slept.

His mentor, Father McCleary, told him once that God had a purpose for everyone, and through his measured hand, his will was always done. *Do not call it unfair*, he said, *do not think it cruel. It is what it is, and following the path to Heaven will reunite you with your son in time.*

Sometimes, Father Alexander doubted. Sometimes he prayed. Sometimes he wept. The rest of the time he spent tracking down Adam and others. Tracking down what some would call the mistakes of God, but what Father McCleary would describe as *tests of faith*.

The dead swayed behind him, their bodies tensed for battle, exuding impatience. He could sense that. They wanted blood. They too wanted to fulfill their purpose. More than likely, they would kill him.

Adam's invitation still hung in the air, full of possibility.

No.

It didn't come out. Not out of his mouth.

Adam shrugged as if Father Alexander had spoken.

"No," the priest said. It was stronger this time, real words reverberating through the air, echoing off the masonry in the church, the sound absorbed by ears and bodies, by cloth and statue.

Adam stood. "I bore witness to the beginning and I intend to bear witness to the end." He finished off the fruit's core and all, save the stem and seeds. These he put into his satchel.

"One cannot have too many apple trees. They always seem to bear exceptional surprises. Sweet fruit. Bitter fruit. It's the beauty of chaos and unpredictability."

Father Alexander removed his long coat, dropped it to the ground, and genuflected, offering a quick prayer: "St. Michael the Archangel, defend us in the day of Battle; Be our safeguard against the wickedness and snares of the Devil. May God rebuke Him, we humbly pray, and do Thou, O Prince of the Heavenly Host, by the power of God, cast into Hell, Satan and all the other evil spirits, who prowl through the world, seeking the ruin of souls. Amen."

When he finished, he stood, sword ready.

Adam shook his head. "I am not a devil. You and me, we're so much alike. As for the Devil, he has been dead for quite some time. Lucifer committed suicide. He recognized the impossibility of his situation and decided he just couldn't take it anymore. There was never a Hell—he fell to Earth. There are still a couple of fallen angels wandering around—you've seen them—but they're as crazy as sin, so to speak.

"The time for waiting is over. The time for action is now." Adam nodded and ran toward the sacristy. He slammed the door behind him and was gone. Again, Father Alexander would have to give chase.

But first, there was a more pressing matter.

Father Alexander turned, sword cocked back, as the horde of dead ran toward him, mouths open, teeth bared. Blood flowed from their every pore like villagers ravaged by Ebola.

Some of the zombies slid and fell in their own fluids as the rest of the bodies bulged forward, hands outstretched. Father Alexander swung his sword at the first three zombies, which were running abreast down the aisle.

The blade decapitated the first zombie, his head rolling under the feet of the undead behind him. The middle zombie crumpled when his spine snapped, but his head hung on by a thin swatch of flesh.

To his far left, the third zombie took a hit to his throat, blood squirting from the jugular. His hand reached for Father Alexander's cassock. The priest split the zombie's head in two above the ear on the backswing.

Father's shoe slipped in blood as he slid sideways between the pews. The zombies filed between the pews in pursuit, but they had to come one at a time, struggling to make it through. As they reached the end, where Father Alexander now stood with his back to the marble wall, it was like cows being led to the slaughter.

He swung his blade, aiming always for the neck, but sometimes just grazing a skull or opening a chest. The blade scratched bone, making a noise as metal on rock. He tried to catch them on the backswing, but had to duck a few outstretched arms. He ran backward in the far aisle as he neared the front of the church. Some of the zombies tried to file through the pews. Others went around the back of the church to come up the aisle, while random ones attacked him from all directions.

The zombies had trapped him.

He looked around, trying to find a way out. He couldn't fight all three lines off at once. Zombies filtered through all the pews now, so he was cut off there. The balcony above him curved out into the church proper and tapered at the sides near the back, but he certainly couldn't jump ten feet into the air. He turned to the wall. It was polished marble for about seven feet and then plaster to the ceiling. But directly above him, attached to the wall, was a Station of the Cross. They were about three feet apart and they spanned both sides of the church. Six on each side.

He could smell the bodies now, the iron in their blood as they reached out, wanting his flesh.

Father Alexander jumped, grabbing both sides of the Station. He felt it pull away from the wall, but didn't want to give the bolts time to dislodge. Holding his sword tight in this palm and using his fingers to find purchase, he pulled himself up and swung his legs between his Station and the next. He managed to hook his legs around the head of a Roman soldier casting a lot for the cloak of Jesus. He felt it crack against his ankle, but at least his body was away from the zombies below.

Their screams and moans made the hair rise on his arm. Some of them jumped, one managing to hook a finger around Father Alexander's belt.

The zombie's finger broke in two places as Father Alexander pulled himself higher. He hooked an arm around the cross on his Station and pulled himself to the top. His legs dangled as the head of the Roman soldier snapped off. The zombies growled in excitement, waving their arms.

Bearing the full weight of the priest, the Station jerked away from the wall. He pulled himself to the top of the Station, stood, and hopped to the next one, nearly losing his balance. The second Station, the one with the now decapitated Roman soldier, shifted.

He jumped from Station to Station, moving toward the back of St. Mary's, barely making it from one to the other as they shifted away from the wall, the bolts unable to support the extra weight. When he reached the last Station, he leaped and caught the edge of the balcony, the strain whitening his fingertips.

He pulled himself over the ledge and tried to catch his breath. But all the zombies who were trying to get him near the front of the church ran to the stairs.

So, they're not completely unable to reason, Father Alexander thought.

Now he was not much better off than before. He could hear them ambling up the steps behind him, heads and limbs banging against the walls in the narrow passageways, moans echoing madness. They would emerge on either side of the balcony, just as angry, if not angrier, than before. The drop from the balcony was about fifteen feet from the top of the ledge, less if he lowered himself before dropping. He noticed several of the zombies looking up at him as he peered over, their arms reaching for him.

If he hit the ground and didn't twist his ankle, he could have time to bring them down before they fell upon him. But it was a gamble. Straight out from the center of the balcony, a large chandelier about twenty feet in diameter hung by chains from the ceiling. He also had the other Stations on the other side of the church.

He sheathed his sword and backed up, getting a few extra steps of running room. The chandelier was huge, so he couldn't miss it, and the chains looked heavy enough to hold his weight.

The zombies reached the top of the stairs. He took his few steps, launched himself from the ledge, and grabbed the chandelier. It started swinging, tilting dangerously back. The zombies' heads below him swung back and forth in time with his movement.

He had misjudged the chains. The links began to pull apart. He kicked his legs, trying to gain some forward momentum, but the chains snapped and he crashed to the floor with the chandelier. Glass shattered, and he raised his arms to protect his eyes; several small shards sliced his cheeks and forehead.

The whole scene stunned the zombies. A few leaned too far over the ledge of the balcony and fell. He tried to push the chandelier off his midsection, but it was far too heavy for him. Father Alexander inhaled. It hurt to breathe. He had probably cracked a rib. He grabbed at the hilt of his sword, but one of the arms of the chandelier had bent around him and pinned it to the ground.

He was an easy target.

Father Alexander grabbed a shard of glass, which bit into his hand and drew blood. Lustful screams filled the church. He tilted his head back and slashed at the ankles of the closest zombie. It fell to the ground with its arms still working. He stabbed at its groping fingers until it withdrew them, but two zombies replaced every fallen one.

Father Alexander pushed a final time on the chandelier. He shoved it far enough down his midsection to wriggle free. He stood, drew his sword, and dropped the nearest zombies. He jumped over twisted metal, hoping that the Pastor of the church would forgive him. Guilt still formed a small rock in his stomach, despite knowing the Vatican would pay for all damages.

As he made his way past the altar, the zombies scrambled over the wreckage. He was ready to kick in the door to the sacristy, but decided to try the knob first, a bit of civilized behavior. He said a little prayer and turned the knob.

It opened.

Father Alexander hurried inside. He closed the door behind him and turned the little lock on the door handle. It wouldn't hold the zombies for long, but maybe long enough for him to escape. The back door appeared to lead into an alleyway behind the church, and the door adjacent to it was closed. Father Alexander tried to imagine where he was in relation to the front entrance, but he was too disoriented after the trek through the church. He would just have to take a chance and have faith.

It was time for Father McCleary to be right, for God to reveal his plan. Was he to perish here fighting the undead, or was he to find Adam and bring him to justice? The sacristy was small with many cabinets and closets, but not much room to fight. On the table to his left, there was a small set of votive candles and a pack of matches. He took a match, struck a flame, and lit one of the small, red votives. He bowed his head and focused on his memories.

A loud bang on the door brought him back from his unfinished prayer. He heard the moans and screams outside the sacristy.

"That was sweet," Adam said. "Memories of his laugh, of his cry. Your son meant so much to you. So in a way, you do understand." He was leaning against the door that led to the alleyway. He certainly hadn't been there before.

Father Alexander drew his sword and charged. Adam didn't flinch as the priest drove the sword through his chest.

Adam breathed in with a great sucking sound. He stared at the ceiling, his breath expelled from the wound around the blade. The odor was ancient, like the brittle parchment secreted away in the darkest corners of the Vatican's library. There was no blood, only dust.

Father Alexander gave the sword a hard twist. He pushed until the hilt was flat against Adam's chest, pinning him to the door.

"For the children of God, I bring you to justice. I absolve you of your sins, Adam. Walk into Heaven with a clean soul."

Adam stared at the ceiling, his mouth agape. Father Alexander peered deep into the man's eyes, looking for something he had lost long ago. He found a lonely darkness. The breathing stopped, and so did the clawing at the sacristy door. It seemed as if time stood still.

There was a flutter. Adam's eyes flicked downward, locking with the priest's own.

Adam pulled in a hard breath. "You are more my children than the children of God. He made me—I am his creation—but you and all your brothers and sisters are my direct descendents. You share my blood. I made you, and it's time for my children to come home."

"We are all God's children." Father Alexander gave the sword another hard twist.

Adam shook his head, his voice soft. "I will love you, Gregory Alexander. I can breathe life into your son. I can bring him back to you."

Again, fingers scratched at the sacristy door.

"To be like the others?"

Adam didn't reply.

"I will not be a pawn in your war, Adam. This is the Kingdom of God, not the kingdom of man. Your arrogance doomed us all in the beginning and soon it will be your downfall."

Adam screamed, a sound of pure anger from deep inside him. He threw the priest through the closed door next to him without a hint of effort. The wood buckled around Father Alexander, splinters scratching his skin, tracing hot streaks through his flesh. Adam wrapped his hands around the blade, twisting and pulling. His back arched as he withdrew the sword from his chest. Then Adam moved out of Father Alexander's sight, dropping the weapon.

The room he was in now was dark, the only light coming from the doorway. Behind him, something moved. He turned, but all he could see was darkness. The light could not make it to the back of the room.

There was a low, guttural growl. His sword was only a few feet away. He scrambled up and sprinted forward. From the dark area behind him, the area where the cloaks hung, a body lunged and crashed into him. They banged into the cupboards, knocking the doors open. Chalices crashed to the floor and communion wafers drifted down like snow. Father Alexander smashed his head and blood squirted from a fresh wound. The zombie priest grappled with him as they hit the floor.

The priest on top of Father Alexander was probably in his mid-sixties, but his face, contorted with rage, betrayed his wrinkles drawing them taut. He had the strength of a young man again, and he pulled at Father Alexander's flesh, threatening to tear it from the bone.

Then, the sacristy door collapsed and more zombies shambled into the room.

Father Alexander searched for his sword—it was too far away.

He grabbed the priest by the throat and squeezed. The zombie priest's trachea buckled under his fingers. That was when the blood flowed freely from the zombie priest's face and throat, pouring over Father Alexander's fingers and into his eyes. He twisted the old man's skin until all movement stopped. Father Alexander felt a moment of pity, but others were approaching. He pushed the warm, bloody body off himself and dashed for his sword. He grabbed the hilt and headed for the door to the alleyway.

A note was taped there, cut in the shape of a fig leaf, like the ones the Puritans used to cover up the genitals in paintings during the Reformation.

Adam's writing was a delicate, perfect script.

*If you survive and change your mind, come look for me.
I am willing to give you another chance. I offer REAL redemption.*

Father Alexander slipped the note into his pocket and ran out the back door of the church, covered in blood, a dead prayer for his son on his lips.

He ran down the alley and into the street. He could hear the zombies from the sacristy grunting and running in pursuit. This street, he assumed, intersected the one he was on before entering the church. He wasn't sure at first which way Adam had gone, but the trail of twitching bodies on the ground, some just now standing, headed east toward the docks. There, he surmised, Adam would depart from America on his way back to his true home. Adam sowed the seeds of destruction that would leave a great nation in waste. He left behind his chaos.

Sword in hand and ambulance sirens in the distance, Father Gregory Alexander, his duty sworn to the Lord and to the memory of his son, followed, unsure of where his path would lead him. Somehow, he knew, he would fulfill his duty, as all things strive to do.

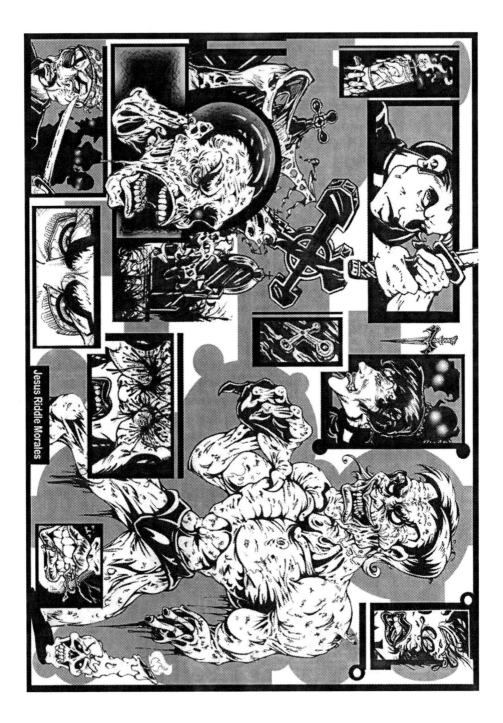

Jesus Riddle Morales

Memory Bones

by Michael Stone

THE SICKLY BUTCHER'S SHOP SMELL GOT STRONGER as he ascended the stairs. The carpet stuck to his feet.

"It be the bedroom on the left, Doctor."

Messinger turned to acknowledge the speaker but the man had already ducked from view. The doctor muttered his thanks and continued up the stairs, his Gladstone bag bumping against his leg. A dust-dimmed window let in just enough light for him to make out two doors, one on either side of the tiny landing. He pushed open the door to the left.

The room stank of open wounds and wet bandages. Wrinkling his nose, Messinger peered into the darkness, trying to discern edges and corners in the flat greyness.

"You must be the doctor."

Messinger faced the voice, and a bed coalesced in the gloom. "Aah. Mr. Lode, I presume." The attempt at humor didn't bring any response. He asked politely if he could draw back the curtains. "I need to see you if I'm to examine you."

The speaker sounded hoarse. "If you must. It's just that my eyes are very sensitive at present."

"I shall take a look at them in a moment, Mr. Lode." He parted the heavy drapes to let in a chink of light.

"That's enough! No more than that."

There was just enough sunlight for Messinger to see a man propped up on pillows, his body hidden by a high-collared, ankle-length nightshirt. The doctor smiled wanly. The nightshirt looked to be the source of the bad smell that pervaded the room. The patient's age was difficult to determine—his hair was as thin and colourless as melting snow, but his long face was unlined, the skin around his jaw smooth and tight. Lode's pupils were pinpricks in pools of baby blue.

Messinger sidled to the bed and eased himself down, placing his Gladstone bag between his feet where it clanked on a bedpan. It was then he noticed the scratches in the wall behind the bed: reminiscent of a prison cell, hundreds of short vertical strokes with a diagonal slash denoting groups of five covered an area of wall larger than the bed's headboard.

"So what seems to be the problem, Mr. Lode?"

"It's not me you've come to see, Doctor."

"Oh! I do apologize. I was told the patient was in this room. By your brother, would it be?"

Lode nodded. "Aye, he weren't having you on." Lode reached out and gripped Messinger's wrist. "You've taken over old Dr. Dimmock's practice, yes?"

Messinger nodded.

"Did he mention me?"

"No, but I didn't actually have the pleasure of meeting Dr. Dimmock. I was appointed by a selection committee after he retired."

"Pity. He was a good man was Dimmock. Open-minded. Are you a broad-minded sort of lad?"

"Well, yes, I suppose I am." Messinger tried to smile.

"Good, because I want you to listen to me. Right?"

Messinger nodded, although he felt things were far from right: Lode's grip was surprisingly strong.

The grip lessened and Lode settled back on the pillow, his blue eyes never leaving Messinger's. "How old do you think I am, lad? You won't find the answer in your notes so don't bother looking."

Messinger straightened up. "And why won't I find any mention of it in my notes?"

"Because your predecessor made up a name and date of birth for me, that's why. Like I said, he was a good doctor; I'm hoping you'll be the same. Now answer the question: how old do you think I am?"

Messinger considered arguing that Dimmock wouldn't have falsified Lode's details because of the minefield of National Insurance, NHS records, vaccination programs and the like, but decided to humor the man. Maybe that was what Dimmock had done; humoured him. It was a fact that consultations went smoother once one had gained the patient's confidence.

Messinger's eyes were adjusting to the dim and dusty light now, giving him a better opportunity to observe the patient's features: the unlined face and clear blue eyes that contrasted sharply with the thin hair and liver-spotted hands. "If I had to guess at your age, I'd venture that you're somewhere in your early fifties, perhaps."

Lode laughed. "Way off, lad, way off. Actually, I'm one hundred and forty-nine!" He laughed again, throwing his head back. Messinger noticed that his teeth were unusually small, very white and even. Lode's laughter snapped off suddenly as he looked squarely at the doctor. "You think I'm mad?"

Messinger gave a non-committal smile. "That's not within my remit," he said smoothly. "However, I'm a busy man with a lot of patients to see this morning, so can we stop playing around?"

"You ought to show some respect for your elders!"

The bed squeaked as Messinger pushed himself to his feet. He heard a corresponding creak on the landing.

Lode shouted. "It's all right, Eustace, the young man is not going anywhere!"

Messinger heard footsteps retreating down the stairs. Disquieted, he sat down.

"I *am* one hundred and forty-nine years old. When I was born, Victoria was on the throne and Britain was at war with Russia. Just accept that. I could verify it by telling you loads of historical details, but you would dismiss them as mere fancies learned from books. My bones are as full of memories as yours are of marrow jelly, lad.

"When I was in my mid-forties—I forget exactly how old I was—something strange happened. I fell under a carriage. It ran straight over my arm here," Lode indicated a point below his left elbow, "severing it completely. I picked it up and ran home to my wife. Screamed my bloody head off, I did!" Lode chuckled at something he'd said before fixing Messinger with a searching stare. He shook his head. "Regular little doubting Thomas, aren't we, lad?" He rolled the left sleeve of his nightshirt up to reveal a thick, ropey scar that circumscribed his forearm.

Messinger peered closer. "There's no way they could have stitched your arm back on in the 1890s," he said. "They didn't have the know-how."

"Nobody stitched it on. It grew back!"

"Of course," Messinger sighed. "Silly me. It grew back."

"Don't get sarcastic, lad, I'm warning you."

"And what became of the arm? Did that grow into a pet?"

"I buried it in the compost heap."

"Pity, you could have hand-reared it."

Lode's lips tightened.

Messinger sighed. "You were saying, Mr. Lode."

By way of answer, Lode leaned forward and raised the hem of his nightshirt to reveal his knees.

Messinger recoiled. "Jesus Harry—who did that?"

"Eustace."

"The bastard must have used a lump hammer!"

"A sledgehammer, actually. Every other Thursday. He seems to think I might run away." Lode sucked on his teeth. "There are times when he might be right."

Messinger jumped to his feet, unclipping a cell phone from his belt. He saw again the scratches on the wall behind the bed, and again he thought of a prisoner counting the interminable days of incarceration. The fives were arranged in columns of ten, and there were fourteen completed columns... making over seven hundred. But seven hundred what? Days, weeks? Surely not months?

"If that's what I think it is, put it away, lad."

Messinger put the phone to his ear.

"If you don't put it away, I shall call in Eustace." Lode let the threat hang in the air.

Messinger shot a nervous glance at the door as a floorboard creaked, and felt the fight in him drain away. "Ah, sorry. Wrong number. Yeah, my mistake. Bye." He broke the connection.

"Now come and sit down." Lode patted the side of the bed. "Come on, lad."

He sat down. "But why—" he began.

Lode held up a hand. "All in good time, lad."

"But this is crazy."

Lode's face softened. "Aye, lad, I know I'm asking a lot of you." He looked at the doctor from under lowered eyelids and chuckled. "The best is yet to come."

"I can't wait."

"I'll ignore that. Anyway, Bessie and me, we kept the arm incident a secret. I lay low, hardly venturing out while the arm and hand were growing back. We nearly starved to death, with me not being able to work. Times were different then. That's when we started the vegetable garden, all the way back then."

Lode's eyes clouded over. "Bess died in 1919 of 'flu. Bloody terrible that was. You young 'uns don't know you're born, I swear. We weren't any more able to cope with grief then as you are now, you know? Just because folks lost babies to disease and brothers and husbands to war, it don't mean we became immune. I was one of twelve children. Only eight of us reached adulthood. My mother used to keep daisies in four little jam jars. *One for each of my little mites in Heaven*, she used to say.

"But when Bessie died, I don't know, I just couldn't cope with it. I was an old man; what did I have to live for? In the end, I went down to the Cotton End Bridge." Lode indicated behind him with a thumb. Messinger realised the man was referring to a bridge over a railway line that had served the local collieries. The track was long gone. He hadn't even known before now that it had a name.

"And?"

"I threw myself under a goods train. When I came to, I couldn't see. I was blind." He looked at Messinger, obviously checking that he was paying attention. "I staggered for a short distance and then gave up and lay down where I was. I could tell by my sense of touch that I was among those tall weeds, the ones with the pink flowers."

"Rosebay willow herbs," Messinger supplied automatically.

"Right. And I could also tell by touch that my head was missing."

Messinger blinked, then slumped and covered his eyes. "Jesus Christ! You had me sucked into your crazy little world then. For a moment, I actually *believed*."

"And so you should," said Lode. "It's all true."

Messinger shook his head. "Oh no. You're not catching me out again. I'm off." He started to rise.

Lode grabbed his wrist.

"You're leaving without examining your patient? What sort of doctor are you, eh?"

"A sane one."

"You think I'm insane? I've been crippled and bedridden since 1952, what d'yer expect? My only contact with the outside world is through Eustace." Lode's eyes flicked meaningfully at the bedroom door. He sat back, breathing heavily. "Please, lad. Stay a little longer."

Messinger sagged. He hated himself for it, but he wanted to hear the end of the story. He knew that all he had to do was peel back that high collar and examine Lode's neck, but he wouldn't—it would be an admission of gullibility. And on a deeper, more primitive level, he *couldn't*. "Okay, but it's against my better judgment."

"Good boy." Lode patted the side of the bed again.

Messinger sat down obediently.

"My head grew back," Lode continued, "just as my arm had. I had no idea how long I lay there among them pink weed things."

"Rosebay willow herbs."

Lode took the correction graciously. "I recovered enough to find my way here and recuperated over a period of several months."

"Forgetting for the moment the sheer implausibility of you surviving decapitation and any subsequent regeneration," Messinger allowed himself a smile, "if what you are saying is true, you wouldn't have any memories. You had grown a completely new brain from scratch. You would, mentally, have been like a newborn. Your story has a plot hole I could drive a bus through."

"We pondered long and hard on that one, me and Dr. Dimmock. He suggested that as cerebral fluid surrounds the spinal cord, it could act as a repository of memories." Lode shrugged and spread his gnarled hands as if he really didn't care. "Anyway, while my body was growing a new head, my old head had been busy growing a new body. Eustace turned up. Eustace, like all my brothers, is *me*. A clone. It was Eustace that started to call me Mr. Lode. It's a joke, you see—I *was* Eustace Orr but now he is, and I'm the lode. He keeps me crippled and when he wants another brother—"

"He removes your head and grows another. Brilliant! Can I go now please?"

"You are being very rude, Dr. Messinger."

"Frankly, Mr. Lode, Orr, whoever you are, I think I'm entitled to be rude after all the crap I've had to take from you." Messinger grabbed his bag and stood. "I shall be sending for an ambulance as soon as I have left here, thereby discharging my obligations to you."

Lode raised a shoulder and let it fall, a one-shouldered shrug that said it was Messinger's loss if he left now. "Before you go, take a look out of that window, lad. Tell me what you see."

"What's out there, the tooth fairy?"

"Just look, will you?"

Messinger rested his hands on the windowsill and gazed out, blinking at the change of light. "There are a few old guys at the bottom of the garden. Weeding by the looks of it."

"They'll be tending the vegetables. We grow our own as much as we can. Look closer at them. Notice anything unusual?"

Messinger narrowed his eyes. He turned back to the man in the bed. He did a double-take out of the window and then back at Lode.

Lode's smile was that of the cat that has found the cream. He indicated the scratches on the wall. "I have spawned seven hundred and thirty-eight of us so far, with another on the way. And some of them have become lodes too, I daresay."

Messinger licked his lips with a dry tongue. "Why?"

"Why what?"

"Why would you want to create so many clones of yourself?" Messinger thought about what he had just said, and added, "That's assuming your story had a single grain of truth in it, which it doesn't, of course."

Lode laughed that bitter short laugh of his. "Haven't you ever dreamed of a world without divides? A world where everyone agreed with one another? One religion, one government, one mind; everyone living in harmony? Eustace has watched the world go to hell in a handcart, watched history repeat its mistakes—correction, he's watched *people* repeat their mistakes. He's taking steps to put things right."

Messinger rubbed his eyes. "My predecessor must have been a gullible old fool if he went along with this lunacy. I'm leaving now, and when I get back to my surgery I shall remove the names Lode and Eustace Orr from my panel. As from this moment you are no longer my patient."

"I've told you, it's not me you've come to see."

Messinger made a show of scanning the room. "So where's my patient?"

Lode motioned with his chin at a deep chest of drawers. "Top drawer," he said. "He's a slow developer, this one. We're a bit worried about him."

Messinger dropped the bag carelessly and crossed to the drawer in question. Glaring angrily at the heavy-looking brass handles, he gripped them tightly to still the quivering in his hands, his nostrils full of the almost overpowering stench of blood and disinfectant. He could hear a gentle sighing, a sound like a damp paper bag being slowly inflated. Was it the soft swish of his own blood pulsing in his ears, or the rhythmic rasp of raw, embryonic lungs pulling air? He whipped his head round and glared at Lode, sitting in the shadows... who grinned right back at him expectantly, his teeth a string of pearls in a peach-fuzzy face.

I have spawned seven hundred and thirty-eight of us so far, with another on the way.

"Bullshit," Messinger growled. Annoyed with himself for even hesitating, he snatched open the drawer.

Spoiled Meat

by Ryan C. Thomas

Yesterday in the park, I fed the zombies, tossing bits of cadaver flesh onto the cold cement as they fought each other like pigeons for the morsels. They're not so different from pigeons when you think about it, driven as they are by a primal need to feed, to sustain.

The pigeons, by the way, are all gone. I ain't seen a four-legged creature in some time. Not even a dead one. They're all just... gone.

Anyway, yesterday, one of them creatures that was feeding—a small girl of about seven or eight, still in pigtails—ate right from my hand, licked the blood off my fingers and moaned for more. That was a first for me, and I thought it was a good sign. I kept urging her to bite, saying, "Come on, just a nip; you can do it, Precious." But she didn't. Frustrated, I drove my hand into her top teeth and drew blood from the veins on the back of my hand. But nothing happened; no sickness overcame me, nor did it get her chewing on my goods. I held my hand out longer and longer until she licked it clean like my mongrel used to do to my dishes after some spaghetti, but she still wouldn't bite. And just like a dog, she sniffed around my chest and legs, looking for meat I might have hidden. But I had no more to feed her.

Clean meat is scarce; uninfected corpses have been hard to come by lately. I know there's one under a car near the bookstore. The zombies have been trying to get him for a couple days now, but he's wedged under there good, his head all sunken and his belly distended. Died from hunger, the poor guy. Hell of a way to go, right? Perhaps tomorrow I'll dig him out and cut him up... if I can get him back to my "home" before the zombies tear him limb from limb. The zombies. The Zees as I call 'em now... just to break up the boredom.

Maybe I could tie the chunks of meat to me and see if that works, see if they take me in the process.

Where was I...

The little girl. Yeah, the little girl, eyeball dangling on her cheek like a cat toy. She finally gave up and went foraging. But the others, they stood around me just waiting, eyeballing me hard, as if I could pull fresh meat from the air and fill their bellies.

"Don't you look at me like that!" I yelled. "I got the freshest meat this side of hell. Look!" I held up my hand so they could see the bite mark from the girl's teeth. "Look at it. Smell it. It ain't bad. Taste it! For Christ's sake, just try it!"

But they didn't listen, just stood there swaying, looking up into the sky, maybe waiting for it to rain. Oh they can hear, don't get me wrong, they got ears like boom mics, but if it ain't alive—aside from me anyway—they don't give a shit. I looked at my hand, knuckles pruned from the little girl's tongue, and I started to cry.

Tears make the time go by these days.

When the sun went down I made my way over to the 7-11 for some fine dining. All around me, the Zees shuffled about, moaning and groaning like the Mormon Tabernacle Choir played at 33 rpm. I used to complain about the noise from my neighbor's stereo, that Satan music, big metal or angry metal or whatever they call it, but what I wouldn't give to hear it now, to hear something different than these things bellyaching all damn day and night.

The 7-11's power has been out since I got here, and half of the store is burned to the ground. The canned food aisle made it through pretty much untouched, though. I grabbed a can of Chef Boyardee and opened it with the can opener I keep in my pocket. Room temperature, but God, food is food, right?

I cried while I ate, that much I remember, sitting there, tears rolling down my face, a Zee staring at its reflection in one of the cooler door windows. I mixed my tears with the imitation raviolis and swallowed it all down.

When I was done, I tossed the can at the Zee to see what reaction I could get. Damn thing didn't move, didn't even notice a can just bounced off its head.

The gun in my pocket called out to me again, like it did every day. Like Romeo to Juliet, in a metaphorical sense, you know. It begged to be used.

But I can't do it. If I take that route... I'm dead. I mean really dead. Gone. Nothing. I don't want to be dead... I want to be undead. I want to feel something, even if it's just aching hunger pangs and a yearning for brains. I don't want to stop feeling.

36

Ain't that what life really is? Feeling?

And so I sat and cried some more—ticktock, ticktock—and eventually I just fell asleep on a candy rack covered in melted chocolate bars.

———

When I awoke this morning in the 7-11, a group of Zees was looking down on me, their drool landing on my chest and soaking through to my skin. How best to describe the odor of Zee drool? You ever—whoever you are, who finds this dog-earned notebook one day—you ever open a trashcan that a baby's diaper has been festering in for a couple days, all out in the sun and stuff? Now cover that diaper in fresh puke from the town drunk... okay, you get the idea. It's like that. Better than any alarm clock when it comes to getting you out of bed, that's for sure.

"Morning, Sunshines," I said. This was met with a witty retort, or what I guess would be a witty retort if I could speak zombie. To me it sounded like one of them didgeridoo things from Australia.

Before all the radios and TVs died, they said the plague was a global problem—what'd they call it, a pandemic?—but I bet some bush people in the Outback survived. Well, maybe. Maybe not. It's been a while. And it means shit anyway because where the hell would I get a plane or ship to get there? It's been... what... six months now? And I ain't seen a living soul. I've driven/biked/walked from Dallas to San Diego, and bupkis.

I rolled off the Hershey's mattress and looked outside, saw it was another beautiful day for being the most unwanted man in existence.

Getting over to the bookstore was a huge pain in the ass, what with the cars all flipped about and the Zees all following me around waiting to be fed, tripping me up like cats running between my legs. Like I got a chef's hat on or something. They know I can get the food.

They can learn, the bastards.

Once I'm gone, I want to keep on learning as well.

I want to be a part of something.

There was a time maybe I didn't, when I wanted nothing but peace and quiet, happy to hole up in the TV room downstairs. Got to the point most people said they didn't want me around anyway if I was going to be like that—which reminds me of the time Brandy asked me what "ostrich sized" meant—and I think at first I was sort of happy bout the prospect of a Zee plague. But now...

As I walked, I started thinking on that whole situation, remembering what it was like in the school basement. Boy, that was dumb hiding down there, with no real way out and nothing to eat but big cans of unsalted corn and beans meant for the school cafeteria.

Someone, one of the town folk I'd never seen before, had a radio, and we'd been listening to static that morning, being as how the airwaves had been dead for over a week. The Zees were scratching at the door, shaking it, making it rumble in the jamb. They'd been doing it for longer than the airwaves had been dead, so we'd kind of gotten used to it. Ain't that pathetic? The radio, however, was pissing me off something fierce.

"Can't you turn that shit off?" I said. "Ain't no one gonna broadcast nothing."

"Some of us are still optimistic," the man with the radio said. "You should try having some hope."

"And you should go chat with what's on the other side of that door. Give all of us some more room to move. Take that damn radio with you."

"You really are a jerk, mister, you know that?"

"I know lots, like you're heating up my nerves. Them things out there want you, they better hope they get in before I beat you dead with that radio first."

I was thinking about taking a swing at this guy when the door swung open. Don't ask me how... must have been all that yanking and pushing and pulling for two weeks straight: the damn thing just gave. Them creatures were piled so high on the other side they literally spilled into the room, grabbing at the nearest piece of flesh they could see. The screaming was deafening as everybody ran around all helter skelter, taken by surprise, swinging pots and pans and yardsticks. I punched, I kicked, I shoved hard, the blood in my ears cutting out the sound of people being eaten alive all around me.

In the confusion, the ground came up to me right quick, Zee feet stepping on me as they went after their quarry, and so I called it quits and lay there waiting for my turn. Ticktock, ticktock.

Want to know the crazy part? I fell asleep. Yup, right there in the middle of all that carnage, waiting for my turn, I fell asleep. I'd heard of guys doing that in the war, some kind of defense mechanism of sorts. What's crazier, of course, is that I woke up again.

Untouched.

When I got up, some of my former compatriots were shuffling around, having joined the enemy so to speak. All around me, the Zees paced back and forth, ambling around with blood on their lips, flesh stuck in their teeth. Thing is, the basement door had shut again and some bodies were in front

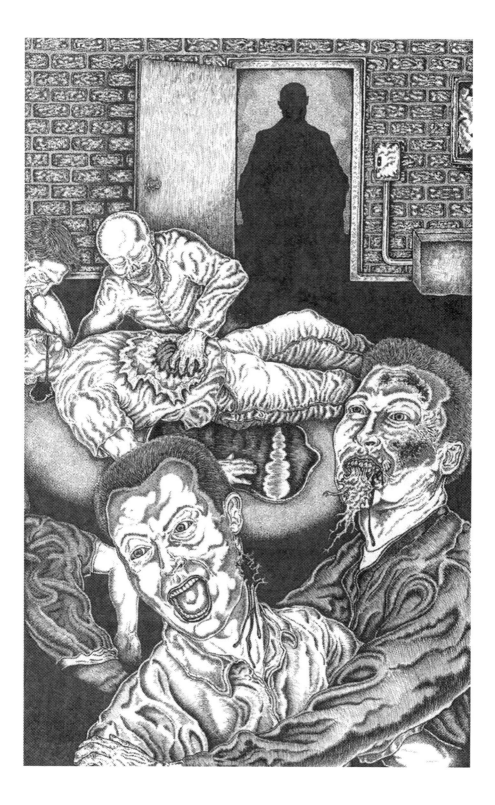

of it, acting as a big doorstop. The Zees were scratching on it, from the inside now, just like dogs. Yeah, like dogs, remember? I got up real slow, waiting for them to notice me, waiting for the inevitable to happen, not really sure why I was still alive anyhow. Not caring about it much neither.

"Hey," I said to the room, "you missed me. Come on, get it over with." I opened my arms in a hugging manner.

They looked at me, looked back at the door, went on pacing.

They didn't want me.

Shit, I thought, now ain't that just a bit off kilter. Why didn't they want me? Didn't make no sense, you know? They should have been all over me, pulling my meat from my bones like I was a Thanksgiving turkey. But they couldn't care less.

What they really wanted, I learned after some time—time spent staring straight ahead, fighting to rationalize my position in all of this—what they really wanted was for me to open the damn door. Because when I finally pushed through them, grabbed a bulk size can of corn off one of the shelves (most of the shelves were tipped over, the cans all ruptured when the others had used them as weapons,) kicked the bodies out of the way, and opened the door, they immediately made for the hallway beyond it, and eventually, the door to outside.

On the street in front of the school, I sat on the curb and watched all the Zees walking around on the sidewalks, on the lawns of nearby homes, down the center of the roads. They all passed me and gave a look my way, maybe stopped and stared for a few seconds, but none came over. Hell, I even took to throwing rocks at them to see if I could get their attention, but they're a one-track-mind kind of species I learned.

The sky was black with smoke from a thousand fires burning all over the county. I didn't hear no birds singing or dogs barking or cats howling. It was just me and the Zees.

At first I didn't know what to feel, but by nightfall, it started to sink in that I was really alone. Not the kind of alone I'd wanted before, where I could turn on the TV and see a ballgame, or get a hi from Jack at the liquor store, or stare at that single mom two houses down who wore them tight pants. I mean really alone. Unwanted. Ostrich sized.

Two streets over was the Episcopal church, so I got up, grabbed my can of corn again, and made my way over to it. The door was open, the stained glass shattered, and there were Zees inside, which seemed a bit disrespectful to me, them being in God's house and all. But then, who's to say all this mess wasn't God's idea, some sort of cleaning method so he can start over fresh. But then why...?

40

I pulled up a pew and stared up at Jesus on the crucifix above the altar. "I don't get it," I said. "Everybody's gone, all eaten and come back as something else. But not me. There something I'm missing here?"

No reply. Nothing.

And then I cried, which was the first time since Korea I'd done that. It was a real cry too, the kind you just can't stop once it starts, the kind that goes on until you're dry inside, the kind you got to fight to breathe through. Some time later, I looked at Jesus again and begged him to take me. "I'm lonely," I said. "I don't want to die. Everybody else, they get to keep on going, even if it's as a monster. At least they got something. At least they got each other. You're leaving me with nothing—nothing! Tell me what I did!"

I threw the can of corn and knocked the cross to the ground.

I fell asleep in the pew.

Where was I...

...tangents, ticktock, tears...

Oh yeah, this morning at the bookstore.

The area outside the bookstore had its usual collection of hungry monsters hobbling around, still waiting to get what was under the car out front. I'd given some of them names, the ones I'd seen around a lot: Goopy and Scabby and No-Arms and Pussface. When they saw me coming, saw the other Zees following me like puppies, they ambled my way as well, as if to say, "Thank God, can you please help up with this big metal doohickey? Our ball rolled under it and we can't get it."

"Yeah, yeah," I said, pushing through their numbers as they sniffed me and played with my shirt (I think they could smell the last bits of good meat I'd tossed out.) "I see your food, you idgits. I'll get it for ya. But first, anybody want an appetizer?" I held up my arm, took out the can opener and ran the dull blade across my forearm. As the blood began to trickle out, a few of them stepped forward and inspected it, but just like the other times I'd tried this, they lost interest and went back to moaning at the car.

Throwing my head back, I screamed at the heavens, "What?! What the fuck did I do?! Why not me?!"

Of course, there was no answer, same as that day in the church. Well, I think one of the Zees farted. Which, really, about summed up what God was doing to me anyway.

"I ain't doing it myself!" I shouted again, just for good measure, pulling out the gun and waving it all crazy-like. "I ain't ending it like that! If you want me, you take me like you took the rest! This ain't fair!"

And I sat down and started boo-hooing again, which lately, had become my shtick. "What's wrong with me, what's wrong with me, what's wrong..." Over and over and over, rocking like a Weeble.

At some point I felt one of the Zees push me, like to say, "Hey buddy, get to it already." Goopy and Pussface were standing next to him, anxious for me to get up as well. Like I said, just like dogs.

"All right, back off," I said, standing up. Past the car, in the window of the bookstore, there was a paperback I'd thought about going in and getting a few times now. Maybe today I would. Maybe it was time to get out of this town—I could use the reading material for traveling. Maybe I should leave tomorrow. The roads are still pretty jammed up with crashed cars and ambling Zees, and I can't ride a motorcycle to save my life, but the Bike shop nearby has some good selections. Maybe Mexico would fare better for me. Maybe I could even keep riding down to Panama or something.

Dropping to my belly, I reached underneath the car and grabbed hold of the dead man's pant leg. His head was all jammed up in the pipes, his eyes still open and dry as chalk, and I had to pull pretty hard to get him out. Course, once his leg hit the sunlight, those Zees pushed me out of the way and went to town, big time.

Hoping against hope, I thrust my arm into the feeding frenzy and felt one take a nibble on my pinky. Hurt like a bitch, but it felt so damn good to be wanted. But the sonofabitch pushed my arm out of the way like it was broccoli on a plate of chocolate cake. Fuckers didn't want me after all. Same old same old.

Yanking some carnage from No-Arm's mouth—in case I needed some for later—I went into the bookstore and grabbed the paperback in the window. It was *The Painted Bird* by Jerzy Kozinski. I'd read it ages ago, and it depressed the shit out of me, but right now, I needed to know someone else felt my pain. Needed to know that someone else out there, even if he was fictional, was as unwanted as me. Rolling it up, I stuffed it in my jacket pocket, made my way back around the Zees, who were all on their knees ripping every last bit of flesh and sinew off that rotted cadaver, and headed back to the park.

The pigtail girl was there again, just sitting on the bench, cradling an unopened can of Coke like it was a baby doll. Let me tell you, when you have no one to talk to, the walls become a real good audience. These Zees were no different than walls, and so I sat down beside her and looked in her eye, the good one that wasn't swishing about on her cheek.

"Hi, Precious," I said. "What you got there? That your baby? What's its name?"

If it had been a real baby it would have been an unhappy one because she tossed it on the ground and growled at it as if it had ruined her life. Satisfied with that, she took up sniffing my coat again and discovered the meat I had in my pocket. Suddenly ravenous, she started to tear into the leather, her strength much greater than you'd expect, so I turned away from her and got my hand on the meat before she rendered me naked. Judging by the look of it, it was a head scrap: an ear and part of the scalp, some hair stuck to it on one end. When she saw it, she lunged at me.

"Hang on, hang on. Jesus you guys don't know shit about patience, do ya?"

So I wrapped it around my fingers because, you know, I had to keep trying, right? Had to hope one of these times the bite would work for me.

And you know what she did, as I gave her my hand and said, "Here comes the plane, into the hanger"? Know what she did? She unwrapped it! Took it off my hand and wolfed it down and didn't touch me at all.

"Oh come on!" I grabbed her head and opened her mouth and stuck my nose in it and pushed her jaws closed until white light erupted behind my eyes and blood ran down my throat. Did that for about ten seconds until I realized I wasn't going to do shit but lose a nose and have to walk around sounding like a teakettle as the wind blew through the new hole in my face.

Needless to say I gave up.

Afterwards, she sat there, blood streaked on her cheek, her dangling eyeball drooping a bit lower, and she just kind of looked at me.

"Brandy," I said, calling her by my granddaughter's name—it just came out of nowhere. She didn't look like Brandy, who'd had blonde hair and freckles before she died, didn't look like her at all, save for the age part. "I miss you."

And then it just came out, out of nowhere, out of that part of my head where important things get buried: "I shouldn't never have yelled at you that day." She, it, whatever, made a sort of cooing sound and dribbled some blood onto the bench, and I chuckled a little bit, which was a good feeling. "I shouldn't never have hit you neither, young as you were. Not for that anyway. Not for breaking a watch I hardly wore anymore. Fact is, I should have laughed at your ingenuity, cooking it in that pot of stew like that. Pretty funny now. Certainly shouldn't have smacked you in the face for it. I get angry, you know, just can't help it. I... I'm... Maybe I can make it up to you? Maybe we can go—"

Before it went any further though, she got up, shuffled over to the coke can, picked it up carefully like it was a crystal vase or something, and walked away into the shadows.

Leaving me alone. Again. With tears. Ticktock. Ticktock.

And so here I am, sitting under the moonlight in a forgotten park, writing to you—whoever you are, who finds this dog-eared notebook—getting ready to head south. The world's most unwanted man. Me. Tomorrow morning, way I see it, I'll grab some Chef Boyardee and get going on down the I-5. Maybe the Mexican Zees got a better bite.

Can't help but keep thinking—hold on... this teenage one's licking my neck... please please please... Shit! No dice. He's leaving now... back to wherever he goes at night, I guess.

Can't help but keep thinking about what my wife said a few weeks before all this began, before she died and came back and ate our granddaughter. She said I was dead inside, that my heart was nothing but a ball of mud, all stinky like skunk cabbage. We didn't get along so great those last years, always fighting and cussing and ignoring each other. And, well, shit, I don't know you—whoever finds this—so I'll just admit that I hit her too. A few times. Great, now I'm getting these words all wet.

Yeah, I hit her. Hard, more than a few times actually. I get angry, you know.

And she said all my bitterness and anger killed any sense of humanity I had.

I told her I didn't care, and went to my TV room downstairs and just stayed there, alone, and didn't come out for... well... until those reports started about the dead people.

I bet she's staggering around back there in Dallas, laughing inside that bloody husk she got as a body now. I bet she's laughing as hard as I used to hit her.

No humanity left.

Maybe she's right.

Because here I am...

Basic Training

by Rick Moore

FOWLER ELBOWED ME OUT OF THE WAY and ran toward the woman. He struck her with the butt of his rifle. Part of her chin disintegrated, covering the rifle butt in viscid black slime. He laughed and said, "Got me a wet one, boys!"

The woman stumbled backward and tripped over her feet. Her back crunched as she landed, and her head thumped against the carpet.

Advancing into the apartment, Fowler twisted the M-16 in his hands and brought it to his shoulder, sighted and ready to fire. He scanned for foes.

"Clear," he called, and moved through to the bedroom. "Clear."

Mitch and I hadn't even made it through the doorway; the door was still swinging from when we'd kicked it open. The bullshit heroics were for Mitch's benefit. Answering the radio call, breaking protocol by coming to unknown territory with half a unit, charging up the stairs and into the apartment—all so the new recruit would think Fowler was some kind of savior to the goddamn planet. It was pathetic.

Our orders were to drive to the training facility and pick up fifteen new recruits, then return to Base. The apartment could have had ten zombies inside. As it was, it just looked like the woman and her victim. But that didn't make Fowler any less of an asshole for risking our necks just so he could play war hero for Mitch, the only recruit who hadn't gone AWOL.

"C'mon in here and take at look at this, kid," Fowler called, locating what remained of the woman's victim in the kitchen.

Mitch looked at me for confirmation. I nodded. He entered cautiously, giving the woman a wide berth.

She was lying on her back, trying to lift her head. Threads of black goop spilled from where her skull had whacked the floor. Every time she tried to raise her head, the tarry threads held it to the carpet, as though she were stuck in a pool of freshly squirted superglue.

I entered the apartment and squatted by her ankles to make an assessment. The woman was naked, and at a guess, in her mid-to-late-fifties. There were chunks of flesh missing from her legs and arms, and she was missing her right ear.

I pressed the barrel of my handgun against the woman's forehead. It was like pressing into putty. A purple bloom spread, dark fluids welling up around the nose of the gun. The woman kept trying to lift her head, forcing the gun deeper. Pinpricks of white roved in her eye sockets, buried beneath layers of black-red crust.

At close range the splatter effect could be fatal—my eyes, nose, and lips all points of potential infection. I stepped away from the woman and took aim, ready to fire.

Fowler came back from the kitchen. "Well are you gonna fuck it," he said, "or are you gonna stand there all day looking at it?"

"Christ, Fowler," I said. "Give it as rest for once, would ya?"

He ignored me and looked down at the woman. "Nice tits. Pussy looks a little runny. What do you think, kid? Feel like taking a dip?"

Mitch grimaced, not sure if Fowler was joking or serious.

"Why don't you take this one, Sarge," I said. "Show him how it's done."

Fowler grinned and grabbed his crotch. "Hey, man, mi casa kielbasa. Maybe I'll do just that."

"Well go for it, Sarge," I said. "Not like we don't got thirty seconds to spare."

Fowler turned on his hard-eyed stare. Grinned. "Better watch that lip, Johnny." He looked over at Mitch. "Hey, kid, you sure you don't wanna get you some head?"

"Right after you get yours, Sarge," Mitch said, playing along now that I'd given him the idea it was okay to give Fowler shit. It wasn't—not with Fowler. He was one of those guys who wanted to dish it out but couldn't take it when somebody gave it back to him.

"Oh, I'm gonna get mine," Fowler said. He looked down at the woman. She growled, pulling against the tarry threads. "Whadda ya say, baby? Wanna give me some head?"

He grinned at me. Raised his boot.

I looked at him with pleading eyes. "Fowler, don't."

His grin didn't falter for a second as he jumped up on one foot and brought the other down. Her head came apart: skin, bones, brains, blood.

Fowler slapped his thigh and stamped a beat with his foot. "They'll be coming round the mountain when she comes"—stomp. "They'll be riding six white horses when she comes"—stomp, stomp.

The kid stood in the little corner of the apartment that passed for the kitchen, watching with huge horrified eyes as his sergeant danced and sang and obliterated the woman's head.

Pantomiming exhaustion, Fowler dropped to the couch and wiped goop from his boot heel with a throw cushion. He lit a smoke and said, "Best damn head of my life."

I was tired of his antics. Fowler didn't care. He got the joke and laughed enough for both of us. I walked over to Mitch.

"Is he always like that?" he asked.

"Fowler? Pretty much."

"He's crazy," Mitch said. It sounded less like criticism and more like admiration. A lot of guys were reeled in by Fowler's thuggish mentality. The man was either too stupid to be afraid, or so insane he no longer cared. Maybe both. But these naïve, scared kids were all looking for somebody to follow now that everything they'd ever known about themselves and the world had ceased to exist. Fowler's bravado convinced them they were safe as long as he had their back.

The woman must have snacked on her victim's brain not long before we'd forced our way into the apartment. The linoleum was covered in dark sticky blood, and the man's head was cracked open like a hard-boiled egg.

His fingers trembled. His hand grabbed the recruit's ankle.

"Shit!" Mitch yelled. He pulled himself free and stumbled away.

The dead thing sat up, white eyes glimmering. Mitch freed his gun from its holster and aimed it at the creature's head.

"Whoa whoa whoa!" Fowler called, waving his arms at the kid and running toward him. Mitch hesitated, looking confused. No matter what they're told in training, they always forget the first time they encounter a Reanimate.

"Lower your weapon," I said. "His brain's already been destroyed. You could empty your clip until there's nothing left of his head and he'd still be moving around."

Mitch lowered the gun. "Sorry," he said. "Sorry."

The victim incessantly moved what remained of his head—left to right, left to right, bubbles of dark fluid forming within the cavity where there should have been a brain.

"Remember," I said. "After you shoot one in the head and destroy its brain, you eliminate the threat. After that they'll stay down for around an hour. When they're about to return a second time, you'll see their fingers twitch. But a Reanimate isn't your enemy. You ever see ten Annies coming at you, and one zombie, be sure to take out the zombie and not waste all your ammo shooting what's never gonna lay down and die."

"Right," Mitch said, nodding.

I continued: "Once the flesh becomes reanimated, you're dealing with something that no longer has a brain. This thing is just cells that have life when there shouldn't be any. Think of them as earthworms in human form. Less than."

Mitch nodded. "I know what it is. It's just I have a hard time thinking of them that way."

"You want my advice?" Fowler said. "Get an axe and chop one of these things up into hundreds of tiny pieces. You watch them bits of innards and fingers and little body parts jumping around, you'll soon enough stop thinking of them as people."

Mitch grimaced. "That's gross."

Fowler laughed and slapped him on the back. "Worked for me!"

* * * * *

Our cargo bucked and thrashed in back, sealed inside body bags, knowing no purpose, and driving me half out of my mind with the constant *thump, thump, thump* as their limbs crashed against the floor. The radio was broken—it was one hundred and ten degrees outside, and we had no A/C. I was hot, bored, and irritated.

My thoughts looped. I'd think about my wife, think about the dead, think about the army, think about Fowler, think about the new recruit—then wonder why I still gave a shit about any of it. Then ask myself if I really did. Then decide I didn't—only to keep catching myself thinking about the same shit all over again.

Fowler was driving—taking occasional pulls from a bottle of Early Times. He handed Mitch the bottle. The kid took a swig and then passed it along to me.

I decided to force down way more than I wanted just to piss off Fowler. Truth was, I'd never been much for hard liquor. But I could see Fowler getting agitated as I guzzled the whisky, and that alone was worth fighting off the gag reflex.

"Hey, what the fuck, Johnny? Go easy there."

I swallowed what was in my mouth, took another long pull, then leaned over Mitch to hand the bottle back. As Fowler reached for it, I wagged my finger in his face. "Didn't your Momma ever tell you, sharing means caring."

Fowler glared at me. There was a time when a disapproving glance would have burrowed inside my mind, making me catalog all I could have done to warrant his disapproval. Back when his good opinion still mattered to me. Back when I looked up to him—*revered* him. But I'd learned to see through a man like Fowler and know what he was really all about. I knew him well enough to know he wasn't worthy of my respect.

Fowler grabbed the bottle by the neck and yanked it out of my hand. All the years on his craggy face disappeared and he was a petulant four-year-old again, snatching back the toy he'd shared because the bribe hadn't bought the other kid's friendship. He breathed the word 'asshole,' then took a hefty swig of his whisky and turned his eyes back to the road.

After a few minutes, some dirty joke must have popped into his head; he laughed to himself and started telling it to Mitch. I'd heard the joke a dozen times before, so I looked out the window, hoping to see something interesting enough to fade the drone of Fowler's voice.

The only thing to look at was the desert, the highway, and a steady flow of trucks identical to ours passing in the opposite direction. Day and night the trucks journeyed from the base, going out into the world empty and coming back loaded with body bags containing dead flesh that refused to die. All the men inside the trucks knew they might not return. Others had already decided not to—knowing everything was going to shit, and that the army was in the thick of it.

I kept looking, hoping to see a stray zombie I could shoot, but all I found were my thoughts: the same thoughts. My wife, the dead, the army, how much I hated Fowler—these were all familiar ground. Only Mitch, or more specifically the reason he hadn't bailed like the other draftees, was of any interest to me. I'd long ago decided to keep my distance from the new guys, just as I did from the guys who'd been around a while. In my experience, soldiers fell into three categories: they were either killed in action, went AWOL, or turned out to be such ingrained assholes that it was better to know them superficially than to endure in-depth exposure. The men I had respected, the ones who'd been my friends, were either dead, or had chosen to protect the only country they could truly still believe in—that of their family.

I tried to speak to Mitch several times, only to find my mouth held nothing but silence. Overcoming my growing sense of detachment made genuine communication more difficult with every passing day. And so we rode in silence.

As the miles rolled beneath us and the sun blazed against my face, I started to nod off. I'd just begun to doze when Mitch jerked in his seat—knocking Fowler's arm and making him momentarily lose the wheel.

"Easy there, son," Fowler complained.

I looked at Mitch, annoyed that he'd woken me.

The kid clapped a hand over his mouth. "Jesus Christ! What the fuck is that?"

The stench of the pits was so ingrained in my flesh that I hadn't even noticed it drifting into the cab through the open window. A few days exposed to the pits and the fumes seep so deep into your skin that the stink never washes off, no matter how long you shower, no matter how much soap you use, no matter how hot the water is. Before you know it, you acclimatize to what was once so unspeakably vile, so much you forget it exists—there's no other choice.

That stench—imagine a city made up of fish markets and slaughter-houses. A city of garbage dumps and open sewers. Top it all off with the fumes of a thousand Meth labs. It was that very same acidy chemical smell of a zombie's breath. The stink of the pits was so bad civilians wouldn't stand within ten feet of a soldier who'd been sent to work the pits, so bad that if a crowd of us on furlough walked into a bar, three minutes later we were the only ones there.

But it was more than just the smell. You could see the fear in their eyes—the civvies. The government was lying to them. Civvies knew it, and we knew it too. Fit for active duty. What a crock. Whatever fucked up shit was making dead people run around and chow down on people was eating us too. Only difference was, we were being eaten from the inside instead of the out. Pit soldiers all had the same look about them, a look that had earned us the nickname "skull-heads." Pit soldiers were going AWOL faster than any other division. But even dressed in civvies, people still knew. Out of uniform they might look like they had the big C or were slamming dope—but no matter how far they ran, they could never escape the way the Pits had marked them.

When he first got into the cab at the training facility, Mitch grimaced and the color drained from his face. All the instructors at the Training Camp had been exposed to the pits, but not so recently as Fowler and I had. As the hours of the morning passed Mitch gradually became a little more accustomed to our stink. But we were nothing compared to the real thing. The recruit went into a coughing fit, leaking tears.

Fowler inhaled deeply and grinned. "Mmm. Smells like home cooking." Mitch dry-retched.

"Better pull over," I said. "Looks like he's gonna puke."

Fowler sighed, his foot switching from the accelerator to the brake.

The kid held up his hand, indicating not to stop. He was determined to prove himself. He looked like hell—pale and sweaty and obviously needing to puke, but as we drove on and the pit-stink got thicker, he didn't make a sound of complaint; he somehow managed to hold onto his breakfast. That was better than I'd done my first time out to the pits—Fowler too—and I could see respect in Fowler's eyes as he gave Mitch a pat on the shoulder. The stench didn't make me want to puke. But that kind of bullshit camaraderie sure did.

If the stench of the pits didn't keep the civvies away, there was no shortage of signs warning them that they were approaching a restricted area. Not that many came to look. They were trying to run from the things we took there—not get closer to them.

Three miles outside Base, we arrived at the checkpoint. Two bored looking guards inside a booth were the only chink in the armor. An eight-foot electrified fence topped with razor wire surrounded the entire compound. Airspace over the Base was also restricted. Anybody who came within five miles received a command to turn back. At three miles they would be shot down. The army didn't want the public seeing the pits. Rumors were one thing; photographic evidence that could cause a public outcry was something else entirely. Thankfully, nobody had decided to test the warning. Yet.

Fowler pulled to a halt in front of the barrier arm. The guard inside the booth looked us over. Satisfied with two of the faces he saw, he raised the barrier, waving us through.

After another two miles of desert, Fowler turned off the paved asphalt that led to the Base, and drove down a well-traveled dirt road. All the way to the Pits, there were high mounds of earth on either side of us.

Trucks like our own were backed up to the pits, soldiers emptying their cargo. Diggers were scooping earth from a fresh pit, making the total seventeen. Each was half a mile across and two hundred feet deep.

As we approached one of them, I tried to imagine how this must have been for the kid. The stink alone had turned his face a sickly yellow and he was dripping sweat. I imagined looking through his eyes at what was inside the pits. Some men had gone crazy the first time they looked inside those holes. Others over time.

"Oh God." Mitch whispered. "God, God, God."

His first glimpse.

I could think of nothing to say to ease the horror of what we'd introduced him to.

Fowler swung the truck in a wide arc and reversed, backing up to the edge of one of the pits. He put the truck in park, pulled the brake, and opened his door. "Time to take out the trash," he said.

"Maybe the kid's seen enough for one day," I said. "Why don't you sit tight, Mitch. We can take care of those two in back."

"Suits me," Fowler said. "If he ain't up for it."

Mitch shot me an annoyed glance. He turned to Fowler. "Who says I ain't up for it?"

"Atta boy." Fowler whacked him in the arm and then got out on the driver's side.

Knowing I might not get the chance again to be alone with him, and knowing the type of R & R Fowler and his boys liked to indulge in, I said to Mitch, "Just watch yourself around that guy. Don't let him talk you into doing anything you don't want to do."

"What do you mean?"

How could I explain? And if I did, would it really make a difference? I shook my head. "Never mind." I climbed from the cab and Mitch got out after me.

Approaching a pit and looking into it never got any easier. But it was impossible not to look. Mitch stood beside me, staring down. Fowler worked the deadbolt loose on the back of the truck and swung open the doors.

There were four other trucks backed up at various points around the rim. The squirming body bags went into the pit with a splash.

They wouldn't stay sealed long. The stuff in the pit had a corrosive effect that ate through the canvas and freed the bodies from their confinement.

Without feeding on living flesh to delay the process of decomposition, the Reanimates liquefy in a matter of weeks. First their skin splits open and the black blood inside them spills out. Their limbs and innards come loose and drift away from the torsos. Their heads fall off. They become part of the bubbling black sewage that flows inside the pits. It flows because it's still animated. Even the silt-beds, one hundred feet beneath the surface, are somehow still alive. To me, the pits looked like pools of crude oil with dead things moving in them. Thousands of body parts that had once sustained human life now living independently.

Below us, a headless torso broke from the inky blackness and went under again, a rope of intestines twisted around it. Upside-down legs went by, feet kicking. A face peered up at us from a body bag that had started to split open. A hand rose from below the surface and skittered across the bag, moving over the face, then dropping back into the blackness and disappearing from sight. On the other side, the same thing was happening in a thousand different places simultaneously—a black stew comprised of moving body parts and internal organs.

Mitch ran screaming. Or tried to. His legs carried him a few feet away from the edge, then buckled. He fell to his knees. Vomited. Sobbed.

Fowler tossed one of the body bags from the back of the truck, and it landed on the ground, stirring up dust. He looked out at me. "Least he didn't jump in. Saw a man do that once." He clucked his tongue, remembering, then ducked back inside the truck.

I went to Mitch and squatted beside him. He turned to look at me, a thread of vomit hanging from his chin, his eyes begging me to make it all disappear, to make the bad dream go away.

I put a hand on his shoulder.

"That's insane..." Mitch whispered. "Insane... Why don't we just burn them like they do everywhere else? Why?"

I knew the answer but wasn't about to say what it was. Not so soon after seeing the Pits. So I said, "A soldier's job is to follow orders. Not to ask questions."

The Pits were an experiment and so were the soldiers exposed to them. That much was obvious. The Government wanted to know what happened when these things decomposed. They tested the air, took samples from the Pits. They ordered us to undergo weekly physicals and give blood, urine, and stool samples to determine the effects of exposure to the gasses the Pits released.

Or at least, that's how it was until about three weeks ago. There'd been no testing or physicals since then. The experiment seemed to have been abandoned. Civilization was falling into chaos. The enemy's numbers were multiplying with every passing day. We were losing the war. But until we were told to destroy the Pits and start burning bodies, all we could do was follow orders and wait.

But Mitch needed to hear something—*anything*. "What's in those pits isn't human," I said. "It doesn't think or feel or understand what it is or what's happening. It's just tissue that refuses to die—just confused DNA that's trying to resemble something it used to be."

Fowler tossed the second body bag from the back of the truck. He jumped down and dragged a bag over to the edge of the pit, then rolled it in.

There was a soft splash, and the kid looked up, watching him return for the other one.

Fowler winked at Mitch. "Don't you worry about losing your breakfast, son. Soon as we're through here, I'll treat you to lunch. Maybe even a few beers to go with it."

Mitch forced a smile and wiped the vomit from his chin.

Looking at Fowler's grinning mug, knowing the son of a bitch had a hidden agenda, I blurted, "And later on, if you'd like, you're welcome to come over to my house for dinner. My wife's making spaghetti. Best I ever tasted. The recipe's so closely guarded that her mother threatened to kill me when she caught me reading it over her shoulder."

Mitch managed a smile.

My wife's mother lived in Los Angeles. My own mother and father, in Atlanta. I didn't know if they were still alive and didn't want to think about it. Their phones still rang, but no one ever answered. The messages we'd left on their machines were never returned.

"Your wife lives with you here on the Base?" Mitch asked.

"Sure," I said. "There are families here too. There are even some families with daughters about your age. Maybe I'll introduce you to a few."

That was an outright lie. The families were long gone. Transferred when requests were approved, AWOL when denied.

"Thanks," Mitch said. "I'd like that."

Fowler didn't. Not one bit. He kicked the dirt and chewed his bottom lip.

In a hushed voice I said, "And remember what I said about watching yourself around that guy."

"Roger that," Mitch whispered. "Truth told, he seems like he's kind of psycho. But he's my sergeant, you know?"

"Come on," Fowler called, "let's go. Before I die of thirst out here."

"I'll write down the address and directions before we drop you at your barracks. Four o'clock sound okay?"

"Sounds great, Johnny," Mitch said.

What was I doing? I'd seen so many of my friends killed. In all likelihood Mitch would be killed too. To keep my sanity, I'd vowed to never care too deeply about the fate of another soldier. And now here I was, doing it again.

* * * * *

What I'd told Mitch about my wife's spaghetti being the best I'd ever tasted was true. But my wife wouldn't be cooking it. She'd been gone close to four weeks. I didn't want anyone to know. So I kept coming back to my house—my shitty army provided accommodation—making like she was still there when anyone asked about her, making like everything between us was fine. She had left no note. All I had for a goodbye was our *last* conversation. I refuse to say final. I keep telling myself one day I'll wake up and she'll be there beside me in our bed. Or that I'll walk in and she'll be there, watching her soaps, or cooking, everything the way it was before the whole world went to shit.

I got a beer from the fridge and walked to the bedroom. The bed was empty. That was where it had happened—where she'd said it out loud instead of feigning sleep, or a headache, like she had those last two months.

"I can't, Johnny," she'd said. "I can't. God, I can't stand it when you touch me. Rubbing that stink all over me. I can't even stand to kiss you—I can taste it on your mouth. And when I look at you... God, Johnny, you look like a cancer patient. You all look like cancer patients. Do you know what people call you? They call you skull-heads. Skull-heads. Do you think I want to end up the same way? You wouldn't want me to become what you've become. You wouldn't want that. Not if you love me, Johnny. Not if you love me."

I finished my beer and worked my way through another two while I made spaghetti sauce. I had no idea what I'd tell Mitch about my wife not being there; but I'd invited him to dinner and planned to make good on my offer. When it was done, I got a spoon from the drawer and set the sauce to simmer. It tasted okay. Just not the same as when my wife made it. I tried another mouthful.

Chewing it, I remembered how my wife would always give me hell for using a metal spoon and scratching away the non-stick coating on the pan. The memory was all the persuasion I needed to crack a fourth beer and head for the couch. I nodded off halfway through it and a news report on the TV about a mass exodus of civilians to Alaska.

When I woke up, it was ten after five. If anybody had knocked I would have woken. I sat there telling myself Mitch could take care of himself, that if Fowler talked him into doing anything, then Mitch was to blame for listening in the first place. The argument wouldn't sell. Two minutes later I was headed out the door for the clubhouse.

*   *   *   *   *

I parked my jeep out front and entered the clubhouse. The bar was already packed, but there was no sign of Mitch or Fowler. The grunts were doing their best to escape the terrors they'd encountered that day, drinking too fast and talking too loud. There were no women—only men. I tried not to look at them too closely. Tried not to notice their deep sunken eyes and skin; it looked too much like wax paper. I ordered a beer, took a deck of cards, and sat at an empty table to play solitaire.

Fowler and his boys came in an hour or so later. I saw the usual faces: Fowler, Hodges, Jones, and Hayden. They pushed through the throng to the bar, swapping friendly insults with the soldiers on their way. Mitch was with them. I tried to push what that might mean from my mind. Tried again to tell myself whatever happened was none of my business. They were drunk. My guess was that Fowler had treated Mitch to a liquid lunch and all thoughts of his dinner engagement had gone right out of his mind. He looked pretty rough—his hair mussed, his uniform rumpled. Like he'd been asleep on his bunk until they'd gone to rouse him from his barracks.

I watched Fowler, looking for the telltale signs that would confirm my deepest concerns. For an hour they drank and laughed and told jokes, and I thought for once Fowler would do nothing worse to the kid than get him drunk.

But then it started. Nudges and winks, whispers and grins. Mitch was completely oblivious to the plotting going on around him. It made me feel nauseous.

Fowler said something to Mitch. He looked back blankly, unable to keep his body from swaying. Fowler repeated what he'd said and Mitch nodded.

When they headed out the door, I stood and followed, catching up outside. I grabbed Fowler's arm. Spun him around. He looked at me bleary-eyed.

"Hey, Johnny," Mitch slurred. "How you doin' man? We was gonna go play some cards. You wanna come play some cards?"

"Don't do it, Fowler," I begged. "It's a mistake."

"Do what?" Fowler asked, a big goofy grin on his face.

"You know damn well what. Just let him go."

He shrugged himself free of my hand. "We ain't gonna hurt him. Just gonna show him a good time."

"Not this kid," I said. "It's not what he wants."

"How d'you know what he wants?" He looked at Mitch, draped an arm over his shoulder. "Hey, kid, you wanna have a good time with me and the rest of the boys, doncha?"

Mitch grinned. "Sure, man. Let the good times roll." Something occurred to him. "Aw shit. You invited me for dinner. Sorry, man, I forgot all about it."

"Trust me," I said, taking Mitch's arm. "You won't enjoy what these guys have in mind."

Fowler slammed into me with his gut and knocked me to the ground. The rest of his boys moved in, boots drawn back, set to give me a kicking.

Fowler whistled. "Hey! Quit it!"

His dogs obeyed and backed away. Mitch swayed, confused.

"Just chill, Johnny," Fowler said. "Time this boy became a man. Ain't that right, soldier?"

One look at Fowler and Mitch was grinning. Even now the kid still trusted him. "S'right," Mitch said. "Let the good times roll."

I watched Fowler lead him away. I got up and followed at a distance. I knew where they were headed. Some called the place "The Woodshed," others "The Shed." For years it was a disused gymnasium, until it was unofficially reopened for other purposes.

Mitch was led through the door. I waited thirty seconds or so, then followed them inside. They were leading him somewhere I doubted he'd want to go. If I was wrong, then all well and good. But if I was right, and they tried to coerce and bully him, to me that made it no different than rape.

I entered The Shed and shivered. Outside it was still ninety degrees, but the Shed was kept almost as cool as a refrigerator. I found them looking down at a "Toy" that was strapped to a cot.

Mitch just stood there, mouth hanging open, eyes uncomprehending. The rest of them were grinning down at the thing they'd brought him to see.

"Pretty sweet, huh, kid?" Fowler said. "Bet you never had a piece of ass that fine before."

"She..." Mitch said. "She's not got a head."

"None of them have heads," I added, coming up beside him. I could see my breath as I spoke. "It was decided they shouldn't look too human. So none of us would ever forget they were only Toys."

"Like blow-up dolls," Hodge said. "Only better. Cause they still get wet down there."

Mitch shivered and I didn't think it was because of how cold it was in there. There were fifty cubicles like this one. Each had a drawn shower curtain in front of it. Soldiers' boots were set outside many of the closed curtains to let everyone know those Toys were taken. Groans and grunts came from inside the occupied cubicles.

The headless thing on the table was strapped at the wrists and ankles so she couldn't move. From the neck down, she had the body of a supermodel. She'd remain that way for a few days, until the rot set in. But there were plenty more where this one came from. Millions. And more with every passing day. The only sign of disease was on her left shoulder, where a zombie had sealed her fate by taking a chunk of her flesh. It had been cauterized and was now a lump of scar tissue.

"Course you gotta wear a rubber," Fowler said. "Cause there's a chance the virus gets passed that way. Me, I always wear two. But it ain't so bad once you get used to it."

He grinned, the skin on his cheeks pulling so taut his cheekbones looked like they'd rip right through. He looked like a living skull. They *all* looked like living skulls, except for Mitch. I suppose I must have looked like one too.

"But she... She ain't got a..." Mitch looked at Fowler, appalled. "You have sex with these things?"

Fowler said, "Might seem kind of strange. Seemed that way to me at first. But think of it like this. You pay a hooker for sex—you're buying the use of her flesh. But there's still a person inside. These days, times being what they are, that just don't seem right. But this way, you're using flesh nobody wants and nobody owns."

I said, "When you think it over, Mitch, you'll see it's better to put these bodies to good use than just toss them in the pit. And we only use them for a few days. Until they start to fall apart. And you're under no obligation to lie down with them, Mitch. It's something we do by choice. Don't think for a second you have to do it if you don't want to."

The Toy pulled against its restraints, its thighs opening, revealing pink meat.

Mitch reeled back from it and pushed past us. He took off across the gymnasium, headed for the door. As he ran his arm snagged one of the shower curtains, snatching it back. A soldier was on a cot fucking one of the Toys. His chin was set on the cauterized stump of her neck. His pants were around his ankles. His ass rose and fell as he hammered away. He'd freed her ankles from their straps and her legs were wrapped tightly around his ass.

Mitch screamed. The sound echoed throughout the gymnasium, becoming one with the grunts and quiet moans and *KY-slap-slap-slap* as soldiers claimed what little reward they could for risking their lives and sanity in a world where every civilian saw them as symbols of death and madness.

Mitch spun around, looking for an exit.

"Happy now?" I said to Fowler.

Fowler shrugged. "Kid had to learn sooner or later."

I found out then what I'd wanted to know for longer than I remembered. I wanted to know how my fist would feel slamming into that big goon's jaw. It felt as good as I'd imagined. Better, because this was the real thing. Fowler fell easy for a man his size. As I stood there looking down at him, I regretted waiting so long to do this. Fowler looked up at me, dazed, rubbing his chin, uncertain if what had just happened could possibly be real.

I said, "If it had been later, after he saw how women treat us, he might have been okay with this. You ever pull a stunt like this again, I will fucking kill you. You got that, Fowler?"

He nodded quickly.

Mitch pushed his way through the door and disappeared into the night. I set off then to look for him and to hopefully make him understand our madness.

*   *   *   *   *

Mitch ran as fast as he could back toward the barracks. I wondered just who he intended to tell. I set off after him, keeping him in sight but gaining no ground on his lead.

Back at the clubhouse, I got into my jeep. Knowing he couldn't outrun me now, I kept my distance and watched to see what he intended to do. Every so often he'd slow to a jog and look at the buildings he passed. He didn't enter any of them. He must have realized the Woodshed had to be sanctioned for it to exist. That meant anybody he might tell already knew about it. Poor bastard. There was nowhere he could turn.

He looked back and saw me following. When he started down the road that led away from the Base, I knew he intended to go AWOL.

He would never get past the guardhouse. Not on foot. And there was no way over the fence. Mitch seemed to realize it. At the entrance to the pits, he turned and walked onto the dirt road that led down to them.

My brights found him at the edge of the first pit, looking down into it. I turned off the engine and climbed from the jeep. He sat there, crying and rocking back and forth. I walked over and squatted beside him.

"I thought nothing could be worse than this," he whispered, looking into the pit.

"It's a lot to take in," I said. "The question now is what you intend to do about it."

His voice trembled as he spoke. "That back there: all those bodies—that's evil. Evil, Johnny. It's an offense in the eyes of God."

"More of an offense than this?" I asked, gesturing toward the pit. "If there is a God, then to allow what's down there to exist when He has the power to make it stop—that's a crime far worse than any we've committed."

"I joined the army to fight for good," he said. "Not to become a part of some sick and twisted little club. How can you guys... How can you..."

I sighed. "There are no good guys and bad guys, Mitch. There never were. That's something you learn with age. There are just people doing what they need to do to get by. I keep telling you, they're not human. Just body parts that won't lie still. All we did was find a way to utilize some of them. Don't us guys deserve that much, given what we do?"

Mitch looked at me. "You think I can just forget all that shit back there, man? Think I can act like I saw nothing? Just say nothing?"

I shook my head. I knew what had to be done.

Mitch would never leave the base again. The order would be given to silence him, and the thugs sent to do the job wouldn't just have their fun; they'd also take their time about it. I'd seen it before.

It occurred to me that we could get in my jeep and run the checkpoint. I could save the kid's life. Even salvage what little sense of decency I had left.

But then I had a terrible self-realization. Just like the body parts inside the pit, I was trying to resemble something I used to be—trying to recapture a time when I was a better man. Before everything went to shit, it was easy to convince myself that an unshakable sense of decorum guided my every thought and action. But now a new truth had emerged: I really did not care. I'd gone out on a limb to protect Mitch—but only because I'd been looking for an excuse to exorcise my long-standing hatred for Fowler.

Mitch said, "What am I gonna do, Johnny? I can't—"

He didn't expect me to do it. Didn't see it coming. One second he was sitting there, trying to make out my face in the dark, the next I hoisted him up from behind and tossed him into the pit. I heard his body tumble down the rocky embankment. Heard a splash as he landed in the foul blackness. Heard his scream as the dead things unwittingly claimed his life, dragging him down below the surface.

I stood there listening, waiting—making sure.

It had to be done. What if he'd somehow made it past the checkpoint? What if he went to the press, and the Woodshed closed? Then what? The bodies gave me a reason to exist. There was no way I was going to jeopardize

that. I was a pariah to my wife, dead to every woman I'd ever encounter from here on out. There was nothing left for me except the Toys.

I returned to my jeep and headed back toward the Base. I wondered if the Toys would always be enough to satisfy the needs of the rest of the men. Or whether, as time went on, they would start to return with different toys —ones that were still alive.

Deadtown Taxi

by Matthew Bey

The fares that night pissed me off more than usual. I got three goddamn lich one right after the other. I hate lich. All they ever do is complain: "You're driving too slow. This isn't the fastest way to the airport. My pelvis is in a knot. Yadda, yadda, yadda." And then they don't tip worth a crap. I wish they would just stay up on their hill, drink their wine, eat their flesh, and stay out of my taxi and out of my life. But I give them their ride and I keep my mouth shut, and I think about the shotgun under the seat and how nice it would be to whip it out and smear them over the back window.

There was one ghoul, pretty early in my shift. I took her from that greasy tenement at 2056 Henry to her job clearing tables at a McDonald's four blocks away. She could have walked there in the time it took me to take the call, but you know what they say: a ghoul and her money are soon parted. At least she tipped more than the lich.

And there was the usual crew of zombies like me. Mostly bartenders at this time of night. Cabbies and bartenders are two sides of the same industry. The bartenders make them too drunk to drive, and then we haul them away. There's always a professional understanding when a bartender is in the back.

It was still too early for the vamps, thank God. They can be some prissy motherfuckers.

So there I was, still fuming about the stupid lich right into the mid-shift lull, when I decided to queue up early at the bus station. I pulled into the first slot, and the whole place was deserted except for her. I knew she was a breather the moment I spotted her. There's a few vamps who try to pull off the "live look," but there's always something a little off. Sort of like the Adam's apple on a drag queen. Now this girl, she was the real thing. And when I pulled up close, I saw her in all her living glory.

She opened the door and slid into the backseat as soon as I came to a stop. The smell of her permeated the taxi. I swear I could smell her brain, all pink and luscious and filled with fresh blood and vitality. I wanted to reach back there and take a big-ol' bite out of the top of her head. In the hungry silence, I could hear her breathe. Breathing's something that don't happen in my cab too often.

"Where ya headed, miss?"

"Oh, yeah, of course. Just a sec." She dug around in her bag. As her head was down, I looked at her through the rearview. My god, she was perfect. She had golden blonde hair and skin flushed with health. She had everything you would expect in a breather girl and more. But there was something about her that tickled my moldy cranium, something that jogged my memories from before the endless drudgery of death.

"Three-twelve Gosford Street, please," she said. "You know where that is?"

"Yes. I'm familiar with that area." I made a show of writing the fare on my clipboard. Gosford is the redlight district of Deadtown. As a cabbie, I knew Gosford like I knew the airport loading zone.

"Is it far?"

I couldn't believe she was in a hurry. I pulled out and started the meter. "No. Not far. Just downtown."

"Ah." She turned her face to the window. She looked clinically despondent. Big surprise. No way no breather would come to Deadtown unless they were totally fucking loopy.

"Did you hear the one about the ghoul who went into politics?" I asked.

"No."

"He loved to shake hands and eat babies."

You could have cut the silence with a machete. My big flaw as a cabbie is my mouth. I'm a talker. I can't just sit there, practically right next to someone, without jabbering my head off. "So. Read any good books lately?"

She barked a laugh, leaning forward as she hugged her shoulders. "Ask me three years ago. Before I got a life and started partying." A crack opened in the cynicism for just a moment. "Sometimes I miss all those books I loved."

I did some quick mental aerobics and figured she had probably stopped visiting the library when she was fifteen.

I pulled up at a stoplight. A lich trundled past in her SUV, pearls hanging about the cracked parchment of her throat. I took the opportunity to ask the question that had bugged me from the moment I laid eyes on my fare. "So what brings you to Deadtown, miss? If you don't mind my asking."

"I got a job here." She held a piece of paper up to the rearview. She had torn it from a newspaper classifieds. I didn't read it. I didn't have to.

I put my arm across the seat back and turned to look at her. She jumped at the sight of my face. I was probably the first undead she had seen up close, and I don't think my own mother would have recognized me. I've been dead for a while, and I ain't been using a lot of beauty cream. I fixed that little breather girl with my milky pupils, and I don't think she could have looked away if she tried.

"Listen to me, miss. There are no jobs in Deadtown for a nice breather girl like you. And certainly not on Gosford Street. Not jobs you would want."

"That's my business." She tossed her head with that pretty pink brain of hers and looked out the window. The way she clenched her jaw in defiance, I'd seen that before; it was so very like someone I once knew—

"The light's green, mister."

The Toyota behind me honked. I sat forward and slowly accelerated through the intersection. We drove another four blocks, and I managed to keep my mouth shut. As we got closer to the red-light district, each block looked seedier than the last. Pushers lounged openly on the corners, hawking their wares, mainly stimulants and Viagra.

The dispatcher read out the next round of calls, the radio squawking out the intersections. We were getting close to Gosford Street, so I put in a bid.

"Cab forty-one," the radio called. A wight named Erika dispatched that night. She was one of the better dispatchers.

I clicked on the CB. "Cab forty-one at tenth and Martin Luther King." I swallowed. My trachea made a dry, crackling sound. "En route to fleshspread."

If the breather girl heard Gosford Street's nickname, she didn't let on. Erika assigned me a new call in the politically correct East Side just as I pulled into Deadtown's sin central.

Lurid is the word for Gosford Street. Neon light striped the interior of the cab. A man can build up a lot of desires when he's dead, and fleshspread is where it all comes out. On the sidewalks, gangly ghasts and night stalkers barked advertisements for chthonic delights. Zombies in brown trench coats stumbled between video parlors. Dismembered hands scrambled into adult gift shops by their fingertips.

I wish I could say I was entirely ignorant of the pleasures of fleshspread, but I've gone through some dark times, and I've done things and seen things that I'm not proud of. I know what goes on behind those doors with the glossy posters.

So when I pulled up to 312 Gosford, what was left of my ichorous heart collapsed a little further. Over the door, a red neon sign blinked "Live Girls." In smaller letters, the handbills promised "Live Death Acts."

I paused the meter. "Here we are, miss." I didn't look in the rearview, but I could hear her rooting for cash in her bag. "You don't have to do this, you know. I can take you back to the station. No extra charge."

"I told you. This is my business."

"I don't think you—"

"Listen. I've been on my own for a while now. And it's not like my mom and pop were much help when they were around." I think she would have cried right then, but she held the tears behind an iron-stiff upper lip. She dropped the fare and a hefty tip on the front seat and got out. She didn't even pause as she walked through the door beneath the red sign.

And there it was again, the tickling of memory. I sat there, double-parked, for several minutes. I listened to Erika calling off the next round. I sighed. For someone who's been dead as long as I have, sighing is a laborious and uncomfortable exercise.

I know she told me it was none of my business, but I couldn't leave this one alone.

I locked up, put on the blinkers, and followed her in. That juicy brain smell of hers still lingered in the vestibule. The inert pile of flesh behind the grill barely looked at me as I pulled out my cash wad and paid the cover.

Light and sound assaulted me as I pushed through the club's steel doors. The bouncer leered at me from his stool. He was a huge thing, possibly a sumo wrestler in life. Since death, his body fat had partially liquefied and sagged, draping over his stool like a garbage bag of pus. He seemed to be chewing on a severed finger.

Zombies and ghouls piled about the bar and around the dance cage. They moaned and screamed with ecstatic hunger. A live girl lay within the bars of the cage, her warm flesh shining under the spotlights. I pushed forward to make sure she wasn't the girl I had taken in my cab. She wasn't. This one was a brunette, but she had the same cynical emptiness in her eyes. She struggled halfheartedly as a charnel thing sent necrotic tentacles around her ankles and up her calves and between her thighs. Her hopelessness excited me.

The club D.J. started to play "Roxanne" by the Police and everything left me except the hunger.

That happens from time to time. My mind just switches off and I join the frenzy of the mob. We all crowded around, all of us zombie Joes, just banging on the cage and moaning, "Brains... brains... brains..."

I came back to my senses as The Police squelched away and the DJ started up with "Friends in Low Places." I felt filthy, as if my scabbed veins ran thick with shit. They were dragging the girl offstage. Now I've seen some pretty ugly things in Deadtown, but that wasn't pretty at all. Smears of blood glued fluttering dollar bills to her desecrated cadaver. They hadn't bothered to rein in the charnel thing. Because they had a replacement for the brunette.

Then I remembered why I was there. I looked over the crowd. The breather girl stood near the back table where the mummified manager prodded her flesh with a finger that was all bone and jerky-dry tissue. They had already put her in a G-string and had liquored her up. She was doing lines of coke, and if I knew anything about the sleezoids who ran a place like this, they hadn't forgotten to slip a roofie in her cocktail. Meanwhile, inside the cage, the charnel thing quivered in a pool of blood.

You know how breathers say their jaw can drop in surprise? Well, it hit me all of a sudden how I knew this live girl, and the shock of it actually popped my jawbone out of its socket.

I hustled back to the door, pounding my mandibles back in place. I stopped briefly by the bouncer and gave him a lopsided grin. "Could I get my hand stamped?"

He ground the stamp into the back of my hand with enough force to burst several of my lesions.

I gave him a wink. "Thanks, pal. Just stepping out for a sec."

Back in the cab, I keyed the radio. "Forty-one. Forty-one."

The radio crackled as Erika responded. "Cab forty-one, go ahead."

"I'm going to ten-seven. You better re-assign my call."

There was a pause as she did whatever it is that dispatchers do when no one is watching. "Sure thing, Otto. Anything I should know about?"

I frowned. "I'm going on that killing spree I've been talking about."

"What set that off?"

I pulled my wallet from my back pocket. The knob on my femur had worked it into a bend, but I could still make out the faces in the pictures inside. There was a picture of me, gaunt from cancer but still brimming with life, and in my lap sat a little girl with golden blonde hair. "I think it's Julie. I think they have my daughter."

"Ten-four, Otto. Just don't wear any company logos."

I knew Erika would understand. I fished out the shotgun from under the seat. It was a twelve-gauge pump. I had sawed off the barrel and most of the stock so I could hide it easier. The spare ammo box was in the glove compartment. I hid the shells in various pockets.

Leaving the engine running, I exited through the passenger door. In a few moments I would need a rapid getaway. Standing there on the sidewalk, I double-checked the chamber. Yep. A shell in the pipe.

I'm not really sure why I bothered with the ticket guy. He was pretty far along. There gets to be a point when a zombie is more decay than man. The guy behind the grill was about four carrion flies from being a pile of damp humus. But I think I wanted to be thorough, and I wanted to demonstrate my own commitment.

I entered the vestibule, put the shotgun barrel through the money slot, and lined it up with the inert pile of flesh on the swivel chair. Out of a sense of obligation, I gave him a one-liner.

"Say cheese."

His head lolled in the general direction of the barrel. I pulled the trigger. He came apart like an éclair filled with viscera.

I always thought buckshot was a good choice for close-quarters work. I was right.

The bouncer had barely got his sloppy ass off the stool by the time I kicked open the door. My ears were ringing from the first blast, so I didn't hear what he shouted. Probably something like, "Mercy, mercy, don't kill me. I've got so much undeath ahead of me." Whatever. I smeared his maggoty head across three shelves of cheap liquor.

The great thing about crowds in confined places is they have no place to run. And you don't have to aim. I stood at the door and hosed down my whole field of fire, grinning exactly like a maniac zombie with a gun. Yeah, I definitely enjoyed myself. I blew smut mongers to pieces left and right.

The surviving patrons jostled to get out the door. One vamp tried to rush me from behind with a broken bottle, but I creamed him pretty bad. Another two low-functioning zombies just stood around, rocking from foot-to-foot and moaning in confusion. I sent them to join the scattered piles of twitching corpses. I crowed a triumphant, "Grraarrrarrr!"

Then I pumped the gun and there weren't any more shells in the ammo extender. I wish I were better at counting my shots. Us zombies, we're not so good with the arithmetic.

As I struggled to get more shells out of my pockets, a lich stepped out of the fleeing crowd. It fixed me with its empty eye sockets. An aura of shimmering necrotic energy drew into it, black runes tracing through the air like squiggly maggot tracks.

Just like a lich to butt in on the action.

I had only just pumped the first shell into the chamber when the lich threw a globe of black light. It hit me about the ribs, stripping away the flesh.

Even when you're dead, it ain't pleasant to feel half your chest dissolve.

I fell and several ribs snapped off and clattered across the floor like pieces of kindling. The lich loomed over me, the energies of unspeakable wisdoms swarming about its fists. It leered a corpse grin at me.

"You... asshole," I said with my remaining lung. "Always... shoot... the head."

The twelve gauge sheered the lich in half where the spine joined the pelvis. The torso flopped around furiously, trying to grab onto its lower extremities. Those lich bastards can be hard to kill.

I saw the manager pulling the girl, my Julie, toward the rear exit, so I dragged myself in that direction. On the way, I passed the girl I had seen defiled in the cage. She hunched behind the bar with a mop in her hand. When this was all over, it would be her job to clean up the mess. It's a long slope from Liveopolis to here. One day you're a star and the next you're just another gaping torso in the crowd.

I limped in a circle to survey the scene. I had pretty much cleared the place out. Whattaya know.

When I turned around again, the manager was using Julie as a shield. He had a length of his burial shroud pulled tight around her neck.

"I don't know who you are, or what you have against my club, but I suggest you walk back out that door right now." He grinned, rows of ivory teeth in blackened gums.

It was tough to speak, so I took my special shell out and held it up so he could see it. A few months ago I went down to the pawnshop and bought all the jewelry the guy said was real silver. Hell, it could have been tin for all I know. The important thing is, the blowtorch melted it all real good, and it formed a fucking big slug about the size of a fifty-cent gumball. I've been keeping that slug for precisely this sort of situation.

I chambered the special slug. The manager jumped a little at the sound of the pump ratcheting open and closed. I sighted down the barrel, aiming right between his shriveled eyeballs. "Here's... the deal... asshole—"

I fired halfway through the sentence. That's one of the problems with being undead. You act really erratic. Whatever. I doubt I had anything interesting to say.

Of course, I didn't fire directly at the manager; that would have been stupid. Everyone knows that mummies remove all their vital organs during the mummification process. I aimed for the row of jars on the top shelf behind the bar. I figured the manager would want to keep his vitals close to him while he worked, so I had looked for them when I scoped out the club.

They were disguised to look like pickled-egg jars, but their tamper seals were intact.

The special slug shattered the jar second from the left. Something not unlike lumpy chocolate pudding splattered across the wall. The manager gave an "urk" and collapsed, even more dead than before. I'm glad I hit something vital on the first shot. It would have been real embarrassing to shoot his spleen or his gall bladder or something.

Julie tore the shroud from her neck and actually collapsed into my arms, which attests to her state of mind, considering how I must smell.

"Thank you," she sobbed, her words slurring. "That fucker tried to choke me."

"Julie... my Julie..."

She just looked at me queer like, her drunken eyes almost as unfocused as mine. I don't blame her for not recognizing me. Julie was so very young when I was living.

We rode back to the bus station. She didn't say much, just slouched in the backseat and vomited at irregular intervals. I babbled as best I could with my remaining internal organs, explaining that I hadn't written all these years because of—you know—the whole brain-eating-corpse thing. I told her that I would lay it on the line for her anytime. I didn't tell her that killing sprees in Deadtown weren't such a big deal. Just a *faux pas* really. Sort of like stealing from a garbage dump.

I waved as she boarded the bus with "Liveopolis" written on the front. She had my cash wad for the night and another chance. I hoped it would be enough.

When I got back to the cab, there was another live girl waiting by the door. This one had dyed-black hair and nostril rings. I noticed the telltale slash scars on the inside of her forearms.

"You on duty, mister?"

"Yeeeesss..." I opened the back door and she slid in, the stink of her brain curling around my head. I stood there, rocking back and forth for a moment, dizzy with the aroma.

When I ducked into the driver's seat, she held up an Internet printout and pointed to some circled text. "I got this want-ad off Craigslist. You know where Gosford Street is?"

"Yeeeessss..." I studied her in the rearview. There was something about this live girl, something that tickled a deep part of my rotten brain, the part of me that remembered the sunshine city of Liveopolis. "Julie...?"

"Huh? Could we get going?"

Julie. My Julie.

Killing the Witch

by A.C. Wise

ake no mistake, Dorothy was every bit the witch—ever as much as the one from the West. The house was no accident.

It was said she met her companions along the way, but that is also a lie. The wild child from out of the darkness went into the forest and found a beast that would be king, which knew no fear, and she taught it to be afraid. She made a man from tin in an image that was her own—with no heart. It was said she loved him first and bewitched him so that he must chop off his limbs with his own axe. She remade him from cold metal and bound him to do her will. It was a cruel love, but without a heart to be broken, he followed her.

Last she made a man, they said, from straw. This was never the case. As with other things, the tale was gentled for innocent ears. Her last companion was made from flesh—the flesh of dead men brought back to life by her wile and will. It did not think as living men do, but yearned with the vague patchwork memory of the dozen men who died to make it live.

It was thus she came—to slay the witch and rule the world. Her hair was dark around a pale face. She was young in body, but there was a terrible oldness in her mind and eyes. Any innocence she had sold long ago to the darkness. Her lips were red and they matched her shoes—both were the color of blood.

Where she walked, the bricks trembled. She came out of the dark into the rude dazzle of color and light and made at once for the heart of the world, the glittering city upon the horizon. She knew power and she would ally herself with it where she could. Onlookers watched her pass in fear and watched her companions with fear as well—the whipped beast still bearing its scars, its maw bloody with the hunger she had taught it; the man of tin as heartless as she, and the patchwork creature of dead men's flesh. As she had made them, so they were; all wicked, hungry, and hers.

☆　☆　☆　☆　☆

In the distance, the city glittered, and one by one, the creatures raised their heads and scented the air. The Witch from Beyond the World was sleeping among the red flowers, dreaming terrible dreams. At rest, she looked innocent, her china-pale flesh a stark contrast to the blood-red petals. Her hair, as dark as the wood they had crossed to reach this place, lay about her like a river, winding almost to her feet where her shoes also shined.

"Is she dead?"

It was the lion who spoke first. His amber eyes glowed with the memory of fire now turned to ember and ash. Deep scars crossed his nose and once-proud face. Where the dried blood had collected, a fly buzzed and tried to land.

The tin man knelt and touched her face with a cold hand. Something shivered through him, the memory of something that he once was, or that he once might have been. Among the poppies, something like dreams passed though his waking metal flesh.

He remembered the softness of skin as white as the moon and dark hair flowing around him like a river. He remembered dark eyes going wide and agile legs with narrow hips wrapped around his waist. He remembered hot breath raising the hair on his skin, a gasp and the wetness of hungering sex surrounding him. He remembered pleasure, but it was only that—a memory and not a thing he could own.

In her sleep, the Witch from Beyond the World seemed to flinch away from his touch, but she did not wake. He drew one shining finger along her cheek. He wanted to hate her, but he could not. The pressure of his finger was enough to draw a thin line of blood from her skin. Again she shivered and twitched, as if near the surface of her dreams, watching them, testing them.

"No." He rose stiffly. "She only sleeps."

For a long moment, the dead thing by the tin man's side regarded the line of blood on the witch's cheek. He was hungry. He knew only that. It was an animal thing, baser than the ravening of the lion, who had been whipped into his appetites by the witch's scourge. This hungering was something else though—it was not physical, but it manifested as such, because the dead man could not tell the difference anymore.

A thousand conflicted emotions rose within him. He had memory, impulse, thought, but none were his own. Like his flesh, they were a patchwork, and one vied with the other, dizzying him. He had been this man and this man and that, and he knew each of their lives and loves, but not his own, and his gut ached with it.

He knelt and touched the wound the tin man had made with only the touch of his hand. He brought his finger to his mouth and tasted the blood. His lips, blackened and drawn back, showed rotted teeth where the blood lingered 'til he licked it clean.

"I was once..." He began, but he could get no further. The conflicting memories, the thousand lives that warred beneath his skin, made his head ache.

The tin man lightly touched the patchwork man's shoulder, his silver eyes trying to convey something like sympathy and something like pain, but like neither, for he had forgotten both. Slowly, the patchwork man rose, and almost as one, the three creatures turned to the city.

"They say," the lion began, "that in the city dwells a sorcerer—even more powerful than our sleeping mistress."

His sides moved in and out, with slow, painful breath. The skin was taut over his ribs, and between those bones that had cracked but had never quite healed, the spaces were sunken, hollow, and in want of food. When he took the scent of the red flowers around them, he could almost remember his own dreams. They were wild things, filled with the hot burning scent of far places. He knew desert sands and open plains and a sun that blazed low enough to touch. He roared and the world trembled. His muscles twitched with the near-forgotten memory of how he had run, how he had tasted flesh, how he had mounted the lionesses of his pride—with all he had lost.

"Perhaps if we could..."

But the tin man touched a metallic finger to metallic lips, which had lost the memory of kisses, and he pointed to the sky.

"It's beginning to snow; she will wake soon."

The thick flakes, drifting down, rested in the Witch from Beyond the World's dark river of hair, clinging and shimmering there like jewels just before melting. They touched her flesh like the memory of the tin man's cold fingertips, and after a long moment, she awoke. Her eyes flashed dark fire, touching each of the three creatures in their secret hearts—fear, memory, and loss. Each shuddered and bowed his head, ready to serve.

Rising, the witch turned her empty gaze to the shining city. She began to walk. In silence, her three companions followed. But as they drew closer to the city, it seemed to hover and draw away, a mirage designed to torment them.

That night, the three sat about a fire while the Witch from Beyond the World slept. "She suspects magic," the tin man said quietly.

She had gathered red flowers from the field as they had walked and had borrowed their dreams once more, sleeping in deep silence while her companions watched over her. In the light of the fire, the lion's scabbed fur shined a dull gold, the tin man's body a dull silver, but the patchwork man's flesh was ever rotten and black, letting in or out no light.

He studied his hands. The fingers she had given him were crooked and malformed, as if the bones had been broken and poorly reset. They were clumsy, awkward things. They could never do fine tasks, like hold a needle or stroke a woman's hair, but they could do other things. As with the memory of love, the memory of violence was in his flesh as well. He thought sometimes how he could, with his brutish hands, crush the witch's pale throat, or bruise her flesh beyond repair with the merest touch.

Sometimes he thought this, but then other thoughts came to crowd it out, and once more, his head exploded with pain. Sometimes the patchwork man dreamed borrowed dreams of lost lives—too many dreams, each overlapping the other. The lion and the tin man would watch him sleep, and when he awoke, they would ask him for his dreams, as jumbled as they were, for only he could still dream.

"I dreamt of the witch," the patchwork man said into the crackling silence of the firelight. The tin man and the lion were still, watching him.

"There was blood on her cheeks, like tears, and my hands were around her throat. She was cold, every place on her was cold, except between her thighs, which was warm, and I was there too. There was blood, and it flowed over me; it made my own dry flesh wet and warm."

The patchwork man's eyes were closed, but he sensed the tin man flinch at his words as though the lost memories of his own flesh were preserved in the dead man now.

"I tore her throat with my teeth," he continued, his words becoming a low moan as he rocked back and forth and the light caught in the seams of his cheeks so that he wept fiery tears.

"I bit her throat, but she didn't die. I opened her chest with my hands and lifted out her heart. I gave it to the tin man and he ate it. I sucked her soul with my breath and breathed it into the mouth of the lion. I cracked her skull and drank her thoughts and her brains. And for a moment, I was still...

"I cried too. She was my mother. She was my child. She was my lover, and I was her son. I did terrible things with my hands, and I did nothing at all. Everything hurt. It still does."

His eyes flew open and caught the light—sick yellow burning to gold, like the lion's dark amber gaze. He rocked in his desperation, and the other two watched. Three pairs of eyes burned with borrowed flame, amber, gold and silver gone crimson, orange and saffron with a heart of icy blue.

"We could..." the tin man mumbled and ran a finger over the blade of his axe, which, though sharp, could no longer draw his blood.

"We could..." the lion rumbled, baring his teeth so they shined with the flame and his red tongue lolled.

"We won't!" mourned the dead man, and he shook and moaned by the fire and wept borrowed tears, which tasted of ichor and embalming fluid.

Morning brought them into the city. The light of dawn made its glittering walls strange. Green became coral and gold—a strange fire such as witches burn. The three creatures shivered as they passed through the massive gates. They felt eyes watching them, but nowhere could they see the watchers. Strange shadows flitted upon facets of emerald; cut gems reflected the light and broke it apart, twisting it and making it anew. It was a sorcerer's city, and they walked through it, ever watched in the city of the unseen.

They came into the wizard's chamber with the Witch from Beyond the World at their lead. The air was filled with the acrid scent of chemical flame, burning green. All three raised their heads as the wizard spoke and the chamber around them trembled.

"You shall have what you want, each and every one of you, if you do one thing—slay the Westlin Witch and bring me her broom."

The creatures turned to the Witch from Beyond the World, all holding a collective breath. She smiled. Her ruby lips curled in her pale face and her dark eyes flashed black flame.

"I shall do better than that. I shall bring you her heart."

And so they journeyed again, to the Westlin's castle now. The Witch from Beyond the World slept in a dead woman's shoes with poppy-scented dreams, and around the fire, her three companions went sleepless and listened to the lonely cold sound of the wind and the sky.

"I dreamed," the patchwork man whispered, raising his face to the stars.

In the seams of his dark flesh, lines of silver light glittered like a network of spider's webs laid across his skin. His yellow eyes shined with the moon, and his voice was low and wistful—it was the voice of a thousand men who had once dreamed.

"What did you dream?" the lion asked, his voice a low purr, as warm as the firelight.

"I dreamt that two witches were one. I dreamt that they bled green blood, that they laughed, and that we were free."

They watched him as he watched the stars, and despite the fire, all three were cold.

In the morning, shadows fell from the sky—unnatural shapes, abominations that the Westlin Witch had dreamed and made flesh. Creatures that were never meant to fly fell upon them and screamed inhuman screams of torment and misery. The Witch from Beyond the World's three companions saw in their eyes trapped souls, misery and terror at their changed forms. The Westlin's creatures fought from pain and fear, and the three companions fought just the same.

The lion swiped at the sky with his paw and brought down one of the shadowy creatures. He tore with his claws at the shadow, which seemed to go willingly to his brute strength. Together, the two animals howled and snarled, a feral sound as much of sorrow as of rage. The lion's wounds opened—new blood on old scars. His muzzle was crimson, and the monstrous creature lay dead beneath his paws. He roared his hollow victory to the hidden sun and to the Westlin's stone walls, but his amber eyes were empty.

The tin man swung his axe. Blood misted the air and fell hot upon the places where his flesh should have been. It fell in his silver eyes and ran like tears down cold cheeks. He swung and swung, and around him, twisted bodies fell and twitched and were still, and he felt neither remorse nor pain, but only the memory of both making him sick and cold.

The dead man reached into the air with his broken hands and tore the wings from things that he could only imagine understood his pain. Like him, they were stitched together from many parts, possessing the memory and longing of each, pulled in different directions fit to tear them apart. It was a mercy when he ripped through flesh and bone with nothing but the strength of a thousand remembered lives—tearing limb from limb and skin from bone.

His hands were covered in blood, and he knelt down and touched the cheek of one of the creatures he had killed. Its eyes were still open, glassy and seeing nothing. They caught the sullen gray light from the sky and reflected it, empty and cold. He shivered and touched the warmth in the cavity he had opened between its ribs. The dark fur around the hole was matted with blood; it steamed in the chill air and glistened on exposed bone.

In all the coldness of the day, it was the only thing that held any heat. The patchwork man bathed his hands in it, covering the seams of his flesh as though the heat could soak through and fill him. He lowered his face and drank to fill the emptiness with something besides ice, something like warmth and life, even if the creature that it came from was as broken and twisted as he.

At last, the black shapes ceased falling from the sky. The ground was littered with broken bodies, like an ebony snowfall, or great flakes of ash. Far above, from the stone walls of her castle, the Westlin Witch watched them. Their own witch raised her pale face, and her dark eyes burned. Through the distance, they seemed to touch each other; through the distance, they seemed to know each other's hearts.

The Witch from Beyond the World led them into the stone castle, and again, the creatures felt the attention of unseen eyes. Every shadow shifted and changed, just out of sight. The very walls echoed a thousand dying screams and remembered the pain of those whose blood had been shed to seal the stones, one upon the other.

They went up through the twisting shadows, and the Westlin Witch waited for them at the top of her stone keep. Her eyes were black like their own witch's, and they burned just the same—darkness so whole and unending it was fit to swallow the world. She looked upon them with scorn and mocking and laughter. There was no pity. She took as much pleasure in their pain as their own witch did.

They watched; the lion, the tin man, and the thing of dead patchwork skin, as one witch faced the other. The broom the wizard had requested leaned against the wall, and as the light of the torches touched it, its shadow jittered large and tossed about the room as if it were alive. The Westlin snatched it up, brandishing it at each of the three as the two witches danced around each other.

"The beast who would be king—a poor, whipped dog with a broken spirit." She pointed at the lion, who bared his teeth, but did no more.

"The tin man, who learned the folly of love only through the total loss of his heart." She pointed her broom at the tin man, whose metallic fingers closed and unclosed upon the haft of his axe.

"You." The Westlin turned upon the patchwork man last. "You, dead thing, are but the memory of other lives and nothing of your own."

She spun at once, shadows swirling about her like a second skin, and she took fire from one of the torches on the tip of her broom, flourishing it at him and feinting forward.

"You crave warmth, but you are afraid. You hunger, but for what? You don't know. You fear the lives you have lived. You fear existence, the spark, the flame, that makes all things alive."

The flames reached for him, licking at the tinder of his flesh. Every life trapped within his stitched skin cried out a memory of fire and fear. Each voice babbled in his head, and he stumbled back, falling and pressing his misshapen hands to his skull. A cry escaped his pulled back lips. He heard the lion roar, heard the tin man step forward and lift his axe. He heard the Witch from Beyond the World speak a word, and all was still.

Somehow, he staggered up, away from the beating of a thousand voices and the minds within his skin. His blind hands groped and touched cold metal. He heard water slosh, a metallic ring, and he hefted the pail without thought. He flung it toward the Westlin Witch and her flame. She screamed, and he knew that, in the moment of her distraction, his own witch had fallen upon her.

He dreaded to open his eyes, but of their own will, they looked upon the terrible scene. The Westlin had fallen, and the surviving witch straddled her corpse. With her nails, she opened the Westlin's chest and took the crimson heart in her small hands while its last blood pulsed out over them. Her lips were the same color, but he could not tell whether or not she had tasted the blood.

A roar, a moan, a cry that might have been his, the lion's, or the tin man's, shook the castle and trembled the stone. He lurched forward, stitched flesh sharing the hunger of the Witch from Beyond the World. He longed to hold the heart in his own hands, to warm himself with its blood and banish the chill. He longed to hear its beat and have that beat silence the thousand voices moving like dark wings inside his head.

His broken hands closed on the white throat of the Witch from Beyond the World. She cried out, a strangled sound, but his yellow eyes were blind with tears. He felt the lion and the tin man watching him, but he did not turn. The Witch from Beyond the World's flesh—so tender—bruised easily beneath his touch. She was all power, but not in silence. If she could speak no word against him, then the brute strength of patchwork lives would win.

At last, beneath his grasp, the Witch from Beyond the World was still. He stepped back, and together, the three creatures looked down at the two witches—both beautiful and terrible in their own way. Dark hair mingled with dark, two spreading pools, like rivers joining hands. The Westlin's blood was upon the stone, but the other's flesh had not been broken, only bruised around the throat, a collar of violets—the impression of a dead man's hands.

"We will take her heart." The patchwork man knelt and touched the still form of the Witch from Beyond the World. "We will bring it to the wizard and say it belongs to the Westlin Witch, and we will be free."

"But…" the tin man began, his silver eyes shining.

"No." The patchwork man rose and faced his companion. "Do not be afraid." He took the man's silver hand and brought it to his dried and blackened lips as he spoke. "This is flesh, this is its way. Here is memory and dream. Be content with what you have and never sorrow for what is gone."

As he spoke, he moved the tin man's hands over his cheeks, over his seamed flesh, over every place he was joined. The lion watched with eyes of smoldering gold, which seemed to liquefy and run in the light of the flames. At the same time, the light on the tin man's face made it look as though the metal eyes wept silver tears.

They walked through the faceted city, three broken creatures bearing the Witch from Beyond the World's heart. The lion's scars had begun to heal, and he carried his head high as he walked. The tin man's stride was easier, and no heavy heart bore him down. It might only have been rigor mortis, but it seemed the patchwork man even smiled. Unseen eyes watched them into the wizard's chamber, and before the great sorcerer, they bowed; the patchwork man spoke and held out the witch's heart.

"Our mistress bids us come with this gift and asks that you send her home. We know that whatever power you have will make all as it should be."

His yellow eyes shined, and again, his black lips seemed to smile as he laid the heart at the sorcerer's feet. Green eyes watched him, and their faceted surface glittered too. Green sight moved from gold, to amber, to silver.

The wizard spoke.

"All is done. The Westlin Witch is gone and will trouble this realm no more. Your dear mistress has departed and will never be seen in this land again. You lion, have found your spirit anew. You tin man, your heart. And you, patchwork man, have more thoughts in your brain than any man could wish for."

Green light slid across his eyes, and then he bowed his head, a smile that was wicked and sad and knowing and terrible all at once. The dead man's eyes returned the look, and the three companions walked together out of the sorcerer's palace, into the shining and watchful city. They tasted the air, and for a moment, standing together, their hungers were less, for they were free and no longer afraid. They could dream.

fin

Fetalfied-Gigolo

by Andre Duza

Part 1

No matter how hard he tried to ignore it, no matter how hard he tried
to sleep, Jack Miller could hear Eleanor, his wife, going through her normal
cycle in the living room downstairs—fumbling through the tapes in the
entertainment center, laughing, crying, talking to herself, then answering back
in a high-pitched, child-like voice.

During her pregnancy ten years ago, she and her ex-husband had kept a
detailed video journal up until midway through her seventh month, when
the fetus—a boy whom they named Daniel—died in her womb due to a rare
heart defect that Eleanor had as well. Because of her own heart condition,
every surgeon/specialist she consulted strongly recommended against surgery
to remove the fetus, which meant that Eleanor Rigdon-Miller would have to
carry her dead, unborn child to term, and deliver it stillborn.

She still had the antique baby buggy stroller—a huge, gothic-looking
thing with whitewall tires—in what used to be her sewing room. Over time,
the room had morphed into a shrine to Daniel right under Jack's nose.

Jack always stepped quickly when he passed the room on his way to the
only bathroom in the house. Afterward, he'd shake his head for allowing
himself to be swept up in Eleanor's psychosis. Had he known about all this
before he decided to fall in love, he might've thought twice about taking on
a woman with such baggage.

*　*　*　*　*

They met in late 1999, September, or was it November? Jack had a terrible memory when it came to dates. He was recovering from surgery to remove a benign tumor from his colon when Eleanor came into his room to deliver an urgent message to Dr. Wettig, his surgeon, who introduced them.

Jack thought she was a nurse, but later found out that she worked in the radiology department filing documents and answering phones. There was something about her that spoke of maternal servitude, an aura that Jack's uber-religious friends would call angelic.

She was a little on the heavy side. Okay, a lot. But Jack was no prize himself; twice divorced, balding, and thin, but flabby. And for a woman her age (fifty-six), her face had a very youthful quality. She could've passed for forty-eight at least.

Twenty years ago, Eleanor's ex-husband had introduced her to Voodoo. She had been training to become a Priestess when Daniel died. The experience drastically altered her priorities. Her place of worship, the Southwest Temple of Voudon, with its glum pretense and its over-the-top rituals, just wasn't Jack's thing. However, the way he saw it, Voodoo was closer to their African roots than his old church (St. Thomas Episcopal), so he ultimately let the goofy shit slide.

The rest is, as they say, history.

*　*　*　*　*

As usual, Eleanor was a mess by the time she came back to bed.

"Good night, love," she whispered to Jack.

At first, he tried to act like he was asleep, which never worked. Eleanor lay facing him and waited him out just like every other time, her long, coffee-stained teeth bearing down from the huge, gummy smile plastered across her face, her lips quivering under the strain. The shaky smile contradicted her flushed hue, puffy eyes, and reddened nose. She looked like a clown, the kind that killed folks, then danced on their bodies.

"Good night," Jack said. He rolled over and tried to will himself momentarily deaf.

"Good night, mommy," Eleanor said in her high-pitched Daniel voice. "Good night, Mister Jack."

Daniel wasn't ready to call Jack "daddy" just yet. That's what Eleanor said.

Fuck if that voice didn't give Jack the creeps every time he heard it.
"Good night, Daniel," Eleanor said as if Daniel was lying next to her.
Again she lay there waiting for Jack to respond.
"Good night, Daniel," Jack grumbled.

*　*　*　*　*

Eleanor was talking to/as Daniel more and more frequently, and she was becoming less and less concerned about hiding it. And not only that, she was starting to fixate on Kevin Niles, the twenty-something, good-looking exotic dancer who lived a few houses down on the other side of the street.

Jack caught her watching him from the living-room window on more than one occasion. Once he overheard her talking to/as Daniel as she watched Kevin wash his car, shirtless. Even Jack had to acknowledge what great shape Kevin was in.

"I bet you would've been so handsome," she said. "You would've put poor Kevin to shame. I'm sure of it."

"Do you really mean it, mommy?" Daniel replied.

"Of course I do. I wouldn't lie ta you, precious. Not evah."

"Do you think I'll ever..." Although she immediately stopped talking when Jack walked in on her, Eleanor didn't seem at all startled, flustered, or scared like she used to get.

She sat dead center on the vomit-colored couch, arms folded across her chest, and she watched Jack try to come up with a reason for walking into the living room. She had a look in her eyes that seemed to say, *Get the fuck out!*

So he did. Better not to get on Eleanor's bad side.

Crazy fucking bitch, Jack thought. As usual when he cursed, he followed it up with an apology: *Excuse me, God.*

*　*　*　*　*

Daniel was an official member of the family now. He ate, watched TV, and slept with Eleanor and Jack—all via Eleanor's high-pitched Daniel-voice, of course. Eleanor made sure to set a place for him at the table and to make room for him on the couch and in bed. And she finally convinced Daniel to call Jack "Daddy."

Jack was growing increasingly distant from her, from them.

The outdoors, especially public places with lots of people, had become Jack's safe haven from Daniel. Eleanor wouldn't dare risk other people seeing her talk to/as Daniel.

It didn't even faze Jack when Eleanor started openly flirting with Kevin Niles. She had changed her entire morning routine just to be outside when Kevin left for his day job. She claimed that Daniel had a crush on Kevin's on-again, off-again girlfriend, Scarlet; Eleanor was only placating his puppy love by giving him a good look at her when she came to drive Kevin to work. Scarlet worked in the building right next to his. Kevin had a car of his own, a late-model Mustang that he rarely drove yet washed at least once a week.

But on the inside, Jack was like a powder keg, waiting for just the right spark to ignite his repressed emotion and cause him to...

SNAP!

*　*　*　*　*

"Why is daddy looking at us like that?" Daniel whined when Jack burst through the bathroom door as Eleanor marinated in the tub, her flabby girth nestled in the embrace of pink suds. She was right in the middle of teaching Daniel about the female body.

The soapy water whipped and thrashed like an angry sea, miniaturized as Eleanor folded her beefy arms to hide her naked breasts. They hadn't seen each other naked in years.

"For God's sake, Ellie, will you listen to yourself!" Jack roared with a passion that Eleanor, and even Jack himself, thought he was no longer capable of.

"Please calm down, daddy," Daniel half-cried. "You're scaring me."

"Well, that's just too damn bad," Jack said, slip-stepping closer to the tub. He placed his right hand on the sink to keep from falling and pointed with his left.

He caught himself about to address Daniel again, and stopped short, his mouth hanging half-open.

"Look, Ellie... you're sick. You need help. Why in God's name can't you see that?"

"Is that true, mommy?" Daniel whimpered. "Are you sick?"

"Don't listen to him, baby," Eleanor said with restrained anger. "That's not daddy. That's the Devil talkin'. He has many ways of makin' the weak do his bidding."

That was it! The last straw... again!

"If he was any kine-of real man, he'd get down on his knees and beg the good Lord for forgiveness," Eleanor said.

She grabbed a towel from the collapsible clothing rack next to the tub and wrapped it around herself as she stood.

Jack wanted to smack the shit out of her. So he did.

"Mommy! Watch out!" Daniel said as Jack lunged, his arm cocked way back to yesterday.

Jack didn't figure that Eleanor would slip and hit her head on the edge of the Formica shelving unit, didn't know that it would trigger a massive heart attack. He didn't think he hit her all that hard. Well, maybe he did, but he certainly didn't mean to. Well, maybe he did.

✳   ✳   ✳   ✳   ✳

The doctors were suspicious right from the start. Jack told them that Eleanor slipped while getting out of the tub, fell and hit her head on the way down. He left out the part about slapping her. Apparently, the slap had left a bruise, which is what the doctors kept coming back to. In order for Eleanor to have sustained bruises on both sides of her face like she had, she would have had to hit one side, bounce, turn around, and hit the other.

Jack was aware that it sounded like a lie; however, he stuck to his story.

Now Eleanor lay in a coma.

The hospital staff was on the verge of getting the police involved in their case until they found Daniel... or the fetus that would have been Daniel. He... it was still inside Eleanor, all shriveled and defunct.

Floating upside down in her thick, aged uterine juices and protected by a calcified lining, the fetus seemed to give Jack a corner-eyed glare when he saw it on the ultrasound. He could've sworn it did.

It was hard for Jack not to smile as he signed the surgical consent forms to remove the thing from Eleanor's womb, and even harder not to let his imagination run with what he now knew. Could it be that somehow, some way, Daniel was really speaking through Eleanor? Could all that Voodoo nonsense really be true?

Nah.

The doctors warned Jack that she might not survive the operation. It was a miracle that Eleanor wasn't dead already due to infection from the fetus, but they were certain that it would eventually kill her if they left it in.

The surgery took about an hour altogether. When they were done, one of the surgeons came out and asked Jack if they would donate the fetus to science, this being such an extraordinary case and all.

"Do what you want with it," Jack replied. "To be honest, I'd rather you just burn it."

The surgeon thought that was an odd thing to say.

That night, Jack left Eleanor in intensive care—still in a coma, but otherwise recovering well—and got himself nice and drunk.

A week later, Jack got a call at work. It was the hospital. Apparently, Eleanor's condition had suddenly worsened. Jack made it to the hospital in ten minutes flat. It usually took him twenty, but it was early in the day, and the traffic was nowhere near as bad as it was during rush hour—he had been coming to visit every day after work.

When he got there, the doctors said there was nothing physically wrong with Eleanor. Nothing that they could find, anyway.

Eleanor Rigdon-Miller died two weeks later at 2:45 p.m. Jack was at work again when he got the call. He never got a chance to say goodbye. Not that it would've mattered, since Eleanor never woke up from her coma.

✳ ✳ ✳ ✳ ✳

"It was 'bout a year ago last week when she passed," said Hank 'Smitty' Smith, the bartender at the Turquoise Lounge.

"Whew... I'm sorry I asked," Kevin Niles replied, speaking out the side of his mouth as he was known for doing. "I knew that old lady was strange, but God-dayum!"

As if to punctuate his shudder-shock, or to burn it away, Kevin tossed back what was left of his drink—an 8-ounce vodka rocks.

Smitty was the guy to ask if you wanted to know something about the neighborhood. He had a way of seasoning a tale with old, wise black-man flair and a deep raspy voice that made the smoke-stained walls of the Turquoise Lounge seem to disappear when he had you hooked.

Kevin had stopped in between jobs to get the real story on the Millers. And man, what a story it was.

"Damn shame if you ask me. The husband, Jack... he used to come in here from time-na-time. In fact, I was the one who got 'im loaded that night after his wife's surgery."

"No shit?"

"No shit."

Kevin leaned against the back of the barstool, stretched his arms, and yawned away his uneasiness. He tucked the tips of his toes under a ridge in the wooden wall of the bar to keep his leaning stool from toppling backward.

He had never seen a dead body until yesterday morning, when two men from the coroner's office carried Jack Miller out of his house in a body bag. The crowd had been whispering that Jack had died of fright. Kevin forgot to tell Scarlet that they had the street blocked off when she came to pick him up.

They were both late for work that morning.

"You shoulda seen him," Dorothy Burke kept repeating. It was Dorothy who called the police to report a strong odor coming from the Miller house.

Jack had been dead for at least two weeks when they found him. His face, or what was left of it after the rats—they assumed—had their fill, was twisted into a horrible expression. "Like he saw Satan himself," Dorothy Burke said.

Although the neighbors knew little about Voodoo, aside from curses, zombies, and dolls that represented people, they were all aware that the Millers were into it; naturally, the rumors about them always had a satanic spin.

"You think it's true he died of fright?" Kevin asked.

"It's certainly possible," Smitty replied. "There's no tellin' what was goin' on in his head after what happened to his wife. Had you seen 'im lately? He was in bad shape toward the end."

"Yeah, I guess I did notice that he'd lost some weight."

"That's the least of it. I used to see 'im talkin' to himself and swattin' at shit that wasn't there," Smitty replied, demonstrating with his hands.

"Like a crackhead?"

Smitty breathed out a chuckle.

"Yeah, kid. Somethin' like that."

It was getting late and Kevin had a second job to go to. He dug deep into his pocket and fished out a twenty-dollar bill.

"You never disappoint, my friend," Kevin said, placing the twenty down on the bar. "Keep the change."

"Glad I could be of service," Smitty replied with a slight bow and a nod to acknowledge the generous tip.

The Miller story was still on Kevin's mind as he gyrated, shirtless, and made his way from end to end of the rectangular stage to *Relax*, by Frankie Goes to Hollywood. The stage was lined with flashing bulbs that hypnotized the screaming bachelorettes, divorcées, soccer-MILFs, and gay men, turning them from ordinary humans into vessels of manifested lust. Kevin was usually able to lose himself in the moment when he performed, especially with the type of song that punched its way out of the speakers. Songs with heavy bass lines helped to drown out the screams and the calls to "Take it off!" Tonight it was also helping to draw his mind away from the sharp pain in his lower back. Yesterday, it was his neck, and his legs the day before. He joked that it felt as if someone was fucking with him.

What the hell was it that Jack Miller saw? Kevin thought as he slid down into a full split and grabbed a fifty-dollar bill from a leather-faced woman with his teeth.

Kevin didn't tell Smitty about the woman that had been stalking him, the one with the antique baby stroller with whitewall tires. She was dressed in a long church coat and a veil that covered her whole head and enshrouded her face in darkness. Eleanor Rigdon-Miller used to wear a coat like that when she and Jack left for church on Sunday mornings.

Kevin would suddenly notice the woman standing in the distance behind the large antique stroller. He couldn't see her face beneath the veil, but he felt as if she was looking right at him. So far he had seen her six times.

It could've just been a coincidence, but something about her made him doubt that very much.

* * * * *

It was 3:00 a.m., and Kevin was driving home from Scarlet's house in Newtown Square when he saw the woman again. She was standing with her stroller on the side of Old Sproul Road.

As usual, Kevin couldn't see her face beneath the veil, but he could tell that she was looking right at him.

She was holding something in her hand—something like a small doll. She held it up for him to see. His eyes, reddened by THC, rolled to the rearview when he passed her.

He was too far away to see her squeeze the doll in her grasp.

The pain was sudden and intense. The sneak attack caused him to yank the steering wheel hard left—directly into the fallen tree that lay across the oncoming lane.

* * * * *

He woke up moments later, surging with the worst pain imaginable. He screamed at the clouds that rushed by.

His car sat twenty feet back on the other side of the tree trunk. A large hole, surrounded by spider-web cracks, decorated the windshield where Kevin had crashed through. Smoke billowed from the totaled front end, which had planted an indefinite kiss upon the cracked and splintered bark where his car made impact. The driver's side door hung wide open. From inside, an ambient rhythm poured from his car stereo.

"You're okay, you're okay, you're okay," Kevin kept telling himself as he tried to stuff his small intestines back into the deep wound in his gut. As the seconds passed, he found it harder and harder to catch his breath or to move from the neck down. "Let me just... Let me just get myself together here. Gotta get it together."

A small fire burst to life beneath the accordion-crushed hood of his car, orange-yellow fingers of flame reaching out from underneath. Over their cackling, and the song's atmospheric qualities, Kevin heard a squeaking sound, like old shopping-cart wheels.

The woman with the stroller stopped in front of the tree trunk that lay between them. She was still holding the doll in her right hand. Now that he could see it, Kevin immediately realized that it was supposed to represent him.

Kevin could no longer feel his arms or legs, or anything else below his neck. It left him with a floating sensation, which he mistook as an out-of-body experience.

"Mmm... Mrs. Miller?" he whispered. "Is that you?"

She nodded: "Yes," to a crackle-crunch of brittle bone and unyielding flesh.

From inside the stroller, tiny fingers, brownish and rotten and clawed at the tips, curled around the outer rim and crunched to a secure grip. Slowly, the thing struggled to pull itself up and over the side. It was a baby... a fetus rather, extremely tiny and slightly unfinished-looking, encrusted in death's rigid texture. Its skin was flaked to hard edges, making it look like a half-constructed puzzle; pieces were missing on its back, arm, and head, where bits of bone peeked out.

It was Daniel Miller in the flesh...

Daniel crawled onto the tree trunk, paused and looked up at Kevin.

After a few unsuccessful attempts to stand—it was his first try ever—Daniel managed to wobble for a moment before falling off the trunk and landing flat on his face in the street below. He climbed up, grunting as he planted his tiny, rigid fingers into the bark and pulled.

Once he reached the top, he tried his second time to stand, but fell once more.

He climbed up again, grunting the entire way. When he reached the top this time, Eleanor Rigdon-Miller cricked her head down to face him. Although the veil hid her expression, Daniel understood her action to mean, "Stop wasting time."

Holding it around the midsection, Eleanor placed the doll at an assisted stand beside Daniel, who sat with his disfigured legs dangling stiff over the side.

Through no effort of his own, Kevin found himself standing, then moving forward one slow, shuffling step at a time.

Daniel giggled through small, crooked teeth stained with dried blood; the spaces between them were caked with a curdled grout. He watched his mother's fingers manipulate the doll's legs, and then he looked at Kevin, who lurched toward them, his head flopping with each step. This was the moment Daniel had been waiting for all his claustrophobic life.

In the background, the flames from Kevin Niles' car snapped and hissed; the music continued to play.

Kevin's twisted expression spoke of terror, which seemed to multiply as he came closer. By the time he reached the tree trunk, his eyes were ready to leap from their sockets.

Daniel reached inside the gaping wound in Kevin's abdomen. He pulled out a rope-like organ, his tiny fingers sliding down it, and then he made a circular motion to loop it around his hand. He lifted it to his mouth and took a healthy bite.

Kevin's head hung limp, facing down, providing a good view of the feast. His thoughts were breaking down into stream of consciousness tangents about hell and suffering for eternity.

With his mouth, Daniel climbed up Kevin's small intestine and bit down, snapping it off when he couldn't lean any farther without falling off the tree trunk.

As he swallowed, Daniel lifted his hand in front of his face and watched his fingers stretch and grow healthy skin around the tips. He smiled and turned to his mother, who nodded back.

Then Daniel wormed his way into the wound in Kevin's abdomen and ate him from the inside out.

Part 2

The new Kevin Niles lived with a gusto that troubled many of his old colleagues, acquaintances, and friends. It started after his accident, which seemed to dumb him down a bit. But at least he was alive. The doctors said it was a miracle he had survived.

The police never found the body in the brush. Once the process was complete, the new Kevin dragged what remained of the old one farther into the woods and buried him.

He forbade himself to acknowledge the name Daniel, even in thought, from now on. Even Mother was to call him Kevin.

At Club Sensations, they tossed around terms like midlife crisis to describe the new Kevin, even though he was only in his late twenties.

Kevin had always been known for his womanizing, but even his platonic female friends regarded it with a certain affection due to his natural charm and the crystal clarity with which his body language spoke to them when he was on stage. They were all victims of its cadence whether they admitted it or not.

They wondered what had happened to make him suddenly become an asshole: rude, arrogant, belligerent. Scarlet, his on-again, off-again girlfriend was the one person who could stand to be around him. Around Scarlet, he acted like a child almost—needy, overly affectionate, and clumsy with passion that often overwhelmed him to tears or laughter when they made love. And he seemed to lose his touch in bed, barely penetrating her before it was all over.

Since the accident, Kevin was always referring to his mother. "Mother," he called her, although sometimes he would slip up and call her "mommy." As far as Scarlet knew, Kevin and his mother didn't get along, yet she had suddenly become the center of his universe. He had even moved her back into his house and, according to Kevin, she wouldn't allow Scarlet, or anyone else, to come around anymore.

"She's sort of old fashioned," he told her. "You know how it is."

It was a sudden and complete shift from that too-cool, half-interested shit that the old Kevin had strung her along with for so long. If he had been like this from the beginning, Scarlet doubted that their psuedo-relationship would have lasted.

Scarlet couldn't shake the feeling that Kevin was keeping something from her. She wondered if it might be drugs. His skin had taken on a pale, sickly color, and his dancing had become stiff and lethargic. One of the other dancers commented that Kevin had lost his rhythm. Somehow, even his voice had been affected, its pitch slightly higher and its tempo eager, whereas before it flowed from his mouth with a sleepy confidence.

Suddenly, the great Kevin Niles was acting like a rookie, bragging about the size of his dick and his overall sexual prowess in mixed company, forgoing his high standards for quantity in his conquests and wearing the questionable women he took home every night—sometimes two or three at a time—on his puffed-out chest as if to impress everyone, especially Scarlet. Recriminations and insults had begun to spread throughout the Club Sensations grapevine.

The more she thought about it, the more Scarlet hoped it was drugs. That would be the only way she could forgive his rampant philandering of late. Sure, there had always been other women. Scarlet wasn't stupid. But Kevin was a catch—intelligent, gorgeous, and progressive-minded. So what if he happened to occasionally stray? They all did. At least the old Kevin cared enough to keep it to a minimum, and to construct elaborate lies to cover his tracks.

* * * * *

The sex was rough and awkward, and probably the worst that Kim Diaz had ever experienced. She caught herself staring up at the masculine shape that pounded away at her desiccated vaginal walls to make sure it really was Kevin Niles on top of her. It wasn't like Kim to keep her eyes open during sex, even in the dark.

How could this oaf be the same guy she'd been trying to get for more than a year? She always thought she was cuter than a lot of the women he hooked up with, and a hell of a lot classier.

As they lay basking in the putrid afterglow of bad sex, Kim wondered if maybe she had done something wrong to elicit such a savage and ham-handed experience. To Kevin, the new Kevin, it was awesome.

* * * * *

From the lit hallway at the bottom of the staircase, Kevin led Kim to the basement. Though finished to look like a bachelor's paradise, it was an intimidating place, small and windowless and overcrowded with expensive furniture, workout equipment, and high-tech audio/visual appliances. On top of all that was a layer of filth garnished with a dusty film. There were empty food containers, two-liter soda bottles, and dirty dishes decorated with half-eaten meals. Soiled clothes were piled on the floor, stray garments dangling from just about anything that would hold them.

The fact that Kim was naked—they both were—made the environment even more of a concern as she peered inside. It was murky, and it stunk of incense and subliminal whiffs of dubious things.

Kim was beginning to regret agreeing to 'try something different,' as Kevin put it.

"Nice, huh?" Kevin said, startling her from behind.

"Uh... yeah," Kim replied with equal portions of sarcasm and trepidation. She gave Kevin the benefit of the doubt though. It might have been different if he was a stranger.

"So..." Kim began, trying her best to maintain her sexy persona. "What exactly did you have in mind when you said 'try something diff—'"

Kevin shoved her into the darkness and the thick musk of incense and dubious-funk.

Before Kim could react, he grabbed her by the back of the neck and walked her forward.

"Hey," she said nervously, "I'm as adventurous as the next girl, but—"

"Shut up!" Kevin's grip tightened as he bent her over the preacher-curl attachment of the workout bench that looked, at present, more like a clothing rack.

"Oww. Take it easy," she said as if she was afraid that her protest might offend him.

"I said QUIET!"

The playful, singsong cadence of sexuality was gone from Kevin's voice, replaced with an impatient, almost callous tone. Kim tried to turn and lock eyes with him, but Kevin pushed down on her head until she gave up. This fear-lust-fear shit was either going to lead to the best climax she'd had in years or drive her fucking insane. Again, if this was anyone else...

"Don't move a muscle," Kevin whispered, letting his hand slide down her bare back. He left the room.

What the hell is he doing? Kim thought when Kevin hadn't come back after a good minute or so. She was just about to stand when she heard him enter the room.

Kim waited on pins and needles, her heavy breaths joining with the slow footsteps that approached from behind.

His touch prompted a primal jolt that arched Kim's back. His hands were colder than before and terribly coarse as he ran them up her back and through her hair. He clutched a portion and twisted it until it pinched her scalp.

Kim moaned at the sensation of teeth against the back of her neck, letting her hips sway. She wriggled to the tickle of sharp edges and... screamed as they clamped down and pulled a chunk of elastic flesh from the back of her neck.

Kim whipped around and broke free of his grip.

"Oh my God, what the f..."

It wasn't Kevin at all. It was a woman (Eleanor) whom she had never seen. She was dressed in a long church coat and was apparently wearing some kind of Halloween mask, strangely dry and discolored, like a relatively fresh corpse. Or was that her face?

Eleanor lunged and grabbed Kim's head in both hands. Kim tried to get her arms up in time to push her away, but Eleanor was already on top of her, her mouth open wide.

Eleanor snaked her head from right to left, searching for an opening through Kim's spastic flailing.

Kim actually thought she was making progress until Eleanor bit down on her nose, cheek, and upper lip, worked it loose, and tore it away her from her face with a snap.

Kim stumbled backward and fell to the floor, sneezing in swift succession and choking on her own blood. With one hand, she inspected the white-hot wound at the back of her neck while she held her other arm out toward Eleanor, who approached with a slow, steady gait, her long, thin teeth jutting out from beneath lips that had shriveled to a perpetual snarl. She was chewing on Kim's flesh.

A few feet behind Eleanor, Kevin appeared and stood naked in the lit doorway that led upstairs. Kim reached out to him.

"Help me!" she screamed through the rush of blood, snot, and tears that amassed in her throat. Somewhere in mid-sentence, she realized, from his relaxed expression, that Kevin had meant for this to happen.

"Nothing personal, Kim," Kevin replied, calm, yet somewhat off-put by the violence and gore. "Mother has to eat."

He wondered if he'd ever get used to it.

* * * * *

The new Kevin Niles had little concern for physical fitness, and after a while, his taut musculature broke down to a flabby thickness. He was even developing a bit of a belly.

Scarlet, his on-again, off-again, considered herself above all that. She was in love with Kevin Niles—the person—despite his shortcomings. These days, the shortcomings were becoming hard to count. For one, he told her that it *was* drugs—blow, to be specific—that had him looking and acting so... different. He knew it was what she wanted to hear.

Club Sensations eventually fired Kevin. The other dancers, along with the bar staff and a few regulars, had been on Doug Crawford, the owner, to get rid of his ass for weeks. They criticized Doug for playing favorites. The reality was that Kevin was Sensations' most popular dancer. Losing him would be a major blow to the business. Besides, Kevin was like family to Doug, and to everyone else as well.

Kevin claimed that they were jealous of his popularity, except he used the word "skillz," and he refused to take any of their attempts at a discussion with him seriously.

Doug begged him to at least lose the weight. "What, are you pulling an Elvis on me?" Doug whined half in jest and half in hysterics. He was the high-strung type.

Kevin thanked Doug for his concern by sleeping with his daughter. She was only seventeen. When Doug found out, he told Kevin that he would blow him away if he ever touched her again or came anywhere near the club. And that was that.

Scarlet even let that one slide. Drugs were known to make people do strange things, things that they would never do otherwise. It was her credo. Scarlet was on a mission to change Kevin. She was convinced that she could.

Kevin's day job fired him a week later. He hadn't shown up in a month at least. He had cashed in on his paid leave for a supposed surgery that he claimed he suddenly needed. Kevin had been a model employee save for a few occasions of tardiness, so they believed him at first, until someone from the office saw him laughing it up with Scarlet at an outdoor café while he was supposed to be recovering. Scarlet warned him that they would find out.

Kevin slowly matured in the months that followed. They were long and hard, and without a job or an education outside of Mother's private coaching, he found himself relying on Scarlet for everything: his shopping, his laundry, his bills.

Mother always told him that women were the root of all evil, that they might seem nice on the outside but they all had ulterior motives. She said that Scarlet was just like the others, but he was beginning to genuinely care about her. He was growing to appreciate her generosity. Scarlet was basically supporting him. Hell, she was supporting them both. Kevin said that Mother relied on checks from the government. That's what she told him to say when Scarlet asked how a woman who gladly takes her money still won't let her come to their house.

"But that all might change," Kevin told Scarlet as they sat watching the moon from the boardwalk in Atlantic City one night. He was starting to realize that Mother was manipulating him. And he was seeing their victims' faces in his dreams now, the way they looked when they saw Mother's face, or when her teeth clamped down on their flesh. He was tired of all the killing.

Scarlet figured he was going to ask Mother to leave just because of her, and she decided to patch things up between them, which, in turn, would put her in a good light with Mother.

In fact, Scarlet was on her way to Kevin's house right now. She considered calling first, but figured it better to surprise Mother with flowers and a smile.

＊　＊　＊　＊　＊

It was Dixie Creighton, Scarlet's coworker, who told Kevin what Scarlet was up to when he called to see what she was doing for her lunch break. He was only a half a mile away at the Goodwill, trying to get rid of all the women's clothing that he had hidden beneath the basement stairs.

Kevin rushed home to find his Mother kneeling over Scarlet, who lay unconscious on the living-room floor, a dollop of blood leaking tears from her forehead. Next to her lay a hammer, its blunt tip smeared with blood.

Eleanor was leaning in for a bite when Kevin planted his entire shin up under her gut and sent her flying into the wall. He could feel her torso crack against his leg.

There was no sign of pain in Eleanor's desolate eyes. He was looking for it to quell the resentment he had developed toward her.

Kevin picked up the hammer and rushed her as she tried to stand, swinging with all his might, rage, and resentment.

Eleanor's hands and forearms were the first to go, crumbling into dried chunks under the hammer as she held them out to defend herself. Moving on to her head, Kevin hammered away until there was nothing left. He continued to swing long after she stopped moving.

The feeling that came over him as he sat on his knees before her shattered corpse was indescribable, "relief" being the only word to come close.

Kevin stuffed the big pieces of Mother's body in a garbage bag and swept up the rest with a broom. He hid it behind the couch until later that night after dropping Scarlet off at her house. She was still too woozy from the attack to drive.

Scarlet never saw what hit her. The last thing she remembered was finding the front door open, walking into the living room, and calling out to Mother.

Kevin told her that she had walked in on a burglar who knocked her out and got away. He even messed up the place to make it appear that someone was rifling through his things. He convinced her not to go to the police.

"There might still be paraphernalia around here that I didn't get rid of," he said. "No telling what the police might find if they search the house for clues."

As for Mother... Kevin told Scarlet she had decided to move out on her own two days ago. He wouldn't tell her where she had moved to, but that was fine. *Whatever,* Scarlet thought.

As to why he had called her at work? Kevin said that he was planning to surprise her with a fancy lunch and break the news to her then.

* * * * *

Later that night, Kevin took Mother's body bag to a popular fishing spot right under the Walnut Street Bridge at 24th. The Schuylkill River was filthy and brown, and he couldn't understand why someone would eat anything that swam around in it. It was the perfect place to dump a body, though. People called it the 'Sure-kill' River. Rumor had it that the Philly Mob dumped a lot of their stoolies there.

Kevin weighted down the bag with a few large rocks that he found in the dirt, tossed it in the river, and watched it sink.

"So long, *Mother*," he said.

* * * * *

Eventually, Kevin and Scarlet had a daughter. They named her Sara. The pregnancy brought back memories of Kevin's past life, but he was quick to circumvent them with trivial pleasantries, most of which had to do with the cute little things that Scarlet was always doing—the way she crinkled her nose at things she didn't like, or her gentle cooing as they spooned together in bed and fell asleep to their favorite TV show.

Scarlet was constantly in and out of the hospital after the pregnancy, which left Kevin to tend to Sara. The doctors could never figure out what was wrong with Scarlet, and each time she'd recover in a few days.

At home, Sara was always getting into things and putting them in her mouth. She had an affinity for things that could harm her: scissors, prescription pill bottles, the cluster of household cleaning products that they kept under the bathroom sink. One night, when Sara was only ten months old, Scarlet woke up screaming from intense stomach pain, vomiting blood all over the bed. Kevin rushed her to the hospital once again.

Two days later, while Kevin was home with Sara, waiting to make his midday trip to the hospital to see Scarlet, the police burst through the front door and ordered him to sit still while they searched the house.

"What the hell is going on?!" Kevin yelled, although deep down he figured they had somehow connected him to all the missing women, or that they had found Mother's body. Both were always in the back of his mind.

Ten minutes later, one of the officers came out of the bedroom holding an old cigar box.

"Found this under his bed. Rat poison," the officer said to another. "Looks like the doc was right."

Rat poison? They had kept some under the bathroom sink, but Kevin had no idea how it wound up under his bed.

"So you like to poison your girlfriend, do you?" another officer said directly to Kevin; he was sitting on the edge of his favorite chair, staring at Sara, who flailed like babies do in her high chair, totally oblivious.

"But what about my daughter?" Kevin said as they cuffed him and read him his rights.

"She'll be as far away from you as possible. How's that?" The officer shoved Kevin back into his seat and walking off to speak to the head officer, who stood by the front door.

Kevin took a deep breath and took comfort in the fact that this was obviously some kind of mistake. He looked lovingly at Sara, who returned a strange stare, one that he hadn't seen in a long time. It hit him like a fucking freight train when she smiled, and the shape of her mouth looked strangely familiar.

"Mother?" Kevin said.

"Hello, Daniel," Sara replied.

Under an Invisible Shadow

by David Bain

(Humanity was still hanging on when I wrote this. But that may not be the case for long.)

Only a few dozen of us have made it this far. Most are Russian, Scandanavian, Canadian, or Eskimo.

Me and Janie, we made it all the way from Florida.

Janie was my guide. I can't see the zombie souls, but she can, and it was primarily her vision that led us here, somewhere deep in the wilds of northern Canada.

I used to say I didn't believe in anything I couldn't see, and that I'd seen nothing I couldn't explain.

But these days I surely believe in ghosts—or rather, I believe in souls, or whatever the hell the spirits of the zombies and the thing we've dubbed The Invisible Lovecraftian Terror are.

Since I've been deemed the most accomplished scribe of the dozen or so English-speaking persons to arrive here at Ground Zero, it's to be my words that are put to paper. See, I once thought of myself as something of a poet. Yes, once upon a time I thought I was above my culture, that I was an aloof observer, sort of floating over it all. Now I realize I was—and am—a disposable product of it. The zombies have humbled me that much at least.

All of this is simply to say that I will write this document in my true, common voice—my human voice—rather than the elitist one to which I sometimes aspired.

Here goes...

The dead started rising from their graves about thirteen years ago.

Before we reached Ground Zero, we had our theories. God released his wrath. Scientists released a bug. Something passed by the Earth.

Whatever the cause, things went down quickly.

The dead arose *en masse*.

Zombies lurched, swarmed, reigned.

Humanity hid, fought, or was eaten.

Political chaos. Military collapse. Anarchy. Mass hysteria. Total communications breakdown—even my beloved Internet was quickly useless.

I was a University of Florida grad student, majoring in biology and working in the field for the summer, deep within the Everglades. Until Z Day, I spent my spare time writing dippy nature poems and faithfully submitting them to the types of magazines that paid in contributor's copies and that were only read by other contributors, if that.

I saw it all go down on the satellite dish until every last station was either overrun or off the air.

Antisocial bastard that I am, I decided to stay while everyone else in my group went back to help. They said they'd send someone for me when humanity won the battle against the zombie legions. Victory was inevitable, they said.

No one ever came back.

For me it was actually idyllic. I knew how to get along in the 'glades indefinitely, eating everything from gator to the indigenous breed of miniature deer, which had been on the verge of extinction until the zombies cleared out its greatest enemy—man.

Plus, for all practical purposes, I was a million miles away from the zombies—I only ever saw three of them in the 'glades, and one looked an awful lot like Jimmy Hoffa. (That's a joke.)

After a while, I found a few TV stations back up, usually run by a staff of no more than two or three. The ones that seemed relatively serious about serving humanity were from Mexico City, Denver, and Berlin. They would play reruns of whatever they felt like—the guys in Berlin were PBS types, the guys in Mexico City liked Mexican soaps and variety shows, and the guys in Denver showed mostly B movies from nearby video stores. Occasionally the people running these stations would do things like offer survival tips, food-gathering advice, and updates on the zombie situation outside the station walls.

Long story short: zombies ruled the Earth for just over a dozen years, destroying and wandering and devouring the brains and guts of any living thing they could get their claws on.

Then a curious thing started happening.

The dead started dying.

Denver reported it first—the dead were suddenly dropping like flies, and the ones that didn't die right off were no longer a threat. I remember one of the Denver guys finally ventured out live on the air and kicked a zombie in the butt just to see what would happen. It barely paid him any attention. The creep just turned, then looked at its claw-like hand as if it knew it was supposed to rip the living guy's head off and dig out the juicy filling, but it had forgotten how. These slow zombies reminded me of late autumn wasps in my native Michigan—drunkenly ambulatory but hardly dangerous.

I remember distinctly that I sighed when I heard the news. Then I held my head in my hands and cried. Then I swore a blue streak and gave in. It was time to cast myself out of Eden and search out other survivors.

I went to the obvious meeting place. The victory had been gained by forfeit, but no matter. Humanity had won the Armageddon Super Bowl and we were going to Disneyworld.

It's a Small World, the countries of Epcott and Main Street, U.S.A., were a shambles. The cleanup of the stinking dead zombies was still going on when I arrived. Most of the survivors were camped around Cinderella's castle.

I'll spare you the tedious, predictable details—the territorial squabbles, the bickering, the stealing, the fights over food, all the dumbass alpha males strutting around, campaigning and contending for leadership.

What matters is Janie, who arrived shortly after me. Janie, and what she saw.

The zombies were dying all right, she said. But souls—or spirits or whatever—were leaving their bodies. The souls were leaving the zombie bodies as they died, and they were flying off in a north by northwesterly direction.

Furthermore, she said, souls which were apparently from other zombie bodies south of us were consistently flying by overhead.

Even after the world had been overrun and destroyed by the living dead, Janie had a hard time convincing people of what she was seeing.

Until, that is, this former supermodel who had done Tarot card infomercials back in the old days suddenly said she saw the souls too—interesting that she hadn't said anything until then, despite the fact that she'd been among the first to arrive.

Then, and only then, it was decided something had to be done. We had to see where these things were going and why. The alpha males advised they were needed to lead the group, and Tarot woman said she had to remain as spiritual advisor.

I volunteered because I don't like people anyway, and especially not this desperate, self-pitying and quarrelsome bunch. Janie went because, first of all, someone had to see the zombie souls, and second, she was as good as I was with a gun.

Although we hadn't met prior to Cinderella's castle, I think we saw something in each other from the start, an independent spirit we mutually admired. We have since become soul mates. The lady's no supermodel, but she warms my body and soul, and that is all that matters.

Without many supplies, we left the next morning, given the precious gift of a Harley-Davidson motorcycle.

I don't think anyone ever really expected to hear back from us. We recently dispatched a crew to reach the Denver station to tell the world about The Invisible Lovecraftian Terror, but, as I said, from here on in, we don't know what will happen.

I'm going to skip a lot here.

We had several "adventures" between Florida and Ground Zero up here in the Canadian hinterlands. If there's time, I'll write them down in detail, but if there was ever a time for the *Reader's Digest* version, this is it.

As we expected, we encountered occasional pockets of humanity. Some were mighty peculiar and some were mighty interesting, but we could never stay; Janie kept seeing zombie souls coursing by overhead.

In what was once known as The Deep South, we ran into a forlorn cult that had given up rattlesnakes and had turned to worshipping the very zombies that tried to eat them—I didn't pay much attention, but it had something to do with the fact that the zombies could take a dozen rattler bites with no ill effects. Now a divided church, one offshoot was predicting a blissful Second Coming of the zombies as we left, while another was preaching Doomsday. The main group was ignoring the splinter factions, however, and was trying to make amends with the snakes.

In Missouri, we met a former Food and Drug Administration scientist who was near to proving, he said, that some sort of virus had animated the corpses—a virus which was now dying off. "Damn lot of good your hypothesis does twelve years after the fact," I told him as I kick-started the Harley. He muttered something about the scientific method and shuffled back to his makeshift lab.

In the Dakota badlands, we met an old Native American who had managed to actually tame a few of the dead buggers. He'd taught them rudimentary skills, like farming his land, which he showed us videotapes of. Pretty resourceful, considering all the horses and cattle had been eaten—but now that all the zombies were dead or dying, the chief was back to scavenging like everyone else. The scientist had told us the zombies possessed a very limited sort of intelligence, but I think even he would have been surprised by how far the injun had come.

Somewhere in there, we switched from motorbike to mountain bike and hooked up with a steadily growing number of crusaders, some of whom, like Janie, had The Sight.

Later we gave up the mountain bikes for snowshoes and found ourselves sitting on dogsleds.

We crested a rise, seemingly in the middle of nowhere, and suddenly everyone who had The Sight gasped. Correction—one or two of the more sensitive ones actually screamed.

Several without The Sight gasped too, for there below, about two miles distant, were dark dots in the middle of all that white. Surrounded by a hundred miles of nowhere, we were approaching an encampment of a maybe a dozen tents.

Some people believe the crater by our encampment was the result of a meteor which must have carried the virus that caused the dead to rise.

But it hardly matters. What matters is the thing above the crater.

Janie and all the other visionaries say the zombie souls are flocking to the air there like homing pigeons. They are flying here from all directions, the visionaries say, zombie soul after zombie soul joining into a single giant being. The Invisible Lovecraftian Terror, floating about a few hundred feet above our heads. This being is said to have a huge, ever-growing amorphous central globe as its main body, with mile-long tentacles flailing out in all directions.

Those with The Sight say The Invisible Lovecraftian Terror appears to be in some sort of stasis, content to simply float and wait, collecting thousands upon thousands of zombie souls unto itself, growing slightly with each one.

If you wanted some exciting, dramatic conclusion, I'm sorry. As I've said twice before, we simply do not know what is going to happen.

The souls of the creatures that once threatened to destroy humanity—that once were, in fact, *us*—might morph into a solid creature and attack. Or the creature might simply rise off into the heavens. Or it might sink into the Earth and poison it forever.

We don't know.

We only know that we've resolved to make a stand here in this cold valley, in the invisible shadow of this horrible presence.

We only know that we can, for now, keep trying to communicate this monstrosity to the rest of humanity.

We know only that we'll continue to fight in the one way we know how—by living within this invisible shadow as human beings, as survivors, raging against it from deep within our hearts.

JESUS RIDDLE MORALES

Ile Faim

by Eric Turowski

Mist blanketed all horizons, blotting out sea and sky, muting the creak and groan of damaged timbers. Sunk near to the gunwales, the vessel pressed heavily through the low chop, seeming to settle deeper into the sea with each passing, desperate moment. Lanterns cast faint yellow globes of light into the milky atmosphere, illuminating the vessel's fine lines and the obvious gashes and breeches of a serious fight. Rippling canvas and burbling wake issued from her passage, as the surviving crew clung to their stations. The *HMS Claw* was, for all intents and purposes, a ghost ship. Then, a cry—cracked by emotion, roughened by alcohol, squeezed by intense joy approaching madness—echoed across the blank sea.

"Land! Glory to God, land ho!"

Feet slapped the deck, and stiff broadcloth rustled as men rushed to the torn rails.

"Land ho, off the larboard side; fifteen degrees port, helm." From aloft, the voice seemed confident, the insane desperation giving way to commanding tones.

"Ahoy the crow's nest, keep a sharp eye for reef or rock." A man slowly came up the companionway, pulling a spyglass from his coat pocket.

The only warrant officer, a carpenter's mate promoted under fire, hurried toward the man with the glass. "Is it true, Cap'n?"

"Aye, Davy," the man said after a time. "Let's have another lantern to the forecastle. Luff the mizzen, and back the main. We'll only land her with the grace of God."

Canvas furled until the frigate crawled ahull toward the shore. Deceleration increased the rate the vessel took on water. Dim on gray, the shape of land loomed; no one spoke as the ship, listing and protesting, headed into unknown shallows.

"Take us in alongside the coast, helm. If she bottoms out, take her hard to starboard. Steady and slow as she goes. Starbolins ready the bower. All available hands, prepare to wear on the main."

Waves hissed on sand, a directionless, distanceless noise. Sailors hauled the sheets, gibing the main course, turning the stern to the wind. Chuffing sand issued through the planks; ears pricked, fearing the low, fatal growl of rock. She listed elegantly to port before coming to a full stop. All was still save the running of water from the scuppers.

"Praise God, a sandy beach." Simon Blackwell, an able-bodied seaman, limped to the forecastle deck and put a hand on the captain's shoulder. "You've saved us again, Tom."

The captain swiped at his brow. "T'was Providence put an island on our course, Simon, certainly not my navigation."

All thirty hands gained the weather deck, from up the companionway and ladders or down the ratlines, making the captain recall the seven score boys, hands, and officers lost. And while thirty hands could manage the frigate, with no real captain, bosun, or navigator, the sixth-rate ship of the line was no more functional than a fishing vessel with gunnage. Tom Caldwell, a naturalist elected captain in the pirate fashion, had little idea where they landed and less so how to get back to Bristol—or even a target as large as Europe.

"Why did Captain Blanchard have to go after that galleon? The days of Marque and Reprisal are over, damn it. The Colonists have a bloody fleet of their own." Former carpenter's mate Davy Martin cast his eyes down at the deck. He had been excited at the prospect of sailing as a privateer, but none of them could have predicted how badly the adventure would turn out. Certainly no one would have imagined plying a sorely damaged vessel through unknown waters.

Caldwell thought it best not to point out Davy's former enthusiasm for piracy. "Have you ever careened the *Claw* before, Mr. Martin?"

"I've worked her in dry dock. We've never put in on my tour."

"I want to go ashore. We'll need a damage report and a plan to make us shipshape. For all we know, we could be ten leagues from Havana."

Caldwell ordered three able bodies, Smythe, Blackwell and Silent Pete, into the boat. Hands lowered the cutter from the davits, and the four of them rowed ashore. The moon rose, a low fire.

Trudging up the beach in fading light, low mountains cast gloom upon them. Jungle canopy hung twenty paces from the shore. Other than the pound of surf, the island sat in silence. "Judging from the terrain, I surmise we've landed in the southern archipelago, perhaps near Carriacou."

"French territory?" Smythe breathed. "Our last heading was Cockburn Town."

The *Claw* beached near an ulvose lagoon, the shores overgrown with heavily rooted trees. Swatting mosquitoes, the quartet continued along the coast.

"Mangrove, wide beach, low mountains—this certainly places us far beyond the Bahamas." Tom Caldwell strode to the jungle, where he crouched to examine the plants. "*Cladium, Cyperus giganteus, Fuirena* and *Grias cauliflora*—we're most assuredly in the southern lesser archipelago. Buttonwood and mahogany," he pointed uphill toward a glowering forest.

Silent Pete squinted into the shadows while Blackwell and Smythe kept muskets to shoulders. "Too quiet about," Smythe whispered.

"Aye," Tom said quietly. "This doesn't seem a settled island."

Blackwell cleared his throat, and Tom looked up to see him pointing. Barely half a shot into the forest, eyes glittered in the lamplight, animal eyes reflecting a brilliant yellow-green. Muskets turned like compass needles seeking north. The air became malevolent, and silent Pete pinched his nose. Smythe fired, the blast shocking on the silent island.

"Hold fire and stand fast." Caldwell slowly stood up, watching the nearly invisible figures for a response. They didn't move, didn't even flinch.

Ramming another ball home, Smythe breathed, "Slaves, d'yer think?"

"With them eyes?" Blackwell fingered the trigger. "Cannibals."

Caldwell pulled a double-barreled Manton pistol, one of a set left behind by the deceased first lieutenant. "Back up slowly, lads. These men may only be curious."

Tom took a step back, and another. When the silent, odorous figures remained still, the able bodies followed Tom. They made the boat with no mishap, but guns were held until Pete rowed them far off the sand.

✳ ✳ ✳ ✳ ✳

The next day, Davy Martin quickly put all hands to work scraping bodies from the hull, felling trees, or configuring a block and tackle to raise and haul the ship. Low tide left the *Claw* fully out-of-water, and a bucket brigade periodically formed to wet the timbers. Armed men stood watch, should the natives reappear. Caldwell took a group to forage for supplies. A smaller group formed a hunting party, returning with fresh foul for the carpenters. Once or twice, men noted the pungent odor of rotting flesh. Constantly, they felt unseen eyes upon them.

Fog returned at sunset, the blazing hot day suddenly snuffed by damp, frigid tendrils. Sailors cast nervous glances at the nearby mangrove forest, and even a meal of spatchcock and fresh fruit failed to lift their spirits. Unnatural silence evidenced their fears—they were not alone.

✻ ✻ ✻ ✻ ✻

A week passed, the days blazing hot, the nights clammy with fog. Men strained at their labor; the felling and shaping of mahogany was backbreaking work, especially trees tall enough to replace the splintered keel. Hunting parties brought back plenty of fruit and fowl, but the men devoured it almost faster than provisions could be stocked.

In the evenings, the hands leaned against the boles of trees, eyes vacant, streaked with muddy sweat. Until the fog rolled up the beach—then most men sought shelter in the careened frigate.

The hunting parties whispered tales of men hidden in the jungle, men who stood silently, watching, perhaps waiting until the ship was repaired enough for them to fall on the tiny crew and make their escape.

"Damn these shallow seas and cool nights." Caldwell leaned on the bowsprit, feeling the tide right the ship. Fires crackled on the beach, the light only deepening the shadows beyond.

Davy Martin put his back to the manline, exhaustion and sun burning lines in his young face. "D'yer think they're cannibals, Tom? The men who've seen the natives, they say they don't look human."

"Aye," Blackwell said, quietly joining them. "Animal eyes, they have."

On the port side, a small group of sailors stood as if listening.

Tom Caldwell lowered his voice. "I can't fathom why you would say such a thing. None of us has clearly seen the islanders. Every tribe we've ever discovered in this region accuses their neighbors of cannibalism. Our explorations are far from thorough here, however."

Davy looked over his shoulder at the quiet group astern. "Some of the lads seem a bit... off."

"We're desperate to a man. The strain of the voyage here, a half-destroyed vessel; landing on some unnamed island. It might be enough to drive a weak man from his senses." The elected captain folded his arms, and stared into the night. Though he found himself sleepless, chased into the dark by anxiety, he could not show it. No one would follow a frightened commander.

"It's not island fever, Cap'n, it's more than that. I can't explain it quite right. And the way the lads eat, until their bellies bloat up, and still they're hungry."

But Tom was hardly listening. Something was terribly wrong on this silent island. He knew if he just had time to think he could suss it out. "Remain observant, vigilant," he mumbled.

Martin and Blackwell continued talking quietly to him, but Tom became deeply lost in thought. After a time, the trusted hands gave up, leaving him to stare at the dim island. At times, though he wouldn't swear to it, Caldwell thought he saw the shadowy shapes of men on the foggy beach. It could well be a trick of the dwindling bonfires.

Finally retiring, he saw the same, silent group of men on the weather deck, their eyes on him. As he descended the ladder to his cabin, he thought he heard them drop over the side of the boat, one at a time. But it could have been the fog playing with the night sounds.

¥ ¥ ¥ ¥ ¥

The day-watch went about their work, the sun hanging beyond the miasma, a blood-red dot. Footprints marked the dampness of the receding tide line, and the refuse of evening meals had mysteriously been carried away. Caldwell sat on a flake of rope, arms folded. When the lads addressed him, he barely acknowledged their presence. The strain he was under, lost so far from home, all of them so alone; and he was not a real captain by any stretch of the imagination.

Guns fired, and shouts echoed in the murk. Tom stood from his seat on the coiled rope. He clambered down a makeshift ladder of ratlines and hit the beach at a run. Near a recently stoked bonfire, two men carried the body of an animal, legs stretched and tied across a pole.

"Fresh pork," one of the bosun's mates cried, setting his burden down on the sand.

Blood still oozed from the stump of the hog's neck and from two bullet holes in the beast's chest. Tom crouched to examine the kill.

"He was sitting at the edge of the jungle, sir, just staring at us. Like them chickens we killed yesterday." The young mate drew a knife from his belt and began sawing the ropes.

"What could it have been wallowing in? The skin almost looks green..."

But when the ropes binding the pig's feet to the pole were cut, the headless carcass immediately began kicking.

"Get back," Tom said.

"It's just like a fresh-killed chicken, Cap'n, won't it run about for a bit?" The bosun's mate jumped back from the struggling carcass.

Somehow, the beheaded creature gained its feet and went charging toward the jungle. Several hands started after it, weaving drunkenly as they hurried.

Chickens and pigs, Caldwell thought—why hadn't he seen it before? "Leave it, lads! There's something unhealthy about that creature."

The sailors looked from the escaping pig to Tom. Sulkily, they returned to the felled trees and lumber as Davy Martin climbed down from the *Claw*.

"Listen to me, all of you." Caldwell counted heads, a few more than half the crew gathered in the shadow of the ship. "It is imperative that we make repairs and set off as soon as possible. There are men on this island, as we've seen. And they are white men, no doubt."

Smythe gave him a puzzled look. "How do you figure that, sir?"

"Chickens and pigs are non-native species on these islands. They arrive with Europeans." He saw the men give each other quick looks. "On ships, perhaps warships."

Davy Martin stepped forward. "You heard the cap'n; hard at it, lads. Let's get her shipshape."

"And the rest of the crew, if you see them, put them to work." Caldwell started down the beach.

"Where are you going, Tom?" Martin called.

Captain Caldwell answered without turning. "To find that other ship. Pete, bear a hand."

* * * * *

At noon, Silent Pete hauled on the halyard to come about as the cutter rounded a promontory covered with low jungle shrub. Beyond, thousands of miles of sea glistened, miles between the island and home. Tom sat astern, spyglass to his eye. "Hard about, Pete, there's a vessel alee."

The captain leaned forward, one hand on the till, one hand reaching for the boom as Pete swung the lateen sail around to tack. In a moment, they sheltered behind the outcropping of forested rock. Standing on the gunwale, Caldwell could reach branches that hung near the water. "I'm going up for a look. Keep her steady, Pete."

Silent Pete, who sustained a severe throat injury in the Napoleonic wars, saluted with a nod.

Tom scrambled into the gnarled, wind-tortured forest. Laying flat on a wide branch and bracing his elbows, he sighted the anchored vessel. She was built for speed, narrow across the beam, with three tattered jibs on the bowsprit and only eight guns. But sheets and lines hung ragged. After several minutes, Tom saw no sign of activity and slipped back aboard the cutter.

"A slave brick, Pete, and less seaworthy than the *Claw* unless I miss my guess. Her crew must have gone ashore."

Pete gestured to the jungle, his face a question.

Tom understood. "They may well be the men we saw. Let's take a closer look at their vessel."

Nervously, they sailed closer, approaching from astern. The legend *Espoir* was emblazoned above the galley windows. Tom snorted. "Hope: an ironic name for a slave ship."

As they neared her, they saw the upper deck overgrown with greenery that seemed to drip over the gunwales like lime frost. Masts looked like trees in a primeval forest, heavily mossed and soft looking. Ropes, hanging limp, resembled fat vines.

"Looks like she's been anchored here a hundred years," Caldwell observed.

Pete shook his head. With one finger, he traced the fine lines of the craft, then the cut of the many jibs. The captain understood. The French ship was a modern vessel, more so than the *HMS Claw*, which had seen decades of naval service before becoming an exploring vessel.

Caldwell and Silent Pete maneuvered to the ship's larboard side where ropes from the davits dangled in the water. Tying the ropes to the cleats, the naturalist and the sailor scaled the sides of the French slaver.

As they gained the narrow deck, they found mounds of verdant matter piled against the gunwales, drifting across the planks like vivid green snow. The stuff crawled up every mast, halyard, and sheet and spread across the yardarms and booms; it hung from the crow's-nest, hung from the bowsprit, hung like Spanish moss in a bayou. Thicker piles of the foliage were so deeply green they were nearly black. Caldwell crouched, running his fingers over the nearest hump.

"I thought I knew most the flora of these islands." He excavated the dark hillock with his hands, finding pale roots that held the mass together. "It looks like moss, but it's rooted like grass. If it gets enough water, it'll pull this ship apart."

They peered down the ladders where open gun ports cast bars of light in the blackness. Veils hung from each gun, the lower deck choked with deep, emerald drifts. "Has it all grown from the hold?"

Tom worked his way down the slippery ladder to the gun deck, feet slipping on the treads. Pete remained where he stood. When the naturalist-captain gave him a stern look, Pete only crossed his arms.

"Fine." In the semi-darkness of the gun deck, the unknown plant seemed even more lush, spreading thickly in the shadows. Mess tables between the guns still held shapes beneath a blanket of deep olive, trays of food hidden beneath a fleshy patina. Moving forward, he descended to the forecastle and found hammocks still strung, dripping with jade icicles. He lit a fuzzy green lantern near the furnace and cast his eyes about. His eyes traced the deepest, healthiest mass of the growth. From the forward companionway, Caldwell descended to the hold.

Soft green fur seemed to fill every inch in the bowels of the French brick, blanketing every barrel and crate. A single skull peeked from the fertile pile as if it had drowned there, blank sockets filled with the foamy material. More skulls formed lumps beneath the rug of jade.

Dragging his eyes from the terrible sight, Tom tried to make sense of it. What kind of plant could grow so mightily from a soil of rice, flour and human corpses?

Sickened, he ascended the ladder three steps at a time. Sliding in the muck on the gun deck, he made his way aft and forced his way into the captain's cabin. He gazed out tall gallery windows dripping with velvety stalactites. Though unskilled in bryology, Caldwell knew the moss looked far too healthy to be growing on the hull of a ship. The cabin itself stood mostly free of the carpet that covered the decks.

On the map table beneath the windows, Tom found the captain's personal log. He flipped it open, glancing at the entries in French. But the close cabin, gripped by the unknown plant, sent a shiver up his spine. He pocketed the book and hurried along the gun deck to the main ladder.

✹ ✹ ✹ ✹ ✹

As he and Silent Pete beached near their careened frigate, Caldwell was discouraged to see little repair. Several fresh planks lay across the *Claw* like gauze on a wound, but she was injured beyond what a few bandages could repair.

Finding a red-faced, disheveled carpenter, he asked, "What's the matter, Davy?"

Martin tossed his hammer to the sand and swiped sweat from his brow. "Half the men have run off. We need to attend a breech on the larboard gun deck, and fifteen men can hardly move this ship."

"I find it unbelievable the men eschew the chance to return to England, or at least civilization. Where have they gone?"

Davy Martin nodded toward the jungle. "Some wanted to find the half-butchered pig, some claimed sickness from the heat."

"But we're shipshape on the starboard side?" Tom inspected the fresh timbers, pitch still smoking.

Davy shrugged. "She'll float. But the gun deck will be awash in high seas. I need men, Tom."

"I'll bring them back. If not, they can remain on this Godforsaken island. Tonight's tide will be high enough to assist our turning the *Claw*. Can we be gone in two days, on the night's tide?"

"Aye, we've got the timber and tar. She won't be pretty, but she'll be seaworthy."

"Then I'll return with all immediacy." Caldwell stalked off into the forest.

Nearly silent save for occasional, entomical buzzing, the jungle was cool. Tom Caldwell understood its lure to the sailors, but not when bearing a hand could mean a faster return home. Tracks of bare human feet led deeper into the overgrown silence, and in moments, he smelled smoke.

In a tiny clearing, he found hastily erected huts and lean-tos, obviously constructed by the hand of Europeans, specifically seamen. But they seemed long abandoned, great webs of *Selenops insularis* spiders covering every door and window. Centered between structures, a fire pit smoked, the skeleton of a pig suspended over the embers. What meat remained glistened bright red in the viridity of the jungle.

"They've gone native!"

Caldwell whirled to find Smythe hiding in the undergrowth. "What are you doing there?"

"We followed them here, the lads who were acting queerly."

"Which lads?"

"Cox, the bosun's mate, Evans, the cooper, the gunsmith, the armorer, the steward, the lot of 'em." Smythe stood up, looking sheepish. "They seemed drunk, even though our store of rum's long gone. Maybe lazy or sun-sick. But they go round together, like a pack of dogs. Have done since our first day on the island. When Simon told you about it, you didn't seem to think anything amiss."

"I don't recall that."

"You told him something about observing, so that's what we been at—observing. They like the jungle, hide themselves here 'til night. This day, they roasted that half-living hog. Kicked in the fire until it cooked, it did. Even then, I don't know that it really died." Smythe made a face, shuddering.

Caldwell examined the clearing, the empty shelters. After circling twice, he came across a familiar *Bryaceae,* the same as the stuff growing on the French ship. From a mass growing between the roots of two trees, he found a skeleton. Boots and blue breeches draped the bones, the uniform of the French. Tom could see the shape of a rib cage beneath a thick green spread, and the top of a skull. Blood flowing in his heart grew cold and fast. "Where is Blackwell now?"

"Following the men still."

"Damn."

"He'll be back afore night," Smythe said encouragingly. Then he took a deep breath. "Cor!"

Near the shrubs he'd hidden behind, another pile of bones lay half-covered in a layer of moss. Smythe crossed himself and stepped away, nearly tripping.

"Let's return to the boat and wait for the men We've got to get off this cursed place."

✶　✶　✶　✶　✶

Moon and fog cast an eerie light on the bleak shore. No watch was set, the men exhausted from turning the *Claw* on its starboard side in high tide. Tom found himself alone on deck as the bonfires burned to coals, no sign of the missing men, or Simon Blackwell. Soon the beach and the ship were lost to darkness. What little noise in the jungle died away.

They came then, skeletal men in ragged clothes. Caldwell could see the glowing green orbs in shadowed faces. Three, six, ten of the men shambled to the beach, staying well away from the smoldering fire pits. Where trees met sand, they stopped in a line gazing up at the *Claw.* For a moment, mist cleared before the moon.

To Tom's surprise, their complexion was neither the brown of islanders nor the white of Europeans, but a shade of green. He reached in his greatcoat for the spyglass. Before he could bring it up, the fogbank closed again, leaving only the dimmest impressions in shadow.

He did not sleep that night; neither did he catch another glimpse of the weird, thin men.

Morning proved clear, the sun blazing the minute it broke over the mountains. Smythe gave his captain a look as he came on deck. Caldwell sadly shook his head. Then all hands began to repair a breach made by a cannon misfire. Planks—warped, hammered, and tarred into place—showed bright against the old wood. Once sealed and painted, the *Claw's* hull would be good as new. They could finish fixing the mast and sail while she was afloat.

Late in the day, Caldwell led a hunting party toward the lagoon in the cutter, while Smythe took men to refill the water barrels. The ship only held half the provisions needed, the men were so ravenous, but also less than half the surviving crew. If the missing men did not turn up, the ship would have supplies enough to reach the Colonies, perhaps even England.

In the hours before sunset, the men regrouped at the *Claw*. Cook and cook's boy prepared a last fresh meal and salted the rest of the meat and fish. Remaining hands dug a deep trench in the sand all the way to the low tide line. Dusk found them at their final repast on dry land, water filling the huge ditch to free the *Claw* from the island. Caldwell ate as much as the rest, feeling empty despite gorging himself.

When the moon rose, the frigate did as well. With block-and-tackle, and two sails, the ship moved seaward.

"Cap'n!" A shout from one of the men at the ropes brought Caldwell to the forecastle deck. He saw the quartermaster frantically pointing. Fishing out the spyglass, Tom sighted the line of trees.

Lit in ghostly silver moonlight, he saw the terror-stricken face of Simon Blackwell as he raced for the ship. In the telescope, Tom could see a gaping, bloody wound on Blackwell's thigh.

Behind him, a line of men shambled from the jungle, most in half-rotted uniforms of the French, stick figures with talons for hands; some he recognized from the *Claw's* own crew. Not a one of them seemed human.

"All hands to the ship!" Tom bellowed. "Quartermaster to the gun lockers, gunlayers to the forward carronade!"

The *HMS Claw* slowed in its transit to the sea when the lads dropped the lines, but she did not stop. Men clambered up over the sides, then raced below to receive a musket, or forward to man the small guns. On the beach, Blackwell continued his desperate run, his injured leg nearly giving out with every step.

"He won't make it aboard unassisted." Tom flung himself over the port side, scurrying down the shroud. Smythe, musket in hand, clambered down beside him.

"Lively, Simon," Caldwell called as he sprinted up the sand. He freed a pistol, aiming at the nearest Frenchman. Blast and cloud obscured vision, but the breeze showed that the ball found its mark: the nearest enemy sailor spun around and fell to the ground.

Two skeletal seamen pulled the injured man apart and feasted on his limbs. Others followed suit, like a pack of lions snarling and hissing at each other. Evans, the *Claw's* former cooper, dug his fists into the downed sailor's abdomen and raised a grisly trophy. Still, others continued toward the ship in slow but steady progress, a score of skeletal men with glittering green eyes.

Caldwell raced to Simon Blackwell, flinging the man's arm over his shoulder. Together, they hurried back to the *Claw*.

"I'll hold 'em off." Smythe fired a round into another wasted sailor, who collapsed to the earth, followed by a horde of ravenous, cannibalistic Frenchmen.

Tom pulled Simon up the rigging, up the side of the ship. "All hands, fire!"

Immediately, musket- and cannon-fire rained down on the island, smashing fragile bodies to pieces. With one good leg, Blackwell struggled to climb the ratlines.

Tom looked back, and saw his seaman ramming another ball into his musket. "Leave it, Smythe. We'll defend from the ship."

Smythe raised the loaded weapon at the same moment a cadaverous sailor reached the frigate. The bullet flew true, piercing the horror's shoulder. The wraith did not fall; instead, it reached for Smythe, bony hands finding no resistance in the flesh of his neck.

Tom looked away as blood sprayed from the carotid artery, sobbing as he heaved himself upwards, shoving Blackwell from behind. Guns still fired, impairing vision with bright flashes and dim clouds of smoke. Finally, the captain made the weather deck. As he did, the guns fell silent.

Men peered over the sides, sighting down musket barrels. "I can't see them."

"They fear the seawater, Tom." Simon Blackwell lay against the forward mast, gulping air.

"Leave the guns," Tom commanded without further explanation. "And unfurl the mainsail! Hop to, lads."

Down the trench, the *HMS Claw* rolled, faster as sails billowed to catch the night breeze. Beyond the beach, the sea glistened, calm and waiting: they were nearly free.

A pair of hands reached over the side, gripping the mainline, knuckles visible through rotting, greenish skin. Caldwell realized his mistake—he had left the deck undefended in his race to get the *Claw* to sea. Glowing, bestial eyes met his own as the creature levered itself on deck.

Caldwell grasped the nearest weapon, a belaying pin from the fife rail. He swung with all his might. Like a rotten melon, the French skull caved in. Gelatinous green matter spattered the deck. Half-blind, the emaciated French sailor came on. Tom swung backhanded, with a grunt, and knocked the wraith into the darkness.

"All hands, repel boarders! Haul up the shrouds!"

By inches, the *Claw* rolled seaward, slower than the drunken shuffle of the emaciated fiends. With bayonets and musket butt, belaying pin, boat hook, or anything at hand, the tiny crew dislodged the boarding horrors. Those that gained the weather deck wrecked havoc on the sailors, biting and clawing like starved beasts. Men fell beneath the carcasses, painfully devoured and torn.

Tom flailed his belaying pin on a man-sized thing, fully covered in a clinging black moss. Emerald slime and red blood spilled across the deck.

Evans and Cox, men Caldwell knew well, leaped over the port gunwale, spattered in blood, with eyes less human than a wolf's. The captain barely recognized the two. Each had a slightly green pallor, their faces and hands leathery and damp. They made for Blackwell, who still huddled against the mast.

Tom beat them with the makeshift club. But they had been alive more recently than the French, and their bodies proved more resilient. Cox grabbed Caldwell's arm, biting deep into his shoulder, teeth tearing skin and muscle. Davy Martin charged forward, armed with a boarding ax. He cleaved Cox's head from his body with a deft stroke, but the sailor's jaw remained clamped, working hard on Tom's flesh.

In disgust, the captain knocked the decapitated head to the planks and kicked it overboard. Evans, claws raised, came at Davy. The carpenter smashed his former shipmate over and over. Finally, a quivering pile of flesh remained, not dead, but segmented enough to pose no threat.

All about, the crew leaned on weapons, panting for breath, wounded and bleeding. No boarders remained.

With the ship running full out, Tom went to Simon Blackwell to tend his wound.

Both men saw the raw bite mark mixed with a gangrenous ooze.

"The Africans must have smuggled the moss aboard the French ship." Tom dressed the wound. "Vengeance against the men who would enslave them. It got into the food stores on the *Espoir*, infected the entire crew as well as the cargo."

Blackwell winced as Tom tightened the bandage. "Ow, that's deep."

"I'm not certain I can save the leg, Simon."

The sailor chuckled. "Long as we're safe from them things—that's good enough for me."

Against the tide, the *HMS Claw* put water between her hull and the beach. "Full sails, and man the bowchasers. Set a course around the island, north by northwest," Caldwell ordered. "Davy, how's she setting?"

Davy Martin dropped from the mainsail, shiny with sweat and blood, a smile on his face. "We're seaworthy enough to make the Colonies, maybe even England."

"Good work, lad." The captain pulled the glass from his pocket. Something else was in his pocket as well. The captain's log from the French brick. He'd have time enough to look at it later. Putting the glass to his eye, he nodded off the port bow when the *Espoir* came into view. "Gunlayers, when she's in range, send her to the bottom."

"Aye-aye. Gunners, fire at will."

The moment the dark hull with fluttering, virid sails became visible to the naked eye, the small carronades at the bow of the *Claw* fired in tandem. The brick jerked and bobbed in the water, the mizzenmast snapping. After a moment, the guns fired again. Weakened planks gave way, and the slave ship sank by the stern until only her bowsprit remained above the surface.

"Helm," Caldwell ordered, "twenty-five degrees port, full sails, west by northwest."

"Let's take her home, lads," Davy shouted the order to the cheering of the crew. Sails cracked merrily as they turned the frigate.

"Help me get Blackwell below," Tom said to Davy. They got the sailor between them and headed for the main ladder. "We'll put him in the artist's cabin for now. See if we can't find a measure of rum for him."

"Aye, Tom." Together, they descended the ladder, helping Simon Blackwell to the cabin on the larboard stern of the gun deck.

"Once we spot land," Tom said, "we sail east with the trade winds. Even the least able-bodied man could follow that course."

"I pray you're right, Tom," Davy said, easing Simon into the hammock. The seaman gritted his teeth, then collapsed into the net, breathing easier.

✳ ✳ ✳ ✳ ✳

Simon Blackwell was the first. The sailor did what work he could with his bad leg, but two weeks after they entered the trade winds, he quietly folded himself up in the shadow of the after mast shrouds, back to the gunwale, and stared off into eternity.

The cook's boy was next. They took his hands from the wheel, where he was doing double duty, and carried his lifeless form away. Tom expected the men to ask him to say a few words, but was happy enough when they didn't. He felt so tired, keeping but one thought in his head: keep the wind astern. If they did that, the ship would practically sail herself home.

An hour into the dogwatch, with time blurring together like one long, stretched out day, Davy Martin woke him as he slept at the helm.

"You need your rest, Cap'n. Cook's got grub waiting."

Dazed, not fully awake, Caldwell descended the aft ladder to the galley. Even though he was the commander, he had been working as hard as everyone else, hauling sheets and swabbing decks, recording their journey in the ship's and captain's logs. He barely had time to sleep and barely enough to eat.

Half the galley was occupied by swinging hammocks. The cook sat on a stool, head in his hands. Tom helped himself to a plate of stew, unfolding a table beneath the only burning lantern.

Scent stirred his gut, but as he bent over the meal, he stopped short. Though the stocks were fresh, the stew looked rotten, the gravy an unhealthy green.

Trying to rouse the cook proved futile, the man responding with unintelligible grunts. Though it pained him, Caldwell left the plate and hurried to his cabin.

Tom had shelved the captain's log from the French ship along with those of the *Claw*, certain English authorities would want to see it. He pulled it down and flipped through the pages. Slowly translating, he read of *Espoir's* progress from the Ivory Coast, the storm that knocked them off course from Martinique. Like the *Claw*, the brick found the island by chance, just as their supplies began to run out.

"*C'est seulement par la grace de Dieu nos demuni mort de la faim,*" he read: "It is only by the grace of God we haven't died of hunger."

"But that can't be." Tom suddenly sat upright. Flipping to the last page, he translated the final entry aloud: "We've restocked our stores. All is well..."

Turning pages madly, he found the rest blank. His thoughts churned as if through mud. The moss wasn't brought on the French ship from Africa, wasn't smuggled aboard by the slaves. It was brought aboard from the island.

He raced for the weather deck, shadows of full sails drawn by the sun setting abaft. Wind riffled his clothes, his hair. Finding the deck empty, he ran for the quarterdeck.

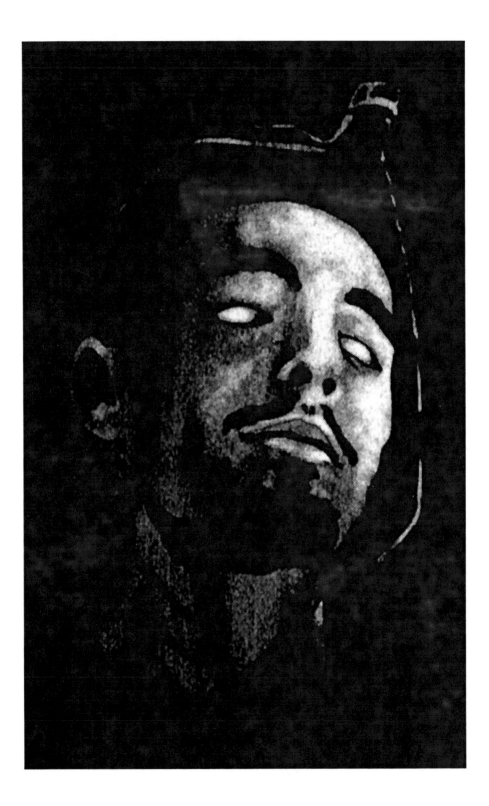

The wheel was tied off. Tom looked at the compass: due northeast. Taking the compass from its mount, he smashed the instrument until the brass, liquid, and glass flew to all corners of the wheelhouse.

"Come, Tom." Caldwell whirled at the sound of the voice. Davy Martin stood before the quarterdeck ladder, a haunch of meat in his hand. "You said even the least able-bodied man could follow this course."

"Davy, we have to turn back. If we bring the *Claw* back to England—"

A coppery smell rose in the air, distracting, compelling. Martin took a deep bite of the meat, ripping it free. It looked raw. "We must be making eleven knots. We'll be home in a month." His voice was a monotone, almost too low to hear.

"That's just it, Davy, we can't bring the moss to England. We could contaminate the whole bloody country!" Tom moved to untie the wheel.

The haunch of meat hit the deck and Davy was on him, hauling him away from the helm. "No, Tom."

He wanted to slap Davy, try to make him understand. Tom froze. Martin's face was covered in wet, red blood. They had no livestock aboard.

"We're going home, Cap'n. Our provisions will only hold out so long. Plenty to eat back home."

Tom looked deep into Davy Martin's eyes, into the green glow of his pupils. Looking at the deck, he saw that the cut of meat had a foot attached—a human foot; probably Simon Blackwell's, from the size.

"Davy, we can't go home."

Davy Martin smiled, revealing gory teeth. "We have to, Tom. We've half gone through the stores."

Caldwell needed to get Davy Martin out of the way, untie the wheel, and set them far off course, maybe into the doldrums of the Sargasso Sea. He didn't know how many of the crew he would have to fight off, but he absolutely could not allow the *Claw* to reach civilization.

Lunging forward, he bit into Davy's neck, feeling a hot spray hit his throat. The idea of changing the ship's course seemed far away. Tom was more concerned with how hungry he'd become.

Shadows collected on the quarterdeck, eyes glinting. Tom growled, but the pack fell on his prize, biting, scratching, pulling it to wet nothing. Grabbing what he could, Tom retreated into the darkest shadows to feast.

The *Claw* continued northeast under a fair wind.

Brownlee's Blue Flame

by David Dunwoody

THE SOLES OF DEATH'S FEET PADDED SILENTLY, catlike, down the tunnel. All around him flickered and danced tiny flames set in candles forged from milky tallow; he felt not their heat, nor did his eyes follow the hypnotic movements of the flames. Death studied the dark spaces in between.

Melted fat pattered on the cave floor at his back. He turned and watched as a spent candle sputtered and died. A life, extinguished; she had been old and ached terribly when bouncing great-grandchildren on her knee, though she'd kept the pain to herself. Death crushed out the smoldering wick and saw her off to eternal rest.

Miles and years down the tunnel, he saw a new candle sprouting to life. Already, the newborn flame was failing in a pool of wax—the boy would die without a name.

Death stood watch until the candle burned out.

Time passed, marked only by the irregular patter of candle wax. Time meant nothing to him.

So it was that Death was walking through the tunnel when one candle among hundreds of billions went out. He reached to pluck the wick from its center and snatched his hand back. Something he'd never felt before—heat scorching his fingertips. And something he'd never seen in all of eternity—a blue flame embracing the wick.

Rubbing his tender fingers and watching them blister in response, Death backed off from the candle. He tried to envision the soul that had been bound to it, but all that came was an impenetrable fog.

The blue flame burned strong yet showed no signs of wearing down its nub of wick. Several times, he held his palm over the flame and let the heat penetrate his white flesh. It wasn't true flesh, but a construct devoid of bone and nerves and arteries; yet his hand reddened, and he felt pain.

After a while, he decided to venture into the living world for the first time in what must have been centuries. Unable to grasp the identity of this flame's bearer, Death could still divine his or her bloodline.

Pulling a black cloak over his naked form, he passed through space into a city: Boston. The living bustled around him in their insignificant business, and their architecture framed great steel canyons atop a suffocated wilderness. Death admired the creative side of Man, admired the uniqueness of their microcosm, even if it was a mere prelude to greater worlds beyond. Unable to create or understand the concept of imagination, Death was enamored by featureless skyscrapers as much as he was by the greatest cathedrals.

He entered a bookstore tucked between office buildings. A spry man in his later years looked up. "Have you finally come for me?" he asked, an inexplicable edge of humor to his voice.

"No," came the answer.

"Then you're here to pick my brain again." Sweeping the tiny store with his eyes to be sure no customers were watching him talk to himself, Rip Baker locked the door and flipped over the CLOSED sign.

"How should I address you?" Baker asked.

"I have no name," Death said flatly. "I am an instrument, not a person."

"You don't believe that."

So arrogant, the living, so quick to assign their own insecurities and quirks to dogs and spirits alike.

Baker leaned on a cane as he led Death through a red curtain, past a hand-lettered sign that said, *Private Readings*.

"The Hindu *Vedas* call you Yama." The old man told him. "Through Chinese Buddhism, you became Yanluo, then the Japanese Enma. The Aztecs, I think, called you Mictlantecuhtli"—he butchered the pronunciation—"and in Greek mythology, you're Thanatos. The Celtic Mórríghan is female. Not an uncommon personification. Do you—"

"I have no true gender."

"Are you an angel, then?" Baker pressed. "Islam says so. Azrael, angel of death. They also say you will die when your work is finished." Baker loved to prod at Death during these appointments. He was lucky his visitor possessed infinite patience.

"I've lost a soul," Death said.

Baker stared at him from across a card table covered by a frilly cloth. "Lost?"

"There is a child bound by blood to the soul in question," Death continued, ignoring the man's puzzlement. *"Ma-ri-Bron-li."*

"You want me to reach out to her mind?" Baker shrugged. "I need a lot more to go on."

His breath stopped, albeit momentarily, as Death produced the child's candle from beneath his cloak.

"Is that—"

"Yes. Don't touch it."

He set the candle on the table. The flame, though untouched by the air, flickered—no, the *entire thing* flickered, like a ghost.

Baker held his hands as close to the flame as he dared. "Ma-ri... Mary. Mary Brownlee. She doesn't know that he died, and frankly I don't know that she'd care."

"His name?"

"Louis Brownlee, her dad. She never knew him. He was in a federal penitentiary. I'm getting all this from her mother." Baker rolled his head to one side, then the other. "His soul is departed... yet not. Not exactly. I can't reach him at all. The cord's severed, but he still walks."

Death took all this in quietly. He eventually spoke. "You desire payment, Baker? Another ten years of health?"

"I'd really rather you didn't," the old man replied. "I've been lonely since you took Linda from me."

"I don't take anyone," Death said quickly; was there a bit of defensiveness there? "I only mark their passing."

He left without a proper farewell.

*   *   *   *   *

Mary Brownlee's mother Stacy was an open book, but not the key. Death sat on a bench in a lovely park and shut one eye so he could watch his candles; time breezed gently by. Five, ten, fifteen years.

Mary was twenty-three now. Louis Brownlee's blue flame was strong as ever. Resurrection wasn't unheard of, but it was always with purpose, always serving the greater Order. Death always knew when a flame was meant to rekindle itself in space. This abnormality—dare he call it a mistake—had escaped him entirely. He stood on the lawn of Mary Brownlee's house and watched insects blink in and out of existence, a constant tide unnoticed by men.

She stepped through the rusty screen door, and he saw that her face was pale and thin, prematurely aged. Was it her father's stolen lease on life that had hollowed her out, or simply the wear and tear of existence? Death compared his skin to hers as she walked past to the mailbox. Troubling in its likeness.

He looked over his shoulder and saw someone in the window of a vacant house across the street: a silhouette, stock-still, focused on Mary.

No, he realized.

It was watching *him*.

*   *   *   *   *

As night fell, the silhouette in the window refused to resolve into a discernable figure. It didn't even move. Death stood rooted in the grass and waited. As each second ticked by, impatience took hold in his temples, his ankles. This abomination was forcing him to abide by its timetable.

It took him a moment to realize the silhouette was gone.

It was after midnight, and Louis Brownlee quietly opened and shut the door of the vacant house. He walked across the yard and stopped beneath a streetlamp. His body was emaciated under a damp dress shirt and slacks. A tie, like an afterthought, looped carelessly around his neck. Gloves covered his gnarled hands, but thin gray wrists were visible, veins empty within.

Brownlee's face, shrunken and cruel, was a parchment that covered all but his teeth and the nasal cavity between his yellow eyes—it was a corpse's face. Creases deepened around an alien smile. He spoke from a throat filled with rot.

"Why are you here? Go away."

Rip Baker, dying of cancer in Boston, would've reminded Death that his Hindu incarnation carried a lasso with which to bind the dead. Perhaps Baker would have been surprised, or just disappointed, to see the traditional scythe appear in Death's hand.

"You shouldn't be here." He took the scythe in both hands and stood in Brownlee's path. "How is it that you are?"

"I asked first." Brownlee's dead eyes absorbed the streetlight's glow and reflected nothing.

Death swung, and his blade passed through Brownlee's midsection without the slightest resistance. He severed nothing.

Brownlee struck Death in the chest with a blue aura that emanated from his palm. Death flew back, powerless, his scythe cutting a swath of decay through the grass; bewildered, Brownlee let his hand hover before him.

And then his eyes *did* reflect something, something older than Louis Brownlee could ever hope to be in this farce of a resurrection body.

"*Flames darker than this dance in your halls,*" he spat. He stepped over Death and headed into the house.

Were he a man and consumed by emotion, Death might have pursued Brownlee. He'd once witnessed a warrior in a forgotten kingdom that, covered head to toe in seeping bone-deep wounds, had wrested the axe from his assassin and turned him to pulp. The warrior, bloodless, with nothing but adrenaline in his body, had not yielded to Death's touch until he was satisfied.

As it was, the Reaper was more concerned than offended by Brownlee's words. He parted the night fabric and stepped into his cave.

In those spaces between, where there were no candles, suddenly there were—black, with twitching blue-purple flames. And he knew, now, that they had been there all along.

And now, Death also knew fear. These things, squirming like grubs, had been lying in wait to take the place of his flames. But for how long? Brownlee had to have been the first. *Had* to. So how long had these others been here, and why make themselves known only now?

He had read many of Rip Baker's books over the years. He knew the names and faces of all his avatars without the old man's teasing. And he knew a common thread in Man's most prevalent mythologies: an end to both life and death. Apocalypse.

Nevertheless, he hadn't considered a day when he would have no purpose. But as still more squirming flames crept into view, Death saw the dawning of Apocalypse, and it cast its cold blue light over him.

* * * * *

Naked, Brownlee sat on the carpet in his daughter's living room. She was spread open on the couch. He tugged a soft bit from her abdomen and chewed thoughtfully.

"Why?" Death asked.

Brownlee answered without turning. "She knew me. She said she didn't love me. She knew I'd come back, for her, and she told me I was wrong to do it." Brownlee sucked the blood from his fingertips. The warmth of Death at his back almost comforted him now; it was coming off the scythe's blade, coated in the dark wax that ran from Brownlee's candle.

"Such things happen," Death said before driving the scythe into Brownlee's back. The wax from the aberrant candle snagged whatever had slipped into the body after the departure of Brownlee's soul, whatever had become this pale mockery of him. It squirmed on the end of the scythe, black and crumbling—then gone.

Bret Jordan 2006

A shallow breath ruptured the blood bubble between Mary's lips. She found herself naked and alone, unable to move, unable to see or feel the troughs carved into her belly. Death stood over her and rested the point of the scythe on her forehead. From some place deep in her shattered mind she whispered, "Daddy?"

He placed both hands on the back of the blade and pushed.

* * * * *

He visited Rip Baker in the hospital one month later.

"I thought you didn't take anyone," the old man said.

"I no longer have a choice." In traveling the world, he had seen the plague of the blue flames taking hold of the newly dead. He was now in constant competition with a mindless, nameless thief; in fact, this Boston hospital was startlingly peaceful compared to where he'd come from.

"So," Baker asked, unafraid, "how does this work?"

Death slipped a lasso of rope over Baker's head.

The old man laughed. "You remembered."

"I thought you might like that." Death tightened the noose around Baker's neck. "What is your wife's name?"

"Linda—"

Death yanked hard, but Baker felt only the slightest tug, and by then it was over.

* * * * *

Three hundred years later, even the hospital's foundations are gone. Within the walls of the forgotten city, the living find shelter in a few skeletal buildings with neither windows nor power. Most who pass through keep going.

The undead hear the throaty groans of their brethren and converge on the city center. A haggard young woman, all skin and bones, is surrounded in an intersection, horrorstruck as those who can speak call to her.

"Come here, to me."

"No, me."

"I won't hurt you."

Thick spittle runs down their chins as they close in.

Then, something shudders at the rear of the mob, and bodies erupt into the air. They twist like rag dolls and land lifeless. The girl sees nothing behind the assault. But the undead see a pale horse charging, and his name that sits upon it is Death; his face is aflame with newfound passion.

As the Day Would Quake

by Kevin Boon

Tis now the very witching time of night,
When churchyards yawn and hell itself breathes out
Contagion to this world: now could I drink hot blood,
And do such bitter business as the day
Would quake to look on.

William Shakespeare – Hamlet

One day you're in your steel mesh, rounding up the positives, dragging them to quarantine, thinking about the new SUV you're going to buy with this month's bonus, thinking about banging your wife, thinking about the two weeks you'll get off in December, thinking about anything and everything except what you're doing, and then you look down and you've got your arm wrapped around a twelve-year-old girl's neck. You see the steel mesh that covers your Teflon suit dig into her pink flesh, drawing blood. Dangerous blood. Contaminated blood. Maybe her blond hair is draped over your forearm. Maybe her terrified eyes are green, like your daughter's eyes, or blue like your mother's, or maybe she's got a cute nose—some damn thing sets you off and you snap. You lose the juice. She becomes too real, too alive, too human to drag off to a Kennel.

And there goes your bonus. There goes your career. And if you go soft enough in the head to listen when her parents offer you money and blowjobs and Peruvian angel dust and beg you to let their only daughter go... to *just this once* forget you found her, because hand-to-God the test was a false positive, and if you just let this one go this time, they'll do anything you want—if you do that, you're dead. Because the agency has got a steel-toed boot for a heart and it doesn't give a rat's ass about how anyone feels about quarantine.

Quarantine is necessary. Quarantine is the law. You come back positive, you go to quarantine. No appeal. No discussion. No reprieve.

Jake Harris knew all this. He knew about that escort down in Florida who, a few months back, had let a seventeen-year-old boy go. He knew the result.

The way CNN told it, the boy was a star running back with a football scholarship to University of Florida—a genetic freak who could run a mile in 3:57 without breaking a sweat and who could catch a refrigerator if it was tossed anywhere near him. The Gators needed a good running back to halt the slide they'd been in for the past two seasons, and the escort assigned to apprehend the kid knew it; he was a dues-paying alumni and a certifiable nut for Gator ball. So when the parents pleaded with him to let the boy go (*false-negative... hand-to-God... false-negative*), he looked the other way. Hid the requisition papers. Doctored the records.

Three months later the boy's kid sister came down with the virus, sneezing into tissue after tissue, her nose filling up with mucus, her throat sore and ravaged by a hacking cough. Thirty-six hours later, she was dead. But she came back. The parents were still trying to convince themselves she just had a bad flu when she came barreling out of her room and took a lump of flesh out of her father's neck. The mother, with the boy's help, managed to lock what was left of his sister in the basement. It must have eaten him alive, knowing that he was the one who had given her the bug, the one who had made her into one of those things.

Within the hour, the father came back and chewed a chunk out of the mother, sending her running for the basement, blood leaking from her arm, forgetting for the moment that her daughter was down there. So the daughter got out, and by sunset, all three were kneeling around the star running back, munching on the juicy bits.

The family that eats together...

Of course it spread. It always spreads.

By the time the wagons and patrols heard about the outbreak, half a suburb was infected. By the time they showed up in the Teflon suits, their riot guns at the ready, their flamethrowers in reserve, the suburb was a write-off. Nothing left to do but clean up the mess. Jake had watched the video on CNN with Susan and Frank Needle, his partner at the agency. It was a bloody holocaust. But the patrols eventually got the outbreak under control. They always did.

No—no one needed to remind Jake of the dangers involved in disobeying protocol.

Protocol was everything.

It didn't matter if the person was a star running back or Jesus-effing-Christ. If he was a carrier, you dragged his ass into the back of the Black Maria and you hauled him off to the Kennel where the lab-techs could deal with him. No last goodbye. No warm fuzzy hugs-and-kisses. No delay. Delay just increased the chance that the virus would spread.

Never mind that Jake sometimes felt like a Nazi storm trooper dragging people off like feral animals to be poked, prodded, and dissected by lab techs. Never mind that they were healthy, vital people who were immune to the virus, people with children and wives and mothers and careers. People with dreams and ambitions. Never mind that every day he became less of a human being.

They were carriers. Even if they weren't sick themselves, they could infect others. Any one of them could inadvertently set off a chain of events that would annihilate the human race.

His job was necessary.

And it paid for his mortgage and for Johnny and Mary's private school tuition and for the cabin on Lake Okeechobee, and for the new high-definition widescreen TV. And it paid for Susan's classes at the college, and for a maid to come in twice a week, and for the lawn service, and on and on...

Blood money.

Despite the psychological drawbacks, escorts had it easier than patrol. Patrol had to deal with the lurchers. Those nasty bastards were always trying to get their teeth into you—even those that didn't have any teeth left—trying to make you one of them. What Jake hated most was the way they leaked fluids: blood, bile, puss, snot, urine, all crawling with virus. He'd never actually known an agent that had become infected by lurcher spit or piss, but he'd heard stories.

Escorts avoided the slimy dangers of patrol, but they paid a price upstairs. It's one thing to flame a rotting corpse. It's another to drag children from their mother's arms. The first one may be messier, but the second one made it tough to sleep at night. Patrol could leave its work at the office (preferably in a vat of acid), but escorts brought their work home with them. It rattled around in their head, eating away at their brain until they got depressed and suicidal—or worse, wound up in the state mental hospital weaving baskets and drooling down their chin.

Jake wasn't going to let that happen to him. He planned to save enough bonus money to retire before it got that bad.

But the bills kept getting bigger and he had to keep digging into his nest egg to keep finances in check.

*   *   *   *   *

The week before his life went into decline, Jake and Frank were sent to Davis Island to pick up a seventh-grader who had tested positive during a routine sweep of the local schools.

Frank was behind the wheel, grinning. Driving the Black Maria made him feel more powerful than he actually was and more important than he deserved to be. He was an attractive man when he took off his visor; he had wavy blond hair, which he wore longer than regulation, and his eyes were sea-blue. Even the path of acne tracks along his chin added to his charm, imbuing him with a regular-guy approachability that more than once had helped him get close to carriers.

Jake's hair was the color of burnt toast and his eyes were the dull brown of dead winter leaves. He was only in his thirties, but next to Frank, he felt old.

The sun courted the horizon as Frank steered the black beast over the Davis Island Bridge. The skyline had begun to light up like a forest of concrete Christmas trees.

A yellow Volvo station wagon turned down a side road to avoid them. A thin, middle-aged woman in a gray Mercedes sat at a stop sign, gawking up at the huge, black beast as it passed in front of her.

"Probably have to clean those expensive leather seats," Frank joked.

Davis Island was an elite address, close to downtown Tampa and surrounded by the beautiful bay waters. The houses sat snugly next to each other, lining the residential streets that snaked out from the main drag. The Black Maria looked like a turd in a punchbowl moving down those wholesome, pristine streets.

Cars changed direction the moment they saw it; drivers slammed on brakes and took illegal U-turns, rerouting their trips, scattering like mice fleeing a flame. The Black Maria meant a carrier was nearby, but it wasn't the fear of infection that made them avoid the large, black paddy wagon. It was the fear that maybe this time the Black Maria was coming for them.

Inside the houses, blinds dropped shut and curtains pulled. Trembling, moist hands twisted locks and shoved bolts in place. Children were hustled into attics and cellars. Televisions and radios shut off. Prayers were offered to mute gods.

"They're more frightened of us than the zombies," Frank said as they rounded a corner.

Jake scratched his chin with the back of his hand and looked blandly out the window. "What's the difference?"

"Hell, I don't *care*—" Frank began.

"No. I mean, what's the difference between us and the zombies?"

Frank looked at Jake, his brow a tangle of confusion.

Jake turned from the window. "Look at it from their point of view. If the lurchers get them, what's that mean?"

"It means they're dead meat," Frank said.

Jake nodded. "And what's it mean if *we* get them?"

"Means they go to the Kennels."

"And what happens to the people we haul to the Kennels? You ever know someone to come back? The dissections, the experiments? You think those are any better than what the lurchers do to them?"

A light flickered behind Frank's eyes. "Point taken," he said finally. "But no one outside the agency really knows what happens to carriers. FEMA keeps it under wraps."

"Still... people get suspicious, curious about what happens to the carriers, start to wonder why they never seem to hear from them again."

"There are the cover stories the agency releases to the press," Frank reminded him.

"Eventually even those begin to sound hollow."

Frank knew Jake was right. Suspicion colored the expressions of everyone they ran into. It lingered behind their eyes in a mist of fear. "I still don't like being compared to a lurcher," he said.

"Neither do I, buddy. Neither do I."

Jake checked the address on the Seize and Retain order glowing on the console. "That's it," he said, pointing. "The blue Cape Cod."

Frank pulled the Black Maria to a full stop in front of the house, the roof of the vehicle skimming the overhanging tree branches. The Black Maria idled low and menacing until Frank cut the engine.

Jake unlatched the door. "Let's get this over with."

They adjusted their suits next to a green mailbox with the name "Miller" stenciled on it. Curious eyes watched them from behind the curtains of neighboring homes. Later, the neighbors would bring condolences and casseroles to the Millers, but right now they were relieved that the Black Maria hadn't stopped in front of their house.

The blue Cape Cod was as quiet as a tomb. Curtains drawn. Doors bolted. If Jake and Frank hadn't already gotten ID-chip verification, they would have sworn nobody was home.

"Should I get the door ram?" Frank asked.

"Wait," Jake said. "Maybe they'll be reasonable."

They approached the door, making sure that the bright red Escort Services logo was visible beneath the wire mesh of their Teflon suits. They carried their visors. It was against regulations, but pickups went smoother when people could see their faces. They rang the buzzer.

Pickups also went smoother when you gave family members a sense of hope, when they believed they still had options, could file legal appeals, have the matter reviewed, unmask some bureaucratic glitch, error at the lab, or secretarial typo. Of course it was all smoke and mirrors. In the twelve years Jake had been an escort, no one had ever returned from the Kennels.

The official FEMA training manual for escorts offered the following guidelines for the retrieval of carriers:

☞ Identify Yourself: During pickup, it is important to create a congenial atmosphere.

> *Use Your Name*: This lets people know that you are a human being who is just doing his or her job and increases the likelihood that they will cooperate.

> *Control Your Language*: Avoid using terms such as "carrier," "escort," "lurcher," "zombie," or other terms that might unnecessarily agitate the carrier and his or her family. Use the less-threatening acronym "FEMA" rather than "Federal Emergency Management Agency."

☞ Be Friendly: The more you are viewed as an ally, the easier the pickup will go.

> *Presentation*: Smile. Refer to the carriers, their families, and yourself by name to create a sense of mutual, human understanding.

> *Information*: Never reveal specifics about FEMA escort procedures. Avoid all references to the Kennels, medical experimentation, infection, and physical and chemical restraints. Never discuss the specifics of the V-testing or the carrier's positive results.

☞ Offer Hope: Tell the carrier and his/her family you are on their side.

- Refer to the procedure as "routine."
- Reassure them that they have many options available. If necessary, tell them that family members are often returned in a short period of time.

- Tell them you understand their concerns and that, although the pickup may appear serious, their situation is unique.
- Encourage them to contact their attorney or doctor, or to call the main office. Cards are available for this purpose. (*Be sure you offer this information after you have the carrier in custody and are ready to leave. Do not let the carrier or his/her family make phone calls while you are present.*)

Jake removed his heavy glove and pressed the buzzer again. When no one answered, he rapped on the door. He called out. "Mr. and Mrs. Miller? This is Jake Harbach. I'm from FEMA and I'm here with my partner, Frank Needle." The house remained silent. "Look, I know you're probably frightened, but believe me, this is not what you think. We are only here on a routine matter. If you cooperate, we can clear this up quickly."

Silence.

Jake rapped on the door again. "I know you're here. Would you please open the door so we can clear this matter up? Otherwise, it might look bad to my superiors, and they aren't very understanding. If you'll open the door and talk to us, I'm sure we can resolve this misunderstanding."

They heard whispering from behind the door. A moment later, the lock turned and the door eased open a few inches.

The man that peered out was Jake's age. Five ten. Thinning pate. His face was blanched.

"Nobody here is infected," he said.

Jake smiled. Frank smiled.

"We know," Jake said. "I'm afraid there's been a misunderstanding. We're just here to clear it up."

From somewhere farther inside the house, a woman's voice said, "They're lying."

"How do we know that?" the man shot back.

"I understand your concern," Jake said. "I had the same thing happen to me with my kid. But it all turned out to be a technical glitch and they got it cleared up in a matter of hours."

"Oh my God, they're here for Maggie!" the woman inside screeched.

The man looked into Jake's eyes. He wanted to believe him—*needed* to believe him.

Jake widened his smile. "May we come in and work this out?"

"I don't know."

"Don't do it," the woman said. "For God's sake, Paul, you *can't*..."

"Listen, Paul—you are Paul, right? Paul Miller?" The man faintly nodded. "Paul, I'm just doing my job, okay? I have to resolve these little misunderstandings or the boys back at the office may start to think something serious is going on in this house. Then they send out the big guns and everything just gets... messy. I'm trying to avoid that."

Paul Miller's eyes were suspicious, but he pulled the door open for them and they entered. Laura Miller was cowering in the corner, her arms wrapped around a little blond girl.

"You can't take her," Laura Miller cried, clutching the girl to her chest. "You can't take her. She's not infected. She's not!"

Jake and Frank smiled and approached the woman. "You're probably right," Jake said, nodding. "That's often the case. And it usually only takes a couple hours to verify that. Then you can put all this unpleasantness behind you and go on with your lives knowing that Maggie's all right—knowing nothing bad is going to happen to her or to either of you. Isn't it better to know?"

"You're lying!" Laura Miller spat. "No one ever comes back."

Jake forced a laugh. "Now where did you hear that? Frank, how often would you say we wind up bringing people back?"

Frank, still grinning, said, "More times than I can count."

"Fact is," Jake said to the woman, "people come back a lot more often than not. Probably eighty or ninety percent of them. Isn't that about right, Frank?"

"That's right." Eventually, Jake was able to charm Maggie from her mother's arms. He handed the official FEMA card with contact information to Laura Miller. "You call these numbers and you'll see. Maggie will be back before you know it." Then Jake walked across the lawn toward the black beast, Maggie clutching his ungloved hand. "Don't worry," he said. "This will all be over soon."

He gently locked her in the back of the Black Maria. Paul and Laura Miller watched in horror from the front door. The hope he'd given them would be short-lived, but at least he'd stopped any futile attempts to prevent the pickup. It would have been tragic if Paul and Laura had tried to intervene. Escorts were authorized by the Department of Homeland Security to use any necessary force to execute a pickup, and Frank had no reservations about killing the parents.

Jake smiled and waved one last time to the Millers. They did not return the gesture. Then he climbed into the Black Maria and they drove back across Davis Island, through empty streets. Jake could hear Maggie in the back softly whimpering.

* * * * *

The Kennels were situated outside of town, beyond Carrollwood, in a large stone building that used to serve as the Whitebread Mental Hospital until the 1970s when such throwbacks to medieval medicine fell under the scrutiny of human rights activists and (more significantly) accountants and taxpayers.

The building cut into the horizon like a mountain rising from the surrounding slums. Before the outbreak, the neighborhood had been middle-class, but after the Kennels were established, no one wanted anything to do with the area. Real estate values plummeted. Now, only the most desperate and abysmally poor would live there. Even they seldom stayed long.

Frank backed the truck into the unloading dock. Attendants in black mesh suits and visors waved them in.

"You mind clocking this one in by yourself?" Jake asked.

Frank shot him a severe look. "That's not procedure."

"I know, but would you mind? Just this once?"

Frank noticed that Jake's hand was trembling. "You all right?" he asked.

"I'm fine," said Jake. "Just tired."

"But you have to sign."

"Sign for me."

"The guards may ask questions."

"No, the guards don't give a shit."

"But... it's *procedure*."

"Fuck procedure," Jake spat.

Stunned, Frank climbed out of the truck. The door thundered shut behind him, leaving Jake alone in the cab. Around back, Frank signed the form twice. Jake was right—the guards didn't care. They dragged the petrified little girl back through wire cages, into the bowels of the Kennel.

Frank climbed back into the Black Maria. He fired up the engine and backed away from the dock. "What's gotten into you?" he asked.

Jake stared blindly out the window. "What do you mean?"

"Is it the carrier? Did you go soft on her?"

"Her name's Maggie," Jake said, feeling the name in the back of his throat.

Frank stared at him in disbelief. "That's what I'm talking about. She's meat, Jake. You get mushy about the meat and you'll drive yourself nuts."

Jake met his stare. "Frank... don't preach to me, okay? I was an escort when you were still in grade school, back before they got the lurchers under control, back when it was messy. I've dragged more carriers out of basements than you can count. Emotion didn't get in the way of my job back then, and it's not happening now. I know my job and I do it."

"But you broke procedure," Frank said.

"I told you—I'm tired. If I'd known you'd turn into a baby, I would've signed her in myself."

"So you didn't go soft on that girl?" he asked.

"What did I just say? I know how dangerous she is. I know what's at stake. She's just another pickup."

Frank sighed. "Maybe I got it wrong."

"Maybe you did."

* * * * *

That night, Susan made a passable meatloaf from a recipe on gotmeat.com. Afterwards, they ate expensive canoles from Santonio's in the family room and watched FOX's *Yes, Mr. President,* on the 42" paper-thin Sony. The format of the show was straightforward. Every week the President, played by an aging, paunchy Kirk Cameron, wanted to seal the Canadian border, bomb Botswana, or enforce a curfew on the west coast, and every week the "liberal" congress fought him, which inevitably led to wide-scale disaster. In the last fifteen minutes, they always tried things the President's way and discovered, to their implausible awe, that he'd been right all along.

Jake could figure out the entire episode in the first five minutes. That was why Susan liked the show—no surprises. You could depend on everything working out in the end.

That night in bed they made an awkward stab at sex. Jake could only manage a partial erection and a hasty conclusion. Susan was not so much satisfied as accommodated.

"What's on your mind?" she asked afterwards.

"Hmmm?" he moaned next to her ear, one arm draped over her bare stomach.

"You seem distracted."

"Do I?" he said.

And that's where they left it, because their lives together had run smoothly so far and neither had any reason to suspect that a serious problem had crept between the sheets of their bed.

The next week passed without incident. Jake and Frank only had three pickups—their lightest workload in two years. Frank didn't bring up the incident of the Miller girl, and Jake gave him no further reason to doubt his commitment to the job.

By Friday, Jake had recovered much of his good nature. He was at the main escort office, chatting with Bob Munson about how damned expensive it was to refurbish a kitchen these days, and looking forward to the weekend. Bob had retired from the escort trade after twenty years, and in appreciation for all his years of service, the department had given him a desk job routing incoming orders and dispatching units. He'd been there during the original outbreak, when the dead first rose up. He'd watched his own mother and father devoured by a gang of recently animated corpses. Somehow he'd come through with his optimism intact.

"It's all plastic, now," Bob was saying when a familiar name flashed on the dispatch terminal behind his back. Jake saw it, fear shooting through him like an icy spike. "No more porcelain anymore. No more chrome."

Jake struggled to keep a smile on his face, glancing at the screen only when Bob's eyes wandered away in thought.

"You all right, buddy?" Bob asked. "You're white as a ghost."

"I'm fine," Jake said. He felt woozy and off-balance, but he didn't dare sit down. If he did, Bob would come around to help him and might catch sight of the name burning on his terminal screen. "I missed my morning quota of coffee," Jake said. "I think I'm getting one of the headaches... you know the ones I mean?"

"Caffeine headache?" Bob suggested.

"Yeah, that's it." Jake pulled a couple bills from his pocket and proffered them to Bob. "Would you mind getting me a coffee out of the machine? I'd really appreciate it."

Bob took the bills without question. "Sure, sure thing," he said, heading off with the bills clutched in his calloused fist.

When Bob was out of sight, Jake slid into his chair. He worked fast, his fingers jabbing at the keyboard. Words disappeared from the Seize and Retain request glowing on the terminal screen. He didn't stop until he was satisfied that every reference to his daughter had been excised. Then he spun around in the chair and dropped his head into his hands.

*   *   *   *   *

It wasn't a question of *if* they would find out what he'd done—it was only a question of *when*. He'd tampered with official Escort Service records. That was a felony. At best, he faced disgrace and financial ruin. At worst, he could spend the rest of his life behind bars in a maximum-security facility. But none of that entered his mind as he drove home, negotiating the heavy traffic, carefully obeying all traffic laws (aware that a minor traffic violation now could undo everything).

What Jake Harris was thinking about as an electric terror surged through him, as his heart pounded against his breast bone, as his skin grew clammy, then wet, drenching his hair and soaking through his shirt, as the memory of his daughter's blue eyes threatened to obscure his view of the road and send him hurling into another car—what he was thinking was this:

What percentage of people tested were false positives?

He'd never heard of a false positive. He'd never even considered the possibility that the tests were not one hundred percent reliable, despite what he may have told the family and friends of pickups. But now, with the type of certainty that is only possible in moments of extreme desperation, he convinced himself that no test is one hundred percent reliable. Too many people were involved in the administration and evaluation of the test. Human error alone would surely account for some mistakes: a lab tech mislabeling a vile, some dyslexic functionary inverting two numbers and sending the wrong person off to the Kennels.

He wasn't going to subject Mary to the horrors of the Kennels based on the questionable findings of some pimple-faced intern.

He'd get a second opinion. Have her re-tested. Of course, re-tests weren't allowed, but he'd find a way. Bribe someone if he had to. His career as an escort was over anyway. He had nothing to lose, nothing but his daughter, and he wasn't going to lose her without a fight.

*   *   *   *   *

Susan was mulling over a steaming pot of pasta when he came bursting into the kitchen. He flipped off the burners on the stove.

"Hey, that's dinner," Susan protested.

"Pack a bag," he said. "Change of clothes. Necessities. Toothbrush. Nothing more."

She complained, but he was firm, promising to explain in the car and insinuating that Mary's well being was at stake. That was enough to get her out of the house in nothing more than jeans and a tee shirt. Jake carried Mary hooked against his hip. Her blond hair was shoved beneath a Care Bears baseball cap, her favorite blanket and stuffed bear clamped securely beneath her arm.

"I don't want to go for a ride," she complained. "I want a kid's show."

Jake had to promise her hundreds of kid's shows, buckets of candy, and rooms full of toys before he could finally get her strapped into the car seat.

When they were southbound on Interstate 75, Jake told Susan about the Seize and Retain request. A torrent of emotion poured from her.

"What's the matter with Mommy?" Mary wanted to know.

"Mommy's fine," Jake told her. "Why don't you color a pretty picture for her?" The strategy failed, and the sound of both Susan's and Mary's weeping filled the car. He let the outburst take its natural course and kept to the speed limit, watching out for the highway patrol, feeling the reassuring weight of his 9mm against the small of his back.

He took I4 east to the Florida Turnpike, then headed south to Yeehaw Junction where he filled the trunk with canned food and bottled water at a small grocery store before picking up 441 south to Okeechobee.

Lake Okeechobee is the largest fresh water lake in the United States, a little north of the Everglades, and it is home to some of the best bass fishing in America. For Jake, fishing was merely an excuse to relax in the sunlight with a cold Guinness. They had bought the cabin two years earlier as a vacation spot where Jake could shake off the stress of his job. So far, they'd only visited the cabin four times, but the locals knew him well enough on sight to not question his presence.

The cabin was secluded near the water, about a mile off the main roads, a two-room shack with running water and a gas generator, but little else in the way of modern conveniences. It sat out of sight of passing boats and stray automobiles. The closest neighbor was Dr. Noble Hardy, a semi-retired general practitioner from Chicago who, for the past five years, had occupied a redwood cabin a ten-minute walk south of them.

Dr. Hardy's wife was dead and his children were all grown, so he maintained the cabin by himself. Hardy operated a small homespun medical practice from one of the three rooms, where he set the occasional broken arm and removed fishhooks from careless fishermen. A year earlier, when Mary had scraped her arm on a rusty nail, Jake and Susan had taken her to Dr. Hardy for a tetanus shot. They found him to be an amiable old man, in full possession of his mind, and Jake had privately hoped he himself would be that mentally sharp when he reached his golden years. Hardy mostly kept to himself, so there was little risk of him dropping in on them unannounced.

It was well past dark when they reached the cabin. Jake started up the generator, while Susan and Mary waited in the car. Once the lights were up, Susan led Mary to the house.

In silence, Jake unloaded the car, stacking the cans of Campbell's soup, refried beans, Hormel chili and SpaghettiOs onto the wooden shelves in the main room and placing the few perishables he had bought in the small Frigidaire. The main room was the larger of the two. A frayed sleep-a-way couch and scarred coffee table occupied the center of the room. A stove, a small refrigerator, and some shelves positioned in the corner of the room served as a kitchen. A small table with three straight-backed chairs sat in front of a small sink. Scenic pictures of the Everglades, cut from magazines, hung from the walls in cheap frames. Susan vented the windows to clear the musty air, then she made up the double bed in the other room and placed new sheets on the sleep-a-way couch for Mary. Mary, who had spent most of the first hour at the cabin complaining about the lack of TV, finally settled down and fell asleep around midnight.

Susan and Jake shared a warm Guinness—one of seven left over from previous trips—and solemnly climbed into bed.

Sometime later, Susan asked, in a small uncertain voice, "Will we have to stay here forever?"

"We can't," Jake replied. "We bought the place on time. There's a paper trail. Eventually, they'll find us."

"What are we going to do?"

Jake spooned against her back, draping his arm over her shoulder. His thumb stroked the back of her wrist. "We won't have to run forever," he said.

A shiver writhed against her spine.

"You don't mean—" she began.

"I won't let them have her," he said emphatically. "I'll never let them have her."

Her tension eased and after a while, he heard the deep inhalations of sleep. An instant later, he joined her.

*   *   *   *   *

Bars of yellow light shot through the cabin, and a breeze danced through the windows, relieving the early morning heat. Mary rose first. When Jake came stumbling out of the bedroom, wiping the sleep from his eyes, he found her seated at the table coloring a picture of a dolphin. A mockingbird outside filled the air with music.

"Hey, punkin," Jake said, giving her head a playful rub.

"Daddy," Mary complained, "you'll mess my drawing."

He smiled. It all seemed so normal... so *safe*. But he knew better. He brewed a pot of coffee and prepared two cups.

"Is that for me?" Susan yawned.

He handed her a cup. They stood next to each other, sipping coffee, focused on their daughter.

"Tell me it's going to be all right," Susan said.

"It's going to be all right," Jake said.

*   *   *   *   *

After a breakfast of Cocoa Puffs and toast, Jake told Susan and Mary to get dressed. They were going for a little walk. While they were busy, he slipped the 9mm into the back of his pants and covered it with the tail of his shirt.

They stepped from the cabin around eight-thirty. The day was green and lush. Wind rustled the trees, and they could hear the distant sound of outboard motors on the lake. Jake led them south into the woods.

From a nearby oak tree, Frank watched them, his fingers wrapped around a .44 Magnum. When they headed south, he followed at a safe distance.

To Mary's delight, Jake began to chant lines from one of her favorite children's books. "We're going on a bear hunt... we're gonna catch a big one... we're not scared... what a *beauuuuutiful* day!"

Whenever nature's chaos forced them to step over a fallen tree or squirm through the thicket, Mary would pipe in cheerfully, "We can't go over it..." Jake would join in: "We can't go under it..." And all three would unite with, "Oh nooooo, we've got to go *through* it!"

By the time they reached Noble Hardy's cabin, all three were in good spirits.

Susan looked at Jake suspiciously. "What are we doing here?"

He smiled. "Trust me," he said, knocking on the front door.

The man that answered the door was older than Jake remembered. Noble Hardy stood only five foot six, and he moved with difficulty. Skin hung from his bones like an ill-fitting suit. But his smile was genuine and his eyes were bright.

Hardy motioned them inside. When Jake told him that they were there for medical reasons, Dr. Hardy turned to Mary and said, "Haven't scratched yourself on another rusty nail, I hope?" Jake was pleased to find the doctor's memory intact.

"You remember that? That was a whole year ago."

"I'm old, not senile. Not yet, anyway," the doctor joked.

He led them into his office and invited them to sit. Susan took up a chair, and Mary climbed into her lap. Jake stood close by.

"What seems to be the trouble?" Dr. Hardy asked.

"It's about Mary," Jake said.

The doctor smiled at the little girl. "Feeling poorly, are you?"

Mary shook her head.

"I need a favor," Jake said cautiously.

Dr. Hardy eyed him. "Oh?"

"A rather large one."

"What would that be?"

"I need you to test Mary."

"Test her for what?"

"The virus," Jake said.

The two men stood across the room from each other. Their eyes locked. "If she was infected, Jake, you would've never made it over here before—"

"I know," Jake said. "I know she's not... *infected.*"

"Then I don't understand," the doctor said.

"I want you to find out if she's a carrier."

Dr. Hardy flinched and took an unconscious step back from the girl. "What?"

Jake repeated the request. The doctor's face twisted with concern. "You need to take her to the clinic in Buckhead Ridge. They have better facilities," Dr. Hardy said.

"We can't take her there."

"If you need a ride, I can—"

"No!" Jake interrupted. "We can't take her there."

Dr. Hardy's face suddenly took on the paternal visage of a seasoned bedside manner. "And why is that?"

Jake studied the old man, determining how he might react to what he was about to tell him. "Because they'll check the NVD," he said. The National Virus Database tracked test results. It linked to all hospitals, clinics, and medical offices. Jake had erased the notice on the computers at the escort office, but the NVD would still have the record in its memory banks.

"If she's been tested already, I can't retest her," Dr. Hardy said, turning toward the phone. "It's against the law. I'd lose my license. The only thing I can do is contact—"

"Put the phone down, Doc."

Dr. Hardy looked back at Jake. The phone froze in midair.

"Put it down," Jake repeated, waving the barrel of the gun at the man.

"I don't have a test kit here," the doctor said, cradling the phone.

He was lying, and Jake knew it. The law required all medical offices, no matter how small, to maintain a supply of test kits.

"You don't want to do this," Dr. Hardy said.

"You're right, I don't. But I don't have any other choice. Now please get started."

"Look, Jake—"

"Just *do it!*"

Mary flinched at the harsh sound of her father's voice and nestled into her mother's chest.

Reluctantly, Dr. Hardy retrieved a sterile test kit from one of the cabinets lining the far wall. The plastic crinkled in his hand as he ripped the package open. "You're making a big mistake," he said.

"Maybe," Jake replied. "Now hurry up."

The little girl was terrified of the needle, but Susan comforted her by singing the theme song to *Dora the Explorer* while Hardy held her arm steady. It took only a few seconds for the doctor to draw Mary's blood. Then he injected it into the sealed vile provided with the kit. It would take just five minutes for the chemicals in the vile to change color. Yellow indicated that the virus was not present in her blood. But if the vile turned purple...

Suddenly the door swung open and Frank stepped into the room, brandishing a gun. "Put down the weapon, Jake."

Jake didn't have time to shift his aim from the doctor. He was caught, and he knew it. "Why Frank," he said, buying some time, "what brings you here?"

"I don't want to hurt you, Jake, but you know I will."

Jake struggled to make his voice sound calm. "I don't know what you heard that brought you down here. But believe me, it's not true."

"She's a carrier, Jake. You know what I have to do."

Jake forced a nervous laugh. "That's the thing... she's not a carrier. It was a mix-up. One of those glitches we thought couldn't happen. But they do happen, Frank. Sometimes they do."

"She tested positive," Frank said. "You know what that means as well as anyone."

"False positive. It was a false positive."

"There are no false positives," Frank said. "You know that. Now drop the gun."

Susan shielded Mary with her body. The girl burst into tears.

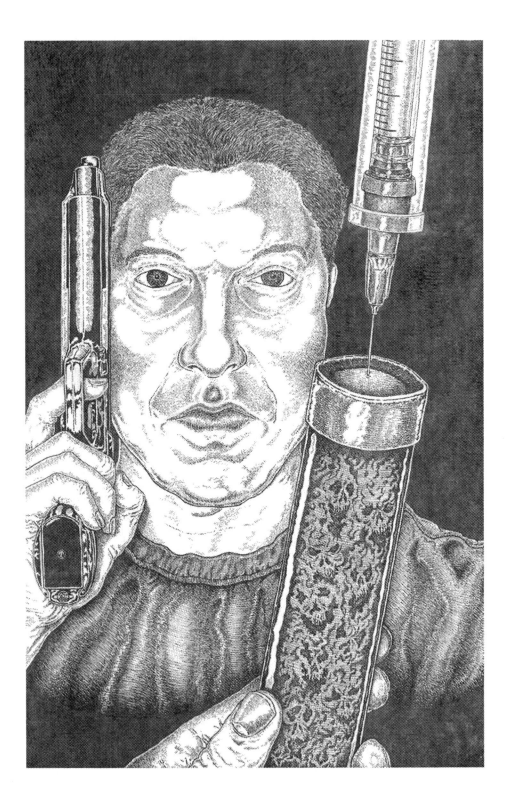

"Sure, buddy," Jake said, making no move to surrender his weapon. The gun slowly inched its way toward Frank. "But she's not infected. Just ask the doctor."

Frank kept his eyes on Jake. "I have to take her," he said.

"If she's *positive*, you have to take her. But she's not. The doctor can prove it. He's running the test right now. Just wait a minute and you'll see."

"Why would I take his results over the official results of a state-administered V-test? No, I have to take her. Now put down the gun."

"Sure, buddy. Sure. Just a minute and—"

"Put down the gun!"

Jake instinctively reacted, spinning the barrel of the gun toward Frank. The .44 discharged a clean shot to the heart. The force of the bullet hurled Jake against the back wall, where he remained, the unused 9mm still in his hand. He was dead.

Susan screamed, clutching her daughter.

Frank paused for a moment, staring down at Jake's motionless body. Then he lowered the gun and stepped toward Susan and the girl. "I'm sorry, Susan," he said flatly. "But I have to take her. It's procedure."

He grabbed Mary's arm and began to pull her to him. Susan fought, but he was stronger and managed to pull the girl from her mother.

With his arm firmly wrapped around the girl's neck, he began to back away. Susan pawed at him, desperate to free her daughter from his grasp.

"You have options available to you," Frank said. "Just contact FEMA, and I'm sure that this misunderstanding can be worked out in a matter of hours. Contact information is available online, if you don't have—" The words were perfunctory—flat and lifeless.

Then they heard Dr. Hardy exclaim in astonishment, "I don't believe it!"

Frank stopped. Their eyes turned toward the vile the doctor was holding in his hand. They could clearly see the yellow fluid pooled at the bottom.

Dr. Hardy almost laughed. "I don't believe it. It's negative." Then he remembered the dead man on the floor, and he became severe. "You have to let her go," Dr. Hardy insisted.

Frank stared at him. His grip on the girl remained firm, the gun still in his hand. Susan's arms were wrapped around Mary's legs.

For a moment, Frank seemed to be considering the impossibility of what the doctor was saying. How could the test be negative? Frank had read the Seize and Retain request himself. Besides, if the results of the first V-test could be wrong, couldn't the doctor's V-test be wrong too? And if the V-test was fallible, what assurance did he have that any result was accurate? No, the doctor must have botched the test, contaminated the sample or misinterpreted the results. *There are no false positives*, he reminded himself. *There are no false positives.*

His face regained its composure. "I understand your concern," he said. "This type of thing happens all the time. If you'll contact the FEMA office, there are procedures in place for—"

"No!" Susan screamed, letting go of Mary's legs and leaping for Frank's throat. He twisted away and backhanded her with the gun, splitting her lip and sending her tumbling to the floor. A thin trail of blood streamed down her chin.

Frank stared down at her. His eyes were empty. "I'm sure this misunderstanding can be cleared up—"

He felt an explosion of pain in his neck. His grip on the girl loosened and the gun fell to the floor. Mary ran to her mother's arms.

"Whaaaa—" Frank groaned. His hand reached up and felt the scalpel jammed into his neck. Blood gushed from the wound.

Dr. Hardy watched him, his lips drawn thin across his face.

Frank collapsed. Susan buried Mary's face in her chest as Frank's life pooled beneath him.

* * * * *

The Escort Service found Jake and Frank's scorched bodies in the smoking ruins of the Miller's cabin. The blade of a large kitchen knife was still imbedded in what was left of Frank's neck, and the coroner found the slug in Jake's heart. The official report concluded that Jake had stabbed Frank to protect his infected daughter and that Frank had managed to get off a shot before he died. The mother and the carrier were not found. The service assumed they had fled and had placed a nationwide APB out for them.

The authorities only stopped by Dr. Noble Hardy's cabin once. He greeted them pleasantly and told them everything he knew. "I seem to remember they stopped by about a year ago for a tetanus shot, but my mind isn't what it was when I was young. That's one of the reasons I had to stop seeing patients. You understand. Mind goes fuzzy when you get to be my age. Now I just worry about hooking bass."

The authorities had been satisfied, and a few weeks after their visit, Susan and Mary felt secure enough to venture outside the cabin. They took easily to lake living. After a while, Mary even stopped complaining that there was no television.

Of course, Jake's death remained with them, a hollow spot in their hearts, but in time, even that pain lessened, and on occasion they managed to put aside the horror of that day.

One night, about six weeks after the incident, Susan prepared a meal of lasagna from a recipe she'd invented herself. The noodles were undercooked, but no one complained. Life felt good again.

Dr. Hardy, whom Mary had taken to calling Uncle Noble, uncorked a bottle of Beaujolais he had stashed in the cabin. He set out three wine glasses. He filled his and Susan's glass from the bottle and poured some grape juice into Mary's.

"I'd like to make a toast," he said. "To the two most charming women in the world." He raised his glass. Susan followed suit.

Mary giggled and raised her glass too. "I'm a *girl*," she said, making them all laugh.

Then Dr. Nobel Hardy sneezed.

"That's strange," he said. "I must be getting a flu."

If You Believe

by Scott Standridge

YOU COULDN'T IMAGINE ANYTHING WORSE.

The door opened and he leapt without hesitation. There was a flash of red fur and black boots, the long white beard whipped suddenly erect with the turbulence of free fall. It was noon the day after Thanksgiving, and from the small Cessna, the mall's parking lot must have been a sea of multicolored dots, a landscape pointillized with the bobble-knit caps of children. Mark had Ginny in his arms; she was laughing, green eyes aflame in the cold clear noon, her small, gloved hand pointed skyward.

"He's coming!" she squealed. "He's really coming!"

"That's right, honey," Mark said. "All the way from the North Pole, just for you." Anne smiled beside them, following Santa with the video camera as he descended. Mall security had marked off a wide red circle with a white X inside, and families ringed the landing area. Mothers clasped mittens with sons apoplectic in their excitement, and fathers held squealing daughters on their shoulders so they could be that much closer to the falling star of the show.

Mark and Anne had brought Ginny to this event for the past three years, ever since she was old enough to know what Christmas was. Every December the mall hired a jumper to put on a Santa suit and fly down to the main entrance, his feathery descent signaling the official beginning of the Christmas shopping season. Usually they hired some hotshot from the skydiving school in Bradford, fifty miles to the south, who needed the extra cash for the holidays. But this year the regular jumpers had taken a package ski trip to Colorado, leaving the organizers scrambling for a replacement. Discreet ads were placed in the paper, and a few radio spots ran late at night when true believers would be in bed.

Charlie Battershell was the only applicant. He had experience—was a trained paratrooper who'd served in Desert Storm—but he also had a history of drinking and irascibility. Since his discharge he'd been fired from every job he'd held; most recently he'd been canned as a vendor at the minor league ballpark for cursing at teenagers who sat during the national anthem. Still, the mall brass was desperate, so they hired him. He packed his own chute that morning, claiming a skydiver's superstition. The pilot thought he smelled whiskey on Charlie's breath, even at 9:00 a.m., but Charlie winked and claimed it was only eggnog in the beard. This detail came out later, of course—afterwards.

For a long time no one realized anything was wrong. Santa floated above the crowd, so high his fall seemed the lazy drift of the world's gaudiest snowflake. But Anne had the video camera zoomed all the way in, and from where Mark stood he could watch in the square viewfinder as Charlie plummeted earthward.

After a few seconds Charlie brought one arm to his chest, jerked it out, and then resumed his spread-eagled descent. He glanced up over his shoulder, apparently surprised not to see nylon billowing above him. He steadied himself and grabbed at his abdomen with the other hand, pulling the reserve chute. He looked again to find the same empty air, the Cessna diminishing in the distance. He abandoned his air-catching pose and rolled sideways, clutching for the top of his closed pack. Anne and Mark stared at the viewfinder, transfixed by the flickering square in which Charlie grew larger and larger.

"Oh my God," Anne said.

Charlie was flailing now, jerking at the pack whose flap seemed sewn shut. Now and then he yanked at the stringy white beard that stuck to his goggles, and finally he turned it so the beard flew out from the back of his head, a mane of white flame. He tumbled end over end, arms thrashing against the battering air. Mark's breath caught. The spin would disorient Charlie, panic him further—he'd never get the chute open like that.

"Daddy," Ginny said. "What's Santa doing?"

Other parents began to realize the jump had gone sour. A few mothers pulled their children back toward the mall, scrambling to get them under the roof in time. One man with a six-year-old boy on his shoulders took off for the main entrance at a jog, ignoring his son's confused pleas to stay. But Mark was frozen. His only movement was to turn away from the camera and look up at Charlie, whose distress was visible now even to the naked eye, as he sped through the last few hundred feet. He came like a bullet, head down,

arms pinned to his sides by the force of the wind. Perhaps, by that point, he was unconscious.

A second before the impact, Anne screamed. Mark pulled his eyes away from Charlie's floundering body. As he heard the bone-shattering crunch, the sick slop of guts and blood on the unyielding surface of the lot, Mark saw his daughter's smiling eyes go dark—like a candle snuffed out on the last flickering light of her innocence.

~ ~ ~ ~ ~

Around midnight, the third day after the accident, Mark dreamed of Charlie again. In this one, parents screamed and children wailed all around him, just as they had on Friday, staring at the red-suited corpse that lay twitching in the center of the asphalt target. Sirens howled in the distance, the police and paramedics who would finally cover Charlie with a plain white sheet.

But while the body lay uncovered, Mark could not look away. He stepped closer, noting the spray pattern of blood from the impact, a red starburst emanating from a terrible focal point. There was blood on Mark's shoes, wet warm drops on his hands and face.

Kneeling beside Charlie's ruined form, Mark lifted the veil of the false beard, thinking in dream-logic to feel for a pulse. One eye stared open from the bloody meat of Charlie's face, every vessel ruptured, the orbital bones shattered to gravel. As Mark looked into the dead black pupil of that red ball of an eye, for just a moment it seemed to stare back—cognizant, aware. And then, to Mark's horror, it blinked.

A rustle of cloth rescued Mark from his nightmare. He turned to find Ginny standing by the bed. She was dressed in a pink flannel nightgown, her red hair all mussed, and she was knuckling one sleep-filled eye while staring at him wide with the other. She yawned, making a small cooing sound in the back of her throat. Mark rubbed his own eyes and whispered to his daughter.

"Hey, sweetie. What are you doing up?"

"Can't sleep," she whispered back. "Bad dreams."

"You want to sleep with Mommy and Daddy?"

Ginny shook her head. "Daddy, is Christmas cancelled?"

Mark glanced over at Anne, who slept soundly beside him. "No, honey. Christmas is still on."

"But what about Santa?"

Mark sighed and pushed himself up on an elbow. They had all been in shock the days following the accident, and neither he nor Anne had found a way to talk to Ginny about what had happened. Instead they distracted her with cartoons and cookies, with new decorations for the Christmas tree. Now there was no avoiding it.

"Honey, it's like you heard on the news. That wasn't really Santa on Friday. It was just a poor, unfortunate man dressed up to look like Santa. It was a terrible accident, honey, and it's okay to be scared and confused about it."

Ginny shook her head again. "I saw him. He came all the way from the North Pole just for me. You said so, remember? Just to see me."

Mark closed his eyes to think, but when he did all he could see was Charlie on the parking lot, the white coroner's sheet soaking red where it touched his body.

"Daddy was wrong, sweetie. I thought it was Santa, but it wasn't. It was somebody else."

"Uh-uh," she said, starting to cry. "Santa's dead. All because of me."

Mark sat up and took his daughter in his arms. She sobbed quietly against his chest as he stroked her hair and shushed into her ear. Anne stirred a little, then dropped back off to sleep. Mark sighed—he could have used her help on this one.

He put his hand on Ginny's cheek and looked into her streaming eyes. He smiled and opened his mouth.

"Ginny, you know Santa is magic, right?"

She nodded.

"Well, then you know he's not like regular people. How do you think he's able to watch you all year long and deliver presents all over the world in one night? He's magic, that's how."

Ginny sniffed, but her eyes softened a little. "What about the mall?"

"That was an accident, and Santa was hurt bad, no doubt about it. But the whole reason he's alive in the first place is because you believe in him— you and all the other little boys and girls in the world. That's how he keeps on, year after year. So if you and all the other children believe in him—if you really, *really* believe—Santa will be all better in plenty of time for Christmas."

Ginny's eyes widened, and for the first time since Friday she smiled a little. "Really?"

Mark nodded. "Honest to goodness, honey. But if you don't really believe in Santa, then I guess—"

A grin broke over Ginny's face like a beam of light in the darkened bedroom. "I believe, Daddy! I really, *really* believe! I believe in Santa, and he'll get all better for Christmas!"

"Well that's a relief," Mark said, stroking her damp cheek. "Now, let's get you back to bed."

A glass of water and a short lullaby later, Mark returned to bed to find Anne staring at him groggily. "What was that all about?" she yawned.

"Ginny had a nightmare," Mark said. "But I took care of it."

~ ~ ~ ~ ~

After that, things settled down for a while. There was a memorial service for Charlie, with a speech by the local Army recruiting officer and a twenty-one-gun salute. A Christmas fund was set up at the bank in Charlie's name for underprivileged children, since he had no family who would need the community's support. The requisite police inquiry ruled Charlie's a "death by misadventure," and the newspaper ran a full-page ad in memoriam on Monday. That, it seemed, was that.

Ginny displayed a childish resiliency that amazed both her parents. Despite their concerns, she insisted that she return to preschool, to see her friends and participate in the holiday activities their teachers had dangled in front of them for weeks. When Mark picked her up in the evenings, she greeted him with a wide smile and flashing emerald eyes, chattering breathlessly about the ornaments they'd made, the games they'd played, and the Christmas snacks they'd feasted upon.

In the hours between school and bedtime Ginny colored her pictures, watched animated holiday specials, and listened as Anne read *Twas the Night Before Christmas* for the seventh time that week. She had no more bad dreams. In less than two weeks after Charlie's death, Ginny seemed to be back to normal.

So Mark was surprised when Anne called him at the brokerage office to tell him Ginny's teacher wanted them to take her out of school.

"What for?" Mark asked.

"She wouldn't tell me much. Just that she wanted Ginny out for a day or two until everyone could cool off."

"Cool off? What are you talking about?"

Anne sighed. "Apparently she attacked one of the other kids. I don't know what it was about—some playground squabble or other—but Mrs. Evans seemed concerned and thought it would be best if we took Ginny out—immediately."

"There's got to be some mistake. Ginny would never attack someone."

"I know that, but what could I say? Anyway, I hate to ask, but I've got a meeting in five minutes and can't get out of it. Do you think you could go meet with Mrs. Evans?"

"Sure," he said. "I'll talk to Gus and go right over."

"Thanks. I really wish I could go, but—"

"Hey, don't worry about it. Team parenting, right? I think I can handle it."

~ ~ ~ ~ ~

Mary Evans was a stout woman with dyed black hair and a severe, doughy face. When Mark arrived just after twelve o'clock, she showed him through the play area to a small room at the back of the building which served as her office. Its walls were decorated with construction paper hearts and bright scribbles of stick figure families. Several featured a snow-woman with the legend "Mis Mary" scrawled over her head. In some, her eyebrows were pointed in an unflattering way, and in others her stick arms were firmly planted on round hips. Mrs. Evans pointed to the chair across from her desk, and Mark sat down.

"I'm sorry to trouble you like this," she began. "But after what happened today, I didn't see any other choice."

"What happened today, Mrs. Evans?" Mark asked. "Anne—my wife mentioned some kind of fight?"

"I think it would be best to bring Virginia in," Mrs. Evans said. "I dislike handing down edicts behind a child's back—it makes them feel grownups are hiding things from them. Donna," she called into the intercom. "Could you bring Virginia McRae?"

Half a minute later Ginny came in. A long pink scratch marred the apple of her left cheek, and her eyes were red. She stood beside Mark without speaking.

"Virginia," Mrs. Evans said, brusquely, "do you know why your father's here?"

Ginny nodded. "Because of Billy Johnson."

"No, that's not right. He's here because of *you*. We want to talk about you now, not Billy. Do you understand?"

Ginny only shrugged. Mark put a hand on her shoulder. "What happened, sweet pea?"

"What happened," Mrs. Evans said, "is that Virginia knocked Billy Johnson down on the playground and kicked him."

"Don't all children get into playground scrapes, Mrs. Evans?" Mark said. "After all, kids will be kids."

"She also encouraged her friends to do the same," Mrs. Evans continued. "She stood at the head of a mob, five or six of them, egging them on while they pummeled him. She was literally screaming for his blood."

"That can't be, Mrs. Evans. Surely this is an exaggeration."

"I saw it myself. It was horrible. Later today I'll have to explain to the Johnsons how their son got two black eyes and a bloody nose in my care. How do you suggest I do that, Mr. McRae?"

Mark turned to his daughter, who stared at her patent leather shoes and said nothing. "Ginny—is this true?"

She shrugged again. "He started it."

"Indeed," Mrs. Evans said. "As you've said, Mr. McRae, we have scuffles between students on a weekly basis. It's to be expected. But this isn't the first incident involving your daughter. Several of our employees have complained about her strange behavior."

"I don't understand."

"Apparently she's started a gang on the playground. Some of the caregivers call it—well, a cult."

"A cult?" Mark laughed. "Mrs. Evans, she's six years old!"

Mrs. Evans stared at Ginny, waiting. "Virginia," she said at last, "why don't you tell your father what your friends do at recess?"

Ginny didn't look up. "We're trying to save Christmas."

"What do you mean, honey?"

"We have to believe in Santa," she muttered. "All of us. Santa's hurt real bad. He might be almost dead. But we can bring him back if we believe really hard, all of us, every day. So we sing Christmas carols—*Santa Claus is Coming to Town, Here Comes Santa Claus*—and we say we believe over and over again. 'We believe. We believe. We believe.' "

"A nice little chant," Mrs. Evans scoffed.

"But today Billy said there wasn't any such thing as Santa Claus—that it was our parents getting us presents. He was trying to make us not believe." She looked up at last, her eyes emerald fire. "I had to stop him! If I didn't, Santa might not come back! If somebody doesn't believe even the tiniest little bit, it might not be enough! Santa might die!" She turned to Mark. "Everyone has to believe, right Daddy? Just like you said."

Mark bit his lip and looked from his daughter's pleading face to Mrs. Evans' glare. At last he put his hands on Ginny's cheeks.

"Could you wait outside a minute, sweetie? Daddy wants to talk with your teacher."

Ginny obediently stepped out of the room. Mrs. Evans' stare got a few degrees colder.

"So you see what I'm up against here. You see why Virginia can't stay, at least for a while."

"Listen, I'm sorry about all this, Mrs. Evans. We were at the mall—you know, when Charlie Battershell fell. Ginny was traumatized, and I guess I just wanted to soften the blow."

"I am of the opinion, sir, that one shouldn't soften the truth. Your daughter is not a baby. If you continue to treat her as one she'll be in for some nasty surprises one day."

"I know that," he agreed, "but it was Santa Claus. I mean, I didn't think believing in Santa Claus would be bad for her, just a little longer."

Mrs. Evans sniffed. "A child's belief is nothing to be trifled with, Mr. McRae. Innocence bought with lies is not innocent. If you tell them a lie, their pure, unsullied belief works upon it, and makes it so. I mean figuratively of course, in their little minds. When they are inevitably faced with an unpleasant truth you've hidden from them, the results can be disastrous. I've seen it. I'm seeing it now."

Mark hung his head. He felt no older than Ginny, ashamed and bladder-tight before a terrible schoolmarm. "Didn't your parents ever lie to you, Mrs. Evans?"

"Certainly," she replied. "Fortunately I was able to overcome it."

Mark drove all the way home in silence. Ginny, enthroned in her booster seat in the back, also said nothing. Every now and then Mark looked into the rearview to find her staring back at him, her eyes hard green stones. When they pulled into the driveway, Mark put the car in park and killed the engine.

"It was wrong of you to hurt Billy Johnson, honey. Think of how his parents must feel. And it got you in trouble, too."

Ginny frowned. "But it wasn't my *fault!* It was Billy—and Mrs. Evans! I bet *she* doesn't believe in Santa either!"

Mark sighed, wondering if he should tell her. But when he looked again and saw her angry little eyes, Mark only cleared his throat and swallowed.

"You have to be *good*, though, Ginny. Otherwise Santa won't come see you."

"I'm being good," she pouted. "It's Billy and Mrs. Evans being bad. They'll be sorry when Santa comes."

"Well," Mark said, "that's just part of life, honey. You can't help it if other people don't believe."

"They'll believe in him when he comes. Then they'll see who's been bad." Ginny glared at her father with cold assurance. "They'll believe, Daddy. They'll *have* to."

~ ~ ~ ~ ~

Christmas Eve was quiet at the McRae house. Anne cooked her famous Pineapple Ham while Mark and Ginny made gingerbread men. Ginny enjoyed creating the little human figures out of the shapeless dough, planting jelly beans, raisins, and licorice in their faces to mold expressions of joy, fear, and surprise. After dinner Ginny was allowed one present—the old-fashioned rag doll Anne's mother had mailed from Wisconsin—and she lugged it dutifully into her bedroom. Mark, warm and sluggish by the fireplace and nursing an eggnogged rum, grabbed Anne's robe as she walked by.

"Ho, ho, hold it there, woman."

Anne grinned. "I have to put Ginny to bed."

"Just a minute." Mark groaned and pulled himself up from the chair. Once up, he leaned into her, looking up over her shoulder. "Well I'll be damned," he said, pointing.

"Mistletoe," she affirmed. "Almost as if it were planned."

"You'll never prove a thing." They kissed long and searching, tongues all cream and nutmeg. "How about if I take care of Ginny, and you go on up and get ready for bed? I've got a stocking stuffer waiting for you."

"Naughty," Anne laughed. "But nice. Don't be long."

Anne bounced up the stairs as Mark leered, then gave him a Betty Grable on the top step before disappearing into shadow. Mark ambled across the living room, shutting off lights as he neared his daughter's door. Through the hallway window, the full moon reflected off a blanket of unblemished snow and lit the yard like noontime. He could see all the way to the edge of the property, where a line of black trees stood like sentries. It was beautiful.

Mark stopped just outside Ginny's door. He could hear her murmuring, saying her prayers. He pushed the door gently and went silent across the hardwood floor to where his daughter knelt by her bedside. Mark hovered in close, hoping to overhear "bless Mommy, bless Daddy," just like in the Christmas movies. Ginny mumbled low, so that for a moment Mark couldn't make out the words. But finally he did—two words only, whispered over and over again.

"I believe... I believe... I believe..."

"Honey?"

Ginny turned to him and smiled.

"He's coming tonight, isn't he, Daddy?"

Mark grinned back. "Maybe. But only if you've been good."

"Oh, I've been good." Ginny kissed her father on the cheek and leapt into bed. "He'll be here," she said. "I just know he will."

~ ~ ~ ~ ~

Mark was awakened by the metallic clatter of trashcan lids out on the lawn. He looked at the alarm clock, which read "2:30 AM" in glaring red lines. The woods near their house were full of possums and raccoons, and every so often the creatures rummaged through their garbage looking for scraps. Mark punched his pillow and rolled over, thinking that whatever mess there was could wait until morning.

But before he could drop off to sleep again, Mark heard something else, faint but clearly audible in the silence of early morning: the crunch of ice and snow under weight, followed by a rasping scrape like a box being dragged across the yard.

Footsteps.

Mark sat up, suddenly wide awake. He had heard of houses being robbed on Christmas Eve, ruthless burglars making off with all the presents while the homeowners slept. But could he be imagining things? Quietly he got up and put on his heavy fleece robe, slipping his feet into the house shoes that lay beside the bed. Anne slept soundly as always and Mark let her—there was no point waking her just yet. He tiptoed over to the window and carefully drew aside the drapes.

The full moon still lit the yard bright as day, but it was no longer a perfect sheet of white. From the black trees at the property's edge all the way up to the house, the snow was crumbled and upturned, spotted with dirt and leaves. The path stretched around to the garage, where the trash cans sat. Mark couldn't tell what had made the tracks—perhaps a raccoon or some stray dogs looking for food. He crept out of the room and down the stairs to have a closer look.

In the living room, Mark flicked on the lights and was relieved to see the Christmas tree still in place, the presents arrayed beautifully underneath. If burglars were prowling the neighborhood, they hadn't made it inside; now perhaps the lighted windows would ward them off.

Still, he took up the poker from the fireplace and brandished it in front of him as he walked toward the front door. There he turned on the porch and landscaping lights, then stood with his hand on the door as he counted to fifty. Satisfied that any criminals would have to be blind not to see that the homeowners were stirring, he opened the door.

The early morning was beautiful and silent. The porch light made the snow near the house sparkle as though littered with diamonds, and beyond the arc of electrical lighting the full moon gave the yard a pale bluish cast.

Mark's breath misted in front of him as he stepped outside, still holding the poker. He trudged around toward the garage, making as much noise as possible. Finally he reached the path he had seen from his bedroom window.

The tracks were human; there was no mistaking that. The footprints had knobby tread deep as a snow tire's—hiking or combat boots. Beside was a trench nearly a foot wide, as if whoever had made the tracks dragged something heavy along with him. Dirt and leaves fouled the snow there, as well as something else—a thick liquid that looked black in the artificial light, streaks of it lining the small trench. Looking to the tree line, Mark could see where the person had left the cover of the forest—regular, evenly spaced footprints all the way back into darkness. There were no return tracks.

Mark followed the trail around the corner of the garage, gripping the poker tightly. He found the garbage cans knocked over, food scraps and paper littering the snow. The tracks stopped abruptly at the garage. Cut into the garage door was a small portal that had been used by their dog Rusty, a black lab killed by a truck the year before. The door had a magnetic lock that opened in conjunction with a small battery on Rusty's collar, thus keeping out strays and other woodland creatures. Since Rusty's death the door had remained closed.

Until now. The Plexiglas panel was splintered, pushed inward with surprising force. The dog door was too narrow and short for a grown man to squeeze through. But the tracks ended here—and the lip of plastic that edged Rusty's door was streaked with the same dark liquid from the trench, which Mark now saw was not black but dark, deep red. The now-empty hole gaped at him like a wound.

Mark ran back around to the front of the house, losing one of his slippers in the deep snow. The ice bit at his bare foot and numbed his toes, and by the time he reached the front door his lower leg tingled as though asleep. Mark pushed through the door and limped across the living room to the kitchen, holding the poker like a club.

As he turned the corner, his breath caught in his throat—the door to the garage stood open, and a trail of mud and melting snow stretched across the kitchen floor. He whirled and saw that the trail continued to the foot of the stairs and upward. Beside the muddy footprints, red swathes stained the carpet. Mark bounded up the stairs and followed the trail to the pink-painted door at the end.

Ginny's room.

Mark ran down the hall as fast as he could. But as he reached Ginny's door something made him pause: his daughter's voice, giggling sweetly, whispering to someone on the other side. He couldn't make out any of the words, but Ginny's voice sounded warm and welcoming, a tone usually reserved for family and close friends. Mark's mind spun, overcome by a sense of dream logic. He carefully pushed the door open.

"...think I'm getting a bicycle," Ginny said. "Is that right? I know you can't tell, I just like to guess..."

Moonlight streaming through the slightly parted curtains filled the room with a dim blue glow. Dolls and other toys littered the floor, and construction-paper decorations hung on every wall. The footprints continued past Ginny's canopy bed to the rocking chair in the corner of the room. The light from the window didn't reach all the way into the corner—Mark could just make out the hem of Ginny's nightgown falling over the edge of the chair, and underneath it two large legs covered in what looked like dirty red fur. Fuzzy white cuffs ringed the top of combat boots, and beside them on the floor lay a canvas bag covered with dark streaks. Ginny kept chattering.

"...said you wouldn't be here, but I just knew you would be. I knew if I believed—Daddy!"

Ginny leapt off the chair and ran across the room to her father. Mark knelt and hugged her close with one arm, pointing the poker toward the stranger who still sat cloaked in shadow. The back of Ginny's nightgown was wet and had a strong chemical smell that reminded Mark of high school biology class.

"You were right, Daddy," she said. "I believed, I believed *so* hard, and now he's here!"

"Ginny," Mark whispered, never taking his eyes off the figure in the corner, "go and get in bed with your mother. Tell her to call the police."

"But why, Daddy? It's just Santa! He came, just like you said!"

"It's not Santa, Ginny—"

Ginny wrestled herself free. "Oh yes it is, I'll show you!" She reached up beside the door and flicked on the light just as the figure started to rise from the chair.

The Santa costume was wet and disheveled—the beard hung off to the side, revealing the mess of tangled blue veins that had burst when Charlie Battershell hit the ground. The hat was too small, but Charlie had tried his best, stuffing his pulverized skull into the conical space and fixing it there with what looked like rusty nails. He swayed unsteadily on his feet, and the shattered bones of his shoulders and chest rose and fell irregularly, making him seem to expand and contract like a bellows. Charlie's eyes were black with old blood, and he stared past Mark and Ginny into space.

At his feet, the canvas bag was open—through its lip Mark could see a mass of jet-black hair and one severely sculpted eyebrow. At the bottom of the bag, another, smaller lump sat, leaking blood.

"He knows who's naughty or nice," Ginny said. Mark looked at his daughter and saw that she too was staring at the bag, a wicked little smile on her face. "*I* was nice—not naughty like Billy and mean old Mrs. Evans." She giggled, and Charlie Battershell came forward jerkily on broken legs. "Can we go open presents now?"

And as Charlie came closer and closer Mark began to laugh, deep in his throat, *ho-ho-hooooah!*, laughing as if he would never stop.

Wall-Eyed

by Kriscinda Meadows

Flatfish are some of the strangest creatures. Pleuronectiformes—we're talking turbot, plaice, flounder, halibut, and sole. While they begin life like most fish—swimming upright, everything symmetrical—they quickly change. One eye, usually the left, begins to migrate up and over the top of the skull, situating itself snuggly next to the other eye.

As this happens, the fish's body turns, its equilibrium adjusts, and it settles, eye-side up, on the murky bottom of its habitat. It's a modification for benthic dwelling, lurking in the depths of the sea, sifting itself through the dark sediments, snatching up its prey in its mouth, which is all akimbo on its face. Its eyeballs turn every which way, the better with which to find, catch, and eat.

They are a mystery. No one knows exactly how any of this takes place. No one can answer with any degree of certainty why the flatfish chose this path on the evolutionary map of morphology. They are confounding. Especially to me.

I started my studies with flatfish twelve years ago. Once I finished my PhD, I headed to Japan to study *Paralichthys olivaceus*—the wild Japanese Flounder—a very important animal to the fisheries of Japan. I study the artificial seeding of these flounder to help ease the reduction in stock size from overfishing.

Truth be told, this doesn't interest me. The proper upkeep of fisheries is important, I suppose, but what I'd like to do is study the workings of the fish—the process of eye migration, and what genes and hormones are involved. It's not exactly medically applicable, but there's a lot to be said about research done for curiosity's sake.

There's only one lab in the world that studies eye migration in flatfish—at Johns Hopkins University in Baltimore, under the stewardship of Dr. Alec Schroeder. I received a letter from Dr. Schroeder about three weeks ago and I've been in a sweat ever since. I hadn't heard from Schroeder in years. He said he's been following my work and feels I'm ready and that I would be an asset in his lab. I tried to decline the offer, but he pressed. He knows this is the area toward which I lean. He also said that if I didn't want to, I didn't have to see Moby.

I suppose this is where I should tell you about Moby Waller.

* * * * *

"What the fuck is that?" Moby exclaimed my first day on the job. I was nineteen, which meant I was responsible enough to be trusted with certain duties but still stupid enough to somehow screw up. Dr. Schroeder was kindly assuming the former when Moby dropped me off at work that morning.

"Those," Schroeder answered, "are called Hogchokers."

Moby and I looked at the good doctor, who looked back at us.

"Hogchokers," he continued, "are found from Maine to Florida, and are so called due to the fact that once upon a time, farmers used to feed them to their hogs, so abundant were the creatures. Unfortunately, the fish's bony body and odd shape caused the hogs to gag and die. So," he added, "I don't suggest eating these fish—I would suggest a nice lean, white flounder."

Combining the smell of soggy feeding pellets with my aversion to seafood to begin with, my stomach churned a little. Moby licked his lips and asked what time I got off for lunch.

In hindsight, I'm ashamed to acknowledge that I hadn't quite figured out that just because you've known someone for a long time doesn't mean you have to be friends with that person. And considering our history up until that point, it's embarrassing that it went on as long as it did.

Moby and I met in sixth grade. We exchanged our first words in the principal's office, sitting next to each other, waiting to be called in. "Whatcha in for?" he asked quietly, as if he were in prison already.

"Makin' fun of the spastic kid," I answered low.

The secretary glared at us then went back to her paperwork.

"No shit!" he whispered back. "Me too!"

Demetri Rieti was in the same grade as us and the product of Mr. and Mrs. Rieti. They were the boys' and girls' gym teachers. I don't imagine Demetri was their dream come true—born with both arms twisted up to his chest, his neck cocked sharply to one side, and a walk that looked more like an uneven march. To top it all off, he stuttered. Strangely enough, he wasn't usually teasing fodder—not until the whole school found out that Mr. Rieti was banging Mrs. Kennicot, the math teacher. That's when Demetri got it.

And so we sat in the main office, awaiting our interviews with the principal, laughing. See, when you picked on Demetri, he got flustered and bunched up even more. His face would screw up, his hands would come farther up his chest to his chin, and his fingers would start fluttering like the legs of a centipede. And then it would come—the retaliation, "Fu-fu-fu-ffffuh-fff-fuh..." and he could never quite spit it out.

And that, sadly, is how Moby and I met. From that day on, our usual greeting was to bring a hand up to our chests, flutter our fingers, and stutter out the first word: "W-w-w-what's up?"—"H-h-h-hey!"—"H-h-h-how's tricks?"

And from that meeting—which should have told me a lot—we stayed friends. Friends through the conflict between his and my family—his thought mine weren't good enough, thought I was trouble. Friends through our first girlfriends—both of which he eventually impregnated, both of whom aborted. I bought the old adage that girlfriends come and go, but friends are forever. Friends through the numerous suspensions from school, where I took the fall because one more would mean expulsion for Moby. Friends through that time my parents posted bail for me because I was in Moby's car during a routine traffic stop and Moby left the bowl sitting in the ashtray, practically waving at the officer.

I can think of a lot of reasons I put up with him for as long as I did, and they all likely express the absolute lack of self-esteem I had at the time. Moby was bad for me. The fact is that, like flatfish, people change as they grow, and Moby metamorphosed into an asshole. And then he metamorphosed into something else. But I'm getting ahead of myself.

* * * * *

My job with Dr. Schroeder was to clean the tanks and feed the fish. They came in all shapes and sizes, depending on the age and species. I didn't know anything about them at the time, but I was open. I was seriously looking at the direction my life was going—which was nowhere—and I was seriously considering getting into college. I wasn't sure what I wanted to study, but I knew I had to do something. I never shared this with Moby, who would have guffawed at me, as he often did about most things anyway. My mere presence in a scientific facility was enough to provoke a certain amount of goading.

My first week passed without incident, and I think Dr. Schroeder liked me because I showed a lot of enthusiasm, which might have been part brown-nosing and part genuine growing interest. He told me that if I really wanted to pursue it, he would take me up to the lab and tell me about what they were doing. He would occasionally start chattering on about his research, but I'd get lost in the technical terms—I'd just zone out and start thinking about a sandwich or something. I meant well, but I just wasn't intellectually ready to immerse myself in the science. Of course, now I know what he was talking about.

His main concern at that time was figuring out the precise mechanism of eye migration and skull development—the line between symmetry and asymmetry in craniofacial and brain remodeling. In other words, what made the eye move and what made the skull's form change?

Schroeder used many different chemicals: methimazole to prevent the iodination of the thyroglobulin, prohibiting the production of thyroid hormone, which kicks off the whole physical process of eye migration; triiodothyronine to speed up metamorphosis from four weeks to four days; calcein to mark bone fluorescently; and various fluorescent lipophilic retrograde labeling substances to trace neurons from the retina to the optic tectum of the brain. There's also physical surgery with microscopic laser ablation, which will destroy certain cells and structures in the eye or inner ear to see how it affects balance.

All of these research mechanisms were important and useful, but none perfect, so naturally, he was always on the lookout for more refined and accurate substances to carry out his experiments.

*　*　*　*　*

Like I said, my job was relatively menial. I cleaned tanks that quickly became slimy again, and I fed fish of various species and stages various foodstuffs. Extremely young fish ate freshly hatched brine shrimp, whereas some of the older fish would eat larger brine shrimp. These came in frozen blocks, and I would often end up with brine shrimp residue all over, trying to break them into the right size for the right number of fish per tank. The Hogchokers ate bloodworms. These are small, squirmy aquatic worms of a creamy pinkish-reddish color whose inclination would be to burrow in the sandy sediments of its natural habitat. We didn't have that in the fishroom, so mainly they just clumped at the bottom of the sediment-free tank until a hungry Hogchoker descended on it with its crooked mouth full of teeth.

When I wasn't cleaning and feeding, I was running fish up to the lab and then back down when the scientists were finished with them. I would also make the runs to pick up newly arrived chemicals and supplies. I was the flatfish flunkie for the technicians in the lab—the Labcoats, as Moby called them. And for some reason, it was quite tiring. At the end of the day, all I wanted to do was go home, take a shower, eat, and go to bed.

I hadn't seen Moby in a week and he was already complaining that I was turning into some sort of intellectual snob, which is particularly amusing considering I really wasn't learning a thing—and that was my fault. Perhaps if I had paid more attention to the details Schroeder was telling me, I wouldn't have done the extraordinarily stupid thing that I did.

So, that Friday after work, I headed over to Moby's for beers and stimulating conversation. He lived in a one-bedroom apartment that his parents paid for. Moby didn't believe in working a job unless it was the job you wanted to work. Unfortunately for Moby's weak-willed parents, Moby didn't know of any job he wanted to work... so he didn't. I was still living with my parents, who insisted that if I wasn't going to go to school, I was going to work and pay some rent, which I did. They weren't mean people; they were just trying to give a stupid kid a hint.

Moby answered the door with the phone to his ear—he brought his free hand up to his chest and gave his fingers a quick flutter; I reflexively did the same. "I have to go, I have to go," he said. "My girlfriend's here, I have to go." He smiled wide at me so that I would acknowledge the comic genius that he was. "I. Have. To. Go. Bye." And he hung up. I set the six-pack on the coffee table and fell into the sofa. He fell down next to me.

"So, w-w-w-what's up, fishboy, haven't seen you in a while." He leaned forward, twisted the cap off a bottle, and took a long, hard swig.

"I've been working. Been busy. Sorry I haven't stopped by."

"Whatever," he said and then launched into a lengthy diatribe about what he had been doing; it basically amounted to nothing. Then he stopped, eyed me, and asked, "When's the last time I dared you?"

Shit. Throughout our relationship, Moby prided himself on the thickheaded things he could coerce me to do. He did so usually by insulting my manhood, as most guys tend to do. And like most guys, I fell for it every time.

"Steal me a fish."

I looked at him incredulously. I asked him to repeat himself.

"Steal me a fish from your work, from the lab. Make it a big one. One of those... what'd he call them... Hogchokers."

I tried to explain that I actually needed that job and I really didn't want to jeopardize it by pulling some half-witted, childish prank. It ended with me saying something like, "No, *you're* the fag. You'll get your fucking fish."

He chortled and then proceeded to drink five out of the six beers I brought.

* * * * *

The following week was work as usual. The Labcoats were excited about some new experiment with some new chemical—Methiphenozythyronine, or MPT—and I caught occasional snippets of complicated conversations. Schroeder explained it to me in laymen's terms. They didn't know what it did precisely. It might affect the movement of the eye and the timing of that movement. It might affect the brain and therefore affect many physiological and behavioral aspects of the fish. Maybe the inner ear. It might do nothing at all.

"I don't know," Schroeder would say, day after day. "It could be something big, it could be nothing. We're going to see what it does and how it does it."

I smiled, wiped the slime from the glass of the tanks and meted out the brine shrimp and bloodworms. Moby had taken to calling the fishroom phone line to ask if I'd picked a fish yet, to make sure it wasn't too big, but not too small. Was Schroeder onto me? Would I bring it tonight? No. Fine. No. No.

In fact, I spent most of my day contemplating my future, so the only time I considered the dare was when Moby called. He would also call my parents' house the moment I got home from work to ask if I was bringing it over that night. Each time I said no, the more girlie I was, according to Moby. By Friday, I knew I had to deliver.

After the exciting start on Monday, the Labcoats seemed a little let down on Friday. One of the technicians brought a specimen to the fishroom, one they had taken up to the lab at the beginning of the week. Dead. At least I thought it was dead. Flatfish, once they reach a certain point following the metamorphosis, tend to lie flat on the bottom for most of the day. They'll lie in the same position for so long that one might think they'd given up this life. I would occasionally squirt them with water from a turkey baster, and even then it was hard to get them to move.

I asked him what, if anything, the MPT did. "Well, it definitely killed it. Would you dispose of this?" Of course I would. Moby didn't say it had to be a live fish.

When finally forced to think about the dare that morning, I had considered that moving a live fish to Moby's would prove difficult. They needed constant aeration, and I wasn't sure how sensitive they were to this kind of thing. It could die in transport to Moby's. In fact, now that I didn't have to worry about all that, if Moby complained that it was dead, I would just say that it died on the way over. Oops.

As the workday came to a close, I waited for each of the Labcoats to go home. Dr. Schroeder came down to the fishroom before he left for the weekend.

"Oh, hey, you're still here," he said as he entered.

"Yeah, I just want to make sure everyone's set for the weekend," I responded. "You know, enough food, clean up the place, all that."

"Good man," he said as he wandered over to the dead fish. The corners of his mouth turned downwards and he squinted one eye at it, closer, and then closer. "Dead all right. Damned shame. I had high hopes for that MPT." He snapped up quickly and beamed a wide smile, actually causing me to jump. "And so a scientist's work is never done! Have a good weekend!" He spun around and left the room.

I stood for a moment, my hands full of aquarium tubing and fishnets, looking at the closed door and then at the clock. Schroeder was usually the last to leave, so I assumed that everyone who had any reason to come to the fishroom was indeed gone for the weekend.

I hung the tubes and nets and then walked over to the dead fish. Leaning over the shallow rectangular container it was lying in, I saw that it was actually quite large for what the Labcoats usually worked with—about seven inches in diameter, and rather thick in the middle. I got closer, and even closer, taking in all the details.

It was a sandy brown, with darker blotches covering its top. I assumed its bottom looked like most other flatfishes, blanched and colorless. It was ringed with dorsal and anal fins that tapered from its head to its tail. Its two eyes, now milky in death, bulged from its body just above its mouth, which sat on it like a normal fish's, looking awkward. It was slightly agape and I could see the little jagged teeth inside. I could also see the tiny bristles all along its surface, and I thought about the hogs that effectively throttled themselves on this little horror of a fish.

And then I thought of the other species of flatfish that Schroeder told me about. I couldn't remember the names then, but I know them now: *Platichthys stellatus*, up to three feet in length and weighing twenty pounds; *Paralichthys californicus*, five feet and seventy-two pounds; *Hippoglossus stenolepis*, almost nine feet, five hundred and seven pounds.

Five hundred pounds of flatfish. As I stared at its bristly brown body, I imagined the Giant Squid and other monstrosities that terrorized sailors for centuries, sea monsters of legend. How about the flatfish, with its Picasso face and eyes that protrude grossly, rotating independently ninety degrees this way and that, searching for prey? Now *that's* a sea-going nightmare.

At that moment, as I lost myself briefly in monstrous daydreaming, gazing vaguely at the fish, one of its eyes moved. I jumped and took a step back. Upon closer examination, and after a squirt or two with the turkey baster, I concluded that it was indeed dead; I was probably just imagining things. I had skipped lunch, after all, and was feeling fatigued.

I found a lid for the deceased flatfish and fitted it tightly so that it wouldn't leak all over the seat of my car. Before leaving, I ordered a pizza to be delivered to Moby's for dinner, and then I headed out, flatfish in tow.

* * * * *

Baltimore is a lovely city, as long as you don't have to drive in it. The streets are riddled with potholes and constantly under some sort of construction and repaving, which sometimes leaves the surface worse off than it was before. After every big bump, I glanced over at the cargo on the passenger's seat. I had fit the lap belt around it so that, when I hit the brakes, I wouldn't have to worry about it ending up a smelly, fishy mess on the floor of my car. I could hear it sloshing around inside, and I hoped the lid was as snug a fit as I thought.

Block after block, I hit all green lights and was making good time. I hoped to beat the pizza there so I didn't have to hear complaints from Moby about paying for it. Over uneven blacktop, bouncing to and fro, the flatfish and I traveled until finally coming to a red light. I was stopped for a few moments before I realized that the water was still splashing around inside.

I turned on the overhead light and leaned closer, peering through the semi-transparent side of the container. I could have sworn I saw the fish inside, a dark blur, thrashing about. But then it stopped. I stared at it.

A horn sounded behind me and I jumped, turned off the light, and drove, eyeballing the seat next to me. The splashing and sloshing resumed as I traveled over the crater garden that passed as a road.

Once I arrived at Moby's, I sat in the car for a few minutes. Again, after I stopped the vehicle, the container seemed jostled for a few seconds, and then quieted. I turned on the overhead light and looked closely once more. Still. I leaned over, popped the glove compartment, and a small Mag-Lite rolled into my open hand. Flicking it on, I cautiously opened the container. The beam gave me a much clearer view of the flatfish than the overhead light alone would have allowed. It stood still, its eyes whitish. And then a twitch.

I jumped a little and then leaned in closer, brow knitted in confusion. As I moved closer, both eyes of the fish sank in a little and then rose upwards again. This was something I noticed flatfish did when you made sudden moves around them. It was a sure sign they were alive even when the turkey baster failed.

I deliberately moved again, and sure enough, the eyes sunk and rose. Then the fins that fringed its radius fluttered, much like Demetri's fingers used to. So it was alive after all. The good doctor had been mistaken.

I moved a finger towards it to give it a harmless, life-confirming poke. It sprang toward my hand. I jumped back in my seat as the fish thrashed wildly, getting water everywhere. I slammed the lid on it and turned off the flashlight. Flatfish don't do that.

I watched the pizza guy pull up and saw Moby heave a deep sigh and pull out his wallet. I couldn't figure out if the fish was alive, or dead, or both. It didn't make sense, but then, I wasn't familiar with MPT—nor was anybody.

Dr. Schroeder *must* have been mistaken. The MPT merely gave the fish the *appearance* of death, that's all. It clearly messed up something else, making it a vicious little thing. The alternative was just too gruesome, and it threw my brain into fits. Unfortunately, that alternative never quite escaped me; it lurked in the back of my mind like a mugger in a dark alley, ready to pounce as soon as I looked the other way—the fish very well could've been undead.

I considered whether I should present Moby with this fish. This fish that stared blindly, this fish that became frenzied, this fish that, I had noticed upon removing the lid, smelled bad. Suddenly, it seemed like a much better idea to just return it to Dr. Schroeder. Besides, this development would probably be important to his experiments. I would just have to deal with whatever bullshit Moby was going to give me. I would have to just suck it up and take it. Moby was a schmuck, but maybe he didn't deserve to be the recipient of a zombified flatfish—*If that's what it is*, I thought, against my better judgment.

I left the fish in the car.

*   *   *   *   *

"You owe me $16.49," Moby said as I walked through the door, his mouth stuffed with bits of my pizza. No usual juvenile greeting. In the five minutes since the pizza guy had left, he had managed to eat three slices and was working on the fourth. He took another bite, maybe just to fill his mouth further before he continued to speak. "Did you bring some beer?"

"No, Moby, I didn't bring any beer." I couldn't sit down; I couldn't do anything but stand there, keys in hand, watching him as he ate. He called me queer and then suddenly stopped chewing to turn and look at me. "Where's the fish?" Bits of masticated cheese and dough and tomato made their way out and onto his shirt, which he quickly dashed up into his mouth again.

"It's in the car, I'll go get it." He was saying something insulting and half-laughing as I walked back out to the car. He wanted the fish? He would get the damned fish. I am half ashamed to admit that, had I known what would happen, I would have still given him that fish. Only half ashamed.

Back inside, I set the container on his coffee table and said something about being really tired. Though three quarters of the pizza was gone by then, I closed the box and started my way out the door—"Sorry, gotta go, tired."

He half-protested, and by the look on his face, was more upset that the pizza was leaving. I heard him mumble something like, "But I'm still hungry," before I shut the door. I went back to my parents' house, where I finished my pizza and watched some TV.

At about three in the morning, I got a phone call from Moby's sister, Martha. She and their parents were just about to leave the emergency room, where Moby had been taken. They'd been there for a few hours, waiting, hoping—but Moby had eventually died. Apparently, he *was* still hungry after I left his apartment, because he ate the flatfish. Doctors pulled bits of it from his throat. To this day, I wonder if they noticed whether the bits were still wriggling.

According to Martha, Moby had been shipped off to the morgue for a more thorough and complete autopsy just moments before she called my house.

I couldn't go back to sleep after that.

*   *   *   *   *

Moby must have disappeared off the morgue slab sometime Sunday night, but I didn't know about it until I came in Monday morning. After getting that call from Martha, I didn't sleep all day Saturday—so when I finally did go to sleep, I slept for twenty hours. That put me in a position Monday morning to go in earlier than usual. When I arrived, Dr. Schroeder was sitting in a puddle on the floor outside the fishroom.

Fifteen feet of rope ran from the fishroom door handle to the handle of the room containing another lab's Zebrafish. He seemed deep in thought.

"Dr. Schroeder?"

I startled him. He pushed himself off the floor with shaking arms. He had made the puddle. His clothes were soaked through. And he wasn't saying anything quite yet, so I stepped past him and started to go into the fishroom, eyeing the hastily tied knots in the rope around the handle. "What's going on, Dr—"

He grabbed my arm and pulled me back from the door. "Don't go in there!" His hands were wet and cold. "There's something in there."

"There's a lot of hungry flatfish in there," I said, smiling. I was trying not to think of Moby. "I should really go in and feed them, Doctor."

"There's no fish in there," he said, and he slid down the wall to the floor again, ready to make another puddle. "Sit down." He motioned to me and I too slid down the opposite wall, careful to avoid any wetness that may have accumulated. "I'll tell you what happened, but I don't understand it, and..." He paused and eyed me. "And you can't tell anyone."

I agreed.

*   *   *   *   *

Dr. Schroeder had decided to do a little work on the weekend and had gone into the lab Saturday night—all twelve of the smaller flatfish that had died from MPT were twitching and shaking in their little containers. One in the fridge—still pinned down for dissection—was particularly active. Active enough to fling the dissecting pins out of the wax, out of its body, and across the room.

At that moment, he stopped his story and looked at me. "Where's the big fish?" he asked, eyes sad yet quizzical.

"I took it down to the incinerator before I left work Friday," I said. I didn't know how much trouble I was in yet.

He sighed in relief and then continued. He had collected all the wriggly fish that shouldn't have been wriggling into one medium sized container and had just left them in the fishroom, as he really didn't know what to do with them. He had to think. And instead of thinking about the things you and I, the average person, would be thinking of, he instead thought like a scientist. What was it in the MPT that was causing such an unexpected reaction in these fish? What part of the brain did it settle and activate in? Were they dead or not? He stopped short of considering the applications and decided to go home, sleep, and think on it some more. He put a lid on the fish to keep any from escaping onto the cold linoleum floor. Then he turned out the lights and went home.

When he came in this morning—extremely early, as usual—he immediately headed down to the fishroom instead of having his coffee and catching up on papers in his office. When he entered the room, he was overcome with an incredible stench. He could taste it in his mouth, which caused him to gag.

He stepped back out of the room while at the same time attempting to prop the large, heavy door open with the small rubber doorstop—this process always took more than a few times to balance it just right so the door wouldn't close with its own weight.

While he fought with the door, he glanced at the table and, with the light thrown from the hallway, saw the container of supposed "zombie" fish lying empty on its side. Water was all over the floor.

Finally the door stuck and stayed.

Taking a moment to get used to the fetor, Dr. Schroeder reached inside and flicked on the overhead light. At that moment, all hell broke loose in a large blue tank situated in the far right corner.

The fishroom is not a large room, so the sudden thrashing caused Schroeder to flinch. His elbow tapped the door, which swung shut. The water in the blue tank splashed high, as if the tank was now filled with hundreds of fish, all surfacing to feed on a breakfast of pellets. But there should have been only fifteen in that tank, and there certainly shouldn't have been any pellets.

As the doctor crept toward the tank, it became less agitated. The thick white plastic cover, greenish-brown in the many corners of its grating, was askew atop the tank, and the aerator was floating in the water, the air from it spraying out a fine mist. Dr. Schroeder peered into the murky waters.

Something from below was coming to the surface. It was hard to make out at first, but he knew it couldn't have been one of the fish, which came in browns and grays. This was an ashen white of another kind of fish. But it wasn't any kind of fish either.

It was a human foot. It came slowly to the surface and then disappeared back into the turbid water. Shroeder was suddenly aware of a sound from the opposite end of the tank—a wet, smacking, crunching sound.

After pacing back and forth for a few minutes, listening to the crunching, listening to the humming and spitting of the airborne aerator, he bolstered himself enough to lift the latticed covering. Something splashed, causing him to pull the entire lid off and jump back. When the water calmed again, the doctor gathered his courage and stepped forward, with much caution.

As his vision cleared the rim of the tank, he felt a mixture of horror and fascination—he was a biological scientist, after all. It was barely recognizable as Moby. It sat in the tank, just its shoulders and head above the surface of the brownish water. Its body was still discernably human, but it was warped, as if ravaged by a horrible, deforming bone disease that twisted its frame. Its skin was patchy with scales that wrinkled with movement and showed off its thick black bristles. Schroeder instantly recognized them, and he moved closer, so slowly he almost lost his balance.

The Moby-thing was devouring one of the flatfish that originally occupied the tank. Its gaping, crooked maw moved quickly on the fish, mashing it mostly; its barely visible row of sharp teeth were obviously still developing. The flatfish thrashed against the assault and stopped only when it started to come apart. Finally, Schroeder looked the thing in the eye and shuddered.

The metamorphosis of the left eye wasn't complete; it wavered close to the middle of the forehead—not over the top of the skull, as would take place in a normal flatfish. And without the benefit of basic flatfish physiology, the eyeball itself didn't have the proper encasement for this kind of activity, so it bulged from between the lids, looking as if it might roll out into the water. The right eye sat in its normal-human place, though it rolled this way and that, occasionally snapping back into a straight stare. It was buoyant, as if on a tumultuous sea, constantly trying to right itself. It sat, waiting for its companion to eventually join it.

Its nose had spread flatter and had moved down a bit, presumably to make room for the roaming eyeball, and its mouth, corners turned downward in a fishy frown, dripped with crushed flatfish. There was some hair left on the head, but not much. The ears were crooked, turned at an angle, and quite deformed. Its entirety, or what Schroeder could see, was covered with a thin film, whether it came from the creature itself, or whether it was a product of a tank that sat over the weekend—waiting for me to clean it this disquieting Monday morning.

Occasionally, the thing would immerse itself, and then come back up—its peaceful munching intermittently rocked by a series of chokes and gasps as its body worked to acclimate not only to its new environment, but its new self.

*   *   *   *   *

I stared as Doctor Schroeder related his tale. He couldn't possibly have guessed that the thing in the tank was once Moby Waller, though he could plainly see that it wasn't a flatfish. It was clear to me what had happened; although, like the metamorphosis of the flatfish's eye, the mechanics of it were a mystery. Whatever it was about the MPT that killed and brought back the fish that I had left with Moby had apparently done the same to him. It *was* a zombie flatfish, and it turned Moby into a zombified... *monster*. That, as Schroeder later pointed out, was most unexpected. The rest was basically expected of MPT—forced eye migration. What kicked off the melding of the two species was completely unknown. Moby was, indeed, a mess.

The half a bagel I forced down earlier began to make its way back up. It wasn't the graphic and gory details of what Moby had become, or was becoming—but the fact that I was responsible for it. In an instant, I was confessing everything, on the verge of sobbing, with some odd little person in the back of my head mildly worried about losing his job.

Doctor Schroeder listened and deciphered what I was saying, as it came in fits and starts. Instead of being angry or shocked, he merely looked on at me, his eyes watching, his brain processing. When I finally finished, he said, "Well, at least we know where to start. It was the MPT—I guess it does something after all."

I stared at Schroeder and thought for a moment that I might make a puddle of my own, trying to grasp exactly what I'd done.

*   *   *   *   *

Twelve years later, my plane touches down at the Baltimore Washington International Airport, and I take a cab past the Inner Harbor, through downtown and farther north, to the University, and hence, the lab. The building has changed little, except that it looks more broken in; it was relatively new when I had taken that ill-fated job.

The receptionist, a somewhat plump and very friendly black woman named Isabel, lets me in through the front door, saying that I am lucky she worked a little late today and that she was on her way out. Doctor Schroeder, she says, is downstairs in the lower levels, probably in the fish room. I involuntarily shudder.

This is the slowest I've ever taken a flight of stairs, placing each foot cautiously, deliberately—drawing it out as much as I can. My stomach squirms inside me, as if full of eels. Schroeder said I don't have to see Moby if I don't want to, though he described him in full detail. It apparently took about five months for Moby to fully metamorphose into the monster that he is now— half flatfish, half human. What's more disturbing are the discrepancies between signs of life and signs of death; though Moby moves, Moby doesn't have a heartbeat.

He is able to sit out of water for a few hours at a time, but has to immerse on occasion to wet himself. Similarly, he can lie on the bottom of the tank for longer periods of time, utilizing the gills he has developed. His eyes are firmly planted on the right side of his face, and his skull has elongated and flattened, but not in a way that is useful. He is misshapen and ill equipped for anything other than being poked and prodded by Labcoats and the doctor himself.

Moby can sometimes become violent, but this is easily defused with a few drops of anesthetic into the tank. Or so Schroeder says.

The farther into the depths of the building I get, the more I can smell the salt water of the various tanks in the many fish rooms containing a number of different species.

As I round a corner, I glimpse Doctor Schroeder as he disappears around another, so I call out to him. His head appears, and then the rest of him as he reverses and takes long quick strides to get to me, smiling wide, his palm thrust forward for the greeting. When he reaches me he shakes my hand heartily and asks how my flight was. I can't think of the flight, and have to remind myself that the doctor sees Moby every day. This isn't a big deal. Or, at least, it doesn't have to be.

I answer shortly, and though I try to hide my trepidation, I launch quickly into a series of questions concerning Moby—most related to whether I would have contact with him. Doctor Schroeder smiles and places his hand on my shoulder.

"Moby is in his tank, down the hall," Schroeder says as he squeezes my shoulder. "I didn't know whether you'd want to see him. And I don't know if he understands or not, but I have told him that you'd be here."

I start at this and feel my face turn red and my forehead go wet, but Schroeder's hand holds firm. "Don't worry. Like I said, I don't know if he understands, but I thought that just in case he did, and just in case you decided to... well, I just thought a fair warning was in order. To be honest, he's never shown any signs of intelligence..."

Not that he did when he was just Moby, I think.

Schroeder smiles. "And again, there's no reason for you to ever see him. We've moved the flatfish to another room down the hall, and there's still plenty of work to be done with them, as you well know."

"I should see him now," I blurt, so suddenly that I myself am hardly aware of it. Schroeder seems to sense this and waits a moment for me to think about it, now that it's been said.

"Are you sure?" he asks quietly.

After a moment of vague consideration, I reply on autopilot, as though what I am saying is obviously something the little man in the back of my head has been contemplating without me knowing it.

"I want to work in your lab," I say. "I want to work on flatfish. I won't be able to come to work every day without thinking of him down here, just down the hall. I should just suck it up and get it over with."

"I think you're right. We can do it right now if you want." I take a deep breath and nod. The next thing I know we are at the door of the fishroom, Schroeder's hand now resting on the handle, pausing to give me a last chance to back out. I decline and steel myself as he opens the door.

The smell of the room isn't much different than I remember, and the sounds are much the same. Air pumps and filters humming along with the fluorescent lights overhead. As I enter slowly after Schroeder, I see that the rest of the fish *have* been removed, and the walls look bare without the racks and tanks. One lone tank sits at the end of the room. It is large—about five by nine feet wide, seven feet in height—and while the old tank that Moby had wandered into those many years ago was blue and opaque, this one is of a clear acrylic. Not that it makes a difference; the water is so murky that one can't see in very well anyway.

"It's hard to get anyone in here to clean it," he explains as if reading my mind. "So I do it myself when I can. He doesn't seem to care one way or the other."

Schroeder pulls up a wheeled step stool with a spring mechanism that responds to weight. "You'll have to step up to get a peek over." He steps up himself and looks in. Satisfied, he comes down and motions for me to take his place. "He was rather docile this morning, but I put a little tricaine methansulfonate in the water, just in case."

"Thanks," I say meekly as I place a foot on the first step and slowly push myself up to the second. Holding my breath, I thrust my head over the side of the tank to peer into it, eyes closed. Opening one, and then the other, I see him. Moby lies half immersed, ghastly and completely changed into whatever it is that he has changed into.

At first, I don't think he notices me as the two eyes stare off into some unknown distance. He has one malformed arm stretched above him, leaning on the side of the tank, and his head lays on his shoulder for support. His skull looks as though it might have conformed a little to his arm in this way, indicating that this is a normal, and presumably comfortable, position for him. I think of Demetri Rieti, the spastic kid from school, and I think of how appropriate this seems.

His eyes shift, but don't look up until I slowly wave a hand above him. They dart toward me and narrow, and as they do, I fight the instant urge to fly from the stepstool, flailing and screaming my way back to Japan. Moby opens his mouth and gasps, then gulps, and gills somewhere beneath the surface flutter and bubble. His teeth are bigger than Schroeder had described, years ago during that first horrific discovery of Moby; they are fully developed now. I take a deep breath of the fetid air around me. *Calm*, I think.

His eyes sink into his head and then push out again, like a camera lens focusing automatically, and as I am just about to ask Schroeder what Moby eats, hoping to calm myself with mundane conversation, I see movement. Moby slowly, with much effort, brings his left arm up his body, allowing it rest on his upper chest. I stare in wonder and disgust. His eyes waver and refocus, and then, what's left of his fingers start to twitch, building slowly into a kind of rhythmic, waving movement. And then a garbled sound issues from the fishy depths of Moby's throat.

"F-f-fuh-fuh-fuh... f-f-f-fuh-fuh..." That was the last I heard before things just went black.

The Legend of Black Betty

by Tim Curran

One

They told Oates it was the yellow fever that did his little Mandy in. Half the county was laid low with it and the other half were remembering the 1878 epidemic of Memphis that had left over five thousand dead. Even then, in that corner of Nevada, people were running scared... of each other, of sudden drafts, of the unburied dead. They were staying clear of what they called "plague-houses" and undertaking parlors, shunning cemeteries and coffin-makers.

"People are saying some crazy shit," Oates told Doc Rifer on the morning of Mandy's funeral. "Saying a lot of things, without actually saying them."

Rifer shook his head, stroked his white beard. "Pay no attention to that rot, Daniel. People around here are a lot of superstitious fools. Your girl went of the yellow fever, that's all and nothing more."

Rifer said they were looking at an epidemic of the fever. Was going to be plenty bad before they got it under control, that was for certain. They'd be closing the lid on a lot of folks before it blew over. But it would blow over. Just had to run its course, that's all. And Oates wanted to believe Rifer because Rifer knew his business; he'd worked malarial camps during the Mexican War and had been doctoring for well on forty years.

"I've seen my share of poxes and fevers and morbid disease, son, and what you have here is surely the yellow fever," Rifer told him.

Oates didn't know what to believe, not really.

Yellow fever? Sure, some were saying that and others were saying there was an epidemic brewing, all right, but it was one of a more spiritual nature.

One thing was for sure: they were all bolting their doors and closing their shutters come nightfall. And it wasn't at all unusual to see things like crucifixes and garlic hanging over doorways at carefully-battened farmhouses.

"Your Mandy had the symptoms, Daniel," Rifer explained. "The fever, the chills, the jaundice, the vomiting. It was all there. Now there's a real smart Cuban physician name of Finlay who's saying the fever is spread by mosquito bites. And you know what? I'm in agreement with him. Now, if I were you, I'd be draining that stagnant crick back of your farm, for that's where the real danger is. That's where the fever mosquitoes are breeding. You never mind that horseshit about spooks and vapors. You leave that to the old women. Yellow fever, that's our enemy."

These were the things Oates thought of as they gathered on that windy hillside amongst the sunken graves and marble markers, the mounds of earth with simple wooden crosses pushed into them, leaning and canting every which way. Rich and poor were buried side by side here, sheltered by tall cottonwood trees, profuse stands of buckthorn and mesquite. There was a calm and serene beauty about the little cemetery, but it was not a place a man ever wished to come. Surely not for himself or for loved ones, and particularly not for a child.

They were going to put beautiful little Mandy in that hole, of all the terrible and unforgivable things. *Mandy*. Mandy with her flowing red hair and bright green eyes, that delightful crooked smile and laughter like wind chimes. They were putting his precious girl down into that goddamned hole and they were burying the best parts of him along with her.

He sniffed away his grief, adjusted the black sleeve garter at his bicep and put his arm around Elizabeth, who was shaking badly. She was not a particularly strong woman, either emotionally or physically, and this was just more than she could bear.

"Just hold onto me," Oates kept telling her.

But Elizabeth seemed impervious to his presence. Her face was pale and pinched, her eyes red-rimmed and swollen like wounds beneath that black mourning veil. She was not crying anymore. She just stood there wavering in her black dress and bonnet, her mind sucked into itself. Oates held her close, and she felt light and insubstantial as if she were nothing more than a bag of sticks. She barely seemed to breathe.

Reverend Fisher clutched his prayer book, said, "I am the resurrection and the life, saith the Lord: he that believeth in me, though he were dead, yet shall he live: and whoever liveth and believeth in me shall never die."

"Amen," the mourners said.

There weren't but six or seven people there besides Elizabeth and himself. All the friends they'd made through the years had not showed, afraid of catching what they thought Mandy carried. And those that had come were standing well away from the casket, pressing handkerchiefs to their mouths and noses, fearing they might breathe in some pox oozing from the box itself. Only Doc Rifer and Reverend Fisher were unafraid.

"We brought nothing into this world, and it is certain we can carry nothing out," the reverend said, pressing his missal to his chest. "The Lord gave, and the Lord hath taken away; blessed be the name of the Lord."

A few people were sobbing now, making muffled sounds beneath the cloths covering their mouths.

Elizabeth had stopped shaking. Instead of leaning against her husband, she stood up straight and tall, her lips set in a grim line. Beneath the veil, her eyes were bright and sparkling like she was seeing something no one else could. She reached out as if to grasp the hand of her dead daughter.

Reverend Fisher said, "We commend unto thy hands of mercy, most merciful Father, the soul of this thy child, Amanda Catherine Oates; and we commit her body to the ground, earth to earth, ashes to ashes, dust to dust..."

Elizabeth threw aside Oates' arms and walked over to the casket. There was fierce resignation to her and no one could have hoped to stop her. She threw her veil back and everyone saw that awful face, the mouth twisted like she was on the verge of a stroke. And her eyes... they were hot and savage and piercing.

"In there, in there, in there," she began to shriek, her voice rising up sharp and scratching above the droning words of Reverend Fisher. "Don't none of you hear what's in there? Don't you hear that? *Don't you?*"

Oates went to her, something shattering inside him now. The mourners were stepping back, and Fisher looked confused, still reciting the requiem for the dead but in a small, mumbling voice. Oates tried to get hold of Elizabeth, but she fought his hands away and dropped to her knees next to the box. The sound of her hands slapping flat on its lid were like thunder.

"Elizabeth," Oates managed. "Come away from there, come away..."

But Elizabeth would not come away. She pressed an ear to the box, listening for something inside. "Don't tell me you can't hear it! That none of you can't hear it! It's Mandy! Listen, goddamn you all, *listen! She's in there breathing! I can hear her breathing! Can't you hear the scraping of her fingers at the lid? Can't you—*"

People were shocked and horrified now. They were crossing themselves and looking on in abject terror. Oates and Doc Rifer took hold of Elizabeth and dragged her away from the box. She came away willingly, but was small and hunched-over, her head cocked to the side like she was hearing something the others couldn't. Her eyes were huge and mad, unblinking.

"Please, everyone," the reverend said, "let us gather in prayer."

But nobody was up to that now. They were all standing around in their Sunday finery, whispering and crossing themselves, looking too frightened to stay and too frightened to run. A wind blew and tree branches overhead rattled together. A wreath of flowers tipped over. A crow cawed in the sky.

And Elizabeth—looking completely deranged and pressing her hands to the side of her head, just overwhelmed with grief and, yes, maybe horror—said to everyone gathered, "You wait... just all of you wait... tonight or tomorrow night, oh yes, you'll see then... *what put my Mandy down will raise her back up again and she will walk among us!*"

Then Elizabeth shuddered and her eyes rolled back white and she collapsed to the weedy graveyard earth.

Two

O ates came awake feeling the night around him.

Feeling it reaching out for him with black, gnarled fingers.

He moved his hand to touch Elizabeth, but she wasn't there. No, she'd had a fit at the funeral four days before. She was under the care of her aunt over in Fallon.

Oates sighed, licking the sweat off his lips. He brushed damp hair away from his brow.

A dream, that's all it was. He'd had some kind of nightmare. And why not? These past days, this past week or so had been hellish. He was remembering it all now and feeling the heaviness of it trying to squeeze his guts out of his mouth.

There in the darkness, he trembled and tried to breathe.

Christ, he hadn't felt like this since Antietam, when he'd woke in a hospital tent outside Sharpsburg laid low by Typhoid Fever. He could remember the chills and the vomiting, all those Union boys around him stacked up like cordwood, all dying of the miasma, drowning slowly in their own filth and bodily secretions. And the smell... good God, the stench of battlefield dressings yellow with pus, flesh gone to gangrene, feces and vomit and piss. Horrible, just horrible. Those men moaning and whimpering, death taking a few more each night as contagion and trauma and despair laid them low. The orderlies taking them out wrapped in stained, graying shrouds. The sounds of shovels digging shallow graves and—

Enough.

By God, it was enough.

Oates threw his legs over the side of the bed, pulling from a bottle of Old Crow on the stand. He pulled out a tin box of hand-rolled cigarettes and lit one with a stick match. The flame made distorted shadows leap on the walls. He pulled off his cigarette, listening and listening and not really sure what for. But something was telling him it was important that he listen. He could hear the wind moaning out there, making the eaves rattle and the farmhouse tremble. It was a lonely sound. A sound of desertion and memory gone to seed.

And the more he listened, the more he was certain that it was not just a dream that had yanked him from slumber. There was something else. A noise, a slight disturbance. If you were to have listened like Oates, you would not have heard anything. But if you knew that farmhouse like he knew it— he'd built it with his own hands, board by board and brick by brick—you would have sensed that something was not right. Maybe a door was open or a shutter left unlatched, but it was there. That sense that something was askew or just off-center.

So why don't you just go look, for the life of Christ?

And that was a good question because Oates didn't know why he didn't go and look. But it was as if something inside him refused to move. It wanted him to stay put, to hide and not dare breathe.

Nerves.

Just nerves.

He was alone at the farm. Elizabeth was completely unwound from the funeral and with her aunt. And Mandy? Well, Mandy was... Mandy just wasn't there anymore.

She's dead... why don't you just quit pretending otherwise? Say it already: Mandy's dead. Your daughter is goddamned well dead.

The idea of that brought a wave of fresh agony rolling through him. Yes, she was dead. There was no doubt of it. She was in her grave up on the hill and his wife was on the verge of nervous collapse because of it. These were the facts that Oates was having trouble with. Thinking them was one thing; accepting them and admitting them to yourself was quite another. There were things a man could do and things that just brought too much pain.

But it was too soon.

For the love of God, she'd only been gone a week now. Not even. And in that time, the mere act of walking and breathing had been overwhelming.

Every morning when his eyes fluttered open, he almost expected to hear Mandy singing or bouncing her ball or playing jacks on the kitchen floor. Like the whole thing had been some wild and terrible fever dream and he was going to be coming out of it any time now, and one of these mornings she'd come bounding in, grinning and giggling, that ocean of red hair flooding her neck and shoulders and—

Shut up, you idiot! Listen! You have to listen now. This is important.

So Oates was listening, something inside his belly clenching like a fist. He did not know what he was listening for, but it was going to be bad.

Those were wild and irrational thoughts, yes, but deep inside he was feeling very wild and very irrational. There was a creeping sensation at his spine and his heart would not stop pounding. Though the night was not especially warm, a trickle of sweat ran down his left temple and rolled across his cheek like a tear. He was tense and terrified and was not even sure why.

Just listen, then you'll know.

Oates heard it then. A sound like something had been dropped, something small. Maybe a pencil. Something that rolled a few inches across the floor. Then he heard another sound... a thud, then a creaking. And that made his guts fill with ice, because he knew that creaking: it was Elizabeth's rocking chair. But if Elizabeth was in Fallon, then *who* was rocking in that chair, back and forth, back and forth?

Oates got up, put his feet on the cool plank floor.

The creaking stopped.

Then started again.

Whoever was out there, he had the feeling they were now aware that he was aware of *them*. Shaking now, Oates could not get it out of his head that he had been intended to hear that. That all this was calculated to have a desired effect, and that effect was absolute terror.

Now, Oates was not a coward.

He'd been through the War Between the States, he'd rode shotgun on a stage, he'd kicked up his heels in some of the toughest mining camps in Arizona Territory... yet, whatever was out there, waiting in the darkness for him, filled him with a fear that was sharp and brittle, beyond anything he'd ever known.

Okay, somebody's here, so goddamned what? Elizabeth had come home early or Raul Penchot had come over to see how he was or—

Stop it, you idiot! You know what's come calling is not that. What's come calling in the dead of night can be nothing good, nothing wholesome.

Oates pulled one of his Colt Navy .44's from its rawhide scabbard. It was loaded. It was always loaded. Cleaned and primed and oiled. You take care of your gun, his old man had said, it'll take care of you.

Oates pulled the Rochester lamp from its hook over the dresser. He lit it with a match and stepped out into the short corridor. He could smell the pine sap in the walls and something much worse. Whatever had come into the farmhouse had brought a noxious stink with it: the smell of rainy caskets and putrefaction.

In the corridor, there were footprints.

Quite a few of them and they were all small and familiar. The footprints of a child, one that had dragged itself through pasture muck and puddles of dirty water. From what Oates was seeing, this child had been standing just outside his door, dripping clots of soil and black water. There was a squashed beetle in one of the prints.

You can't be thinking these things, you just can't.

But he was. For those prints were telling him things that destroyed something inside of him, laid him raw on some primal level. Those prints were like the prints of an eight-year-old girl, one that maybe died of the yellow fever like so many in the county. Except this girl she had—

What put my Mandy down will raise her back up again.

He could hear Elizabeth's voice shrieking in his brain, echoing down corridors and through empty rooms.

Oates was scared white now.

By God, what he was thinking, what he was feeling, and, yes, *knowing...* it was not good, not good at all. His breath would barely come and his limbs felt rubbery. There was a weight in his belly that did not belong there.

He cocked the pistol.

He stepped into Mandy's room.

The stink was worse in here... like bile and bad meat. Whatever had come into the house had spent some time in this room. By the light of the lamp, Oates could see a dirty stain on the bed coverlet like somebody filthy from the fields had sat there. Elizabeth had packed away those precious few toys of Mandy's... the wooden blocks and spellers, the flaxen-haired dolls she'd made for her, the rubber ball and crayon box. Sure, they were all packed away, but there on the floor, amongst the dirty prints and stink, Mandy's jacks all laid out as if she had been playing with them.

And maybe she had.

As he came out of that room, sweating and shaking, Oates realized something that he hadn't before. Something that he should've thought of right off. The dog. Boots, their old hound... he wasn't barking. Goddamned dog, he barked at anything. The moon slid behind a cloud and he barked. And right now? Out in the yard... it was dead quiet.

Where the hell was that damn dog?

He followed the prints into the little parlor and there was Boots. Blood was splattered right up the walls, dripping off the arm of the loveseat. Looked like a calf had been slaughtered in there. But it was just the dog. He'd been eviscerated, gutted right there by the hearth, his jaws wide and foaming and red, his viscera pulled out in a tangle of snakes. His throat had been torn out. From the trail of ichor smeared across the floor, Oates figured the dog had been killed outside and then dragged in here.

He was still warm.

Elizabeth's rocking chair was still moving. The seat cushions were black with dirt. A loop of the dog's intestines was tossed over one of the chair's armrests, just abandoned there like a scarf someone had been knitting. Whoever had been sitting in the chair had been playing with it, gnawing on it, just waiting and waiting, covered with dog blood and hairs, smelling the stink of slaughtered dog and maybe enjoying it.

The prints were black with blood now. Oates followed them to the steps leading up to the loft above. He held up the lantern, expecting to see some smiling white-faced wraith staring down at him, but there was nothing. Only those bloody prints that led up, but did not come back down. Whoever had made them was waiting up there, behind that door.

Oates let out an involuntary groan.

Yes, it was there, all right.

As he climbed those narrow stairs, he could hear it breathing. It was waiting for him with teeth and claws or a purloined knife, but it was surely waiting and there was no love in its heart... just a riven, unspeakable blackness that it had brought out of the grave.

Do what you got to do, son. That ain't yer daughter waiting in the darkness. Can't say what it is exactly, only that it ain't human. It's just something that came out of its crypt with murder in its heart. Walking meat. Meat pretending to be a little girl...

Oates couldn't take it much longer.

There came a point when even stark madness was better than the things you saw in your brain. The graying faces and dead eyes and pale mouths swimming in for a kiss. No, sometimes it was just better to look insanity in the eye and be seen.

When he got to the top of the steps, he could hear a voice humming behind the door. A scratching, sibilant voice that was like Mandy's, but not exactly. More like Mandy being impersonated by something that had been gargling with glass shards and cemetery dirt, chewing on meat.

Oates grasped the brass knob.

It began to turn in his hand and he gasped.

The door swung open and Mandy was standing there, mildew grown green and thick at her throat and down the sleeves of her dirty burial dress. Her eyes were yellow and reptilian and glaring with a stark madness. An earthworm twisted fatly in her hair. Something black was smeared all over her pale, bloated face. She reached out with shriveled fingers, rank earth dropping from her in clots, a vapid grin on her face.

"Dad... dee," she gurgled.

Oates felt something like a scream shatter in his head. He took one flailing step back, words coming to his tongue, nonsense even to him. Mandy stepped forward, stinking of hot, boiling carrion. He could smell her breath... cold and offensive with the reek of dog bowels and dead things she'd been chewing on.

"God forgive me," Oates said and brought up his Navy Colt.

He pulled the trigger.

Three

Two days after he'd buried his daughter's remains for the second time, Oates finally came out of the madness that had shaken him like a wet dog. There had been fever and nightmares and a cool acceptance of insanity, but now, like a storm that lays waste to the countryside, it was passing. Oates couldn't remember much after he put that bullet in his dead daughter's head. Just some weird confused mess of him wrapping her in a blanket and carrying her back out to the graveyard, putting her back in her ruptured coffin, filling in the grave with his bare hands, crying and cackling beneath a full moon. Then coming back to the farmhouse, cleaning up the mess she had made... the dog's remains, the muddy prints, that which had sprayed from her skull when he pulled the trigger. Other than that? Just drinking whiskey and sometimes screaming his throat raw, falling to the floor and pounding his fists.

Now all of it seemed distant and unreal.

Mandy had come back from the dead and there was no getting around that. Like Lazarus, she had kicked her way out of that box and come calling.

But it wasn't Mandy.

Oates knew that like he knew his left hand. Mandy was sweet and caring and loving, but what had come out of the grave wearing her skin, well, that was something else entirely. It had been no more human, no more capable of love and compassion than a leech sucking the blood from your leg or a jackal gnawing on bones it had pulled from a tomb.

But how to explain it?

How to take something like that in and keep standing, not fall down and scream yourself mad? There was only one way to do it and Oates found it: hatred. Bitter, unrelenting hatred that burned like sulfur in his belly, seething and consuming until his very soul was blazing hot and white. This is what would get him through the weeks to come and this is what would feed him and keep him alive. This is what would put him on the trail of whatever had done this to Mandy.

His madness evaporating in the burning light of vengeance, Oates made himself a hot bath and scrubbed himself clean, shaved and pulled on a pair of striped trousers, vest and frock coat, high-shafted trail boots. Then he made some coffee and drank it from a tin cup out on the porch, thinking and remembering and plotting. It was morning and the air still carried a chill. He stared out over his alfalfa fields and corn, the barn and cribs beyond. The countryside was beautiful. Green and lush and rolling, cut by stands of cottonwood and aspen. In the distance, the mountains rose up, looking purple and red in the early morning light, the slopes green with juniper and pinion pine.

Yes, it was fine land, rich and healthy and vibrant. Beautiful.

But beneath that beauty there was a horror that was real and wasting. For there was a malignancy chewing at the belly of Churchill County, something that had fastened itself like a parasite and was sucking the blood off drop by drop. Oates did not know what it was, but he could sense it there, growing fat and full on purloined life, something insidious and ravenous that had slipped up from the slimy cellars of hell, stuffing its guts with the bones and men and women and, yes, children.

Such a thing could not be allowed to exist.

Oates knew it wasn't just Mandy. He could think of two dozen others that had died in the past month, people he'd known and worked and drank with. Farmers and storekeepers and miners. Just ordinary folk that had been put into their graves by an unimaginable contagion.

Now, Doc Rifer was saying yellow fever, but the epidemic facing the county was surely not yellow fever. Maybe it mocked the symptoms of the black vomit, as yellow fever was sometimes called, but it was surely something else. Doc Rifer was a good man, a wise man, but there were things even beyond his scope, beyond the ken of all mortal men, and this was surely one of them.

Sitting there, Oates pulled out one of his home-rolled cigarettes and showed it some flame. He pulled off it, letting his mind drift off. Yes, quite a few that he knew had perished of the fever and quite a few more that he did not know. People in that county were simple. Farmers and miners and retailers, they understood what they could hold in their hands. Most went to church and most said they believed in the Lord God, but Oates knew that sometimes faith was not so much deep-felt as a matter of tradition. If it's what your parents did and what your neighbors were doing, then you would do it, too. True faith was exceptionally rare, regardless of what people said or pretended. The people of Churchill County were a good sort, hard-working and mostly honest. They did not let religion and superstition steer them more than necessary; they worked the land and raised their families and drew their strength mainly from the good earth itself. They had very little patience with the unknown and the unseen.

But now, that had changed.

People were clutching crucifixes and Bibles, sleeping with prayer books under their pillows. They were hanging garlic and St. John's Wort at their windows, nailing horseshoes over their doors and sprinkling salt at their thresholds. Many were inviting Reverend Fisher and Shockley from the Congregational Church to come and bless their homes. And quite a few had even asked Crazy Bob, the tentshow revivalist, to do the same.

Oates did not see this as a deep conversion of faith, but as a symptom of the disease taking root all around them. For here was a disease, an ailment, something intangible that Doc Rifer could not get under his brass microscope or separate in a test tube, and it scared them. They were afraid of shadows and vapors and knocking at their doors in the dead of night. There were vague whispers, some of them not so vague, concerning the dead that would not stay dead.

Oates had dismissed it all, spooks and ghost stories and witch-tales, but now he knew better.

Yet he wasn't about to hide from any of it. There was something evil afoot and it would not be vanquished by hiding and praying and making Indian sign outside your door and hanging charms about. No sir, Oates was going to hunt it down. He was going to get his hands on whatever was responsible and crush it beneath his fists, feel its bones snapping and its vile blood running out in creeks and rivers.

With that in mind, he went in the house and began to make plans.

Amen to that.

Four

Throughout the day, he made the rounds on his dappled mare, doing that which pained him, but which had to be done. He visited farms and ranches, cabins and far-flung mining camps in the hills talking with laborers and farmers and hardrock miners, just about anyone who had lost a family member or friend to the fever. Some would not speak of it, but a surprising amount of others invited Oates into their confidences, speaking of the fever, the burials, and what had taken place afterward. He heard horror stories that day, but he listened and accepted and they gladly shared these things with him when they learned what he had been through and that he planned to run this contagion to ground, to burn it out at the roots.

The stories were pretty much the same.

Kin was buried and several nights later, they showed up, pounding at doors after midnight, slaughtering animals, and opening graves, feeding on what they found inside. Quite a few that witnessed these things went mad. A few had been murdered by their newly-risen wives and fathers, brothers and sisters. It was all insane and incomprehensible, but the pattern was there for eyes that wished to see.

Those that died of the fever were returning from the grave.

And not as haunts that tapped at windows or moaned in the night, but as demented and predatory things, ghouls that fed on the dead and cannibals that preyed on the living. Oates had put a bullet in Mandy's head. That had put her down and this seemed to be the accepted method.

Aim for the head every time.

Yes, Oates heard all manner of tales that day. Things about the walking dead slipping into houses and biting kinfolk or simply laying in their old beds or sitting at supper tables and saying the most awful things. Secret things they could not know. But what was the most interesting was that the name of a town in the desert called Crowley kept coming to the fore. Something had happened there that nobody really wanted to talk about and it all had to do with some negro whore called Black Betty that had supposedly raised the Devil.

These were the things Oates told Doc Rifer about that evening in his book-lined study. Rifer argued with him, of course, but not for long.

"I'm going up to Crowley, Doc, and I'm going to burn this blight out or die trying," he said. "You can believe all this or not, but I plan on running this evil to ground and there ain't a damn thing you can say to stop me."

Rifer didn't bother trying. "Crowley. Yes, I've heard about that pesthole and more than once. Place is deserted now, Daniel. If you plan on going out there, you might want to stop by a little village called Compton on your way. It's maybe three or four miles this side of Crowley. You want to know about that place, Compton would make a good beginning."

"Was planning on stopping by anyhow," Oates said.

Rifer swallowed. "Daniel... have you ever heard the term 'zombie'?"

"Not that comes to mind."

"It's essentially a superstition from the West Indies, Haiti and Guadeloupe. People there believe that a witch doctor of sorts has the power to raise the dead."

"Maybe that's what we got right here. Maybe that Black Betty came from there. Don't know and don't honestly care, Doc. Because I know where that bitch is going and that's straight to hell."

Five

Oates did not see himself as a savior, some messiah coming down to ride herd on the Devil. He was just a man, no better and no worse than any other man. Only difference between himself and the others was that he had had enough. This sickness, this fever, this plague of sorts had been allowed to take root and fester. And if it hadn't, maybe Mandy would have still been alive. Maybe and maybe not. Now its roots were running deep and it would be no easy matter to cut it out, but Oates figured it was time somebody got their knife out, and that somebody just happened to be him.

The day he rode into Compton on his mare, he was riding about as high and randy as any man a week on the trail. He was blown with desert dust, his teeth full of grit. Dirty and worn, he looked desperate and dangerous, a man riding the edge of something sharp and lethal. As he came in, most that looked at him quickly looked away, maybe not liking the gleam in his eye, a gleam like gypsum winking back yellow moonlight.

Compton wasn't much.

A few rows of tall brick-fronted crackerbox buildings with false cornices, some plank shacks and log houses set in-between, a couple dirt roads intersecting the lot. Oates saw a tent-roofed saloon, a couple bunkhouses, a boarded-up dance hall and lots of signs weathered illegible by the wind-driven sand. He saw the finger of a church steeple in the distance, but other than that, not much. The place was dying a slow death out in this dry, suffocating desolation. There'd been a gold mine and refinery up in the hills at one time, but that had played out a few years before and now Compton was anemic and looking for a deep grave to crawl into.

Oates kneed his mare into a walk and pulled reign outside the saloon, tying her off at the hitch rail out front. He stepped out onto the warped board sidewalk, pulling his sawed-off American 12-gauge from the saddle scabbard. A couple Mexicans were sitting out front, eating peppers from dirty jars and smoking thin brown paper cigarettes.

A kid came running up, stopping just before Oates and giving him the once over. "Ya'll want me to water and hay your mount, mister?"

The kid was grimy with a sodbuster hat and corduroy trousers with holes in the knees. Oates wasn't sure if those were freckles on his face or spots of dirt. But, then, that was this whole goddamn town... nothing but dirt and dust every way you turned.

"Be obliged," Oates told him.

"She'll be down at the livery yonder when you need her, mister."

Oates went into the saloon, the rough-hewn batwings creaking on leather hinges. Inside, it wasn't much. A few beaten-looking men were sipping beer and playing hands of Seven-up and five-card. A round, greasy man behind the bartop was mopping sweat from his brow. He didn't even ask Oates what he wanted to drink.

And that was the feeling Oates was getting from the rest of them, too, and maybe that whole goddamned town as well: lethargy, inaction, stagnation. They were sticks of furniture, inanimate things watching the dust settle and the flies buzz. Jesus, like wooden Indians standing outside cigar stores waiting for pigeons to shit on 'em and little boys to scratch their initials into 'em.

"Whiskey," he said, setting his shotgun on the bar, hoping that barkeep would tell him to put his gun someplace else, because way he was feeling, he just might.

As Oates drank his whiskey—kind of gritty, as if it were full of sand like everything else—he took in the atmosphere of that place which wasn't far removed from an alley privy: just close and crowded and dim, stinking of sweat and time and silence. The men slouched over drinks and gripped oily dog-eared cards with grubby hands, just an extension of the saloon itself. None of them would even look Oates in the face as if maybe they were afraid of what they might see in his eyes and what it would tell them about themselves.

Oates sipped his whiskey, pulled out a cigarette and lit it. He stood there in his dusty wool pants and gray vest, his sweat-stained shirt and pinch-crowned Stetson. He had his pair of Colt Navy sixes set in low-slung gunbelts, butts forward. Usually, in a place like that, the kind of hardware Oates was carrying would have attracted some attention, mostly the wrong kind. But here? No, just blatant disinterest. *Welcome to Compton, stranger. Sit a spell and have a slug of whiskey. Please excuse us while we don't give a high-stepping fuck.*

Oates drew off his cigarette, still trying to make eye contact with someone. No dice. Seven men and not a stick of curiosity to be had.

"Gentlemen," he finally said. "Name's Daniel Oates. Got me a spread outside Stillwater up north. Reckon you've been through there, you hung your hat in Nevada Territory any length of time. Here's to you and yours. Round of whiskey, barkeep."

There were a few grunts of assent from those gathered. Not much else. The bartender passed out the whiskey and the men drank it with all the enthusiasm of bored cats lapping up milk. Again, disinterest in just about anything.

There was one with a spark in him, though. An old party with a tangled white beard and a dirty flannel shirt. He sat in the back well away from the others. He actually looked at Oates beneath his Southwestern sombrero, nodded, and tapped the blackened stem of his corncob pipe on the table.

"Thanks kindly, stranger," he said.

Oates flicked the ash off his cigarette. "Now that we've made acquaintances, maybe one of you would like to tell me about a town near here. Deserted, they're saying. Some kind of funny business about it. You know the place I mean? I'm guessing you do."

"Crowley," a voice said.

One man swore under his breath and left his whiskey untouched, went right out the door. Another followed quick on his heels, grumbling and kicking a stool out of his way. That whittled down Oates' new acquaintances to a lean five. And other than the old man who kept watching him with a surly grin, the others just plain pretended he did not exist. Or maybe that he was a bad stink that would clear, you gave it enough time.

"Yep, Crowley would be the place I'm thinking of, boys. Been hearing some funny things about what went on there and what might be still going on."

One of the men playing five-card, laid his hand flat on the table. He stroked a well-waxed mustache. "Ain't nobody in Crowley, mister. Was some silver veins near there, but they's all dry now. Just as dead as Crazy Horse's left nut."

A few men grunted at that. Maybe it was supposed to be laughter.

Oates just nodded. "Don't say? Not what I been hearing at all. Folks is saying some mighty peculiar shit went on up in Crowley. I think I heard something about dead people that don't wanna stay dead."

Mustache laughed at that, but it was tinny, off-key laughter that sounded awful pained. "Shit, boy, only Lazarus ever did come back other than the messiah hisself."

"Well, I'll tell you, what I'm talking about here has little to do with Jesus and the saints and everything to do with the Devil." Oates took a drag off his cigarette. "Now, question is, are you boys gonna sit there and dance a jig with me, take turns blowing smoke up my ass, or are you gonna start telling me the way things really are? What do you think?"

"I think," Mustache said, "you ought to get back on your horse and ride back up to Stillwater. I'm figuring you ain't gonna like Compton much. Because Compton ain't Stillwater. And Crowley? You'd best just leave that lick of hell alone, hope it leaves you alone."

Oates crushed his cigarette under his boot. "So that's it, eh? The lot of you are just going to sit here holding them goddamned chairs down while that cancer breeds on your doorstep?"

"Sometimes, mister, sometimes it's best to walk around a rattler rather than trying to stomp it," Mustache said. "Some things got teeth. Some things tend to bite if you interfere with their ways."

There was logic there, Oates figured, but not the sort he cared for. Sure, you might not get bit if you kept your hand out of that den of rattlesnakes up in Crowley. But on the other hand, sooner or later, those snakes might decide they needed more living space. Maybe another town.

Oates said, "Okay, boys, I'm done greasing you. I came here looking for men to ride with me on Crowley. Men who'd had enough, men who were ready to burn out that graveyard up there. But I'm guessing you boys are not those men."

"You guessed right," Mustache said. "And the last goddamned thing we need is for some stranger to be riding up there and stirring things up. So do us all a favor and go on back home."

"Well, friend, I'd dearly love to do that, but my home ain't exactly much of a home anymore," Oates said. "See, this epidemic we got in the county, it ain't just thick here in Compton. It's everywhere. People are catching some sort of fever, dying, and then a few nights later they're climbing back up out of their graves—"

"Shut up," Mustache said. "You just shut up with that crazy talk."

Oates just shook his head. "Nope, don't plan on it."

"Then I'll be leaving, because I don't have to listen to this."

Oates pulled one of his Colt Navy .44s. He brought it up fast and without hesitation. And he put it right on Mustache. "Now, I don't consider it real friendly of you to walk out in the middle of my story. In fact, I think it's downright fucking rude. So either sit your ass down or they'll be sweeping bits of your skull out the door come morning."

Mustache sat down. He was pissed-off and reckless right then, but he wasn't wearing a gun. His friends were, but none of them liked the idea of drawing on Oates. You'd been around enough hell-for-leather mining camps, you got to know when there was murder in a man's eyes and there was no doubt of it with Oates.

"So where was I? Oh yeah, now that fever's spreading. Nobody knows how. Maybe it's that hot dry wind that's been blowing. Who can say? Only thing anyone can figure for sure is that it's blowing straight out of Crowley." Oates took another slug of whiskey. "Now, a couple weeks back my Mandy Catherine got sick, real sick, you see? Fever and sweats, skin gone yellow like the camp fever took her. Vomiting black blood and just wasting away 'til she just couldn't fight it no more. So we put her in the ground, we put my little girl in the ground. Eight years old and we put her in the fucking ground—"

"That's enough!" Mustache shouted, standing up and making for the door. "I won't listen to this! You can't make me listen to this!"

Oates didn't hesitate. Burning up inside and just sick with the memory of Mandy, he pulled the trigger and put a slug right through Mustache's back. It threw him up against the wall, leaving a glistening spray of blood and tissue in his wake. He staggered two or three steps and went face-down.

"You killed him." The bartender said. "You killed him."

"Yes, I did. Same way I'm going to kill the next man that opens his pisshole and interrupts what I'm trying to say." Oates lit himself another cigarette. "Okay, so we put my girl in the ground and a few days later? Well, a few days later she comes home. Decides to kill our old hound and then sit in my wife's rocking chair and chew on the guts. Now ain't that a pretty fucking picture? How can such a thing be? That's what I asked myself. But I didn't have any good goddamned answers until I waltzed into this stinking shithole. Then I knew. God yes, I knew. My daughter died because you goddamn ass-sucking cowards were too damned afraid to take care of business! Too damned afraid to get some iron in your pants and ride up there and set things to right!"

"Don't you think we wanted to?" one of the others said now, his eyes just sick and scared. "Don't you think we all wanted to go up there and burn that snakepit out? Don't you think we're just dog-sick of hiding behind locked doors when the sun goes down? Do you think we like jumping every time a stick snaps out in the yard or there's a knock on the door? Do you think we like that?"

Oates leathered his Colt. He'd had enough. "I'm guessing you must. Well, good day to you all. I can't honestly stand the sight of you people anymore, so I'm riding up to Crowley. You can expect me by nightfall. I'll be bringing Black Betty with me, on account she's real anxious to make your acquaintance."

With that, Oates stepped over Mustache's corpse and went out into the blazing sunshine. He'd barely made it down the road before someone came up behind him. It was the old man from the saloon. "You looking for them what eats folks, eh? Well, then, you're gonna need some help."

Six

Pumped hard with attitude and about as ready as he figured he'd ever get, Oates went over to the livery and got himself a fresh mount, a coal-black gelding rippling with muscle. Once he'd transferred his double-rig saddle and bags, he mounted and started riding out.

Weeds was with him, of course, riding on his gelding.

And once Weeds started talking, look out, he was like a leaky faucet you just couldn't turn off. Try as you might, you just couldn't put a kink in his hose. As they rode out of Compton, the words flowed and flowed out of the old man. It seemed there wasn't anything he hadn't done or hadn't seen. He'd cut trail with Jim Bridger in the Rockies and hunted buffalo in Kansas, been a Confederate sharpshooter at Gettysburg and laid track for the Union Pacific line, panned for gold during the California rush in '49 and fought the Bannock in Idaho back in '78. And that didn't take into account getting drunk with Wild Bill Hickok, fighting the Comanche in Texas, or how he helped corner Sam Bass and his gang at Round Rock.

"Yes sir, I would suspect I've done just about everything and been just about everywhere," Weeds said, seemingly proud of himself. Then he frowned, spit tobacco juice over his left shoulder. "Course, stranger, there are certain things I've never had much interest in doing, certain holes I'd prefer not to be sticking this old pecker of mine if a choice is offered. I'm figuring Crowley is one of them places."

"Maybe you ain't up to this, old man," Oates said. "You turn back now, I won't think any less of you."

"Turn back?" Weeds looked like he was ready to start swinging. His hand actually went for the Remington Army .44 in his holster. "Son, now you listen to me and you listen real good. I might not look like much and maybe you think I'm full of more shit than a greenhorn's pants, but get this: I don't tuck my willy between my legs and run. Never have, never will. I've ridden hard since long before you had hair on your little balls. I've been beaten and shot, hanged and stabbed. A Kiowa war party tried to roast me alive one time and when I was an Express rider, I pulled arrows out of my ass like quills from a porcupine. But I didn't back down and I didn't turn tail. I've pissed blood by the buckets and grinned whilst I did it. Now, I don't know, not really, what we're riding into, but I'll be at your side. I'll fight with you and I'll die with you and if we make it back out, I'll get drunk with you."

"Okay, old man, don't get your dander up."

"Don't get my dander up, he says. Shit and shit."

Oates almost smiled at that and he hadn't smiled for a long time now. "Okay, old man. We should be riding into Crowley within the hour if your calculations are correct—"

"They are."

"—and before then, I think you better tell me what I need to know. You can start talking anytime now."

Weeds cut another chew from his plug and worked it between his jaw and gum. "Well, stranger, I know most of it, I'm thinking. Maybe more than I care to know. See, about ten years back, Crowley had itself a couple silver mines run by the Silver Horn combine out of Utah Territory. Had a pretty refinery up there, the works. Sure, there were near on five thousand people squatting in Crowley and then things went to shit.

"I'm not sure which happened first. Maybe the veins dried out or maybe that hoodoo nigger bitch Black Betty blew in on a storm of disease and misery." Weeds shrugged, studied the hardpan desert that stretched as far as they could see. "All I can say, is that it was about that time things started getting a little funny in Crowley."

Maybe "funny" wasn't the right word for something that was damnably disturbing, demented, and just plain spooky. Black Betty was a prostitute out of Baton Rouge, came to town in a wagon with a dozen alley cats, bought herself a hotel and turned it into a high-dollar brothel within six months. Black Betty christened it the Dark Star, maybe on account of her skin color and the fact that she'd once worked for a cathouse called the Star of India in Baton Rouge. No matter, wasn't long before Betty and her crew of meat-eaters were turning greenbacks by the buckets and pissing gold coins.

"But there was some pretty damned crazy talk, stranger, I'll tell you that much. Horseshit about them girls practicing root-lore and witchcraft and herb-doctoring. Even heard a few tall ones about Devil-worship and the like. No matter, maybe some were concerned about that shit, but men in general didn't stop going to the Dark Star to get a taste of that imported kitty up there. And weren't none of it cheap, mind you. Most of them alley cats in Black Betty's stable would cost you four or five hundred Union for a slap and a tickle. But that's a mining town, ain't? When money's being pulled out of the ground, prices tend to inflate."

Well, Weeds said, things went on and on as they do. He couldn't exactly say if there really was any truth to the Devil-worship business, but there *was* something he had seen with his own eyes, not that it honestly amounted to much. But all those girls at the Dark Star, they all wore a funny necklace or amulet around their throats. Weeds said it looked like a crescent moon with a snake coiled around it. A very odd thing and quite a few people had commented on them. But they were always commenting on something about the Dark Star. Things like the voices you might hear in the next room that sounded like they came from some old hag speaking a language that didn't sound natural, or the fact that Black Betty ordered an awful lot of livestock for her and her girls. Livestock they butchered themselves.

"Just between you and me and the sweat on my nuts, stranger, I'll be honest as a Christian coming to preach and admit to you, here and now, that I did not care for those girls. Don't look at me like that for chrissake. I mean, sure I liked to look at 'em because these were some sweet imported candies... but something about 'em, well it just left me cold."

Weeds fell silent like he was thinking over what he had just said. "There was something funny in their eyes. Something that got down inside you and just didn't want to leave. Looking in their eyes, I don't know, but it was like staring into the eyes of a cow skull in the desert, you know? Nothing in there, nothing warm or human exactly, just this sense that whatever was *supposed* to be in there had been picked clean."

Weeds admitted that it didn't make much sense. About all he could say was that those whores were hollow where they should have been full. Something inside them was gone and something else was living there. He likened it to hermit crabs you'd see on the beach. They'd steal snail shells and the like, crawl inside and set up housekeeping. The girls were sort of like that... just shells. Wasn't nothing inside 'em, so something else had slipped in there.

Oates listened and did not judge. It all sounded like some high and happy horseshit, but after what he'd seen and knew to be true, he wasn't about to laugh any of it off. Devil-worship and storybook witches flying on brooms? Well, sure, why the hell not?

Weeds kept talking as they made their way across the salt desert. The sun was blazing overhead, nothing the eye could see below but sand and rocks, some stands of giant cacti, yucca plants and agave. Now and again some greasewood or creosote brush. They saw a few sidewinder rattlesnakes, some spiny lizards skittering amongst the rocks, not much else. Now and again, a turkey vulture would circle high above looking for something gamy to peck on.

Weeds wiped sweat and flies from his face, said, "Now I suppose I should tell you about one of Black Betty's girls, the one they called Georgia Peach. Now she was something... blonde and blue-eyed with tits that would make your mouth water. She was a real Fancy Sal, that one. She was some kind of European treasure from across the pond and couldn't speak much of the King's English, but with them looks, nobody cared. Least, not at first. Georgia Peach was a real dainty dish, stranger, and if you wanted to jump that stuff it would cost you a grand. And there were plenty that paid it."

She was real popular, despite the high prices. Mainly it was mining executives that could afford her, some of the ranchers from up north. But eventually some real strange things began to be said about Georgia Peach. She was fine to look at, but you had to be careful if you touched her. She got pretty wild in the hay, Weeds said, and stories circulated about her biting men and scratching them up real bad. There was a dirt evil streak in her and you could see it in her eyes, that hunger that made you feel like a joint of meat pulled from a roaster.

It came to a head of sorts when it was claimed that Georgia Peach had slit some miner's throat while he was putting the business to her. One of his friends came in saw her chewing on the wound, licking at what spilled out. People said it wasn't the first time. That Georgia Peach had slit more than one throat.

Weeds wiped tobacco juice off his chin. "Now I knew the feller what discovered the crime. Name was Lyle Denehew, a hardscrabble miner that struck the mother lode. I saw Lyle a few weeks after his friend... some investor out of Detroit... was killed. Lyle told me all about it. Said he heard a funny sound next door. Him and his lady were all finished up, said he heard something like rain strike the wall, then a gurgling sound.

"For some reason, it set on him wrong. He went next door and stepped inside. Saw it all by candlelight. That friend of his was right on top of Georgia Peach and she still had those long legs of hers wrapped around him and was grinding into him. And that would have been fine, but there was blood all over her... splattered on the wall and her mouth was at his friend's throat. Even when he came in, he could hear that she-devil sucking at his throat.

"Lyle said something went cold inside him just looking at that horror. Georgia Peach saw him and pulled her mouth away from his throat, had a razor in her hand that looked like it had been dipped in red ink. She pushed Lyle's friend off her and he hit the floor with a thud like a hundred-and-fifty pounds of cold Texas beef. Then Georgia Peach? Well, she slid off the bed, just soaked with blood. Her arms were covered in it, her tits and belly, her face. When she grinned... and she *did* grin, Lyle said, like a hyena with a mouth full of carrion... her teeth were stained red, bits of tissue hanging from her mouth like confetti..."

It was a repellent, hideous story, but Weeds saw it through. His friend Lyle ran out of there, wearing nothing but his britches, and he never came back. When the marshal got there—some hot gun name of Rawley Cook—stewed on Mescal, he found a lot of blood, but no body and no Georgia Peach. Bed was soaked red, spirals of blood sprayed over the walls. The window was wide open and the sill had bloody prints on it, but that was about it. It looked like the body and what dragged it off went right out the damn window two stories up.

"Did they ever find her?" Oates asked.

"Oh yes, she showed a few days later, claimed ignorance of the entire event. Black Betty was tight with the Silver Horn execs who controlled Rawley Cook, the marshal, and the whole thing was swept under the carpet. And Georgia Peach? Well, stranger, no jury would ever have convicted her, maybe she was some kind of bloodsucking witch in the sack, but out of it, just as a fine and beautiful of a lady as you could imagine. Those blue eyes would have melted anyone."

But it was hardly at an end.

Georgia Peach was taken off the market by Black Betty. Maybe so she'd stop killing men and maybe because Black Betty was afraid somebody might decide to put a stake through her heart. One of the rumors circulating was that Georgia Peach was locked up in some room in the attic and fed raw meat, but Weeds said that was probably just a story. Who could say? But one thing was for sure, the girl liked to wander about town in the wee hours dressed in a cloak, and folks were always afraid of meeting up with her on some lonesome road. People didn't see much of her, but when they did, they said she was awful pale and those eyes of hers were enough to melt paint off a door. Whenever she was out, a couple of girls went with her.

And then, one night, she slipped out on her own.

"Here's what happened, stranger: Georgia Peach had a real nasty reputation by that time, folks saying she was a hellwitch and a vampire. Some squatter's kid went missing and people were pretty certain who'd gotten the boy. Kid's window was open and, well, people figured some evil wench in a cloak had slipped in there and taken the kid away. Maybe up to the graveyard yonder to have herself a midnight feast. They never did find the kid's remains. Which is probably a good thing.

"Now, one night Georgia Peach got out, was walking around town by herself and she met up with some friends of that Detroit investor. Lyle claimed he was not among them. They took her to a barn somewhere and took their turns raping her. Yes sir, raped her harder than the U.S. government raped the Sioux Nation. That's the story that was told, anyhow. But all liquored up and out of their heads, these boys got carried away even further. They took a couple axes and chopped that bitch up, sectioned her like a Christmas hog ready for the spit. Then, apparently, they bagged her up and took her parts over to the Dark Star and dumped 'em on the porch. Stuck her head on the newel post like a Halloweeny pumpkin. And that, my friend, set off the mother of all firestorms.

"See, Black Betty loved that girl. Loved Georgia Peach like she were kin. And the girl's murder put her right over the edge. Black Betty was this tall, leggy negress with a butter-soft Louisiany accent that would make you shoot your load right in your pants. Yeah, tall and high-titted, all that dark hair hanging down to the middle of her back and green eyes, green eyes like fine emeralds sunk in sweet chocolate. I saw her only once and despite those looks, she was not the sort of dark wood a man would want to split. Not if he favored his business, that was. On a good day, those green eyes would make your knees weak and make your heart pound, make you want to cross the street if she put 'em on you. But on a bad day? That look of hers would strip the meat from your bones."

Black Betty, story had it, was not just some fancy chocolate whore out of Baton Rouge, but some wicked witch that had been run out of town for casting the evil eye and bringing the plague, all manner of things. It was said she liked to lay around nights wearing nothing but a necklace of animal bones and reading to her girls from rotting leather books written in Latin.

"Well, Black Betty was beside herself. Rawley Cook, never exactly sober, made an investigation and it amounted to nothing. Black Betty closed up shop, shut the Dark Star down for mourning and it never did open up again. People said she zipped it up tighter than a pine box. The girls were not seen outside of those walls. You could see lots of candlelight in the windows at night, like the girls were going up and down the stairs and from room to room in a candlelight procession. That only fed the wild rumors of Devil-worship and witching and all that pagan business.

"Black Betty wasn't trying to discourage it either, on account her porch was decorated up with all manner of spooky voodoo shit. There were these garlands hanging from the porch overhang made out of the boiled white vertebrae of rattlesnakes with dozens of little rodent bones sticking out at all kinds of crazy angles. Those garlands were set with the skulls of cats and rats and you name it, like crazy skeleton sculptures. When the wind blew, those hanging bones rattled and clattered. There was some kind of decoration over the door made out of a wagon wheel of cow femurs with a big gape-jawed wolf skull sitting right in the middle. Lots of pelts, wax-and-feather gris-gris, and dried plants hanging about. Pots of some smelly concoction simmering away night and day. Goddamn porch was looking like a witch doctor's hut from what people said. It scared the shit out of everyone, but there was no law against it."

Weeds said that what happened next was just as weird.

One night during the dark phase of the moon, Black Betty climbed up onto that sharp-peaked roof of the Dark Star and started chanting things and calling out words into the sky above. Whatever she had been saying scared the piss out of everyone and people locked their doors and bolted their windows. Saloons emptied and churches filled.

That night, as she screamed those vile words into the wind from her high perch, things happened. The clouds boiled black in the sky and Crowley shook as if from an earth tremor. Windows shattered and lean-tos and tumbledown shacks fell right over. The cross high up on the steeple of the Congregational Church fell right off and was found the next day completely melted like somebody had tossed it into a blast furnace. But the very worse thing was that the graveyard up on the hill shook and rumbled like an empty belly. The gates were blown off their hinges and tombstones fell over; graves were ripped open and the marble vault of some rich miner was desecrated. The iron doors swung wide and half a dozen coffins were spewed out into the cemetery, what was in them scattered in the weeds and bushes. Weeds said it was like that sepulchre couldn't hold down what was in its belly and decided to vomit it out into the grass.

"I'm surprised by this point," Oates said, lighting one of his cigarettes, "that the people of Crowley didn't go on a witch-hunt and burn Black Betty."

"Maybe they wanted to and maybe they just didn't dare," Weeds said. "Things settled down for a few weeks and I suppose people were hoping it had passed, but it hadn't passed. Black Betty was still holed-up in the brothel and she stopped ordering livestock, but instead she wanted all the fresh meat she could get. And it was an awful lot of meat from what people were saying. Now, stranger, about that time the fever began. People started getting sick and dying, the mines ran dry, and Crowley was just a coffin waiting for its lid to be thrown shut.

"Now, if things weren't bad enough, something else happened. Something that was witnessed by some very reliable people."

"And what was that?" Oates asked, almost afraid to.

Weeds looked suddenly sick like he'd bit into something rancid. He wiped his mouth and then wiped it again. "On near sundown, but the sun still bright enough where you could see plenty fine... Georgia Peach comes walking right up the road. Sounds like horseshit, don't it? But it's true enough. I knew three people who saw her. Del Whipple ran a smithy shop there, good friend of mine. He saw her same as the others. Del said he almost lost his mind. A couple of folks took one look at what was dragging itself down the road, maybe making for the Dark Star, and plum fainted dead away. You couldn't blame 'em.

"Georgia Peach had come down from the cemetery maybe, kind of pulling herself along, sort of dragging one leg behind the other. Del said she was naked, gray and blotchy like tombstone marble, all puffy-looking, had this dark fungus-looking stuff growing up from her privates and onto her belly, down her throat and onto her tits. But not so much that you couldn't see that she had been stitched back together like a rag dolly what lost its limbs and stuffing. Black stitching held her arms and legs on, ran from her business to her throat to keep her goodies inside. Her head was threaded to her neck and it hung off to the side like her neck was broken. And her face... yeah, there were stitches running over it like branching lightning, her nose set off to the side, one corner of her lips drawn too tight so that it was up on her cheek. She didn't have but the one eye, the other being a socket packed with graveyard soil. Her hair was full of dirt and worms, flies all over her, maggots dropping from her mouth like rice.

"Del said she stank like spoiled pork, a dirty smell that made your stomach jump into your throat. She was making a funny hissing sort of sound that could maybe have been breathing, or maybe that wrecked throat trying to speak. Del said that one eye was wide and staring, just insane and bloodshot, and when she put it on you, it made your guts run like sweet jelly. Sure, she was a walking corpse, rotten and stinking and wormy, but there was something in that eye. Something black and deranged and *aware*, something that knew things and had seen things that would make your mind go to sauce. Del told me that Georgia Peach looked at him like a spider might look at you if it was smarter than you and hungry and you happened to be caught in its web.

"Well, most people ran off, but Del and a few others stayed. They put their guns on her and she laughed at them and that sound was enough to turn your hair white, make you want to crawl under the bed and suck your thumb. Just a scraping, shattered glass sound coming from that throat full of dirt. Del admitted to me that he actually pissed his pants. Undertaker Clem was there. She looked right at him with that one good eye and the blood drained from his face.

"She started talking with this awful scratching voice, telling everyone there things she couldn't possibly know. Things about how Clem had been doing things perverted and unclean with the bodies of certain females that had come into his parlor. She talked liked she'd been inside those corpses when he was... well, humping on 'em. Then she started talking about Clem's daughter Margaret who had passed of the fever a week before. Said how she had dug the child up and bit the tongue out of her mouth, how Black Betty herself had made a shawl out of the girl's skin and had salted her death mask and hung it on the wall.

"But it wasn't only Clem that Georgia Peach... or the thing inside her... directed her ire against. She told another fellow there how his father had been raping his kid sister years before, how he made her suck his cock and swallow what came out. That fellow ran off screaming. Then she turned on Del, told him... told him in his *dead mother's voice* why she had committed suicide when he was five years old. And it wasn't because Del's infant brother Joshua had died of the crib death like everyone thought, but because she had lost her mind, gotten tired of his constant crying and pressed a pillow down over the baby's face until it stopped making noise and stopped moving. Del was crying like a baby himself when he told me that part. He said that witch said other things, but he would not... *could not*... repeat them.

"See, stranger, what was living inside of Georgia Peach's shell was not human; it was just black and dirty and foul, something without a soul. Something that was never meant to be born. It had seen the other side, torn through the veil of death, and it knew all the tormented secrets of the dead. Things no man should ever, ever know."

Despite that sun burning down above and that salt-dry air that sucked the moisture right out of your skin, Oates was chilled right to his marrow, and the sweat that beaded his brow was like ice water. "What... what did they do with her?"

Weeds laughed without a trace of humor. "They were out of their minds with what she'd been saying, so they killed her... if you can kill something already dead. They opened up on her, blew her to fragments right there in the street until she stopped moving. And then... then the worms started coming out of her, just boiling out of her with hot-corpse gas, thousands of fat maggots—"

"All right," Oates said, swallowing down his stomach. "That'll do."

But Weeds was far from done.

He told Oates how the fever was taking people and no sooner had they been put in the ground, than they rose back up again. At night, there were dozens of them in the street knocking on doors and scratching at windows, all wanting to be let in. More and more walking dead all the time, screaming out terrible things in the darkness, opening graves and eating what they found inside, gutting livestock and murdering folk that were fool enough to be out after dark. Entire families disappeared in the dead of night and sometimes they'd show up a few days later pounding on the doors of kin, wanting to be let in.

There was one woman they called the Screamer. She wandered the streets at night in a shroud, crying out for her lost child. Rawley Cook, drunk and out of his head, went after her one night to kill her and she looked at him and said something to him that made him put his gun in his mouth.

"Around that time, people dying and nightmares walking the night, Crowley depopulating itself, a posse went into the Dark Star to burn the poison out. There was no one left alive in there. Not a one. They couldn't find Black Betty, but they found the other girls sure enough. Down in the cellar, they were all laid out in open shallow graves and every one of them was grinning. The posse dragged a couple of the girls out and chopped their heads off, but it all sickened them and they ran. And that, stranger, was the end of Crowley. The mass exodus began, people running to get away from the fever and the shadows that crawled out of their graves after sundown."

And that's how it must have happened, Oates figured. People were just scared, so they ran as far away as they could get. And that cancer has been breeding ever since, spreading through the belly of the county. Poisoning and consuming and eating what good meat was left. In time, if this wasn't rooted out, the entire county would go bad.

"Now all that I say to you, stranger, happened no less than ten years ago, but it has never stopped. A year ago I buried my Alice in the plot outside my place in Compton. No... natural death, her heart was bad." Weeds was having trouble with this. "I started having bad dreams right off. God, how I loved that woman. She was all that held my world together.

"One night, I woke up after midnight and the front door was wide open. I found a trail of filth leading into the kitchen. I had a smoked ham in there and something with muddy feet had gone in there after it. Had ripped it right off the bone and then vomited all that meat on the walls, the floor, you name it.

"About then, I heard something outside. A wet crunching sound and something like a slimy sort of breathing. I went out there and there's this boy, maybe fifteen or so, except that he's dead and most of his face has rotted off the skull beneath. He's all dirty and black either from dragging himself up out of the grave or digging in others. Because, see, that's what he was doing then and there. He had dug up my Alice and he was chewing on her. He had nibbled most of the meat from her throat and breasts. When I shot him through the head, there was carrion dropping from his mouth."

The old man was quiet for a time after that and it was just the two of them winding out toward Crowley, both having suffered and both having seen things that would forever blight their souls.

Finally, Weeds said, "So that's it, stranger. You know all I know. Maybe some of it's bullshit, but I don't think so. Now you might understand why those in Compton are too afraid to ride out here, why some of those boys have all they can do not to put their neck in a noose and jump off a stool. Now you know what we're riding into and what waits for us there. All I can say, stranger, is may God help us."

Way Oates was seeing it, there was nothing left to be said. They had guns and attitude and hate and not much of anything else. God willing, it would be enough. The table had been set and now it was time to eat lunch with the damned.

Seven

If Compton was anemic and looking for a grave, then Crowley had already found one... only some fool with a shovel had dug its moldering hide back up again, brushed off the dirt and worms and tried to pass it off as a town. But Crowley was not a town, not anymore. Some things belonged above ground and some things belonged below it and there was no doubt where Crowley fit in.

As they came in and Oates got his first real look, it made something in his guts twist like a corkscrew. For it was a dead, diseased place, just rotting and bleak and skeletal, blown by a wind of hot pestilence. He could smell the corpse slime and dry rot seeping from those close-packed houses and shacks and buildings, and he had all he could do not to turn and ride back out again.

Remember why you're doing this, he told himself. *Just keep that in mind. Whatever's breeding here in the warm darkness and cellar-damps took Mandy from you. It started a chain-reaction that has gutted your family, pulled out all the good stuff in wet loops, let all that you love and care about bleed dry.*

Sucking in a breath of gritty air, Oates let himself feel it all again... the hatred, the pain, the despair. He let all those suppurating wounds on his soul spill their vile fluids until that poison filled him and made him want to scream, to get someone or some*thing* in his hands that he could snap and rend, pull apart like a doll.

Easy now, just easy now.

Don't lose your head. Let the pain work for you. That's the way.

"Can you smell it?" Weeds asked, drawing his Remington Army .44 from the scabbard and holding onto it so tightly his knuckles blossomed with white half-moons. "Dirty, black smell... Jesus, like things buried and other things gone to mold. Take a good whiff of that, stranger, then ask yourself if I made all that crazy shit up... go ahead, just ask yourself because the proof is in the pudding. Only this pudding, I'm thinking, is made out of bonemeal and bad meat."

But Oates did not need to ask himself that.

Because he knew deep in the papery rustle of his heart that Old Man Weeds had not made up a thread of all that business. He only reported what he had seen, what he had been told, and what his wily old brain had concluded. For maybe Weeds acted like some half-ass Sagebrush Willy, but he was tough and he was smart and his brain was firing just as smooth and pure as a steam calliope. It didn't miss nary a note.

And Oates?

No, he believed there was an evil here, a darkness that was invidious and infectious and reaching out for their throats even then. The horses knew it. They were getting skittish and whinnying. They knew bad when they smelled it and this place was about as bad as bad got.

Crowley was a close-packed collection of high brick buildings and narrow wooden structures fronted by plank sidewalks, lots of shacks and shanties squeezed in-between. There was a rusting cannon in the town square, livery barns and rooming houses, a cinderblock jailhouse and plenty of taverns. Up in the hills above, you could see the old hoist shacks and towers and derricks from the mines, all of it looking decayed and stripped like the exoskeletons of immense insects sinking into the mounded earth.

Maybe Oates didn't like the feel of Crowley or what waited there, but there was something that was sitting on him just fine: the old town was a firetrap. Way it was pressed together like that—crowded and leaning, some buildings sharing common walls, and when there was an opening, a privy or a tent-roofed hut was jammed in place—it was going to work out just fine. You lit up one building, the entire place was going to go... and especially with that hot wind blowing.

"Well, stranger, we'd best make for the Dark Star," Weeds said. "Ain't nothing else to see in this graveyard. Whole goddamn place has gone toes up."

As they rode, Oates became aware of the buzzards circling overhead, how they were sitting on hitch posts and roof overhangs, spreading their wings. They knew there was dead here and they were waiting for it to show itself.

The Dark Star was a high two-story structure set between a gambling hall and a rooming house, sagging and boarded-up, weathered a uniform gray from the sand-driven wind. A sign creaked on posts, but it was unreadable. The roof was sharply peaked and Oates had to wonder how Black Betty had stood up there that night, screaming words into the sky. A dozen buzzards were roosting up there now, cawing and picking at each other's feathers.

The porch was much as Weeds had described: lots of bones dangling overhead, many more having fallen, scattered over the planking. They were all yellow and ancient, some of them going to powder. Oates filled the deep pockets of his old, thin army overcoat with shells for the 12-gauge. Weeds carried his Remington .44 at his hip and a Hood double-barrel shotgun in his fists.

Using the barrel of his American, Oates knocked that grinning wolf skull aside and grasped the brass knob. A funny tingling went right up to his elbow. His fingers actually recoiled like they had touched the lid of a casket.

"Locked," Oates said.

"Step aside."

Weeds put both barrels of the Hood against the latch and pulled the triggers. The lock and knob blew right into the foyer with a lot of wood. The door swung open.

Weeds broke open the Hood, cast aside the spent and smoking shells, jammed two fresh ones into the chamber. "That's how you do it, son."

Oates figured if anyone hadn't known they were coming before, there was no doubt of it now. Old signboards creaked down the street, dust devils whirling up the boardwalks. Nothing out there but wind and sand and nothing inside but death and silence. To Oates, the town in general and the Dark Star in particular reminded him of things embalmed, things salted and mummified and blown dry in the desert. As he stepped inside, a murmur of terror spread through him.

"Hey, you dead ones," Weeds called into the foyer, "we come to do you a hurt."

True to form, everything was dry and splintered and dehydrated inside. The fancy wallpaper hung in dirty strips, holes chewed in the wainscoting by mice. The hardwood floors were warped, the ceilings bowed. Dusty sunlight filtered through shattered windows and gaping holes in the walls themselves. They could hear pigeons cooing from somewhere above.

"Where first?" Weeds said, licking the salt off his lips.

"The cellar. Let's take care of what's down there first."

Weeds knew the way and Oates had to wonder how many times that randy old goat had been to this place. They followed a corridor until it split and there was a door right in front of them. Its panels were filthy as if generations of dirty hands had been touching it. An old, rusted iron catch was twisted to the side.

"Wait a minute now," Weeds said and took off down the hallway. He came back with a kerosene lantern. He scratched a match off his boot and lit it. "No sense feeling around in the dark whilst something might be feeling around for *us*."

Down the stairs they went, the individual steps creaking and sinking beneath their weight, but holding. The stink was awful down there, just noisome and dry and nitrous. The floor was dirt and it didn't take them long to find the shallow graves. There were about a dozen of them, only half of which were occupied. The whores rested inside them, hands clasped over their bosoms. One of them had decayed down to a skeleton and Oates didn't figure she'd give them any trouble. They were all dressed in fine white burial dresses of lace and silk that had gone to gray and rotting rags much like the remains they covered.

Weeds held the lantern over one of them, black shadows crawling over the cadaver. She was emaciated and threadbare, gray, leathery skin stretched over a framework of sticks and pipes. There were great holes eaten into her face and throat. She had no eyes. Spiders had spun webs over her face and had woven cocoons in her eye sockets. Her jaws were sprung wide as if in a scream.

Oates had a hard time believing that something like her could actually move, actually walk. She looked like a mummy, something from a tomb, and he told Weeds as much.

"Well, let's see," Weeds said.

He handed the lantern to Oates and picked up a shovel nearby. Maybe it was the same one that had been used to dig the graves years before. Weeds was breathing hard, his jaw was set. He took the shovel and pressed the blade to that corded deadwood throat. He looked over at Oates one more time, swallowed.

"Do it," Oates told him.

The old man sucked in air, raised the shovel, and then brought it down with everything he had. The blade sliced right through that neck with a sound like an axe into kindling... a crackling, snapping sound. The head was severed just that easily.

"Not so bad," Weeds said, wiping sweat from his brow. He picked up his shotgun and took the lantern from Oates. "Maybe that's all we got to do, just lop them heads off and—"

The head moved.

Actually *moved*. The mouth hooked into a sneer, the teeth chattering together, a dry sibilance of air blowing out as if it were trying to talk, and they were pretty sure it was. With each scraping gasp, a little puff of dust came out from between those shredded lips. Blackened, eyeless sockets fixed on them and you could almost believe that they could see.

Weeds made a choking sound in his throat.

Then the body came alive, arms coming up, hands whipping about and trying to grab something they could tear and rend. The body thumped and writhed in the grave, legs kicking and torso thudding up and down, up and down. Oates brought his 12-gauge up and pulled the trigger, blasting that leering head to fragments.

The body shuddered, went still.

Oates just stood there, breathing hard. He felt just locked up and immovable. Yes, he had seen his dead daughter walk and that was horrible beyond imagining, but this... this was somehow worse. Like seeing a window dummy come to life or a scarecrow begin to breathe. It was absolute madness.

"C'mon, stranger. Just hold the light."

Trembling now, Oates took the lantern from the old man as they went to the next grave. Weeds did not hesitate. He put the barrel of his Hood to the dead woman's forehead and pulled the trigger, blowing that skull to fragments like a shattered vase. One of the hands twitched, but that was about it. Then to the next one. He pulled the trigger.

That was three.

They went to the fourth and the corpse sat right up, that fissured face looking over and up at them. The eyes snapped open in the head, black and shining things like spills of oil. With the butt of his American against his hip, Oates fired one-handed without even thinking. The buckshot almost tore the dead whore in half. Her breasts and upper chest literally exploded into a rain of debris and something like plaster dust that hung in clouds. She screamed at them, thrashing and clawing and trying to rise, but crumbling even as she did so. Finally, she collapsed back into the grave, snapping her teeth and staring up at them with a consuming malevolence, a hatred born in the blackest gulfs of non-existence, those fingers like sticks and twigs scratching at the earth around her.

Oates fired again, that living head spraying apart with something that hit the far wall like gravel.

The other two were pulling themselves up from those sunken graves, one dressed in a raspberry taffeta dinner gown with pearls at the throat and the other in a sky blue bustle dress. Both garments were decaying like their owners. But whereas the others were mummies from sandy tombs, salted and cured things that crumbled as they moved, these two were rancid and moist, their ruined faces furry with grave fungi that hung like garland from their throats.

Both Oates and Weeds were about to start shooting, but something was happening.

Something weird and frightening that they could feel along the napes of their necks and along their spines. The earth beneath them trembled and split open in dusty crevices, and the dead began to rise in earnest. Somebody, somewhere, had sung a song of resurrection and that parched soil heaved and ruptured like ancient wounds tearing open and, dear God, what was spilling out. What was seething and oozing from the ground all around them. Fingers broke the dank, dripping soil, followed by hands and flyblown faces. Yellowed and ruined eyes studied the cellar. Lungs filled with dust and insects gulped in the hot wind. The dead rose and hissed, helped the weaker from their beds of dirt.

They were rising everywhere, dozens of them.

Hands broke that crust and searched for legs to grab and worm-holed faces looked for ankles to bite.

It was utter pandemonium as the dead continued to rise, first a dozen then twice that, a profusion of the living dead, clawing and shrieking, faces rotted to pulp and looking to steal a kiss, others shrouded in webs and looking for hot meat and hotter blood.

Oates and Weeds stumbled back to the stairs as the earth around them lifted and bulged, mounds breaking open and grinning faces gnashing their teeth. Weeds kept shooting until his shotgun was empty, then he pulled his Remington Army .44 and blasted away until the pistol was hot and smoking.

Oates jumped over a heap of rising cadavers and tossed the lantern. It struck the wall and vomited a rolling wake of flames across the floor. But still the things pulled themselves up and out, ever forward. Creeping things and spidery things, faceless things and hungry things. But the very worst might have been those undead babies, crawling things thrown together out of slime and bones, faces boiled down to unformed skulls.

Weeds led them up the stairs as Oates filled his shotgun and blew zombies in half, in quarters, in pieces. Those things were shrieking and wailing and screeching, living skeletons and limbless husks.

But the flames were rising.

They had climbed the walls and tasted the old beams and dry planks and found them to their liking. Everything so dry and splintered, it caught instantly, flames mushrooming everywhere. The cellar was filled with smoke and shadows and screaming mouths.

Oates had almost made it to the top when Weeds above him grunted and fell into him, a hot spray of blood splashing into his face. A hatchet was buried in his head. He slipped past Oates and tumbled down the stairs to those ravening and clutching things below.

There was nothing Oates could do but vent the scream that had been building in his throat for so long. Weeds was engulfed in a sea of putrescence. His body floated for a moment or two, then sank, coming apart as mouths bit into it and greedy fingers tore flaps of meat from him in a grisly feast.

But Oates didn't have time to think about any of that or register the horror of it, a scene that would haunt his dreams for a lifetime.

For standing at the top of the stairs was a woman.

She was dressed in a black brocade dress with a high neck made of cream lace. Which was probably a good thing, because she had no head to speak of. White, hooked fingers reached out to him and he brought his 12-gauge up and gave her the final round. It threw her back, splattered the wallpaper with black blood and rancid tissue. Oates dove up there as she came forward again, tripping over him and thudding down the stairs.

He threw the door closed after her.

The rusty latch would barely move in his hands. He could hear them coming up the steps, slithering and drooling and rustling, things dropping off them, flies vacating them in clouds. Finally, as the first three or four marble-gray hands reached around the lip of the door, the latch came free. Oates kicked the door shut and slid it in place.

The dead pounded and hammered with fists that were hard like stumps and soft as rotting apples.

The air smelled not just of putrefaction, but of smoke now.

The Dark Star was going up fast.

Oates, his mind just shut down now, a white silence breathing in his head, pulled his Colt Navy .44s and raced down the hallway.

He made it to the stairs and saw a little girl with a tumescent and bloated face waiting for him. She had no eyes, her flesh gone to a soft mucilage like hot wax eager to melt from the skull beneath. She held a baby in her arms... or something like a baby. It was more skeleton than flesh, a creeping bag of bones that only wanted to be held. It grinned up at Oates with white milk teeth, reaching out its rotting hands for him.

Oates fired one of his Colt Navies.

The first round knocked the baby from the girl's arms and scattered its moldering bones like dice. The second round splashed the girl's face from her skull and cored the brain beyond. She fell straight over like a fence post.

Then the stairs.

More tricks and more treats.

Another zombie was coming down to call on him, but this one was regal enough to give you pause, take your breath away. This cadaver was that of a man who'd really been something in life. He was dressed in a purple velvet clawhammer coat with long tails, matching trousers, and pointy-toed lizard boots set with rhinestones and gold inlay. There was a pink silk cravat at his throat and a silver watch-chain at his belly. Atop his head was a high stovepipe top hat upholstered in that same garish velvet.

His face was just as ruined as the others, but even this had an almost patrician charm to it. He had no eyes and he moved gracefully down the steps, tapping a cane before him with a golden wolf's head on top. The skin of his face—what there was of it—was leathery and sliced and gouged like a well-worked barber's strop and the color of a new moon. The mutilated musculature beneath was stretched taut and bloodless over a finely proportioned skull.

"Mr. Oates," the mouth said with a voice like wind through a catacomb. "The dear lady herself waits you upstairs. A real gentleman never keeps a lady waiting, so—"

Oates couldn't help himself.

As a peal of demented, almost girlish laughter bubbled up and out of him, he put a .44 slug right into that high-stepping cadaverous dandy before him. Then he put another and another. The dandy's head disintegrated and he rolled down the stairs, coming apart in a dusty heap like an ancient parchment.

The smell of smoke was getting very strong now.

Oates could feel the heat welling up out of the cellar.

There wasn't much time.

Black Betty wants to meet me, he thought, *and I sure as hell don't want to disappoint the lady.*

He ran up the stairs and went from room to room until he came into a bedroom that must have been fine before the mice ate the stuffing out of the silk pillows and shifts, before age had faded that cherry woodwork, and before spiders had spun webs from the canopy of that bed to the feather mattress below.

There was something on the bed.

Something that rose to face him now.

Here was the mother of whores and devils, that hell-witch and conjuror and flesh-eater. Here was Black Betty, a thing of blight and burnt offerings, mummy dust and cerements and graveyard earth. She was dressed in a faded and worm-holed silk reception gown with a long bodice and finely pleated sleeves that must have been khaki once, but was now gray and black from all the filth she had vomited down the front of it. She drifted forward like a wraith from a plundered tomb, smelling of mildew and bones and rot. Her breath was like carrion.

Oates let out a yell and put two bullets in her that didn't even slow her down.

She still had that long train of lustrous black locks, but it was now attached to a charnel scalp like something tanned. Her face was an atrocity, looked like it had been picked by buzzards... pecked and nibbled and chewed. That ebony skin was hanging in flaps, great holes eaten through it so you could see the accursed yellow skull beneath.

As she came forward, Oates saw that her dress was ripped from breast to crotch and that her abdomen was split open... and inside, things rustled and scratched and squeaked.

She was filled with nesting, slat-boned rats.

Pistols in hand, Oates dove at her even as she came to meet him. She took hold of him, trying to crush him against her and he battered her face with the butts of his Colts and she threw him down with a strength he was helpless against.

Then she jumped on top of him, straddling him and holding him down, that decaying face swimming in for a kiss. Rats poured out of her, clawing and biting and nipping and Oates was screaming as he felt those teeth sink into him, felt those greasy gray bodies flood over his own. Black Betty's jaws opened wide and a tongue like a bloated black worm slithered out and licked his lips.

With a chlorotic grin on that embalmed face, she spoke in a powdery and broken voice: *"Now you're getting what you came for, Daniel Oates! You are having me as I had your daughter! How helpless you were watching her flower fade before your eyes! Letting her die like a sick dog! Did she scream when you murdered her the second time? When you put her down, did she scream the name of her father or did she reject the poison hypocrisy of your love?"*

And Oates, though he was certainly half-mad or maybe completely mad, interrupted her by saying, simply, "Fuck you."

Then he stuck the barrels of his Colt Navy .44s right into her mouth until she made a gagging sound. He pulled the triggers, blasting her skull in shards, all that filth inside vomiting up and out in a cloud. And the rest of her... she went quickly. Her skin blistered black and fanned out with cracks like candy glass. She went to rags and dust and squirming things, the rats melting away into clods of fur. She was nothing but filth and worms and broomstick limbs attempting locomotion.

Then just a heap of rot.

Oates brushed her off him and stumbled into the hallway. The corridor was thick with smoke. Flames were climbing the stairwell. He turned back into the room, kicking through the dirty glass and seeing the porch roof directly below him. He knocked away the rest of the glass with the barrel of one Navy and jumped out, hitting the roof and rolling off. He thudded into the dirt street and found his feet, immediately going face down.

But he got up again.

Weeds' horse had broken the tie rail and had bolted.

But his gelding was still there. He untied him and climbed unto leather. All around him, as the sun set, they stumbled out of doorways and climbed through windows, slithering from crawlspaces and attics and dark, webby places.

The walking dead.

In shrouds and burial suits and dirty dresses, they stepped out to greet the night and not a one of them did anything but stare as Oates galloped past them, making for the desert beyond.

Even an hour later, in the cool saguaro country of the Nevada desert, he could see where Crowley was behind him in the darkness. It was a glowing orange conflagration that flickered and blossomed like a fire flower, consuming and wasting and spreading.

The town would be wind-blown ash by morning.

By the time Oates reached Compton, he was ready. Ready to pick up his life and hold his wife against him. Ready to begin mourning his Mandy properly.

The End

Roses of Blood on Barbwire Vines

A Zombie/Vampire Novel

As the living dead invade a barricaded apartment building, the vampire inhabitants must protect their human livestock. Shade, the vampire monarch, defends her late father's kingdom, but Frost, Shade's general, convinces his brethren to migrate to an island, where they can breed and hunt humans. In their path stands a legion of corpses, just now evolving into something far more lethal, something with tentacles—and that's just the beginning.

"A marvelous dark fantasy—filled with ruthless vampires, flesh-eating zombies, and enough action to leave you breathless. Intense, gruesome, funny, and fast-paced—it has all the ingredients needed to satisfy even the most jaded fan of horror fiction."

—Jonathan Maberry, Author of *Dead Man's Song*

Shade, the vampire monarch, has learned that zombies are penetrating the vampires' barricaded apartment building, threatening their human livestock. Using magic and seduction, General Frost convinces Shade to migrate to an island, but now, as she looks out over the city, she begins to regret her hasty decision…

ʿΩ

L eaning against the parapet, Shade stared at the barricade. The rain had stopped, but its smell haunted the air. It would return. But it would never wash away the reek of dead bodies.

When her scouts last explored the city, zombies dominated everything: the metropolitan area, the housing developments, even the outlying apple orchards and dairy farms. "They're closing in," the scouts reported. "They're in the billions."

Now, legions clotted the city's arteries and veins, lured to the Haven by the stink of a still beating heart. They lamented, groveling and beseeching entry. They rattled the garage-door armor of the blockade and clobbered its cement keep. They were beggars, the whole world turned homeless and panhandling, the little children showing ribs through bloody shirts, their parents carrying baggage beneath sunken eyes.

Two of the beggars had scaled the cemetery gate: a businessman, his scalp peeled like a hairpiece, and a punk, his right arm merely bones and phalanges. Barbwire had snatched the cuffs of the businessman's Armani suit, and the corporate zombie scuffled with the creepers. The punk had wriggled his way beneath the wire, through crevices and gaps in the concrete slabs, through shattered windshields and busted-out window frames. Spikes of green hair poked up from a gap, then disappeared as the punk stumbled upon a new crawlspace.

Shade sighed and gazed out at the city, at the brownstones and glass, at the white spires of a Catholic church and the air-conditioner-choked windows of other apartment buildings, all dissolving in the darkness. She clutched the pentagram, points digging into her palm.

With Frost's glow faded from her cheeks, she grew frigid. He had charmed her, and in his afterglow, she had watched her father's kingdom crumble. The necklace had grown dim against her chest, and she had smiled.

Some of the Undertakers had despised Roman's decision to enthrone a woman after his death. The soldiers thought females were too weak to lead. Shade was beginning to believe them.

She looked north, toward the river, toward Frost's boat. She closed her eyes and returned to the beach of her fantasy. Waves had worn away her human quarry. She could discern nubs, what remained of the man's legs, but the tide had washed his blood from the purple shells. Hair, like brown seaweed, floated on the surf. And farther down the beach, close yet unreachable, her father's castle still crumbled into the sea. The flying buttresses of its cathedral slowly gave way.

"Rejuvenate the roses," Roman had told her the night he had died. They stood atop the Haven, looking over the buildings. He did not wish to give the city a new name. He wished to revive one of its oldest; he wished to restore its meaning. The City of Roses: it had once been his home.

When he faced Shade, one corner of his mouth frowned, his eyes sad yet steadfast. He had known something then, had known something would go wrong. He had gazed into the seer's eye, no doubt, and had seen the theater, the assassin in the shadows. Had Shade been perceptive, she might have seen his fate reflected on his iris, might have seen his killer, a face, a name. She had not.

"I must go," Roman said, and he embraced her, her father, her family. Together, their blood was strong. Together, they were undying.

"Defend our home," he said, and then he departed.

Yes, he had known, had hidden it in his words, and Shade had not been smart enough to decipher his message, had not been wise enough to save him. And to her, the incompetent, the *woman*, he had entrusted his legacy: "Rejuvenate the roses," his last wish; "Defend our home," his final command.

Someone had killed him.

Shade opened her eyes.

The punk was halfway through the blockade, crawling over the hood of a burnt sedan. His leather jacket squeaked as he moved.

Shade pointed her 9mm. The hollow point lodged somewhere in the punk's skull, and he slid off the car, suspended and twitching in a web of concertina wire until the black widow Death sucked his cursed life.

The businessman had surpassed the barbwire and was stumbling through a maze of parking meters and pedestrian crossing signs. Lengths of barbwire stuck to his sleeves and suit lapel, to the lava-rock-colored legs of his dress pants. Shade began to squeeze the trigger, but he disappeared behind a stack of parking curbs.

"Damn."

She holstered her gun and bounded over the parapet, plunging head-first and shaped like a missile. Her cape flapped against her legs, and her hair moved in torrents where not matted with blood. Pavement, bricks, and marble all rushed up to meet her.

Before splattering against a plane of old sidewalk, Shade spread her cape into bat wings. It caught wind and she rose, soaring to the front of the barricade over heaps of supermarket shelves, park benches, lampposts, and chain link fence.

Lowering her legs, she used her cloak like a parachute to land on a column, one of the many perches that towered over the debris. Most the columns were Doric with plain capitals, taken from the courthouse, but this capital sported the scroll-like volutes of an Ionic.

As Shade landed atop this more ornate capital, dust kicked up beneath her boots; pebbles ticked down into the ruins. The businessman looked up, his cheeks hanging in ribbons, his nose dangling by a thread.

Shade shot him once in the face.

He fell against a pile of stop signs, clanging the red metal. His head slumped on his shoulder, its third eye weeping oily blood, the Puppeteer deceased.

Shade dropped to his side and ripped a piece of barbwire off his suit. Both ends had a clean face, except for burrs at the bottom, as if someone had snipped it so that, with a little torsion, it would break. A second piece reinforced this suspicion.

She tucked a segment into her belt loop and sprang onto the column to crouch.

More zombies crested the gate, headed toward the barbwire.

Shade flipped onto the last pillar, drawing her gun midair and blasting the closest ghouls. One fell over the edge, his teeth shattering as he bit the bullet.

Dropping to the barbwire brambles, Shade clutched a vine and examined it. About every foot, the cable was notched. The segments broke off with a twist.

Before installation, each spool of barbwire had been inspected. Weak and rusty wire had been used for minor snares, whereas the strongest wire had been bundled around the front of the barricade. Had the wire been originally notched, the inspector would have used it elsewhere, most likely in one of the apartment snares. Someone had snipped the wire on purpose.

Groaning, another group of corpses rose from the cemetery gate. Shade leapt onto the column. She clenched her fists and watched.

A dead Latino swiped at the barbwire. He pulled back, and thorns ripped the sleeve of his windbreaker into blue ribbons. The hombre plowed forward, striking. At first, the wire did its job, tearing and springing under pressure. But then scraps busted off, and the zombie tromped a path beneath his Rockports.

Shade cursed.

Jumping from column to column, she visited another patch of barbwire. This one grew farther back in the barricade, congesting a narrow alley between piles of shopping carts. Again, the wire had been scored. Shade twisted a section. It fractured just as easily. She tossed the wire into the carts and returned to the burnt sedan.

Drawing her bone saw, she walked to the pit of razor wire. She slotted the segment of barbwire into the punk's mouth. It grated his molars and caught on his tongue ring. Shade yanked, wresting his cheeks into a joker's grin. She wrapped the barbwire around his head and lifted him halfway onto the car. Her bone saw cut easily through his neck, through the muscles and arteries and spine.

The cadaver fell back into the razor wire, decapitated. Shade held the head on the roof and sawed into the crown, working her way around the cranium. Pulling out a dissection kit, she checked on the invading ghouls.

The zombie in the windbreaker was no longer foremost. Instead, a businesswoman in a pinstriped dress suit led the pack, clambering out of the rubble, following the punk's old path. The left side of her face had been scraped off, an anatomy-book cutaway that revealed muscle and the pearly knob of her cheekbone, the seashell rim of her eye socket, the quartzite rocks of her molars.

A vagrant in a grime-saturated parka and an equally insulating beard trailed close behind. Something had taken his left eye, now just a dark pit. He fixed Shade with his other eye, grinding his teeth like shards of bottle-brown glass.

From the kit, Shade selected a scalpel. As she pried the punk's skullcap with a trowel of scrap metal, she used the blade to slice connective tissues and cerebral meninges. The cap opened with a viscous sigh, like a clam. She tossed it aside.

Inside the cranial cavity, most of the punk's brain stewed a raw pink, a dead gray, and a marbled red: a corned beef boiling in fluids. Shade's bullet had failed to mushroom and had dug a small tunnel, rather than the usual cavern, through the left hemisphere.

Attached to the inside wall of the skull's frontal plate, a black heart pulsed. Its tentacles had suckered onto the brain, probing into the tissue, the tendrils fading into the pink depths toward the brainstem. The heart's oil had permeated the frontal lobe and had started to percolate into the parietal lobes as well. Little black veins meshed all the important centers of the brain, so as to manipulate them, control them.

This blob, this parasite, was the puppet master of the deceased. A castaway of covert Nazi experiments, the Puppeteer was designed to reanimate fallen soldiers; it was initially called Hitler's Heart.

Under private funding, contemporary American scientists had continued the Nazis' development, enhancing the parasite with stem cells. They accidentally bred a mutant strain communicable through the respiratory tract: the parasite shed microscopic eggs through the nasal passage; it also infected the blood and the mucus membranes. The parasite subjugated the host, dead or alive, within twenty-four hours. Only a small population proved immune to the airborne spawn, but no one survived a bite, including Shade.

She had seen it happen to an Undertaker before. In less than ten minutes, the soldier's veins had burst and his skin had sloughed off. He had not reanimated, though. His superior immune system killed him to destroy the germs in his blood.

Dangling from the strings of another Puppeteer, the businesswoman reappeared from the wreckage. Her nylons had gaping runs, and her legs were scratched and cut. The bottom rhinestone button of her dress suit had popped off, exposing her belly, stained green with decomposition. Only a jut of concrete separated her from Shade.

Detaching the Puppeteer's gristly mantle from the punk's frontal plate, Shade nicked one of the parasite's arteries and dodged a spray of black fluid. The parasite lashed out, shooting a tentacle toward Shade's face, octopus suckers groping. She slashed the feeler midair and it thumped to the car's roof, writhing and oozing black.

Three more tentacles suctioned to the car. They constricted and toppled the head, dragging it toward the edge. Tofu giblets of brain matter tumbled from the bullet wound.

Surprised—she had never seen the parasite defend itself before, had never seen it try to escape—Shade cut through the tentacles. She set the head upright, and the Puppeteer cringed; it tried to shrink away.

Using the steel trowel, she extracted it, along with a slice of frontal lobe. She shoveled the diseased tissues into a baggie, where the parasite shuddered and squirted oil across the plastic. It deflated, severed tubes spitting, spluttering, dead.

Floundering over the last jut of concrete, the businesswoman lunged. She reached for Shade with long, cracked nails painted blue. She had slashed her left wrist along the radial artery, and the slash was now a dried incision.

Throwing the steel trowel like a knife, Shade buried the metal deep in the woman's eye. Bone splintered and eye white splattered. The zombie's stirrup pump caught in a fissure and her ankle twisted. With a snap, she collapsed.

Stinking of whiskey-preserved rot, the vagrant crawled over her body, his lone eye seeking and glazed with a cataract, bits of flesh dangling in his whiskers. A new eye, slick and jittery, poked into the empty socket. It was the same sick black as the Puppeteer, only with an opalescent pupil and the nictating membrane of a frog. It blinked and oozed its lubricant. Yet another new ability: never had the Puppeteer generated body parts.

Shade collected her tools and slipped the brain sample into a canister on her belt. She booted the punk's head into the razor wire and leapt onto a leaning column, springing off the fluted sandstone onto the fire escape railing. The bottom portion of the escape had been sawed off. Approximately fifteen feet separated it from the rubble.

Climbing onto the platform, Shade turned to the vagrant. Atop the sedan, he groaned and reached upward. Shade blinded his new eye with a hollow point, glad to see it vaporize, glad to wipe out that bit of twisted magic. The beggar slid off the car and joined the punk in his razor-wire grave. He grew no more eyes.

Along the fire escape, boards covered the windows and entrances, eyelids to block out sunlight and other irritants. Shade climbed to the roof. A rifle barrel met her at the top.

"Your Highness," Edward said, lowering his weapon, a PSG-1. "I apologize."

Edward was a Sexton, specifically a sentry, meant to guard the building from ahigh. He offered a hand, but Shade refused. She did not need a man's assistance.

Edward took a step back as she climbed over.

"You didn't notice me down there?" she asked.

He switched his rifle from one shoulder to the other. He was embarrassed, but his smooth, pale cheeks were unable to flush. "No," he said, "I just started my watch. Came out the door and heard something, thought I'd check it out. Sorry."

Shade peered into the puddles of Edward's eyes, seeking any shady glimmer. "They have breached the barricade," she announced.

His eyes widened; the puddles swelled.

"At the cemetery gate."

He glanced around her toward the drop, as if to verify, but he stopped himself and gave her his full attention. His surprise was obvious. Nothing lurked beneath the mud swirls and drowning earthworms that colored his eyes. Shade's stomach muscles relaxed, but she upheld her posture, never daring to slouch. Not in front of her soldiers. Not in front of the men.

"Keep them at bay," she said. "And call for reinforcements if necessary."

Edward nodded, straightening his own back. "As you wish."

Shade left him. She knew without looking that he had gone to see for himself.

Usually, two sentries manned the rooftop from dusk till dawn, yet when Frost had led Shade here earlier, the roof had been deserted. She hadn't noticed then, but was wise to it now. Had Frost dismissed the Sextons beforehand? Had he vacated the roof so he could moisten long-deadened sexual tissues? And who had snipped the barbwire?

As Shade opened the metal door into the stairwell, she rested her palm atop the canister on her belt: an offering for the seer, a bribe for answers. She looked toward the river, toward Frost's beach, then toward the theater where her father had died.

She went down the stairwell toward the fifth floor. The door clapped shut, and Edward took his first shot, an echoing message, a lonely ode to the nightingale, singing forevermore.

HTTP://WWW.ROSESOFBLOOD.COM

About the Authors

David Bain has had fiction and poetry accepted for publications such as *Poems and Plays*, *Blue Unicorn*, *The Columbia College Chicago Story Week Reader*, *Weird Tales*, *Mythic Delirium* and *Strange Horizons*. In all, he's published more than 100 pieces. He is the editor of *Whispering Worlds*, a large free e-book of speculative poetry which received an "Internet Hot Spot" nod from Ellen Datlow and was named the most impressive such online collection by *Black Gate* magazine. It's available free via his website at:

http://www.geocities.com/davidbainaa

Bain has an MFA from Columbia College Chicago. His thesis is a novel entitled *Gray Lake*.

Matthew Bey is a writer and editor living in Austin, Texas. He is the co-editor of SPACE SQUID: "the zine for people who no read" and the RevolutionSF.com fiction page. He has sold fiction to *Andromeda Spaceways Inflight Magazine*, *Black Gate*, and several online markets. Like every adult male in America he has already worked out how to defend his home in the event of a zombie attack. The plan involves standing on the roof with an improvised weapon called "cinderblock on a rope."

Kevin Alexander Boon is the author and editor of eight books, including the novel *Absolute Zero* and a number of books on Kurt Vonnegut, F. Scott Fitzgerald, Ernest Hemingway, Virginia Woolf and other writers. He is also an award-winning poet and short-story writer, a skilled composer and musician, and a produced playwright and screenwriter. Kevin lives in Pennsylvania where he teaches writing, film, and literature at Penn State and coordinates the English Program for the Mont Alto campus. He is currently researching zombie literature, working on a zombiestudies.org website, and promoting his new novel, B.O.O.T. His website is Kevin.Boon.us

Steven Cavanagh is based in Sydney. He grew up on an Australian cattle farm, which taught him about guns, guts and crawly things. He won the Australian Horror Writers Association's 2006 flash fiction contest, and has appeared in *Shadowed Realms* and *Andromeda Spaceways Inflight Magazine*. Horror anthology appearances include *Shadow Box, Black Box* and *Book of Shadows Volume 1* (Brimstone Press). He suspects zombies just need more coffee. Steve's writing blog is at http://stevecav.blogspot.com

Tim Curran has been fascinated by story–telling since a young age. He spent his formative years listening to his father and uncles tell stories of their depression–era childhoods and experiences in World War II. His neighborhood was filled with interesting, unusual characters who spun tales with great abandon. It wasn't long before he was telling tall tales himself. His influences range from H.P. Lovecraft to Elmore Leonard, Jack London to Ray Bradbury, E.C. horror comics to film noir. He is the author of the small press novels *Grim Riders, Skull Moon, Skin Medicine, The Hive*, and *Dead Sea*.

David Dunwoody lives in Utah with his wife and two cats. Recent publications featuring his short works include *Read by Dawn 2* from Bloody Books, and Permuted Press' novella collection *Headshot Quartet*. He also writes fiction and reviews for the magazine *The Hacker's Source*. In 2006 David serialized a novel online, which can be read at EmpireNovel.com

Andre Duza is a member of the Bizarro movement writing under the sub-style Brutality Chronic. His novels include *Dead Bitch Army* and *Jesus Freaks*. He has written stories for *The Bizarro Starter Kit* and *Undead*. Look for his third novel, *Necro Sex Machine* due out this Fall. In addition to writing, Andre is an avid bodybuilder and a certified instructor of Spirit Fist Kung Fu. Andre's martial arts background also includes boxing, Taekwondo, and Chinese Kempo.

Walter Greatshell is the author of the novel *XOMBIES*, published by Berkley. He can be reached through his website: WalterGreatshell.com

Matthew Masucci resides in Southwest Florida with his wife and two children. His work has previously appeared in *AlienSkin Magazine, Aoife's Kiss*, and *Bloodlust-UK*. Visit his blog at www.emeraldcite.blogspot.com

Kriscinda Meadows is a student of Gothic literature and Zombie Studies, formerly wrote for the website All Things Zombie, and currently operates the zombie blog, Zombie-A-GoGo, which features zombie film reviews, interviews, and general news updates. She lives in Gettysburg, Pennsylvania with her significant other, Peter Dendle, professor and author of *The Zombie Movie Encyclopedia*, and their pet Spook. You can visit her blog at:

http://zombie-a-gogo.blogspot.com/

Rick Moore is an Englishman who now resides on American soil. His fiction has appeared in *Dark Animus, Chimeraworld 3, Embark to Madness, History Is Dead* and *Bound for Evil,* alongside such authors as Ramsey Campbell, M.R. James and H.P. Lovecraft. In 2004 Rick co-founded *Red Scream Magazine* where he was fiction editor for 2 years, before taking a back seat to focus on his writing. Visit his MySpace page at myspace.com/zombieinfection

D.L. Snell is an Affiliate member of the Horror Writers Association and an editor for Permuted Press. Award-winning author Brian Keene "dug the hell" out of Snell's short zombie/vampire story, "Limbless Bodies Swaying," which Snell expanded into his first novel, *Roses of Blood on Barbwire Vines*, available from Permuted Press. For more information and to read sample chapters, visit www.rosesofblood.com

Scott Standridge is a writer and editor from Little Rock, Arkansas. His work has appeared in *City Slab, Whispers from the Shattered Forum,* and many other small press magazines. In addition to writing fiction and nonfiction, he recently completed his online Sonnet Project, for which he wrote a sonnet a day for a full year. You can view the results, many of them horror-themed, at http://thesonnetproject.blogspot.com. He is also Fiction Editor for *City Slab Magazine*. Read more of his stories and post comments on his website, www.scottstandridge.com.

Michael Stone was born in 1966 in Stoke-on-Trent, England. Since losing most of his eyesight to Usher Syndrome, he has retreated from your world to travel the dark corners of inner space. To put it more prosaically, he daydreams a lot. Michael's work has appeared in numerous organs including *Continuum SF, Dred, Electric Spec, Pseudopod, Fusing Horizons, Robots and Time, Down in the Cellar, TQR, Twisted Cat Tales* and *Butcher Shop Quartet*. August 2007 will see a collection of his work from Baysgarth Publications. His vanity has a name: www.mylefteye.net

Ryan C. Thomas works as an editor in San Diego, California. His first novel, *The Summer I Died*, was released by Coscom Entertainment in 2006, and has become a cult favorite among extreme horror fans. His short stories have appeared in numerous markets over the years. You can usually find him in the bars on the weekends playing with his band, The Buzzbombs. When he is not writing or rocking out, he is at home with his cat, Elvis, watching really bad B-movies. Visit him on the web at www.ryancthomas.com

Eric Turowski is an internationally published writer and author of "Willing Servants." He is the general manager and part owner of the Alameda Sun newspaper in Alameda, California, where he also resides. Currently, he is working on his next novel.

A.C. Wise was born and raised in Montreal, Canada and currently lives outside of Philadelphia. Wise's work has appeared, or is forthcoming, in several publications, such as, *Realms of Fantasy*, *Insidious Reflections*, *Lone Star Stories*, and the anthologies *Into the Dreamlands*, *Shadow Regions* and *Read by Dawn Volume 2*. For more information visit www.acwise.net

About the Artists

Paul Campbell is an accomplished professional in both the writing and illustration fields with more than 15 years experience. He currently has over 75 published stories and countless illustrations. Some of his more recently renowned work would be his illustrations for *Baen's Universe* produced by Baen's Books where he's illustrated stories written by but not limited to: H.G. Wells, Joe R. Lansdale, and Bob Shaw. Having previously owned and operated a publishing company with a readership of over 50,000, Paul has once again decided to step back into the field of publishing with a new venture: RAZAR Magazine. www.RazarMagazine.com

Blake Clouser is a film maker and visual artist living in Chicago, IL. He has studied drawing and painting in Italy under the renowned landscape painter Daniel Lang. His previous works have been diverse creations in the form of poster art, websites, album cover design, videogame character design, music, screenplays, and comic book art. He is the eldest of 4 boys in his family.

Matt Hults lives with his wife and two children in Minneapolis, Minnesota. His fiction appears in the anthologies *Echoes of Terror*, *Fried*, *Fast Food, Slow Deaths*, and *Horrors Library, Volume 2*. His first horror e-book, *Skinwalker*, will soon be available from Wild Child Publishing. Come sample more of Matt's work at his web site, NewHorrorFiction.Com

Bret Jordan is a 39 year old Texas resident. He is married and has four children, all girls. By day he programs computers for a local business, and by night he works as a freelance artist. When not working, drawing, and spending time with his family, he reads and writes stories. Samples of his artwork may be seen at: www.bretjordan.com

Clint Leduc is an artist and aspiring amateur filmmaker. He lives in a small town outside of Worcester, Massachusetts where he attends college as a Graphic Design major. His work for *The Undead: Skin & Bones* and *Flesh Feast* marks his first foray into illustration.

Jesus Riddle Morales is an illustrator and Graffiti-Art-Style muralist. He is also a freelance commercial artist and Internet author. He, along with his counterparts in the Synoptic Knight Templars and "BTB" crew, co-created a system of stylized art called "Hyper-gothics." Hailing from Chicago's Southwest Ghetto, "Riddle's" work is well known throughout the U.S. His "Zombie Bible" tales are a staple in the West Coast college scene and his alluring, Hyper-Gothic art can be found in many underground books, websites, and other forums. Visit Riddle's art-page at:

http://www.myspace.com/darkriddle

Permuted Press

delivers the absolute best in **apocalyptic** fiction,
from **zombies** to **vampires** to **werewolves**
to **asteroids** to the very **elements** themselves.

Why are so many readers turning to
Permuted Press ?

Because we strive to make every book we publish feel
like an event, not just pages thrown between a cover.

*(And most importantly, we provide some
of the most fantastic, well written, horrifying
scenarios this side of an actual apocalypse.)*

Check out our full catalog online at:
www.permutedpress.com

And log on to our message board
to chat with our authors:
www.permutedpress.com/forum

We'd love to hear from you!

The formula has been changed...
Shifted... Altered... *Twisted.*™

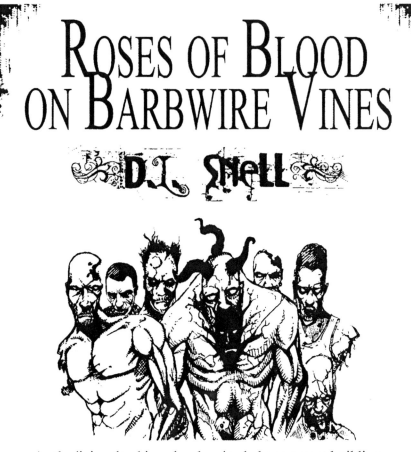

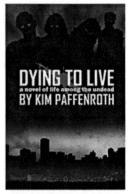
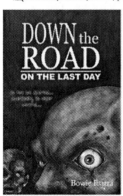

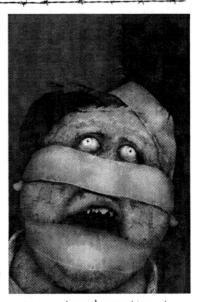
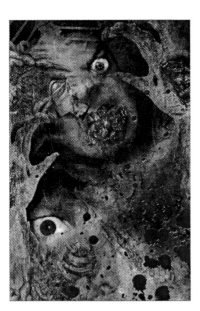

Printed in the United States
134352LV00002BA/118-330/A